Praise for

'Ruth Figgest demonstrates how to make a story about more than one thing at once. Her astute young heroine faces the prospect of plastic surgery to render her looks more pleasing to her lovingly fault-finding mother but simultaneously arrives at a new understanding of the state of her parents' marriage and the ambivalent purpose she has to serve within it.'
Patrick Gale

'Ruth Figgest has a deep understanding of the human condition in all its many guises and depicts it with razor-sharp accuracy. Her characters are emotionally vulnerable, self-sabotaging, and prone to exhilaratingly outrageous behaviour, but they somehow never lose our sympathy. This is psychologically acute, perceptive and witty writing that can make you laugh out loud and wince with discomfort at the same time.'
Umi Sinha

'A thoroughly compelling read: pointed yet subtle, it skewers middle-class American foibles with biting humour and authentic compassion. Figgest's voices are so real and tangible they leap off the page into your ears and into your bones.'
Martin Spinelli

'Ruth Figgest has as firm and careful a grasp on the delicate texture of relationships as any writer since Henry James. This painful—and often, disconcertingly, funny—exploration of a moth........................p, growing old, g............................d accretions of exp...........................e and more ....vel.'

Magnetism

Ruth Figgest

First published in 2018 by
Myriad Editions
www.myriadeditions.com

Myriad Editions
An imprint of New Internationalist Publications
The Old Music Hall, 106–108 Cowley Rd, Oxford OX4 1JE

First printing
1 3 5 7 9 10 8 6 4 2

A CIP catalogue record for this book
is available from the British Library

ISBN (pbk): 978-0-9955900-6-9
ISBN (ebk): 978-0-9955900-7-6

Designed and typeset in Palatino
by WatchWord Editorial Services, London

Printed and bound in Great Britain
by Clays Ltd, St Ives plc

*This book is dedicated to Cara Bentham,
Kate Crouch, and Valerie's daughter,
Jane Olsen. With love.*

1976

The Quickening

Carl says, 'My money's on failed suicide.' He rocks his chair back to lift up the front legs and balance on the back ones, just like you're told not to do at school. I recognise that this is a skill that has taken a lot of practice to perfect. He is self-contained and whenever he speaks his voice is surprising. It's very gentle and soothing, almost a whisper. There's something familiar about his speech: I recognise a bit of a drawl; maybe he's not always been from around here.

He is talking to Wilbur and they're talking about me. Both sexes mix together in this ward and right now the three of us are sitting at the edge of the communal area. I got here first when I finished my cereal and when they finished breakfast too they came to sit either side of me. No one sits on the sofas in the morning; we will do that later. You have to make some changes just to break up the day and in the morning you need the hard seats to make you realise that yes, you are awake and yes, you are here. You are still here in this place, and you can't leave. No one knows when they'll be able to go home.

Wilbur scoots his chair even closer to mine and turns to study me. Wilbur has gorgeous hair, like David Cassidy. I notice how it swings forward when he moves close to me and imagine how soft it must feel when it tickles his neck. I don't move a muscle and I do not blink as he studies my face, and his eyes drift down to my breasts, my stomach, my legs. He looks at my arms and my wrists, my hands.

He looks right in my eyes. His voice is a hiss. 'That is by far the largest cat-e-gor-y – ' he spaces this word out, every one of its syllables distinct and clear, his mouth movement large, as if he thinks I might possibly be deaf ' – and there's nothing wrong with that, honey,' he says. I'm keeping still as the red-hot tip of the cigarette he holds between his fingers comes closer. He strokes my face with his thumb and then he withdraws and settles back in his chair again. I can feel the trace of his hand on my skin as if it has come up in a welt.

Now Wilbur takes a deep drag of his Virginia Slim and blows the smoke out. The smoke floats up above us and it is mesmerising. He waves his hand about to shoo it away from his hair. I tip my head to watch it all disappear near the ceiling and I realise how much I need to lie down. I am as heavy as the smoke is light. The weight of my head is too much, the muscles of my lower back cannot hold my spine erect, I ache with the effort of sitting here, of being here. Of being.

2

Carl laughs loudly and all the tension I feel is momentarily broken. I know that he is not laughing at me, nor is he laughing at Wilbur, he is just laughing. The place is crazy and the sound he makes is deep and unbroken – not a chuckle, a real laugh – and it must be contagious because Wilbur laughs a high-pitched squeal, and I know I would like to as well, but I don't know how to move my face to make it laugh and I cannot make a sound. I am still as the two of them laugh either side of me as if the funniest thing was on TV or something.

I've been told that the mirror mirror on the wall is a one-way window into the nurses' office, but Florence, a big black woman, one of the nursing assistants, still pops her head right out of the door to see what the commotion is. She smiles when she sees the two of them laughing and Wilbur reaches around me and slaps Carl's back. He points back to Florence and now she waves and laughs as well and goes back inside the office.

We are not allowed in our rooms during the day. On this, the fifth floor, we have to be in the communal area from six in the morning until eight in the evening and no one is ever allowed to lie down on the sofas. Everyone says it's okay to do nothing but sit, but no one seems to understand that it's too much even to do nothing. I want to sleep. Actually, I've thought about this a lot. Mashed potato is served every day for dinner and I feel like mashed potato: heavy and gloppy and inert. You have to eat something at each meal. The nurses make notes all day long and what you eat goes down on your records. You also have to stay in plain sight for at least two hours after meals. Wilbur explained to me that no one is allowed to use the bathroom for a while after eating because some people are here because they make themselves sick after meals. He told me that when I first got transferred to this floor, even though I didn't ask, didn't want to know and it wasn't something I'd ever done. He said it can be quite effective but it ruins your teeth. 'Not my bag,' he said. He opened his mouth to run the tip of his tongue across his own teeth, so that I could see that they were white and perfect and evenly spaced, like a movie star's. I wondered if he'd had braces.

As long as you stay on this floor, if you eat then you are allowed to wear your own clothes, and this means whatever you want, apparently. There's a man who dresses like a woman and that's still okay. Since I've been here I've eaten every meal, but for the last three weeks I've been wearing these corduroy pants and this pale yellow top, which is what I was wearing when I was admitted. Mom brought in some underwear and new jeans and T-shirts for me, but I'm happy with what I've got on. I change my panties but the rest can be my hospital uniform, now that I'm on this floor and am allowed to wear clothes.

Mom has been here every day since I arrived, even though they wouldn't allow her to see me for the first week when I was upstairs. My father hasn't come. She says it upsets him too much, to think about this, that Dad has always been the sort of person to shy away from difficult things; she should know, she said. She was sorry that this was a disappointment for me, but he didn't mean anything by it, it's who he is, she said. That's all, just the sort of person he is. 'A person who finds it difficult to change,' she said.

The new things she's brought for me remain in the pink overnight bag under the bed in my room, along with some books she thought I might like to read: *Dr Atkins' Diet Revolution: The High Calorie Way to Stay Thin Forever*; *Yoga 28 Day Exercise Plan*; and *How to Live with Yourself*. That last book has a bright red cover with a white border, like a big stop sign. I've put it at the bottom of the pile.

Wilbur gripes every day that all the stodge they serve up for our meals is ruining his figure. The first time he said that to me he untucked and lifted his dress shirt and stroked the flattest belly I have ever seen on anyone, man or woman. He must do a hundred sit-ups a day. 'You know,' he says to me now, 'you might as well smoke. I think it's real good that you don't, but you might as well. You're allowed, so I say, why ever not? Why not?' he repeats. 'Do you want one?' He offers me his pack.

I don't take it. I don't move. I shut my eyes. I am not here. 'She doesn't smoke,' Carl says. 'Leave the kid alone.'

Now the ward door buzzer goes off and I look at the clock. It's seven-thirty. I've been awake for nearly two hours. It's half an hour since breakfast finished.

'They're back,' Wilbur says. 'Right on time. They run this place like a bus terminal. Coming and going. No peace.'

Dolly, Florence and Leanne come out of the nurses' room. Florence starts putting out bowls and spoons and laying the places at the smallest of the three breakfast tables and then Henry comes in first, with his big clipboard, followed by four patients wearing hospital pyjamas. I don't know the names of the two old men in the group and in fact I've never seen one of them before, but I know the two women: Franny and Alice.

Alice's husband comes to see her most days. She has a beautiful face and lovely blonde hair and he sits next to her stroking it all the time he's visiting. Wilbur says that her baby died and she killed it. I think he's lying – they'd have put her in prison if she killed a baby – but she doesn't stop crying even all the time her husband plays with her hair, as if she's done something terrible, so maybe she did.

The four of them stop in a line and Leanne and Dolly go forward to guide them to the tables. Leanne is a scrawny white woman and Dolly is dark brown and plump like her name. They're nursing assistants like Florence, but Henry is a registered nurse. I'm not sure about the others that come on duty now and then, and especially the night staff, because not everyone wears a badge, or they wear it clipped in an awkward place you don't want to look, like on their belts dangling above their groin, or else upside down. No one has a last name on display.

The four in blue pyjamas trickle over to the tables where they sit down like obedient first graders. Florence is waiting and glops oatmeal into metal bowls from a tray and puts one in front of each of them. They're asleep, really, even as they lift the spoons into their gaping mouths, but they chomp and chew and suck their way back to being awake.

They look like zombies and there's something terrifying about it, but I can't help watching. Outside, staring at other people is rude. Inside, there's usually nothing else to do and it's all we do at times even when there is something we could do. The open areas are littered with puzzles, magazines, decks of cards and board games, but here we kill time watching everyone else killing time.

Wilbur is watching them too. He's pretending not to be scared by it. He says, 'You know, almost everyone gets the ECT, in the end. Not me, mind, but I am a complicated diagnosis. Until they straighten that out, I am *not* going down that road. No, sir-ree. No. Don't you think?'

Carl's expression in return is beautifully, defiantly blank. No one could know what he was thinking and I'm pleased he doesn't answer, but the lack of acknowledgement or agreement annoys Wilbur. He must have been a terrible gossip in normal life. Wilbur says to Carl, 'Well, fuck you. Excuse me for trying to have a conversation,' but he's not really angry, he's just desperate for something – so he wants to know what's wrong with everyone here, but in a way that's all, now, that any of us have to ourselves. We're both holding out; Carl won't tell and neither will I.

I haven't spoken a word for at least eight weeks.

'Fried brains or not, *Franny* will at least talk to me,' Wilbur says. 'You watch.' He goes over to the table, squats next to her chair and strokes her head.

Franny is old, about sixty, and her grey hair is long and very frizzy. Franny and Wilbur are always so close that I wonder if they were friends from before here, or maybe they're just good friends because they've both been here longer than anyone else. I wonder why she's here, and why she's on the list for ECT twice a week, every week, and then I wonder how long until I'll get out, or if I'll end up like her. I don't know what will happen but, even though I don't want to be like her, I don't think I'll ever want to leave. I can't imagine being that old. It's a creepy thought, she must have been my age once.

When Franny turns to look at Wilbur, she appears surprised then a couple of seconds later recognition flickers over her face. Then she smiles at him broadly, cleanly and honestly, just like a two-year-old. Wilbur turns back to us to see if we're watching. He wants to know that we've registered the power that he has. He has woken Franny from sleep – brought his friend back from the dead.

'He's like some fairytale faggot prince,' Carl says now, which makes me jump because I didn't realise he might be able to read my mind.

2013

The Tornado

I am at work when the phone call comes and it takes me a minute to understand who is speaking. I finally grasp that it's Gus, who is this ancient guy who goes to Mom's old church and takes care of her yard. He's phoning from Phoenix.

'Gus,' I say. 'How are you?'

His voice wavers. 'Your mother, honey. It's bad news.' I sit down.

When I get off the phone I go to tell my boss that I have to leave. Jerry is the head of public information and marketing.

I explain that just now I had a call to say my mother has died. I tell him that my work is right up to date. I can provide him a quick handover for events and where we've got so far and he'll be able to pick up on anything that might be coming up. 'I can email you anything you need to know in my absence. But,' I say, 'I think I really have to get on a plane.' I start to shake and he gets up from behind his desk and takes my arm and leads me to sit down in the space he's vacated.

Just as I am sitting down, his secretary interrupts us. She appears surprised to see me sitting in his place behind his desk. Candy, a massive middle-aged woman – my sort of age – is wearing a sticky-out brown A-line skirt below a baggy blue turtleneck, and brown penny loafers. She is as different from spun sugar as a cactus from a dandelion and therefore, of course, her nickname is Cotton. Jerry asks Cotton to get us a coffee. He takes her to the door and intends a whisper but I can hear him tell her that my mother has passed.

By the time Cotton returns with two mugs of steaming black coffee I am unable to stop my legs from jerking up and down. 'I'm sorry,' I say. 'I don't know why I'm shaking.'

'It's the shock. Have a sip and take a bite of a cookie.' She passes me a box of animal crackers. 'Shock can kill a person,' Cotton says, 'And you're way too skinny.'

Her definition of skinny is warped, so this is not true, but I probably do weigh near a hundred pounds less than she does. I say, 'I've got reserves enough, but there'll be stuff to do. I don't know what to do.'

Jerry is reliably definite. '*Yellow Pages*, or the internet. Find a funeral director and he'll walk you through it. It's their job. They'll know what to do and how. You don't have to decide anything. They're professionals. Let them do what they need to do and let it happen. Keep your head low and go with the flow.'

I'd expect nothing less from Jerry. He is what people call a born leader, a very likeable guy. This is exactly why he got this job. He sounds decisive and confident but he never makes a decision he can be held accountable for and everyone else does everything. He doesn't actually do a thing.

I thank him for the advice and then Cotton kindly arranges the tickets and a cab and I phone Gus back to tell him when I'll be arriving.

I go to the airport via my apartment and I collect spare contact lenses, a pair of glasses, and a change of clothes. I don't have to take much. I can't really think about what to pack anyway. The driver waits for me and, though there is traffic, we get to the airport in time for me to check in and sit and wait until it's time to board.

I look around at the people waiting, like me, at the airline gate. There are people travelling in pairs talking to each other, others travelling alone, reading magazines or staring out the window at the parked planes. Perhaps some are afraid of flying, some are tired and going home to see their families, instead of going somewhere they don't live and facing something unexpected. There's a woman who is around my mother's age. She looks perfectly healthy, and, the last time I saw her, Mom did as well. People in their seventies probably die all the time, but plenty of them don't. I'd put money on this woman living at least another ten years. She is holding a magazine. Her reading glasses are propped on her nose but she's not looking at the *Reader's Digest*, she's looking around her at the other passengers. Our eyes meet momentarily until I look away.

It is now that my mother's death hits me. That not only will there be things that have to be done, but it'll be up to me to do everything – but now, no one to tell me I'm doing it wrong. She always wanted me to move to live near her and I didn't want to. We spent a lot of time together anyway, and I won't consider that she might not have died if I'd been nearer.

When we're called to stand in line in order of boarding assignment, I watch the same woman struggle with her carry-on bag until a young guy helps her. I'm a 'D' – two letters behind – so she boards before me and I pass her aisle seat on the way to find my own near the back of the plane. She is settling herself in and I see that she's looking at her magazine again.

This is a direct flight, less than three hours. They probably won't even bother with snacks. I find my seat and, though I'm squashed between two big college students, no one bothers me. I pretend to read the paper and cry silently.

My old lady has left the plane and is gone before I get off. Gus meets me, we hug awkwardly and he drives me straight to Mom's house. When we get out of his car he apologises about the yard; the grass is overgrown. He explains that he didn't get round to doing it in the morning as he'd planned. When there was no reply to the doorbell, he went around the back and looked in the windows because the dog was barking like crazy. He saw her in the den, on the floor. 'I had to break a window and climb through. But it's okay, I've secured it with some wood. You'll be safe. When the paramedics got here they went in the front door.'

'But it was too late?'

'Yes,' he says, and I imagine this elderly man peering in, and then having to climb through my mother's ranch house window, finding her dead and then phoning for an ambulance. It must have been awful.

'I'm glad it was you. She likes you.'

'Well, your mom is something else.' Then he corrects this. 'Was,' he says, 'Terrible stuff when she was a kid, but God, she sure rose above it and had quite a life, didn't she? She sure was something else.'

'Sure,' I echo. I don't really know what he's talking about, but it's nice that he liked her so much.

We are at the front door. He pulls out her meagre bunch of keys with the rabbit foot keychain. The sight of the keys starts me off crying again, but Gus doesn't notice. I follow him into the house. The lights are off. He switches them on and the house lights up. Everything is dingy and dirty; she can't have dusted for months. It wasn't like this when I was last here.

'There's no real mess,' he says as I continue to follow him past the open door to the living room and through to the den. 'It was all … well, no mess. Oh, and I took the dog to be boarded. They'll keep it there until you decide what you want to do. Poor thing was barking and barking like mad, real upset he was, but I know you're allergic. I didn't want you ill, so I got them to come and collect it. Phone number is in the kitchen. She'd used them before. She told me.' He points and I look around the room. 'See, there's no real mess. That's a blessing.'

The allergy is a falsehood and his comments about this room, too, are untrue. There is no blood on the carpet, but the room is far from clean – there are used mugs and plates, and piles of papers on the surfaces. It is a *total* mess.

It turns out that I don't have to decide on the funeral director. While he puts on some water for coffee Gus tells me he's taken care of that as well. 'I used this guy for the wife on a recommendation, and he'll do you proud too, don't you worry,' he says. 'Your mom,' he says, 'has already been moved to their premises.'

Although I'm grateful, I seem to have lost the power of speech. I keep expecting Mom to arrive home any moment and ask what the hell we're doing because my mother is like a tornado – the biggest person in any situation. All my life she's whipped in without warning and changed the landscape and I've repeatedly been swept up and along in whatever unpredictable direction she takes. Surely she wouldn't leave me and little old Gus in charge. She never lets anyone else deal with the big stuff. This is some sort of mistake, or joke. 'I can't believe it,' I say. 'What is she thinking?'

'I know.' He nods slowly, then again more slowly, and finally, almost imperceptibly, he moves his head once more.

After another few minutes of sitting in silence completely still and looking at the space on the floor where the small couch and coffee table have been shoved aside – presumably where they attended to her – Gus leans forward to drag himself up to standing. He puts his hand on my shoulder and says softly, 'Well, I'll be getting on, and let you get some rest.'

I'm suddenly terrified at being here in her house alone. I try to sound conversational. I remember he's a widower and that his wife's name was Nora. 'How long has Nora been gone? Tell me about her. I'm sorry I don't know much about you, Gus.'

'We were married for forty-three years. The Lord works in mysterious ways and he decided to take her before me.' He pauses. 'Listen, honey, do you want me to pray with you?' He is asking me tentatively and when I shake my head he appears relieved. Then he says, 'I can send my pastor around, if you like. Maybe tomorrow?'

'Thanks,' I say. He passes me the bent-up card from the funeral director and suggests I phone them in the morning to arrange an appointment. 'Hard,' he says, 'being an only child. But at least there won't be any arguments. Lots of stuff gets thrown up at these times. My kids were hardly speaking to each other after Nora passed. I had to referee.'

I desperately want him to stay. 'I didn't even know you had children.'

'Not nearby. One in Maine and the other, the girl, in California.'

'I should have lived closer to Mom.'

'No.' He shakes his head. 'I was always saying that kids doing their own thing was the best way, and your mom agreed.' Now he says, again, that he's really got to be going.

I try, 'I guess you must miss your wife a lot? It must be lonely at times.' Gus doesn't bother to respond, and thinking of attempting to seduce this nice old man just to keep him in my dead mother's house is as ridiculous an idea as any I've had this year. I should be ashamed of myself.

Finally, I decide I can't kidnap him so there's no avoiding it. I've got to let him go. I see him to the front door and we say goodbye and then I go down along the corridor to the room that she told me, whenever I came to visit, was mine. I don't want to look into any of the other rooms. I don't want to see this place without her in it because I will see her everywhere and she is nowhere now.

'My' room appears to have become Mom's store room – there are stacks of boxes against the walls. The sheets on the bed seem clean. Even if they weren't I wouldn't care. I don't wash. I don't unpack anything. I strip off my clothes and climb beneath the covers, exhausted.

It's still pitch black outside when I wake, just gone four a.m. Perhaps the time difference accounts for some of the sudden, dreadful surge of energy that sweeps through me now, but not for all of it. I have to do something. What I really need to be is Superman, flying around and around the world, turning back time to before she went and died.

2011

The Blind Sentinel

My mother has been broken in a car crash – a leg and ribs – and the two of us are in the guest bedroom where there is room for a mattress on the floor beside the bed. This is where I'm lying now, listening to the steady snoring above me and wondering when she will drive again, and whether she should drive again. I've told her she'll feel better in the morning, but that's probably a lie.

I think about the road kill I see by the side of the highway back home. 'No one plans accidents,' someone in the waiting area at the hospital said earlier. 'They wouldn't be accidents if they were planned.'

Dan, her neighbour opposite, was a big help. I could never have moved this mattress from 'my room' in here on my own. He was the one who suggested we sleep in the guest room, once he'd had a look at her overcrowded bedroom. Her last boyfriend supposedly slept in here when he was with her, but I won't think about that now – I'll never sleep if I think about Philip.

Mom is lucky to have Dan nearby, but then she's always been a lucky person – a lucky person who's never had any idea how lucky she is. Like Mr Magoo, going through life unwittingly escaping mishap and leaving mayhem in his wake, that's exactly how she is. She could have been killed today, but, instead of realising the close call, she's snoring away and I'm lying here unable to sleep.

My body is exhausted but my mind is wired tight. I know I won't sleep because it has been so stressful. By the time I got from the airport to the hospital the dust storm was long gone, but everyone was still talking about it and I was trying to put together fragments of information to figure out what happened. On the news before we finally bedded down tonight, we learned that there were tons of other car accidents across Phoenix. That's why it was so busy in the ER.

I can hear her dog breathing heavily in the hallway outside. He scratched the door for a while, but finally gave up because I wasn't about to let him in and I won't relent. He needs to know who is boss. He's been getting away with too much for too long.

I can't believe how boring it is lying awake listening to someone fast asleep without a care. I wish I'd left the curtains open because some street light in here would be good. Perhaps I could use a flashlight to read or something – she must have a flashlight somewhere – but I don't want to risk waking her up by rooting around in the drawers. I decide to count sheep.

I'm somewhere after sixty when she whispers my name and I'm pulled up from the airy no-man's land between wakefulness and sleep – and momentarily startled to find myself on the floor beside her bed. Then I can feel a rush of energy and I'm wide-wide awake again.

I wear contacts, but I can't sleep in them and I am as blind as a bat, so I always put my glasses under the pillow. I grab them now and push them on to my face. 'Mom? Mom, are you okay?'

'I think I should take something,' she says all breathy and childish, sounding like a drunk Marilyn Monroe, 'Please let me have Poopy. I wish you'd let him in.'

'No.' Though I'm only whispering, I try to sound firm. Simple statements. 'You don't need anything. They gave you a bunch of Vicodin and a shot at the hospital. The dog is already asleep. You've got cuts and stitches. It's unhygienic. He can't come in. He's okay out there. He's fast asleep. Just go back to sleep yourself.'

Then, on cue, the stupid animal starts to whimper and scratch on the hall carpet outside the door again. She should never have got a dog. When we talked about it on the phone she said she was thinking about getting one because she was lonely, that she wouldn't be lonely if only I moved closer, but, if I wouldn't live near, then she was going to get a dog.

'I can't,' I said. 'I've got a job.'

'Then I'm down to the pound tomorrow.'

And I laughed. 'You know you have to walk it and clean up shit if you have a dog. You'll never do that. Dog poop has to be picked up and, besides that, they are helpless and need looking after. Have you thought about that? You'd have to take care of it.'

But the very next day she did as she said she would and picked up a miniature poodle. She chose a neurotic dog that also craps a lot, probably just to prove me wrong.

'I haven't been able to sleep at all,' she says now.

I raise my voice trying to cover up the scraping and snuffling sounds the dog is making outside the door, before she might notice them. 'Well, you did a pretty good imitation of sleeping. You were asleep.'

'I wasn't. I was faking. I was just tired of listening to you droning on and on. I wanted you to relax because I know you need your sleep. You can't sleep while you're talking. You know, honey, sometimes you just need to shut up. You should learn that.'

'Why would you think I could relax? You could have been killed.' I don't want to scare her, but perhaps she should think about what happened. 'I don't want to scare you, but perhaps you should think about what happened,' I say. She wasn't wearing a seatbelt. She hadn't put the headlights on, and, the police also said she was talking on her cell phone. 'Killed, Mom. You could be dead now. D. E. A. D. and then there would we be?'

'Well, I guess that it wouldn't be my problem,' she says quietly.

She still hasn't adequately explained what she was doing out near interstate seventeen. When the police asked about it at the hospital, she was evasive and then the doctor told them to stop questioning her. He made excuses, saying that she'd had a shock and that really elderly people often don't immediately recall the details after an accident and that we must all be patient.

18

'She's early seventies,' I said, 'that's hardly *really* elderly, nowadays.'

She piped up from the stretcher, 'Hey, doc, I've had some work done. Is my face still okay? I can't afford to get another lift done.'

Here in the dark, she says, 'I'm not dead and don't worry about me, honey. I'm a very strong person. This is no big deal. I'll be fine. I'll be good as before in a jiff. Don't sweat it. You'll get yourself all worked up.'

'Yeah, well,' I say, 'I *am* sweating it. I am oozing sweat with worry about you. I am soaked with sweat from all this crap. And I'm exhausted. You need to rest. Try to go back to sleep.' Again, I mean to sound like I'm in charge, that I am now the mom talking to the kid but, unfortunately, coming from the floor it loses all possible impact.

'So, go on and get me my meds. I need something to help me sleep. Fetch me my Ambien.'

'No, Mom.'

'You are *not* a doctor. You're not even a nurse. Or a nurse's aid.'

It's two-thirty in the morning local time, because Phoenix opts out of daylight savings. Four-thirty a.m. back in Oklahoma City. I sit up, then I stand up and feel suddenly lightheaded. It's pitch black and I can hardly make her out on the bed. 'Do you want the Elavil? How about that?' This is a new prescription for her and I think it'll be okay with the Vicodin and it's also a whole bunch better than Ambien, which she shouldn't ever take because she sleep-eats when she takes it. People can choke on food if they don't know they're eating. Mom has devoured whole bags of candy, boxes of chocolate, bags of nuts and entire punnets of fruit in her sleep. On more than one occasion she's woken to find her sheets stained, packaging detritus scattered around the bed, and a trail of spilt food leading along to the kitchen and the open refrigerator door.

At the hospital she didn't tell them about the Ambien, or the rest of her stash. She's always had good insurance from Dad's benefits and it's rare she has to do a co-pay, so every single prescription gets filled and she never, ever throws drugs out. She has several gallon-size Ziploc bags stuffed full of vials with labelled prescriptions from various doctors she falls in, and out, with. Even if out of date by years, they're still secreted away, just in case.

Earlier at the hospital, when I interrupted the doctor's questions to list for him all the current meds she takes regularly, and those old prescription drugs I'm sure she takes on occasion, she waved me to shut up. She said, 'My daughter has problems. I can speak for myself.' In front of him she told me to go and get myself a coffee. 'Scram,' she said. He looked embarrassed and shrugged and I walked out. Later he told me to be patient with her. I should have told him to try fifty-one years with someone like her.

She says now, 'No. I want the Ambien. Go get my pills. Under the vanity unit. I'll only take a half. Take the edge off it.'

I guess she won't be able to get up to get anything to eat and because I'm too tired to argue any more I say, 'Shut your eyes. I've got to put the light on.'

'Don't put the light on.'

'I have to put the light on. Make sure you're taking the right thing.'

'Don't put the goddamn light on. I know which ones by feel,' she says. 'I have the super-senses of a blind person.'

'You're crazy.' I stride across the room and punch the light switch and blink. The room looks smaller in the bright light. It's dusty, faded. She's smaller too. I can see she's annoyed but she can't stop me: she can't get up.

'I need to get word to Philip. He'd want to know I've been hurt. I'm sure he'll be concerned. *He* would care. *He* wouldn't treat me like this.'

'Forget it. It's been more than ten years. You think that freeloader would take better care of you than me? I could remind you. He was gone like the wind.'

'*You* could find him. You're very resourceful. We both know how resourceful you can be when you want.'

She doesn't really want him. This is a strategy – her feeble attempt to make me feel disposable. She thinks that, if she threatens Philip, I'll be more agreeable. I nearly feel sorry for her, because their relationship ended badly and if she thinks he's an option she must be feeling desperate. She wouldn't be able to find him again after all this time anyway. I will say nothing.

In the hall, the animal is wagging its tail and begins sniffing around my ankles. He's a dangerous trip hazard and she's stupid for thinking she's going to be able to keep him. She should never have got him. Sooner or later he's going to be unwanted and neglected. But there's no telling her anything. Being around my mother is like trying to fly a kite in a storm. She will always do what she wants and she is inherently reckless not only with herself, but with everyone else. She doesn't keep a calendar for recording appointments. She won't make plans ahead of time. She loves surprises and surprising people, including herself. She won't be tied down to anything and that's why I know she'll get pissed off with this animal before long, and put it down, and then we'll have to pretend that he just died.

Since Dad's death she's been like a helium balloon untethered and I am someone trying to catch hold of the string. I have a recurrent dream lately in which the roof of my house is tipped open, like a lid, and air and rain let in, and I know this is because my mother is getting old and I don't want her to go anywhere, to leave me behind on one of her whims.

I shouldn't have told her she could have died. I shouldn't have said that. I find her drugs underneath the sink in the bathroom off her bedroom and identify the bag containing various types of sleeping tablets.

When I get back to the guest room her lips are fixed in a tight straight line and she reaches up to snatch the bag from me. Then she screws her eyes tight shut and fishes in it with one hand. It takes seconds. Before she can open the selected vial, I prise it from her hand to check it's the correct one.

It is. She still has her eyes shut. She doesn't say anything. I hand her back the Ambien pills and take away the others.

'I know exactly what I am doing,' she says.

And this is the thing that frightens me most. I might pretend my worry is about her, that she's incapable of taking care of herself, but it's me that I am worried for. She's in charge. It is hopeless trying to stop her.

In desperation I decide I might as well take a pill as well, and finally twenty minutes later I sleep.

At some point in the night the dog gets in. I must have left the door open a crack earlier and he was wily enough to wait until we were both out for the count, because here he is with us in the morning, not on her bed but on the floor with me. He's got that awful doggy breath and he's trying to lick my face. I push him away and feel for my glasses. They're not under my pillow.

Mom, above me on her bed, is snoring still soundly asleep. Fortunately, the dog is too squat and fat to jump up to her bed unless I lift him there, but where are my glasses? If he's gone and chewed them, not only will I not be able to see right now, but I'll have to get a new pair made and that will mean leaving her alone for at least a couple of hours.

Then the dog is back with something orange and the size of a plate in his mouth. A Frisbee. He's waving it back and forth in my eyeline. I can't imagine that Mom throws a Frisbee for the dog, but perhaps she does. He's thwacking it at the legs of the furniture and against the divan, trotting around in a figure of eight – around her bed, around me on the floor and then back to the bed again.

Her staying asleep is best for both of us but the wretched animal has no consideration for people and is going to wake her up. 'Stay asleep,' I whisper upwards. I squiggle myself to standing. I still can't find my glasses and the dog rushes at my legs. I hate the rudeness of mornings on the best days, but having to deal with a wild animal first thing is ridiculous. He wants to play Frisbee, I guess. Every time I reach down to take it from him, he runs away.

I climb over my shoes, still worrying about my glasses. I fumble for my sweats in my suitcase, which is open on the floor at the foot of my mother's bed. As I'm pulling them up, Mom's voice behind me says, 'You'd better put him out. He needs the bathroom.'

'Shush. Rest. You should sleep a bit more. He's okay.'

'He'll make a puddle if you don't let him out. He needs a pee.' At the sound of Mom's voice, the dog gets excited and starts running about more wildly.

'He wants to play Frisbee,' I say.

'Frisbee? That's nice. Good. He'll like that. Let him out.'

'I can't find my glasses.'

'Where did you leave them?'

'They're not there.'

She leans over the bed as well as she can and, at first without opening her eyes, she calls the dog to her in that silly soppy voice, 'Come to Mommy.' Then she tells me that the little shit has got my shower cap. It's not a Frisbee! She says did I give it to him to play with?

'The hell I did!'

'Well, he's enjoying himself. You have to make an effort so that he can learn to like you. Dogs don't like people who don't like dogs. They can sniff out insincerity at a hundred miles and you should think about that. Dogs can always tell good people from bad.' Now she produces my glasses from under her blanket and waves them at me. 'Go and put them on *him*. The glasses and the shower cap,' she suggests as if we were six years old. 'He'd look so cute. Do it.'

'The hell I will.' I am shouting now, and I grab the glasses from her. They are smudged and slightly bent but as I slide them up my nose my surroundings come into focus. They go from a blurry swirl of soft colour to something smaller and more defined. Mom's bed is like a throne in the middle of the room and Poopy is in front of me. I look down to see him raise his leg over my suitcase and begin to urinate on my belongings. 'The hell you do,' I yell and grab him. He's a fat wriggle in my arms and he doesn't stop peeing. There are dribbles all over the floor as well.

'He can't help it. Don't be angry with him. You should have let him out. Poor little boy.' she says at my back as I storm out with the whimpering dog held out in front of me, its hind legs pedalling the air.

'Get yourself back to sleep,' I shout back. 'I'm not telling you again.'

When the wash cycle has finished and my clothes are in the dryer and I've dabbed the carpet clean, washed out my suitcase with diluted Clorox and dried it too, I think about making Mom some breakfast. Poopy is now strictly confined to the back yard. He's barking and crying out there, but he needs to think about what he's done. I ask her what she wants but she says she wants Vicodin first. 'I never eat breakfast. I can't eat breakfast.'

I don't point out that this is because for years she hasn't got up until after midday. I say, 'You've got to eat something.'

'I'll have some peanut M&Ms. They're in the icebox.'

'That's not food. Toast or cereal, or toast and cereal. Or eggs, or waffles?'

'God, you're torturing me. I never thought you could be so...so...nasty. My own daughter,' she says. 'Just give me my pills.'

I've never had a two-year-old to deal with but I imagine it might be something like this. 'Not until you eat something.'

'No. I won't.'

'Yes, you will.'

'I won't.'

Obviously, she is beyond reasoning with. So much so that, as we continue to argue, I realise I've forgotten the justification for insisting that she eats before the pills. This moment seems entirely inevitable and, though I realise I've lost myself in my own stubbornness, there's still something exhilarating about her dependence upon me. Maybe I *am* the cruel control freak she's saying I am.

I take the bottle of pills from the bag on the table, show her the label and rattle the Vicodin in the air. She glowers at me as I wave them and then I put the vial right into my pocket. It's a tight squeeze, but very effective theatre. 'Their street value must be something. Huh?'

'Don't you dare.' We stare at each other a moment, then she says, not averting her eyes from mine, 'Toast. One piece.' And all the tension is released, not immediately like a balloon popping, but slowly it seeps away, like an old balloon deflating.

'Good, Mom. Good.'

'I'm not a pet,' she says. 'And I'm not senile. Don't talk to me like that.'

I fetch the toast feeling very, very smug. We can do this, I think. It won't be impossible. She will eat her toast and the dog will stop barking and realise who is in charge. I put margarine on the one piece, our agreement, and march it through to her. I leave her with the toast and go back to the kitchen to get her a coffee and a glass of water for the Vicodin, which she takes from my hand.

In a few minutes she asks for the dog and, because she's complied with my demands, I think it's only reasonable for me to go and get him. When I return, I put him on the bed with her. She's got a nice druggy smile already, and I'm just thinking that I might put the TV on and watch with her when I see her slip Poopy the piece of toast.

She doesn't know I've seen it. I have a choice: I can ignore it and we both win, or I can call her on it. Just then the phone rings and I don't have to decide.

'If it's Brenda tell her I'm okay and I'm asleep. If it's Louelle or Patty, tell them what happened, but I don't have the time to listen to what's up with Patty's divorce or Louelle's daughter so don't let them get into it. And if it's Frank, tell him I'll call him when I'm a bit better,' she says. 'Don't say too much if it's Frank.'

'Are you expecting a call from this Frank?' She has never mentioned a Frank.

'No. No. But if it should happen to be him – I'm just saying – let him know I'm not able to get to the phone. But restrain yourself for once. Don't tell him everything about everything.'

'It's right there. Tell them all what you want yourself.' I point to the princess phone on the coffee table next to the bed.

It's ringing in chirps. 'Want to be responsible and listen to me, or shall I hand it up so you can take the call yourself and then if it's this guy you can tell him whatever you want to?'

'You know I don't want to speak to anyone.' She looks down at the phone. It's been ringing maybe twelve rings by now. 'Okay. Get the call. Do this for me. I'll do what I'm told. I give up. You win.'

'Hello,' I say and it *is* a man. And this man says he's Frank. He's heard about the accident, he's been concerned. 'Oh, thanks for phoning, Frank,' I say.

Mom's eyes are bright with excitement. She is hanging on my every word.

'She's being so brave. Yes, I'm her daughter... No... She's strong. She's amazing, actually.'

I hold the phone away from my ear so that she can hear him talk about her. He's got a nice voice and he's saying how worried he's been – not only him, but how worried they will all be at the club.

'Yes, yes. Of course. I'll give her your love, Frank.' She grins at me. 'A visit?' Mom's eyes widen and she shakes her head frantically. 'No, I don't think she's up to that. We have to be sensible. Give me your number and I'll ring you tomorrow?' I find a pen and the blank back of a bill envelope to scribble his reply down. Then I say a grateful goodbye to Frank, who has given us something new to talk about for a little while.

The dog is settling down in the curve of her waist; he sighs dramatically and shuts his eyes. She strokes his back tenderly. I wonder if she ever was tender with me like that.

Only three hours later we are beginning the argument that is the preamble to lunch. The dog is still lying beside her halfway under the blankets. When I ask what kind of

27

sandwich does she want, she says she's not hungry and she doesn't want to eat anything, she just wants her next lot of pills because she's starting to hurt again.

The dog opens his eyes, wriggles a bit then rolls on his back. Mom tickles his belly and then awkwardly leans over to kiss him on his snout. She repeats that she's got no appetite and smugly adds that that she knows pain relief works better on an empty stomach anyway. She says that in fact she's been thinking about losing a bit of weight lately, and then she says it wouldn't do me any harm to miss a meal as well. The winter has been over for half the year; I should try to use up some of my winter fat reserves. Then she starts to laugh at her joke.

'God, Mom. I presume that's the pills talking, so, for that reason, and that reason alone, I will not take offence.'

She doesn't apologise. 'I'm your mother,' she says, and shrugs. 'Who else can tell you the truth? You're fatter than ever.'

'Well –' I point at the dog ' – just so you know, if anything happens to you, the very first thing I'll do is put that dog down. You should keep up your strength if you care about it. I'm fetching you lunch and you are going to eat what I fix and then I'll let you have the pills.'

She whispers, loudly, into the dog's ear. 'Don't worry. She's just jealous.'

I walk out leaving the two of them there, and five minutes later, when I come back with the plate, I'm pleased to see that she eats the chicken sandwich I've made. She eats it very slowly. Eyes on me and her one free hand firmly on the nasty little dog.

2007

The Cockatoo

The leaflet says, *Plastic surgery is a sensible option for the common problem of ageing.* And Dr Chartaine's credentials are on the back. I don't know what all the letters stand for. Chartaine sounds enough like a charlatan to make me suspicious, but Mom said his name didn't bother her at all.

Then the door opens and he's here in the flesh. Gleaming white medical coat. Huge white hair in a kind of crest on his head. Huge warm smile. Sparkling teeth. The only improvement would have been a halo, and I've got to admit that he is one good-looking man. His face puts him around forty, I'd guess, but then he might, I suppose, be fifty, or sixty, or seventy even, with that white hair. Surely they don't let people operate on faces at seventy?

He sits down behind his large mahogany desk. Mom is beaming back at him. This guy has already done a job on her.

'This is my daughter,' she introduces us. 'She will be staying with me after I have the work done, just to keep an eye on me. She works for the city,' she says. 'Not here. She's come all the way from...' My mother pauses and looks confused, as if she's forgotten where I live. 'A long way away,' she finishes.

'Oklahoma,' I say.

'The panhandle state,' he says, looking deeply into her eyes.

'Like a saucepan,' she says. 'That's the one. Not a nice place, if you ask me.'

'So, what are you planning to do to my mother's face?'

He turns his smile to me and I can see it is designed to disarm. So are his words. 'Good to see you here. Such a support,' he says. 'You must be a good daughter.'

'No, she *is* a good daughter,' Mom says. 'We do everything together.'

'It would be normal to be worried about your mother.'

Yes. 'Damn straight I'm worried.'

'She has a bit of a mouth on her,' Mom says. 'Don't pay any notice.'

Then, without taking his eyes from mine, he gets up and comes over. He stands beside my chair and puts his hand on my shoulder, as if he's a priest and I'm taking my first communion. He says to Mom without turning, 'No need to apologise at all. She's delightful.'

He strokes my hair, and I find that I let him. He tilts my face to look upwards to him. 'Great cheekbones. Good chin, fantastic nose, durable skin. You'd get ten years back with a peel.' He has deep brown eyes and long eyelashes. I'm sure he's wearing mascara and I'd put money on eyeliner as well. His aftershave is woody and fresh and his teeth are as white as a ten-year-old's but his breath smells of something off. An unpleasant and slightly familiar smell. Ketones. He's on a low-carb diet.

Mom says, 'She takes after me, except for the nose. I can't take credit for the nose.'

I mutter, 'Dad had bone structure too.'

'Well, you've been doubly blessed, then,' he says. Then he slides his hand down and strokes my back. His hand feels strong and purposeful and, though I pull away, I still feel a finger making a definite circle in the small of my back. He has the hands of a pickpocket.

'Your father's looks weren't all that.' Mom sounds annoyed: he's paying attention to me, not to her. Astutely, Chartaine retreats behind his desk again.

'It's a quick procedure. Quite routine but we'll want to do some pre-op workups just to make sure everything is shipshape. Just jumping through hoops. You know the drill.'

It's a whole hour later, after heaps of paperwork and forward appointments to schedule, and we've just walked into the underground car park which is cold, dark and stinks of gas fumes. I'm going to have to start parking my car on the street when I go back to work: these fumes, I have just learned from the receptionist as we left, are particularly toxic for the skin.

The place looks different from this angle and I can't hold my breath any more. I've got to figure out where we left the rental. I should have paid attention when we arrived, but we were arguing about whether or not popcorn has nutritional value.

'He's an asshole, Mom. How much are you paying for this? Are you sure you want him near your face with a scalpel – and what's with his hair? He looks like some kind of tropical bird.'

We start down another row of cars.

'I think he's nice and Brenda recommended him. He did her daughter-in-law's nose, and threw in some decent breasts for free. I got a good price. Where's the car?' she asks.

'We're looking for it.'

'You should mark the row on the ticket. This place is huge.'

'I have never, ever – not once – seen *you* do that.'

'When did you last see me lose a car? You should pay more attention.'

We start down the fourth row.

'You were with me. You could help.'

'The driver is responsible. We were late. I was worried he might not see us.'

'You made us late. And for the amount you're paying he'd have made a house call.'

'No doctor makes house calls.'

I'm looking for a dark blue car, but I'm starting to wonder if the rental was, in fact, another colour, and then she points. 'There it is, it's got the Hertz sticker in the back window.'

'Nothing wrong with *my* eyes,' she says when we get to the exit.

Which just annoys me because now I can't find the ticket in my purse.

'Mom, did I hand you the ticket?'

'No,' she says. 'You'll have to tell them and they'll charge you for the whole day.'

'It's got to be here. Somewhere.' I tip the contents of my bag on to my lap. Two lipsticks missing the caps. Grubby packets of Tylenol. My migraine meds. Four pens, a bunch of receipts for junk I bought, some coins, hairy hard candies stuck to each other. Couple of bobby pins.

'You need to get more organised, honey,'

Finally, I remember that I put the ticket in the glove compartment because I was worried about losing it. 'I'm organised just fine, Mom. Do you want to fucking walk from here?' I scoop the stuff back into the bag.

'Honey, you're very cranky lately.'

And of all the criticism she's aimed at me so far this week this is the worst because it's true. Just like the Seven Dwarves of Menopause in a cartoon someone put up in the ladies' room at work, I've been bitchy, itchy, sweaty, sleepy, bloated, forgetful and a bit psycho lately. I've not had a period now for six months. I'm sure my OB-GYN will be happy to confirm it, at the cost of a vial of blood and a hundred and fifty bucks, but what's the point? It's perfectly natural. I just need to accept it, and ride it out. In silence, I put the ticket in the slot and the arm lifts to let us out.

'I'm sorry,' she says. 'I do appreciate you coming to take care of me.'

'No, *I'm* sorry, it's not you.'

'I know, honey.' She pauses and sighs. 'You know, he thinks I'm terrific for my age, and if he thinks that, I could tell him a thing or two!'

'He thought I needed a peel. Do you think I should have a peel?'

'At *least* a peel. You're looking your age lately.'

'God, Mom!'

'I'm your mother,' she says. 'My job is to tell you the truth. Nowadays there's no reason to look your age.'

The blood workup goes okay, and the nurse is happy with Mom's weight and blood pressure. The operation is going to be done at Memorial Hospital and we are supposed to be there by six a.m. It's not easy for either of us to wake up that early, but I'm up at four, and Mom makes an unusual heroic effort, which means we manage to arrive only half an hour late.

I've brought the sunglasses and scarf that the leaflet recommended and I put these in a drawer near her bed. She's scheduled to share a room but the other bed is empty, so she swaps the charts to get the window view. As worried as I am, Mom is in good spirits. When they come with the pre-med she gulps down the pills with one of those small paper cups of water, and makes a joke about getting a legal high, but all I'm thinking afterwards is how small she looks lying there, waiting.

A few minutes later the anaesthetist comes to see her. He seems competent – asks some good questions and actually looks at her when she replies. Then, her voice changes. She's slurring her words as she tells him that he's handsome, that he must have to beat the ladies off, and that just to have his hands on her makes having this operation worth it, whatever it was costing. 'What's your cut?' she says just before she suddenly falls asleep.

I burst into tears.

'She'll be okay. Don't worry. We'll take care of your grandmother,' he says, and I don't correct him. I tell him thanks.

Chartaine comes to see her next. This time his impressive tuft of hair is contained in a scrub cap. When he sees she's already asleep he rather sweetly strokes her head, as though he really cares. I think about how she should have had her roots done before this. It's going to be a month before she can get another colour on. She might have to dig out her wig or something. 'Just checking,' he says, 'does your mother have any false teeth, or bridges?'

'No, she's got good teeth.'

'Why am I not surprised? She takes good care of herself.'

I blurt out, 'I think I'll have a peel while I'm in town.'

'Well, one thing at a time. Let's get your mom's face fixed.' He picks up her wrist and she wriggles a bit, but remains asleep. 'Steady heart.'

'She won't look like a freak, will she? She'll still look like herself?'

'She'll look *more* like herself. Muscles sag; skin loses its tone.' He glances at my chest. 'Breasts drop.' Now he looks at my belly and I reflexively suck it in. 'After kids, without surgery, a woman's stomach is never the same again. It's like that. Things take a toll. *Life* takes a toll.' He sighs like he understands about how that might be, about how everything might be, all the disappointments, and how time runs out on you nearly every day. He doesn't wear a wedding ring. He's probably divorced. He's a doctor. He must see crap all the time. No wonder they have the highest suicide rate.

I let my abs relax. I whisper, 'I've never had kids. I couldn't.'

He nods knowingly and looks me straight in the eye and says, 'Well, you'd have made a great mother.' He stops speaking and we look at each other. He doesn't drop his gaze. He squeezes my shoulder and says, 'Hey, we'll do that peel and you'll be fantastic and, meantime, she'll be fine. I know what I'm doing. I promise.' Finally he tells me what we already know, that she's got to stay in for two nights and then she'll be home.

While the surgery is going on, I go down to the gift shop and choose a bouquet of flowers for her room for when she wakes up, and a couple of magazines and some chocolates. There really isn't much choice in the store. The box I choose is heart-shaped and all the chocolates inside are strawberry-flavoured. It probably a leftover from Valentine's Day but they are still in date. I don't like strawberry, but Mom will.

The surgery should only take two hours, so when it runs beyond three hours I'm getting a bit antsy. 'Is my mom in recovery yet?' I ask at the desk.

'No, they let us know when they go into recovery, so I'll have to say, not yet.'

'Has something gone wrong?'

'No, they let us know when something goes wrong, so I'll have to say, probably not.'

'Can you call them?'

'Ma'am, the operating theatres are very busy environments. They've got a whole lot of people to take care of and need to devote their attention to that, not to phone calls. I have to say I think we need to let them do their job.'

'What's your name? Because *I* have to say – ' I point ' – you are not wearing a name badge.'

'Susan.'

I look at my watch, 'Twenty minutes, and I'll be back, Susan. If anything has happened to her and you've not told me, there will be questions. I'll want answers.'

But, before another five minutes is up, a nurse comes to tell me that Mom is in recovery and will be back to the room in an hour. He tells me that she's okay, done really, really well and that he'll be with us to go through the information on aftercare around four o'clock.

I eat the entire contents of the box of chocolates I bought for Mom in the next ten minutes. I shovel them into my mouth and gobble them up – one after the other. I feel sick from all the sugar and fat, and also plain disgusted with myself. A facial peel won't deal with an extra twenty pounds of weight. I'll need lipo. I've got to operate some self-control.

When I've finished, I remove the evidence by dumping the empty box at the nurses' station.

She's home three days later and looks dreadful, but this, we're told, is to be expected. 'Do you think I'm too old to have a facelift?' she asks as soon as we get in the car.

'Mom, it's already done.'

'Do you think it worked?'

She's had her eyelids and the bags under her eyes done at the same time as the facelift. Even so, her actual eyes are visible, but the rest of her face is covered with bandages. She could be a stranger under there, except for the voice, and the fact that she's wearing my mother's clothes. 'Sure, of course it worked.' Then I know for sure she's my mom because she asks if 'this time' I've remembered where I put the ticket.

When we get home, the phone is ringing. Brenda is the first person to call to find out how Mom is doing. Brenda is one of her longstanding Mah Jongg buddies. They're a group of widows – each as obsessive about the game as the other – and I've figured out that when Mom won't say where she is, she's playing Mah Jongg. The tick-tick-tick sound of the tiles would drive me nuts. Mom tried to teach me a couple of years ago, but declared I wasn't up to it, and she never tried again.

'She's doing great,' I say. This makes Mom shake her head maniacally. 'Well, not that good really, I guess,' I add – puzzled. Mom starts nodding. 'But we're trusting that she'll improve.' The shaking starts again. 'That she might improve. We're bearing up,' I finish. Mom nods her approval at my lies.

Brenda sounds concerned and says everyone is missing her and that I should wish her well.

'Why didn't you tell me what you'd told them, before I had to field this shit?' I ask as soon as I hang up the phone. 'I feel like a midget playing basketball.'

'I didn't tell them what kind of surgery I needed.'

'Brenda knows you've had a facelift. She's the one who recommended Chartaine. She's your friend.'

'By the time I get back, I'll just look rested. We don't need to talk about it,' she says. 'No one wants to discuss plastics.' And that's the final word.

Gus, Mom's friend from her church, comes to do the work in the garden on schedule, at two o'clock. At the sound of the doorbell she goes to hide in her bedroom with the curtains drawn and I have to make out that she's having a rest because, of course, she doesn't want him to know either.

Even if she is determined not to see him, with Gus around, technically, she's not alone, so I take the opportunity to go out to the store. Now she's back I've got a list of stuff to get and I need to get her Vicodin prescription filled.

The displays in the drugstore are now all about the fact that Hallowe'en is only ten days away. There are decorations to choose from and countless bags of treat-sized candies: mini Hershey bars, bite-size Reese's Peanut Butter Cups and Tootsie Rolls and we should stock up. I get a sign to put on the lawn, which is a ghost wearing a top hat that says *Trick or Treaters Welcome Here* and pile bags of the candies into the shopping basket.

Ten minutes later, on my search for the pharmacy counter, I find myself stuck in feminine products. In Aisle C there appears to be a stepped graduation from bright glamorous boxes of various types of tampons one end of the aisle, to duller boxes of sanitary towels, to disposable douches, to feminine hygiene washes and wipes, to incontinence underwear (male and female) and bed pads.

It makes me feel ancient, knowing that I can remember the time before Tampax was suitable for girls, and before old ladies gave up stockings for pantyhose. Sanitary belts, garter belts, girdles: all those contraptions womankind discarded only a few years before I was scheduled to wear them. No self-respecting woman would ever wear a girdle now – but what's different about Spanx, really?

This aisle of horror ends at a T-junction opposite the pharmacy counter, with shelves there stuffed full of suppositories, boxed enemas, jumbo containers of Metamucil, Ex-Lax pills, other constipation treatments and then haemorrhoid creams, wipes and aerosol foams.

I drop Mom's pain med prescription to be filled and then, while waiting pick up some eye ointment that Chartaine suggested too, I wander around the store.

Mom likes Fresca; there's a special offer on, so I get two dozen cans. I get a copy of *People* magazine, and this month's *Reader's Digest*, and a copy of the *National Enquirer*, which I begin to read when I return and have to sit and wait for the pharmacist to do the final check of her tablets. On page three there's an article, with pictures, about men in China who developed seizures from playing Mah Jongg, and another one on page six about botched plastic surgery: 'My surgeon turned me into a werewolf'.

I read it from cover to cover while I'm waiting and then decide not to buy this trashy magazine. Finally, I get a DVD for us to watch. On the way home I stop at Safeway and buy some cheese and bagels, popcorn and a bag of ring donuts. I can't think what else to get. We can order takeout if Mom wants different.

Gus is just finishing. He's put some new mulch under the trees in the front yard, and has weeded the flowerbed by the driveway. The lawn looks good. He's set up the sprinkler and tells me that I should switch it off at nine o'clock this evening. Even as I listen to what he's saying, I'm trying to remember to remember it. 'Say hi to your mom,' he says as I wave him goodbye.

1408, the film, is good. Of course, it's a horror film and we share a bottle of wine and three bags of popcorn. I tell Mom that she should keep the bandages on until after Hallowe'en so that she can answer the door. I say she looks like a real mummy, and this makes us both giggle even more, but then she keeps saying, 'No, no,' and tells me, through gritted teeth, that she can't laugh because, when she does, it feels like it's stretching her stitches. I tell her about the Mah Jongg epileptics. She makes these funny desperate squashed laughter sounds, and this increases the hilarity. We haven't laughed so much together for years.

When it's time for bed she says, 'You should get it done, your face. He'll take good care of you. It's okay.'

A week later I arrive at Chartaine's office without make-up and feeling optimistic. Even though he tells me to be silent, Chartaine talks throughout the twenty minutes it takes for him to apply the goop. His breath is a bit better, but still a bit bad. He tells me that he enjoyed taking care of my mom and that he likes living in Phoenix for the sun, then right away he says that I'll have to use a factor 70 sunscreen forever. Did I know that? I mustn't forget that. He moved here from Ohio then his wife left him for a tennis pro. But he enjoys golf and the golf courses here are the best in the country. Finally, he tells me that the greatest effect from the peel won't be today or tomorrow but over the next week.

'It's like a sunburn,' he says. 'Your skin will get redder and redder in the next three or four days. That's normal. I'll give you some cream to use; don't use anything else. Nothing else, honey. We'll follow up in a week and we'll take it from there.'

At the very end, as he's moving the chair to upright again, he says, 'Fantastic job,' as if I've been doing the treatment, not him. He squeezes my hand and, for the first time in ages I have a surprising and uncomfortable rising sense of excitement that reminds me that, despite the onslaught of menopause, my libido has not entirely checked out. I want him to kiss me. I want him to do more. I can feel my body warm to the idea, and at that thought I think I begin to blush, but I can't tell, because suddenly my whole face now begins to feel as though it's on fire.

By the time Hallowe'en night comes Mom has puffy and purple-ringed eyes, green and yellow bruises on her cheeks and jawline, and the stitches running around the front of her ear and into her hairline are still bright red and angry. The zinc-white ointment I've slathered thickly on my face makes it look like I'm wearing a Kabuki mask. There are fewer children than I thought would come and those who do step back when we open the door. A few actually run away.

We have fifty Tootsie Rolls and a whole bunch of Peanut Butter Cups left over. When we finally switch off the hall light, we decide to finish them off, and down another bottle of wine together. 'I like him, Mom,' I say, about Chartaine. 'It was a good idea. Why not make the best of your looks? Why not?'

'I'm getting my eyebrows tattooed,' she says. 'They've gone so thin. I want definition.'

'We all want definition,' I say. 'I think that's the main problem.'

At first I am disappointed to see Chartaine's assistant, instead of the man himself, for the follow-up appointment. He's probably off playing golf. She introduces herself and

41

apologises for Chartaine's absence. I recognise her name – she's the one who took out some of Mom's stitches. Marla is very professional, and meticulous as she takes a careful look at my face. She tells me that rosacea, should I develop that, can be fixed with laser treatment, so I mustn't worry. She can't tell me the odds for sure, but I get the feeling I should start to plan financially.

She honestly seems pleased with the results of the peel, and I tell her I am too.

By the time I leave Phoenix the swelling is going down on Mom's face and she's starting to look normal, and better than before. When I return to work, everyone says I look refreshed, that the time away did me good. I schedule my next lot of vacation time for Thanksgiving. Mom's hygienist already has us booked in for tooth-whitening.

2005

The Wind

'I'm not coming and you shouldn't go either. This weekend is five days away and Mississippi is right next door to Louisiana. They've evacuated there too. Things are in ruins.'

I'm at work and we're on the phone. It's my mother.

'I have to be there for Patty,' she says, 'She's one of my oldest friends. I really can't go alone. Please just get the tickets. I'll pay for yours too. It'll be fun to be together.'

'Mom, it might mess up her plans if you don't go to her wedding but she should have cancelled it – or postponed it. My phone hasn't stopped ringing with people cancelling plans. I'm real busy with rescheduling loads of stuff. She *will* understand, for sure.'

'She can't reorganise. She's got a deadline. They've got a honeymoon booked.'

Then my supervisor, Brad, walks in and I have to pretend that I'm talking to a client instead of to my mom. 'So, exactly what dates are you looking at?' I say.

'Friday. Friday 2nd September. We'll travel that evening and rent a car. The place she's chosen is real rural, but I know it. It'll be fine.'

'And how long do you want?'

'Just two nights. I'll meet you there. Get two flights that arrive in Greenville around the same time and we can both fly home Sunday morning. Please come.'

'I'll have to check, and get back to you. Can I take a number?'

'You know my number.'

'Uh huh.' I scribble something down that might look vaguely like an out-of-state phone number. 'I'll ring you right back after I review our availability. Looking forward to doing business with you.' And then I hang up.

'A booking? Finally, a booking,' Brad says. 'Anyone would think that the world had come to an end.'

'For thousands of people it has. I don't know why they weren't evacuated quicker. I think it's really bad, really.'

'Rome wasn't built in a day. Big things take time. They know what they're doing, and people like you who don't know all the facts shouldn't overreact,' he says.

I don't respond. I read in the *Reader's Digest* that if you want to do well in a job it's best to let the boss have the last word and this is true, I'm sure, even if he is an asshole like mine. Brad's latest line is that no one can accuse him of discrimination, because he hates black people and gay people equally.

'I still say she should have postponed or chosen some other place.' We are whispering. The wedding, being held in a place known as the catfish capital of the world, is about to begin.

'This venue is not available again for another two months.'

'Well, it's hardly available now. Some of the glass is covered with Saran Wrap. Who wants to get married in Belzoni? The town sounds like a pizza.'

'You shouldn't be such a snob,' Mom says.

We are still arguing as the music starts up. Patty's Mississippi groom walks down the makeshift aisle, backslapping, shoulder-squeezing, high-fiving and talking to everyone as he makes his way to the front. I'm glad we're not sitting on the aisle.

The first thing you notice about Gary is his moustache and receding chin. He looks a bit like an old chipmunk. At first his hair doesn't look long, because it's pulled back in a ponytail. We keep getting a view of a large round bald patch on the very top of his head when he bends down to speak to the seated guests. He is wearing a white suit that must be pure linen because it looks so bedraggled. This was a really bad choice, because it is crazy humid; Patty is getting married in the hot-house of a sort of botanical gardens. There is a terrible stench of lilies and the strong earthy smell of some mulch they must have used to pack in the flowers. Some of the orchids look tilted, wilted and dying. However, all of the flowers everywhere are oversized – like this place is the 'after' of genetic engineering gone wrong.

There are plenty of empty seats around. Someone should suggest we squeeze up, but it doesn't look like anyone is taking charge of the event. I can't spot an MC. This kind of thing irritates me because, professionally speaking, when people don't know what to do they experience anxiety.

My hair is beginning to frizz up and I'm starting to envy Mom's wig. It might be artificial but hers is the only hair within fifty feet that looks like it probably is supposed to look. A couple of years ago she bought this wig for use in emergencies and she didn't have time to get her colour done before the trip. It looks exactly the same as her own hair – short and ash-blonde, the same style she's had for years now.

I try to remember when she cut her hair because when I was a kid it was quite long, but maybe it was gradual. As women get older their hair needs to be coloured more and more frequently, and in middle age there seems to be an unspoken rule that it should be cut. Shorter and shorter the hair goes and then it starts to thin, so finally, I suppose, a wig is the neatest, most reliable solution. Liz Taylor used to wear one all the time.

Speaking of Elizabeth Taylor, I haven't seen Patty in at least a decade and, since I last saw her, she's put on a hundred and fifty pounds. Even the *Jurassic Park* flowers here can't disguise her size as she waddles towards the podium where Gary and the lady officiate are waiting.

There are no bridesmaids and, although this is her third or fourth marriage and she's my mother's age, Patty is wearing a white wedding dress with a cream lace veil over her face. She looks like a slightly toasted marshmallow. An extremely old and small man with a walker escorts her. Mom nudges me and whispers, 'That's Patty's uncle.' When some little kid starts to wail the sound distracts him. He lets go of the walker to straighten up and look around, puzzled, like he's forgotten where he was or what he was supposed to be doing. Patty tugs on his arm to encourage him forward again.

'Alzheimer's,' Mom says. 'Pitiful.'

As soon as they get to the front, Gary pulls the uncle towards a waiting chair and uses the walker to block him in place. Patty lifts the veil off her own face and dumps the flowers on her uncle's lap.

We are called to order. The officiate begins by saying she is here, with us, to participate in our experience. She says her role is to ensure it is all done according to the laws of Mississippi. Her title is 'celebrant' and she fully anticipates that she will celebrate with us today. She makes a little clapping motion. I begin to be entranced by her large, expressive hands, which she uses to emphasise otherwise familiar words in the marriage ceremony. Perhaps referring to Patty's previous series of unsuccessful marriages, she gestures with her right thumb over her shoulder and tells us, 'The past is there, in the past. Locked away – ' she mimes turning a key in a lock ' – safe and secure, not to be revisited.' Now her face becomes serious as she indicates the four sides of a box, or safe perhaps, and she pauses, allowing this information to sink in, before she continues. 'Time to come…' She stops and points to indicate that the future is situated in the lobby, 'is yet to arrive.' At this her face lifts into a big smile. We should be happy about the future. I'm beginning to wonder if she perhaps was the only hearing child in a household of deaf people.

Mom whispers, 'Does she think we're all idiots?'

'Shush.' I like this woman's sincerity. This is probably a second career for her. I'm sure people don't set out to do this kind of work until they've acquired a bit of life experience because it must be difficult to command a mixed audience like this. She looks a little bit older than me – in her fifties probably – and she's wearing a sensible outfit for the occasion, for her large size, and for the heat: a flowing dress in thin material, grey background with small geometric patterns randomly set.

Now she's talking about the highway of life – she indicates holding a steering wheel – 'with all the potential of a lot of different paths to take.' She turns her head all the way left and right, convincingly like a confused driver. And then she does another long pause for us to catch up and finally she concludes, 'Patty and Gary have decided to go this way … here … today.' Using both hands, she dramatically points to the ground immediately in front of the feet of the bride and groom. Everyone seems to lean forward in unison to look at whatever she's pointing at and at this movement the old man, Patty's uncle, suddenly stands up. The bouquet falls to the ground and he shouts, 'What the hell is happening?'

Patty rushes over to calm him and gets him seated again and the woman quickly sums it all up by announcing Patty and Gary 'wife and husband.' For my part, I'm a bit disappointed that she decides to end it so abruptly, because not only have I been enjoying the dramatics, I've concluded that this style of talk would also do nicely for a funeral service, and if she could go on for a bit longer it would test the theory more soundly.

After the ceremony, over champagne and cloying strawberry tartlets served by bored-looking waitresses, Gary continues to work what would be the room; his interaction is easier now that people are no longer stationary and everyone is nearly eye-level. 'Just call me Gary,' he says when he wanders up to Mom and me. We're huddled together near the drinks table. She's had three; I'm on my second glass.

I ask, 'So have you got another name we could use?'

He looks at me blankly.

Mom tells him first that she and Patty have been friends forever and then introduces me. 'This is my daughter. She begged to come with me. Support, you know, and Patty knows her. She positively adores Patty. We're very close.'

I'm not sure if Mom means she and I are close or that she and Patty are close but Gary seems to understand well enough that we're all good buddies. He nods. 'Uh huh.' There is a brief, polite, pause then he changes gear and says, 'So, have you heard the joke about the guy out hunting in the woods?' I have already heard Brad tell this stupid joke a hundred times. 'So, anyway,' Gary says without acknowledging my nod, 'this guy shot his friend. Hunting accident. He phones 911 and he tells them there's been an accident and he's shot this guy and the girl on the phone asks, is he dead? She asks, is he dead? First thing, can you check and see that he's dead? And then...and then...ha, ha, ha...there's another shot... The guy comes back to the phone and says okay, now he's dead. Ha, ha, ha,' Gary says, 'what do you make of that, hey?'

Mom starts up with fake laughing.

'So exactly how long have *you* known Patty?' I ask.

'Oh, years. Long time,' he says. He is looking over my shoulder.

'Hilarious joke,' Mom says. 'Ha, ha, ha.'

He drifts away again and Mom says to me, 'She's got some terrible taste in men, but there was no need to be rude.'

'I can't think when it's this hot. I'm sweating like a pig.'

'Yes, imagine poor Patty. How hot she must be – the size of a baby elephant.'

'So, what happened? Stomach balloon removed?'

'She was in fashion. I guess when she retired she wanted to eat.' She pauses to look around. 'Honey, I've got to find the restroom.' Now she puts her empty champagne flute to her cheek then her forehead. It tilts the wig a bit, makes it a little crooked and it's suddenly obvious that she's wearing a wig. Before I can say anything Patty waves and heads our way. She makes a grab for Mom. They air kiss and the hair moves a little more. 'Let me look at you,' Patty says, speaking to Mom. 'How long has it been?'

'Let me look at *you*. There's sure a lot to see.'

'I know.' She looks around. 'We chose the place because it's just so unusual. Hey, you grew up around here, didn't you?' She doesn't wait for a reply and breathlessly rushes on. 'I'm so, so, so pleased you made the effort. I know Katrina rather stole the show. Did you meet my man Gary yet?'

'We sure did,' Mom says.

'Isn't he just one sweet guy? My man. *My* man,' Patty repeats.

'He is that. Funny guy. And it's all legal, done and dusted.' Mom puts down her empty and reaches for another glass of champagne from the tray of a passing waitress, and, again, rests this one against her cheek. It moves the wig once more. 'Ah, that's better.'

But Patty isn't listening because she's spotted this and gasps. 'Are you okay?'

'It's a sauna in here,' Mom says. 'Never mind blushing, you must be the boiling bride.'

'Honey, do you need any help? Can I get you anything? God, all this time and life just goes so fast and then it's over. Oh, I'm so sorry, I shouldn't have said that.'

'My mom is not dying,' I say.

Mom says, 'Patty, you are the most bouncy-back person I will ever know.'

'Oh, honey, you are just so kind to say something like that.' She looks like she's about to cry. Underneath all that blubber she's got a pretty face, and she obviously really cares about Mom. 'Coming from you that means loads. I don't know anyone who has overcome as much as you.'

I say, 'We were just on our way to the restroom to freshen up. Where can we find it?'

'Over there.' She points to near the entrance. Then she leans over and hisses in my ear, 'I'm so, so sorry. Thank you for making this effort to come along. You must let me know, won't you? Oh, God.'

'She's fine,' I say. 'Really. She is.'

'So brave!' she calls after us. 'So, so brave.'

'Let's get out of here,' Mom says. 'I can't believe you let me come.'

We go straight past the restrooms and out the entrance into the slightly fresher heat the other side of the double doors. 'Who in their right mind would have a wedding this time of year?' Mom says. She wobbles on her feet as she gets into the taxi – probably waiting for someone else – outside.

'Well, who'd get married?' I reply.

But I guess Mom has absorbed something of the wedding talk and she's been drinking. 'You know, honey, sometimes I even miss your dad, God rest his sad little soul, and you must miss something from when you were married to the midget.'

'He wasn't a midget.'

'Dwarf, then.'

'He was the love of my life.'

'Suppose a person doesn't notice height when you're lying down.' She laughs at her joke.

'I do kind of miss regular sex.' This is true. I frequently miss having someone near me in bed at night. I suddenly realise how much I want to be wanted like that by a man again. I wonder if I'll ever be wanted like that again. 'Maybe Patty did a good thing getting married. She'll have done a pre-nup, of course.'

'Oh, yes.' Then Mom sounds wistful when she says, 'Me, I'd have liked the opportunity to miss regular sex. But your father ...'

I interrupt. I don't want to hear about whatever they got up to in bed, or didn't.

'Love,' I say. 'Patty must just love Gary. God knows why, but that must be it.'

'You know, nowadays you can have regular sex, honey – as much as you want or as much as you need – with whoever you want, whatever you want nowadays, no one needs to be married any more, unless you want an excuse for an event, I guess. People can sleep with other people. It's okay.'

'I know that.'

I spot that the cab driver is following our conversation with interest. He is looking at the two of us in his rear-view mirror and smirking.

Normally I'd have given him the finger, but in this backwater dump in an unfamiliar state and given the content of our conversation, it wouldn't help the situation, so I just look out the window and calculate how much his tip would have been now that he's not going to have one.

It's a long enough drive – around twenty miles back to the motel – and Mom seems to doze off. Where we stayed last night and will stay tonight is halfway between the wedding venue and Mid Delta Airport outside Greenville. We didn't rent a car because there was nothing available when we arrived. It's such a small place clearly not even rent-a-wreck can be bothered to make the effort. I saw some diner within walking distance where we can eat tonight, but there are no bright lights in Belzoni.

When we get back to the room, the TV is blaring out. 'You forgot to turn the TV off.'

'No, I didn't,' she says.

'I went to the office to get the cab and left you here. You didn't turn it off.'

'The maid must have been watching it.' She pulls the wig from her head and throws it on her bed. 'I'm going to take a shower and cool down. Turn the AC up. This humidity and heat is just awful.'

'I know you left the TV on,' I mutter. I sit down on my bed right in front of the screen where images of the hurricane aftermath are crowding in one after the other accompanied by commentary about the too-little, too-late evacuation. There are more amateur video clips, then still after still of stranded people. Almost every single one of the people in the pictures is black. There's one of a mother trying to hold her small child above the water, of a man in a boat struggling to paddle it with a plank of wood, of what appears to be a dead body floating in the floodwater.

'You should change the channel,' she calls through from the bathroom.

Instead I turn up the AC as she requested. Cool air blasts into the room from the unit.

I think about the past and future of these people and of the place. Poverty is a life sentence, sometimes a death sentence. Poverty ties people to places for generations.

This county here seems really deprived, full of inbred trailer-trash rednecks. Patty said Mom grew up not far away, which is hard to believe, but Mom didn't disagree. She never talks about her childhood. She had a couple of sisters that she hated and, once she moved out of state with Dad, I think she never saw them again. Most seniors bang on about the past, but not Mom. Where we lived when I grew up, and where she lives now, are a different world from this one. I momentarily regret withholding the tip from the cab driver.

Mom comes back into the room, dripping wet and wrapped in a towel. 'I agree with Patty.' She glances at the TV. 'You can't always focus on the bad stuff. Put on the shopping channel.'

I don't move. The president is being interviewed in Mississippi. 'Bush is in Biloxi,' I say. 'It's real bad there too.'

'That's hundreds of miles from here.'

'Two hundred.'

The coverage cuts back to stills of the damage. There's a dead dog at the side of a pile of slurry; an aerial view of the tops of houses, like Monopoly pieces in a puddle; a helicopter tries to rescue a woman and what looks like a boy, but might be a girl, or another woman, the two of them are clinging to a rooftop. Then there's a video clip of a helicopter circling a family group – a man holding a baby, a woman and another small child. The helicopter flies off suddenly, apparently abandoning the rescue effort.

'How can they leave people like this?' I say.

'Don't upset yourself.'

She goes back to the bathroom and I hear the hairdryer going. 'Shut the door,' I shout, but she doesn't reply. Maybe she can't hear me, but, then, she never actually listens to me. I turn up the volume. It looks like reports from a war zone or something and it reminds me about how Vietnam invaded our home when I was a little kid.

The entire landscape will never be the same again. It'll take a quarter of a century before it starts to look okay. There are more and more photos. People in distress crying, devastated houses. The ticker-tape at the bottom of the screen reports that the Superdome roof is leaking and the building is now flooding. The conditions inside are dire and there are reports of violence, drugs and rape. None confirmed, it adds, but three evacuees have died there already. Buses are to evacuate the stadium and also the tens of thousands of people currently housed in the New Orleans Convention Center. They're taking them to Texas.

Mom comes out again. She puts on some underwear and pads heavily barefoot around her bed to stand next to me. 'You should change the channel. Or at least turn it down.'

I don't move. 'I'm watching this.'

'Come on.' She reaches over and tries to grab the remote from my left hand. I fixedly transfer it to my right hand, then to both hands. 'I can't hear myself think,' she says. She is now standing directly in front of the screen, between me and the TV. She's still just in her underwear. I can smell her skin, the soap she uses, her deodorant and her shampoo.

I shift to try to see around her, but she's like a bear – too big, too close to the TV. She is obliterating my view.

'Move.' Now I am shouting. 'Move. Move. Let me see. Let me see.'

She leans forward to grab the remote again. She says, 'No. This is not good for you.'

It's the way that she says it that makes me look at her. Her face, like her voice, is blank, flat, like a stranger, someone who I don't know, who doesn't know me, let alone care about me, or for me.

'Don't,' she says. 'Stop.'

We lock eyes for a couple of seconds – no more – then she turns around to do something to the TV, but then I drop the remote and she bends down and picks it up from the floor.

She holds it with two hands, squints at it, and then she punches at the buttons with a thumb. She changes the channel. The sound of some drug ad for depression blares out at us, reciting numerous possible side effects of taking the drug to make you feel normal, and then she finally manages to mute the sound.

'You should get changed,' she says. 'In that get-up you look like a bridesmaid or something. Why don't they have a minibar in the rooms?'

'The wig you were wearing makes you look like you're on chemo. You looked like a dying person.'

'Well, I'm not,' she says. 'I'm not. I'm not dying here.'

I shower and dress in shorts and a top. It's too early to eat dinner, really, but at the diner they're happy to accommodate us – because the place is empty. We both order burgers and fries, coleslaw and onion rings. They don't serve alcohol except for beer, but that will do. The cold drink and air-conditioning helps a lot.

Mom tells me stories about Patty's previous husbands and why they got divorced. She had a kid once, who died as a baby. She'd wanted a big family because she was an only child but it didn't happen. 'Won't happen now,' Mom says. 'Way, way too late.'

The woman had a crappy life, I guess, and Mom is trying to be a good friend. I'm kind of glad we came to the wedding after all.

Once back in the room we lie in bed to watch the ABC Movie of the Week and I fall asleep before the end.

For some reason the airport looks even smaller than when we arrived. Mom's plane is scheduled to leave a whole hour before mine departs and she's got a much longer flight. After saying goodbye I read a newspaper for a bit, then I watch the people working – at the ticket desk, the two cleaners, the people waiting like me. Airports small and large are all alike: transitory places full of people on their way to becoming something different. I moved to Oklahoma City for a fresh start, in the same way that my mother persuaded my father to move to Arizona all those years ago. But I moved alone, whereas she dragged us with her, unwilling, halfway across the country on what seemed like a whim.

I wonder about the thousands of people who will be displaced by the authorities now. Louisiana to Texas is quite a change.

When we land, I am relieved. The trip is in the past. The airport in Oklahoma City is reassuringly more modern and bigger than the hokey one in Greenville and it's even more of a relief to arrive back at my apartment. I unpack quickly, check the clock to see when Mom will get to her house, and then phone when I expect her to be back. She is. She sounds fine. Everything is as it should be.

Work is busy the first week of September and for days I try not to listen to the news. When I do, it is still preoccupied with Katrina. Dick Cheney and his wife finally go to visit and to offer their support. Everyone's been saying he stayed on vacation for too long because everyone wants someone to blame. Then there's an announcement that Al-Qaeda say they're planning attacks in California and Australia. Life is precarious, perpetually outside of individual control, so maybe it's not a bad thing to make an effort to change the small things when you can. The only man I spend any time with lately, my boss, is a total jerk. I'll buck the trend and grow my hair longer. I turn down an invitation to the movies from Linda and instead make plans to update my resume on the weekend. I should date more. I could join an agency. I even think that it's not too late to try again to have a child. Maybe.

On the phone Mom tells me that she's had her hair colour done. She doesn't want to wear the wig again. Not if people think she's got cancer. I tell her to keep it. You never know what might happen. 'You might *get* cancer,' I say. 'And then you'll really regret it.'

She doesn't laugh.

'I'm only joking,' I say. 'I just think it's good to keep all options open. Guess you haven't heard from Patty. How long is her honeymoon?'

'It was a Caribbean cruise. It got cancelled. She's going on a diet because she saw the wedding pictures. She's got to drop fifty pounds and then she can have some lipo. I need you to tell me if I look ridiculous. I'll tell you. We've got to look out for each other.'

We live a thousand miles apart. 'Yeah, well,' I say. 'I'm okay, Mom.'

'And if I get sick?'

'Sure, Mom,' I say. 'I'll tell you if you get sick.'

1999

The Weasel

It's been a jam-packed flight and with a last-minute booking I got a bad seat assignment. I was positioned next to a woman with two rugrats that cried continually, and right in front of some fourth-grade monster who spent most of the journey kicking the back of my seat.

Though I'm pre-menstrual, headachy and feeling grimy as we finally exit the plane, I walk along the concourse feeling freer with every step. I'm hoping that, because I was late checking in, my bag might be one of the first on to the conveyor belt, so it won't be long to wait.

It's May, the beginning of the summer, and through the glass I sense the familiar dry Phoenix heat – it'll be a good ten degrees hotter than Oklahoma out there – and I'm excited that I will see my mother soon and I know that this is a good thing to do. In fact, it'll be a relief to see her and healthy for me to have some vacation time. A fresh start.

And then something really does go right. It's no wait at all. The tenth suitcase that drops through the flaps is mine, and when I come out of baggage collection there she is – waving madly and right in front of me.

She looks different. When we hug, her body feels as though the stuffing has been removed, and her hair smells like a health food store. Since I last saw her she must have dropped thirty pounds. Her face is pale, gaunt and wrinkly. It's always nearly impossible to get facts from her when we're face to face but when it's only her voice down a phone line I have no idea what's happening and she's been exceptionally evasive lately. She's got too much insurance to be sick, and is too young to be senile, but I've worked out that once this guy Philip came on the scene she began giving up all her friends. A couple of months ago she explained that she felt she had to abandon some stuff. 'It's important to do things together and my friends bore him,' she said. In fact, it sounds as if she doesn't actually do anything any more and he's there all the time. It's as though my mother is fading away, or turning into someone else. Someone I don't recognise. Seeing her appearance now doesn't help.

It's not like I don't know that he's important in her life, but, when we walk out from the airport to the parking lot hand-in-hand and she points him out, I'm still shocked to see someone else sitting behind the wheel of Mom's car.

'Is that him? Is that Philip? He came with you? And you let him drive your car?'

'It's nice to be the passenger. And there's my toenail.'

'The toenail is on the other foot. And since when are you the passenger?'

'I'm thinking about getting one of those Subarus.'

'You love your Malibu. We've always bought Chevrolet. Dad always liked Chevrolet.'

'Your dad didn't know a thing about cars and things change. We have to move on.' Then, as we get close to the car, she tells me to deal with my face. 'No one wants to look at your miserable expression, honey. Try to look happy. First impressions are important.'

Aren't they just? I think. How could she have neglected to tell me about all that facial hair? When this guy does his version of a smile you can only really tell because a dark pink hole opens up between the overgrown moustache and the grubby grey beard. His teeth look yellow.

He doesn't get out to help with loading my bag into the trunk, or even to open the door for Mom.

I climb into the back seat. 'Mom, *I've* always loved this car; why would you replace it? I don't know why you'd think of changing it. It drives okay.' I remember how we went together to buy it and the salesman helped us out with a good deal because Mom charmed him and played up the fact that she was recently widowed. She did that for a long time, telling everyone she met about the shocking tragedy of losing her husband. Adding flourishes to the story, reducing the truth with every telling, and expecting me to play along. We argued on the way home from the lot. Knowing that the car we were going to collect the next day was going to be a thousand bucks cheaper than the showroom price, that it would be specially cleaned, the tank filled and that she had an extended guarantee for exactly no cost but her appreciation, she explained that it wasn't because she'd manipulated him, but it was because men always find vulnerable women appealing. 'It brings out that knight in shining armour that they all want to be. And you might want to think about that yourself. You have no idea how to behave around men. You batter decent people with your nasty mouth and scare men away. You could learn something. Even your father wanted to save the day,' she said.

I was missing Dad, and still angry. I said, 'What do you mean?'

'He was what was he was. I held up my end of the deal. One hundred and fifty per cent.'

I said that he'd have done anything to make her happy. He was always trying, but she was forever running off somewhere. What had he ever got out of the relationship but a lot of heartache? She shook her head and said she refused to dignify my question with an answer. 'There's lots you don't know,' she said. 'And you wouldn't understand what it was like.'

'Try me.'

'That's it,' she said. 'Enough. My life, my marriage, is none of your business.'

Now as we leave the parking lot Philip waits while Mom and I dig around in our purses to come up with payment. So, this guy is also a cheapskate. I'm quicker than Mom and pass forward the four bucks. The springs in the back seat beneath me ping as I shift my weight. They're worn out and the engine doesn't really sound great. The car, I guess, really is very old now, but she has always taken care of it. I wonder how that guy Randall, who used to deal with the car, is feeling now that this Philip is hanging around. If she has to replace the car she could get another Malibu. Randall would have recommended an updated Chevrolet, not some foreign car. I settle back again. 'You know Americans have a duty to buy American, Mom.'

'That's a very narrow-minded view,' Philip says, looking directly at me in the rear-view mirror. 'It's a global economy and we need to think about the environment. Other manufacturers do a better job.'

I mouth, 'Fuck you,' and he has the nerve to grin right back at me. I give him my meanest 'don't mess with me' stare (the one that should have worked on the twelve-year-old on the plane) until he chooses to look at the road again rather than risk an accident.

This is not a great start.

When we get into the house, Philip gets out fast and strides on ahead of us. He's wearing shorts as teeny as hotpants and flip-flops on his feet. I wonder if this is his key or if he's using Mom's car keys. Has she given him a key to the car and the house? From this distance I can't tell, but I am struck again by his appearance: his legs are sinewy, tanned and very hairy. It finally comes to me what he looks like: my mother has got herself tangled up with a weasel.

She waits with me while I unload my bag and trundle it up the path.

'When can I speak to you on your own?'

'We'll have plenty of time.'

'How on earth did you meet him?'

'Who?' she asks. We're at the door and she rushes on ahead before I can say we both know exactly who I mean.

The house smells earthy, and it looks dusty and untidy. I go directly to my bedroom, only to discover that my childhood bed which was moved from our previous home has been pushed against one wall and my vanity unit, which should also be in there, is gone. There's a desk now, with a big, expensive computer. I dump the bag on the bed and go to find her.

Mom is sitting at the kitchen table, smiling. Philip has removed his T-shirt and replaced it with one of my mother's pinafore aprons. It reaches down to his knees. He's not only topless, he's barefoot as well, and I can see his hairy, long toes. His arms are scrawny with muscle and his armpits dangle limp grey hair.

'You've changed my room,' is all I can say.

'It's the study now.' Philip says.

I will not look at him, or reply. I'm waiting for Mom to tell him to butt out but she doesn't. Finally, she says, 'I thought you'd like the computer, honey.'

'There's a password on it,' Philip says from the stove. 'Just tell me when you want to use it.'

I address her. 'When did you get a computer?'

'I don't use it. But I can, if I want. I think I'm going to take a class.'

Suddenly the weasel becomes animated again and forces his way into our conversation. 'The world is a small place now.' He waves the chopping knife around emphasising his words. 'It's fantastic how you can find out all sorts of things with the Internet. I'm always telling your mother how it's possible to see sights you could only imagine. Better than books ever were in that respect. Everything instant. It's such a wonderful thing. You can shop, manage your money, talk to friends, do everything on line. I couldn't live without it.'

As he prattles on, I notice that the kitchen windows are grimy and I wonder what's happened to Don who used to come and wash them weekly. I say, 'The house smells different, Mom. Have you changed your laundry detergent or something?'

She says, 'I only use natural products now. Better for the environment.'

I'm wondering when my mother started caring about the environment but that'll have to wait until we can talk on our own. 'I guess I can check my emails. That's good.'

'No problem,' he says. 'I'll set you up a user account after dinner.'

Mom never said that he had moved in – he's never answered the phone when I've phoned – but right now he looks very comfortable and at home.

'You sure look pretty handy in Mom's kitchen.'

'Philip is staying in the guest room. We don't sleep together,' Mom says.

He says, 'Of course not. Absolutely not.' And then the skinny, furry, ugly bastard turns and winks at me.

'So, where is *your* home?' I ask.

'Shall I say wherever I lay my hat?'

Mom sort of giggles. She sounds ridiculous, like she's thinks she's a teenager, and the kind of girl who laughs at any stupid joke a boy might make, just because he's a boy.

'I'm surprised you wear one,' I say. 'Since you wear nothing else.'

'Part of the reason I love Phoenix is the sunshine. I worship the sun and it does a body good. Hey, I hope you like mushrooms,' he adds. 'I'm making mushroom stroganoff for dinner.'

'Philip loves to cook.'

'Let me guess: vegetarian?'

'I got in the habit many years ago when I was living in Asia.'

'When was that?'

'Stop grilling him.'

'I'm sure you want us to get to know each other.'

'She wants to find out about the new man in her mother's life,' he says.

'No, I don't,' I say. 'I was only being polite.'

Now there's only the smell of frying onions and the sizzle of the big mushrooms as he slides them into the pan.

He wipes his hairy hands on the apron fabric and suddenly I remember. We were on a family vacation before Chip and I split and I bought this for her. Against the yellow background, the blue slogan reads *Pour one for the cook* and it's an inspiration for this situation. 'How about a glass of wine, or something?'

Philip says, 'We don't drink alcohol.'

She says, 'I can get some from the market. We don't mind you having a drink. I might find something in the garage.'

'I'm sure she can go without for one night.'

'I don't know that I can. Give me the keys, Mom, I'll go.'

It is, however, Philip who tosses me the car keys after digging into the pocket of his shorts. If there's only one set of keys this means that they do everything and go everywhere together, which means this situation is worse than I thought and I have arrived just in time.

Things have changed at the Bond Street store. It's all upmarket now, with a big delicatessen section. A sign blazes *Everything for the Gourmet Chef*. Prices have shot up, too. I spend fifteen bucks on a bottle of wine that would have cost me ten at most back home. I take my time getting back, and drive around the neighbourhood a bit. It's a good area: there are kids playing on their bikes, and the neighbourhood tennis courts are all busy. House prices have been on the rise as well, no doubt. What a freeloader.

The food is ready when I get back. When we sit down to eat, Mom explains that Philip is into something called 'foraging'. He picked the mushrooms himself; he's very experienced at finding food. I say, 'I'm surprised you found so many, and in May. Here in Phoenix, in May. You must be *very* talented, or a magician.'

The same headache from earlier presses forward on me again. I don't know how to cope with it, nor with two other things: I am sitting opposite a half-naked old man for a meal in my mother's house and he obviously thinks he is the host. His brown nipples look obscene. I feel simultaneously disgusted at the sight of his sagging skin on his skinny, hairy chest, and disappointed with myself for feeling that I mustn't mention anything about it. I want to ask him to go and find some clothes.

I just can't believe my mother is putting up with this. I down a glass of wine.

When he lifts the casserole lid and says, 'Help yourself, there's plenty,' I see that he's cooked a staggering amount for only three people. The smell makes me gag. Where would he have found the mushrooms? Are they poisonous? At the same time as recognising this is an irrational thought, I can't stop thinking that it's only me standing between him and my mother's life, house, and money. Why wouldn't he poison me?

Beside me, Mom serves herself a large portion. I wonder, from the look of her, how much she's been eating lately. A person would have to be starving to eat this. But until they're married there'd be no point in poisoning her. She's safe. Today it's only me he intends to kill.

Phillip also piles his plate high and starts shovelling the food in, leaving his mouth open as he chomps and slurps loudly. I watch bits of food drip from his mouth on to his beard. 'Go ahead and dig in,' he says when he spots me watching him. 'Don't hold back.'

'I thought mushrooms could be dangerous if they're the wrong sort.' Just to be polite, I ladle a small spoonful on to my plate and I refill my glass.

'I know what I'm looking for,' he says. He talks with his mouth full.

'I trust the supermarket for my mushrooms.'

'Yes. We've got Safeway —'

He interrupts Mom. 'Unless labelled organic it can't be trusted, and can you even trust what is supposed to be organic when there's money to be made in it? I don't think so. You know, I'm surprised at you. Your mother here said you were a smart woman. But with everything you've said so far, the jury is out on that one. Me, I'm not so sure.' At the very end when he says he's not sure, he looks up at me with those small feral eyes – a direct challenge.

Mom says. 'Oh, why don't you two just lay off each other? I'm going to fetch dessert.' As she clears the table she doesn't comment on the fact that I haven't even tasted his mushroom stroganoff. I ate the rice and the salad but his creation still sits on my plate, like a fat cowpat – from a thin cow with a severe gut disease. She piles up the dishes so that my plate with all the forks is on top.

As soon as she leaves the room I say, 'I'm a woman who likes to operate my free choice as an American to shop at my local supermarket.'

'Are you aware of how hostile you are?'

'I am hostile because of what you've done to my mom. My mother is not herself. She's a shadow of herself. She's weak, isolated and timid. Not herself at all. It's obvious that all this is your doing. That's why I'm here. I'm here to protect her, and I will protect her.'

He laughs. 'She's improved. She needed to lose weight. Any dog or cat owner knows that you have to feed an animal properly in order to keep its weight under control to ensure it lives a long time. People are no different. Before we hooked up, your mother was drinking too much, eating junk, and wasting her time doing meaningless things. She told me that since your father died she was lonely and bored. She is now on a healthy diet and a regime of appropriate supplements ... Believe me, she's not bored, she's a very satisfied woman, and her mind is active without being unregulated.'

'Unregulated?' I say. 'My mother is not anyone's *pet*.'

'You are deliberately misconstruing my words. The fact is, people become what they focus on. We've been working on a mind exercise programme to visualise health and wealth. The goal is prosperity in every aspect of our lives.'

'Sounds like a whole bunch of complete crapola.'

'Well, it's made a huge difference to her outlook, and you shouldn't dismiss the idea. My initial and abiding impression is that you have the bloated look of a wheat addict. I'm sure that's the root of all this unhealthy anger. You are unbalanced. Emotionally and mentally. And let's not start with your issues with alcohol.' He pauses. 'It's normal to fear change, but your attitude is infantile and fuelled by unnecessary chemical surges. I could help if you'd let me. If you stopped being so defensive.'

'"Initial". "Abiding". Huh? For your information, I don't fear change. I relish change. I love change. I adore change. I invite change to step in and change away. But not for the worse. Just tell me this: what's happened to all her friends?' I pour another glass. 'Tell me that. It's classic abuse. You're isolating her. You don't even want her talking to me. Her daughter.'

He says that people move on, and that I'm not a kid. When I hear Mom returning from the kitchen all I can do is to quickly suggest that he should move right along too, right out of my mother's life, the sooner the better.

Mom puts three bowls of what looks like some sort of yellow oatmeal on to the table. She explains that Philip has made a grain pudding for dessert and I say I'll have to pass, I couldn't eat another mouthful, which is true.

She takes a couple of spoonfuls. 'It is rather bitter and gritty,' she says.

'The problem is you've still got a taste for refined sugars. Try to experience the true flavour within the food. You'll appreciate the fibre tomorrow.'

'Leave it, Mom. Have some Metamucil if you need fibre. You don't have to eat pig swill like that.'

He glares at me. She looks at me, then him and compromises by taking another half-spoonful before she says she's full. Then she offers to get us some peppermint tea. I ask if they've done away with coffee as well.

'No, no, honey. Of course you can have coffee. There's some in the cabinet.'

'If you can't do without your fix,' he says.

Once she's out of the room I ask him, 'How long have you been here? Where did you come from? You don't fool me. The question is, how on earth did you manage to fool her? Because my mother is no fool.'

'You're really having problems with this, aren't you? You've clearly got unresolved attachment issues. You're probably loveless as well as childless and I'd guess you're just very, very jealous.'

'You don't know squat about me. But I've got your number. Let's cut to the chase. How much do you want? To leave. How much? What would it take?'

He fakes surprise and shakes his head. 'I don't know why you can't be happy for us,' he says as Mom comes back in with the drinks, and he turns to her. 'Your daughter was just trying to bribe me or something, to get lost. To leave you.'

I laugh as convincingly as possible and finish my glass of wine. 'What a jokester. Ha ha. Very funny,' I say. 'Philip was just worried we're not going to get along. I said any man my mom likes is fine by me. Actually, Mom, it's great being here with you and I'm going to go ahead and extend my ticket. I'd love to get to know the area better again. What do you think?'

'I think that would be just wonderful,' she says.

I ask her to tell me how they met. She tells me that it was on a flight from Vegas. 'One of those skinny long planes, you know, the kind that you wonder if the back end might just crack off. And that was right where I was sitting. We hit a dust storm. Philip was next to me and he grabbed my hand; he was scared something awful.'

'I was being nice. *You* looked frightened,' he says.

'No, it was definitely you. Well, the crew buckled themselves in. The whole back end of the plane was buffeted up and down, sideways, every which way. Philip kindly offered me some pills to take. I'd finished my drink and there was no way I'd get another, so I said I'd try them. Then we just got talking. It went from there.'

'What pills did he give you?'

'Oh, I don't know, something mild,' she says. 'Innocuous. Nothing really.'

'I'm a qualified herbal prescriber. I gave your mother a natural tranquilliser. Herbal. We've finally ironed out your mother's moods.'

'There was nothing wrong with my mom,' I say.

'Two of them makes me just terrific, honey.'

'Philip is not a doctor, Mom.'

'I'm state-certified.'

'That's a funny phrase. Like you're crazy or something. Nuts, you know. Certified.' I laugh loudly and am pleased when Mom joins in and that's the point that I realise I am pretty smashed.

Then she says, 'You know, that was a hell of a trip. I'd won big. Real big. I was feeling on top of the world. I knew the plane would be okay. They make things to last. I wasn't

71

scared one bit. You know, I used to feel invincible.' For a second she looks and sounds like Mom again, which makes me think maybe there is time for her to come to her senses, it's not too late. But for some reason this thought makes me feel tearful rather than optimistic.

'Yes. You were,' I say.

The bottle is now completely finished and we take our hot drinks through into the den. Just for the hell of it when she's not looking I mouth, 'Fuck you,' to him, again, once, twice and three times, to make one hundred per cent fucking sure he gets the message.

They go to their separate rooms at nine o'clock, telling me that Philip will be up early – he likes to watch the sunrise – but Mom is likely to sleep in.

I'd hoped that Mom and I would finally be able to talk, but he says she's always more on top of things when she gets adequate sleep. I don't want her to stay up for my sake but I go to my room very disappointed that we can't talk in private tonight.

Philip has signed me in as a user on the PC. I check my emails. Then I check his; he hasn't password-protected the password change screen. After that I take a look at his boring online activities history. He's been looking at stuff about roadkill finds, some pseudo-psychology and science about nutrition, and ecology crap. The most boring thing I discover is that there's a forum for mushroom-finders, and the most interesting thing I come across is about nudist sunbathing sites.

As I get into bed, I notice that four or five boxes have been stored underneath it. I lock the door before I drag out the first box.

Beneath carefully folded men's clothing – mostly jeans and T-shirts – I find several photo albums. This, then, is the weasel's past. There are dramatic landscapes, exotic places that I don't recognise at all. There are few pictures of people but when I come across a run of pictures of him in the third album I realise he's had that ugly beard for most of his adult life. There it is on a beach somewhere, next to a surfboard. Another in which he and his facial hair are hiking somewhere. He's got proper footwear on in that picture, but he's otherwise invariably topless, lean and tanned, wearing as few clothes as possible.

In the third box, beneath plates and a thin box full of cheap cutlery, there are some legal papers. He's divorced. This appears to be all the documentation from 1978 dissolving his 1964 Las Vegas marriage to a Marie Fortner. I've come across a number of pictures of women in his albums, from what might be that time period, but none to identify which of them might have been Marie. There's no indication that they had any children, but likewise no indication that they didn't. But, if they'd had children, surely he'd have some photographs of them.

Then I am startled as I spot a spider scooting along in front of me, heading under the bed. It's brown. It might be a brown recluse; they have that violin shape on the back. I stare into the under-bed gloom, wishing that I had a flashlight. It's scurrying away so fast that it's now completely disappeared. I quickly drag the bed away from the wall, trusting that this will stop it getting into bed with me and killing me in the night, before I can save my mother.

Finally, I climb under the covers. Trying to calm down, I breathe slowly, and remind myself that I've had a lot to drink. All houses have spiders. Most of them are non-poisonous.

I know I have to come up with a strategy more intelligent than my first plan just to stick it out. This has to be short and sharp. Maybe I could kidnap her?

I hear a coyote yowling outside somewhere.

I wish I'd discovered something horrible about Philip from his belongings. If he were a convicted serial killer I'm sure she'd get rid of him, but the worst thing I found out was that he's had a bad beard for a long time, has been lots of places and was married for fourteen years and got divorced.

Now I tell myself to try to see something good in this. No one is all bad, after all. For years Mom has wanted to lose weight. Finally, she has achieved her goal. Being thin is supposed to promote longevity; if he's made her thin, why do I think it's a bad thing?

But this is wrong. No one has the right to cut my mother down to a smaller size, least of all a weasel like Philip. No one has, no one will. She's always taken care of me and now it's my turn to step up to the plate. I cannot let her down. I decide as I fall asleep that somehow I have to ensure she sees what's happening with this guy, and rely upon her independence and strength of character to resolve the situation.

I wake later than I'd planned and with a hangover. I feel desperate for coffee. In the hall I notice that, at some time since my last visit, my parents' wedding photo has been replaced by a framed certificate of completion of a diploma in Nutrition Science from University of Nevada at Las Vegas University 1990.

There's no milk or creamer for my coffee, just some nut milk in the icebox. Even though it smells okay and I want my coffee, with this almond stuff in it, every sip reminds me of Philip. I find myself re-reading the same story in the newspaper, about what's happening with the downtown area, when the patio doors open and he steps into the house, wearing only his skimpy grey undershorts. I maintain eye contact and ask if he wants me to fix some breakfast for him. I'd rather do the cooking than him.

He tells me that he's already had his morning energy smoothie. He offers to make me one if I want to try it. No, thanks, I say, I hate smoothies. Then I tell him that I've decided to run out and get some jelly doughnuts. He's got to give me the car keys.

On the drive to the market I consider that now I will have to actually return with doughnuts and probably actually eat one. I haven't eaten a doughnut for years. The calorie count is astronomical. I think about when I was a kid and Dad, Mom and I used to go to the doughnut factory just out of town some Saturdays to watch them being made. The back wall of the shop was glass so that customers could see right into the factory. We'd watch the newly fried doughnuts get loaded on to the conveyor belt that took them to where they were injected with different fillings: some of them were going to become custard doughnuts, some jelly, some cream. Then the line would move into another area and they'd get their toppings. Icings, sprinkles, chocolate, some of them plain with holes. You could buy bags of doughnut holes there too.

I wonder if Mom thinks about Dad at all any more. We avoid the topic of their marriage and we also rarely talk about him, or what happened to him at the end. I have wondered if she felt guilty, but have concluded that she's rewritten it completely. Mom doesn't like to think about anything that might be unpleasant. Well, no one does, but Mom *really* doesn't.

In the store I buy some croissants as well as one token doughnut. It's a plain doughnut, a kind of compromise – it's not going to be too bad for me – but the yeasty smell of it as the girl bags it at the checkout is very inviting. I ask for another one, to eat in the car on the drive back. I don't go straight back to the house. I drive beyond her neighbourhood. I park and the sun comes in through the windshield, warming the car nicely. The sky is huge and the earth beside the road is baked a beautiful orange. Scarred Oklahoma is a long way away. I eat the second doughnut slowly.

The house is quiet on my return. Philip must have gone out, but I can see from the light that there's a message on Mom's answer machine. I wonder if he receives phone calls here now, too, and also if he's dictated the current voicemail greeting. I play the message. It is from Susie, the daughter of Mom's old friend Charleen. Charleen died ages ago, but I know Susie has always kept in touch – Mom is always telling me about Susie's high-flying life. She's a stewardess and now she's saying she wants to visit on a stopover and she's left her cell number.

When I've taken the number down, I go and make Mom a strong cup of black coffee and take it upstairs and down the hall to her bedroom.

'Hey, sleepyhead.' I open the door. 'Are you awake?'

She hauls herself up the bed.

'Want them open?' I nod to the heavy drapes. 'It's dark in here.'

'No. I can see you fine. Sit here.' She pats the bed next to her and I sit down. I ask if she slept okay and she says she slept *nearly* enough.

'I've got coffee.' I manage to put the mug on the bedside table, squeezed between clutter, a couple of rings, a vial of pills, odd earrings, her watch, a small pile of books, two half-empty mugs of something, and a full glass of water.

'I need a pee.' She is naked, of course. Her breasts hang and, though thinner, her skinny backside still wobbles as she walks from the bed to her bathroom, past the unused

76

running machine which now is the base for numerous piles of clothes. Some are freshly laundered and some still have labels on them; these will be eventually headed back to the store. Real shopping for Mom is like internet shopping for me. I fill up a basket from my wish list and then empty almost everything before checkout and completion, and Mom almost always buys and returns.

There are knick-knacks on every surface in her room. She gets the craziest stuff, buys cheap trash everywhere. Whenever I've asked why she's wasting good money on garbage, she says it makes her smile, that I shouldn't begrudge her this pleasure now that she can buy things she might want. Gift shops, souvenir shops, entrances to historic churches and museums – she's always picking things up, and keeping them. A little doll, a pottery bell, a dusty lace handkerchief...bits of trash piled up on top of each other. Objects that meant something for the entirety of the two seconds that she held them before dropping them into a bag to bring home. Everything is thrown in a tumble. The rest of the house isn't so bad. She knows it's abnormal to live like this, so it's confined to here. Her bedroom is where things accumulate. I assume some of this crap might be valuable because she's told me that when she dies I must go through it and check everything before throwing things out.

But perhaps she was just referring to the money. She got a bundle with the insurance after Dad died but, even before he died, whenever she could she would squirrel away wads of withdrawn cash in unworn shoes in her closets. Stacks of hundreds are wrapped in foil in the garage freezer, disguised as meat ('if someone breaks in they're never going to check out the contents of the freezer'), and odd hundred-dollar bills are hidden in the pages of books and magazines elsewhere in the house.

It all seems to be inept preparation for something. It's as if she expects some sort of disaster, and instead of stockpiling food, water and maybe guns, as a normal person might, she stores cash.

For a moment I wonder if Philip is already depleting her stores, but I doubt she's told him about this habit. It is our secret. And, Mom has never been one to put all her eggs in one basket. I don't think the weasel would realise that yet.

When she comes back she's got a dingy housecoat on. She climbs back into bed. 'Where is he?'

'Out. I guess he had some errands to run or something.'

She makes no comment. Without looking she picks up a pill pot, drops out a pill and downs it with the water.

'Want the coffee now?'

She doesn't reply. She throws herself back against the three pillows and I think maybe I should have let her sleep instead of waking her just because I want some time on our own together. But, instead of saying this, I plough on.

'Susie phoned. There was a message. She wants to come over.'

'Oh, no,' Mom says. 'I don't think so.'

'You like Susie. You can't neglect all your friends.'

'I don't neglect people.'

'You're neglecting me.'

Now she grins. 'No, I'm not, honey,' she says. 'Look, he's okay,' she adds. 'I want you to get used to him.'

'I don't want to talk about the asshole.' I get up and pick up the phone from the bedside cabinet. 'I'm calling Susie back.'

'I don't know ...'

I press the buttons and the phone begins ringing at the other end. Mom takes a noisy sip from the mug. Mom always liked her coffee black and strong.

Chicago is ahead of us, so it's nearly twelve o'clock there, but Susie *is* home. She has this reassuring Midwestern way of speaking – monotone and flat and always the same pace – but, even so, I can tell she's pleased to hear from us. That's how I pitch it after saying who I am and why I'm phoning, not Mom, who is looking at me warily. It's 'us' she'll be coming to see. 'Hey,' I say. 'Mom would love to see you, and me too. Old times and everything.' We fix it up for two o'clock, when she'll be flying in. She'll get to the hotel, take a cab out here and we'll go from there.

When we get off the phone I tell Mom that Susie sounded great. 'It's an upbeat thing to do. We need things to look forward to.'

'I don't know how Philip will feel about this.'

I don't say that I can guess. What I say is that, if he loves her, then he'll be pleased for her, surely? Then I say, 'You're not thinking of marrying this guy, are you? That would be a big mistake.'

She doesn't answer.

Susie looks great. I hear the cab pull up and open the door to greet her. Momentarily I think that she's been wholly exempt from ageing, until I realise that I'm thinking about her mother Charleen and my childhood memory of her before she got sick. Even so, Susie has taken care of herself. She's probably ten years older than me but from here she looks ten years younger. She's still in uniform.

She turns to wave at the cab driver, presumably to let him know that she's at the right place – she's always been a friendly person – and then she walks in and gives Mom a long hug.

Now that stewardesses are called 'cabin crew' they don't have to look as glamorous as they used to. With compulsory retirement rising more than thirty years I guess this is inevitable, but Susie now still looks glam and like a Susie, not a wear-worn, careworn 'Susan'. There's none of that dried-up-skin-and-sagging-muscles look that I regularly search out on my face in the mirror and, unlike me, she looks like a person up for life, going places, doing things.

When she releases Mom, she sniffs the stale air before she turns her attention to me. Perhaps she can smell Philip. She must be noticing the shabby carpet, which could have done with more than my half-hearted vacuuming efforts three hours ago, and the film of fine dust everywhere.

Susie's perfume is sophisticated, and delicious. Her Barbie-doll physique feels firm and contained beneath her clothes. She could easily make me feel inadequate but the warmth in her forthcoming smile and how she says how great it is to meet up makes that fleeting sensation disappear. She is one of those people, I realise, who just always puts others at ease.

'Come right on in,' Mom says, 'the den is this way.'

Then Philip suddenly appears, to spoil everything. He is topless, of course. He strides across and shakes Susie's hand. 'Hi,' he says, 'Welcome to our humble abode.' Like he belongs here. Like it's his.

'Mom's friend,' I explain, before Susie can think it's anything more.

'Do I know you?' Susie says. Once he's released it, she puts the hand over her brow to shield her eyes and squints at him. 'You look very familiar.'

And, strangely, wonderfully, he just says that he'll leave us gals to catch up. He explains he's got to get back to the garage. He's got an engineering project. He's rigging up some contraption to stretch spines or something. I'll have to make it clear he's not to use it on Mom, but the possibility of *him* coming to a bad end and hanging himself upside down strapped to the metal frame he's constructing makes me hopeful.

Susie sits down in the armchair facing the window. The light streams in on her face. She says that the last time she saw me was when I was really still a kid, a teenager maybe, but she knew me earlier, when she was a teenager herself. She says, 'You were just in grade school when you told me about a boy, Jimmy Fontaine. I even remember the name because of the look on your face as you said it. He carried your books from the bus every day. Like a Prince Charming. Do you remember?' She and Mom wait for a response.

And, though I haven't thought about Jimmy Fontaine for very many years, I feel myself blush at the thought of him. I remember being excited and amazed that he'd chosen me, had asked me if he could carry my books.

'Gee,' I say. I'm about to explain that until she'd said his name I'd forgotten all about Jimmy and can't imagine why she'd remember. But Mom interrupts my thoughts.

'You know, that was real weird: Philip is usually so sociable. I know he's busy but he loves to talk to people.'

'That's because he's a complete know-it-all.'

At this I sense Susie scrutinising us. 'Funny things, families,' she says.

Mom says, 'So, tell us what you've been up to.'

'Mostly thinking about my plans for retirement. Once I stop being here, there and everywhere, I'm going to get myself a dog. They're good company. I always regret having had to put Mom's dog down when she went, but once I was back at work I couldn't keep up with her. She was so old, too, and I just couldn't take care of her.'

'I remember your dog.' I am sad at the idea of Susie having to put that lovely Labrador down because she couldn't keep it.

'It was the kindest thing to do,' Mom says very quickly. 'Sometimes you have to do these things. For everyone's sake. Hey,' she says, 'Susie, you look terrific. Have you had any work done?'

I offer to make us coffee and leave the room.

When I get back we arrange to go out for a meal at Grimaldi's. It's a place that one of Susie's colleagues has recommended. She will meet us there later. Now she'll head back to the hotel to freshen up.

Only when she's left do I ask Mom if we should find out if they do Philip-food. I'm pleased to see that Mom doesn't seem to care. 'He can phone and we'll take it from there,' she says, but I make the call, and relay to them both when Philip comes in from the garage that they can cater for any particular diet.

He says, however, that he doesn't want to go out. He's reached a crucial point with his project so he'd prefer to stay in and, remarkably, he says he doesn't mind if we go without him. Mom makes what I know to be a poor effort at encouraging him to come, but his mind is made up and it's decided that we will go without him. She says she's going to get changed.

The idea of the weasel being left in the house going through things, maybe discovering her secret money bundles, is not appealing. But neither is the idea of any unnecessary time spent in his company. I'm not sure what I should think about this, but the decision has been made anyway. I go to get showered and changed too, and as I strip off I'm relieved to discover that my period has started; it means that within a day my clothes will start to properly fit again.

When I'm ready and walking into the kitchen I overhear Philip telling Mom that he doesn't like Susie, that it would be impossible to like a woman who has gone and got herself 'bolt-ons'. He says perhaps Mom should cut her, and the past, loose and get herself some new friends so as not to drag the past into their present. 'It's finally time for you,' he says, 'for us. For me, too.'

I decide not to add anything to the conversation. The best thing I can do is stay out of the way. Surely this kind of statement will help her realise what he's trying to do? So instead I walk in, compliment her on her outfit and announce that I'm very sorry he's not coming with us, because Susie is such a good friend to the family, it would have been nice to have him there too.

They both know that I am lying.

The restaurant is downtown. Mom orders a glass of pinot noir on arrival, and when the waitress comes for the order she chooses a fillet steak. It takes Susie and me longer to choose.

Susie is animated and talks about her work and makes both of us laugh, and then she talks about her mother. I watch the two of them engage in memories and I feel like an observer. I envy their ease together. This is silly because I know that if anyone should be jealous in this situation it's Susie, because my mother is still alive and here, laughing and good fun. But then I see that their friendship isn't like that; it's not like that kind of mother-daughter relationship at all. It's as if, after Charleen went, Susie just slid into the vacated place.

She asks about Uncle Pete, which surprises me, because Mom never, ever talks about him, and the way Susie says to Mom, 'How's Pete?' implies that Mom might know and that Susie is more informed about my uncle than I am.

Mom says, 'I heard he's still working. I think he's all right. Got a family. I imagine a weatherworn wife. Not the sort of life I'd have liked. Not really.'

'Where does Uncle Pete live, Mom?'

'Didn't Richard chase him all the way to Oregon after you got married?' Susie asks.

'Something like that.'

The whole situation here between them makes me feel even more left out and sad, so, rather than exploring the possibility of discovering something, I decide to change the subject and ask about Charleen. 'How did you meet Susie's mom, Mom?'

But before she can answer, Susie jumps in gleefully. 'I guess you might say that my mom sort of dated your dad before your mother turned up.'

'Dad dated Charleen?'

'For no more than a minute,' Mom says. 'Just long enough for her to figure out she wasn't his type.' Mom and Susie laugh loudly at this.

'And you stayed friends with Charleen?'

'No. They *became* friends,' Susie says. 'Comrades in the experience.'

Mom says quietly, 'It's in the past.'

Between the entrée and dessert, Mom says that she needs the ladies' room. She leaves Susie and me waiting for the cheesecake we've all ordered. I watch Mom weave her way through the restaurant. Susie is hardly drinking; she and I are sharing a bottle of white, and I've had the lion's share.

'You know, it's the funniest thing about your mom's boyfriend,' she says. 'It's suddenly come back to me where I thought I knew him from. There was this guy who used to hit on flight attendants. He'd done it for years. The airline I was working with at the time didn't seem to worry about that, you know, they expect us to put up with idiots hitting on us all the time, but when he turned his attention to other women, to women passengers travelling alone ... well, he got banned from flights with us and they circulated a picture of him. Ridiculous.' She shakes her head. 'I'm a hundred per cent sure it wasn't him. But I've been thinking about why he looked so familiar all day. It was probably the beard. I'm pretty good with faces and, even though I'm getting older, I hate to not be able to figure that sort of thing out. I finally just remembered the picture. I didn't want to say anything to your mom, though. It's just silly. It can't be him.'

She confirms the airline for me. 'A creep, huh?' is all I say.

My heart is thumping loudly as Mom returns from the restroom saying she's not felt so full, or happy, for ages. The waitress serves the cheesecake and the portions are so large that none of us can clear our plates. We say goodbye in the lounge. I hope to see Susie again soon, is what I say. The two of them hug and I watch them, feeling detached.

In the cab, I tell her. I leave out all Susie's reservations about what she'd initially thought. I tell her Philip is preying on her and that it's not the first time he's done this sort of thing. That there will be incontrovertible proof, if we need it.

'But I don't travel with that airline. They're cheap. No nuts. No cookies.'

'Exactly,' I say.

'But why didn't she tell me?' Mom says.

'Because she didn't want to hurt you.'

'And you?' she says, and I cannot reply.

Back at the house there is an almighty argument. Both Mom and Philip are loud. Mom is drunk enough not to hold back with the assumed revelations. I go to my room and leave them to it. I hear him deny everything, say that he will prove it's not him, that he'll sue 'that artificial slut' for slander. How could Mom believe such lies? That he's sure it's me who's at the root of this. That we have an unhealthy relationship. That she's stuck in the past. That she's doomed to be lonely. That she is mentally ill and in denial. That it's no wonder her husband jumped off a roof. That no one will ever really care for her the way he does and that she'll know that one of these days. Then I hear him tell her she's basically just a hypocritical fat lush who will die young from abuse of her body.

There is a moment of silence and then, finally, she shouts that he's got to get out. 'Now!' And, of course, no one could expect to make up after saying a woman is a fat lush.

All this time I've been standing on the other side of my bedroom door ready to rush out and defend her should the fight get physical. It's a relief that he's pissed enough at her rejection to storm down the hall and call a cab when she tells him to go. He takes leave himself to wait for it outside, abandoning his framed certificates and the boxes under the bed, and he doesn't say goodbye.

When he contacts us the next day I say, truthfully, that Mom does not want to speak to him. I explain that I'll arrange storage for his things and send him an email about where he can collect them. I ask him for an email address and write it down. He says. 'I thought your mother knew me,' and I tell him that we're changing the locks.

1999

The Mutt

'Is it just me, or is everything really crap?'

When I hear my lover Mikey's voice, I realise that tough love appeals to me mainly because I'm just not tough enough for any other response lately. His depression is in a downward spiral. Compassion and empathy are only for the brave. 'I'm hanging up if you say anything else depressing,' I say. 'I've got enough to think about. I'm at work.'

There's a long gap, then he says, 'I guess maybe see you later, then?'

Next to me Helen scrapes back her chair and leaves the room. We share an office and she'd be fetching us coffee around now anyway. She knows about Mikey's depression but not much else. Then I screw it all up by telling him, on impulse, 'I'll wear that sexy outfit you bought me for my birthday.'

I don't know why I do it. My current bedtime reading, a gift from Mom, *Women who Give, Give, Give Learning to Take, Take, Take*, would not approve of such a statement.

He sighs and says, 'But honey, oh, God, I just feel like I'm drowning.'

'Wrong answer,' I say. I put down the phone.

I have to unlock my computer to see what I was working on, because it's set for a very quick timeout. This week my password is *Thisjobis100%shit*. No spaces – a very strong security rating. Security tensions generally run high this time of year. Tensions run high. Two weeks ago was the fourth anniversary. They began working on the memorial in January, and at the ceremony their relatives threw tributes over the glass wall. Even though the speech on the day was all about the planned memorial – about the future, not the past – really the area is just a construction site with a massive hole. A huge empty space.

But I can't think about that; right now I've got to find a location for an indoor shuffleboard conference in seven months' time. The guy wants just before Christmas and it'll be easy to slot them in, but instead of taking the booking straight away I've got to make like we might not be able to accommodate it, and then phone him back after a couple of hours. Brad says we need to promote the image of a centre under constant demand. I don't know why when we're so desperate and this tactic just leaves me hoping that I'll be able to catch the client later before he opts for elsewhere. Timing is everything.

When my cell rings it's Mom. It's early in Phoenix. 'Hi. You okay?' I ask her, on speakerphone, as I continue to look at the computer screen for when the shuffleboard event can happen. I spot that we can manage the week after Thanksgiving. Mr Shuffleboard should be happy enough with that.

'I thought I'd call before I go to the hospital for my surgery.'

'Oh.'

'I knew you'd forget.'

'Remind me of the detail.'

'My toenail. My left foot.'

'That's podiatry, not surgery. I'm at work.'

'I'm nervous.'

'Mom, it'll be fine. Call me when it's done.'

'I just hope I survive. Anyway, I can't talk now,' she says, and hangs up.

On the way home I pick up stuffed eggplant from the delicatessen at the strip mall, to reheat for dinner. Mikey is sitting in his car outside my building when I pull up. He may have been there for hours. He used to have a key but I took it back last year because he started spending all day at my place, doing nothing, and I thought that he should do that at his own house.

He waves limply, gets out of the car, and drags himself up to the door. He's scratching his head like a dog with fleas. He looks a mess.

'I got some food,' I say.

'I don't know if I can eat.'

'Do you just want to go home?'

'I guess I can eat.'

The eggplant that looked so appealing in the store is slimy and limp on the plates. The texture makes it hard to swallow, but somehow he's found his appetite and I watch as he goes at the food with gusto, and then finishes off some from my plate too.

He has not always been like this. We met when he came to discuss arrangements for an event at the Civic Center to commemorate the first anniversary of the Oklahoma City bombing. He'd helped with sorting donations immediately afterwards, and had been going to a regular support group for people affected by it. He was socially aware and thoughtful, definitely in touch with his feelings, and I was pleased to be with a sensitive man. I was hopeful for a relationship that might last and was buying books like *Building a Relationship for the Whole Nine Yards* and Mikey seemed perfect. Over the first few months I met some of his friends and by all accounts he'd had a good job in sales, and been cheerful and confident, before he got made redundant two months before the bombing. That, everyone said, was when he really began feeling depressed; that was the *real* sequence of events, but somehow Mikey was able to focus only on the bombing. It's as if that was the point at which he lost everything – which he didn't. He wasn't anywhere near when it happened; he just decided to get involved with the aftermath, and hasn't been able to let it go. He completely gave up looking for a new job the summer after I met him, because one of his aunts died and left him a near fortune. For this reason – the money – alone, he could dress better, I think, but he's got a thing about shopping for clothes. He says that too much choice is overwhelming for him, but I've noticed they always put sports clothes near the entrance. He's afraid of getting trapped. He also bought a place out of the city, for the same reason.

The fact that McVeigh is never going to be tried for the remaining 160 charges of murder is his continuing obsession. He was sentenced to death for the killing of eight federal officers and there's no worse punishment, but for Mikey it's not enough. He says after all the appeals and delays, in twenty or thirty years maybe, when everyone outside of OK has forgotten what he did, McVeigh will be quietly killed in Denver and he'll never have to face justice *where* he should.

I have decided I have no feelings about the bombing whatsoever. Mikey has enough for both of us. The visit to his shrink, Dr Sayer, is the highlight of Mikey's week, and I know that I of all people should be more understanding, and I wish I *were* more understanding, but he's just not getting any better.

Mikey eats a bowl of ice-cream for dessert while I describe my day to him. The noise he makes as he slurps up the Baskin-Robbins is like an animal. I also tell him I've got to find out about Mom's toenail. He helps himself to seconds from the freezer and I wonder if he's going to want to stay over. If he does, I wonder if he'll remember about the stupid outfit and whether there's any way of skipping the get-up.

I pre-empt any request for sex. 'God, I'm exhausted.'

'Phone your mom. She might be dead.'

'Mikey, the relationship is not working for me.'

'She's your mom, for God's sake.'

As he helps himself to a third bowl of ice-cream, I leave to make the call and she answers after the twentieth ring. 'I can't talk long,' I say, 'Mikey is here.'

'Who?'

'Mikey.'

'That one with a baby name. *Another* one with a baby name.'

'What's up with your foot?'

'The doctor was wonderful. I can't feel a thing, though. I'm sure it should have come round by now.'

'What can't you feel?'

'The toenail.'

'Can you feel your foot?'

'I can move it.'

'When are you going back for a follow-up? Is he going to see you again?'

'Tomorrow.'

'Let me know how it goes. I'll speak to you then.'

Then she hangs up the phone again without saying goodbye, just like they do in the movies. I'm not putting up with that. I call her back. 'You didn't say goodbye.'

'I can't talk,' she whispers. 'And you said you were in a hurry.'

'Okay, goodbye.' I say. 'Goodbye, Mom.'

But she's already hung up again. I am left looking at the phone, annoyed with her, and disconcerted. I know her. Something's up.

The next day Helen is at work before me. She's flustered. She says, 'Thank God you're here. Did you know that ovaries just shrivel up when they've finished being needed?'

'No.'

'It's like, as a woman, when you're done procreating, then you're no longer a woman.'

I ask Helen why she's thinking about this and she says it's something that Tom, her husband, has mentioned. 'I figure he's getting ready to dump me.'

'You're solid. Why'd you think that?'

'He used my hairspray.'

'Hairspray, huh?'

'Yes, and he bought hair dye.'

'Dye, huh?'

'And …' She takes a deep breath. 'He's been going to the gym.'

'Hey,' I say, 'it's all good. He wants to look good. That's good.' But I think she's probably right. Her marriage is headed for the rocks and maybe she should take note of the blinking lighthouse.

'Do you think my ovaries are shrivelled up?' she asks. 'I should have had kids.'

I remind her that she still gets her period, and say that I doubt it and that she could still have kids if she wanted them. I suggest that it's Tom's brain that has shrivelled up, that it's his problem, not hers. 'You two are great together,' I say. 'But maybe check out a lawyer anyway. Keep your options open. Have you thought about storing your eggs?'

She's still crying when Brad arrives. Fortunately we don't see him in person all that often and Helen manages to pull herself together. He asks about bookings for next January and I have to say we don't have any yet. 'We never have any regular bookings for January.'

'Think about a strategy. We need to expand our horizons,' he says.

'Sounds like Tom,' Helen says, as soon as Brad has left the room.

In the afternoon, I speak to Mom and she tells me that she's seen the podiatrist again; her toe is healing up and she has no pain any more.

'You didn't have pain.'

'You are so pernickety.' Then she tells me that she and her friend Philip might come for a visit. We could do some stuff together.

'Who? No one wants to come here for vacation. Why would they? Downtown is a bombsite,' I say, which, of course, is exactly the opposite of what Brad tells us to tell all our customers.

'Well, I want you to know that I'm just fine and very, very happy,' she says. 'There is no need to worry at all about me.'

'What are you saying, Mom? What's going on?'

'Got to go. I've got plans,' and she puts down the phone.

I'm on the phone again with another client, and in the middle of agreeing a booking for a Barbie Believers Convention next summer, when the sirens go off. Gretchen, the Barbie-lovers organiser in California, can hear it her end of the phone line too. 'What the hell is that?'

'Probably nothing. Listen, we'll firm the dates up tomorrow. Can I call you back, tomorrow? Is that okay? Eight your time?'

I join Helen to look out the window. Our office is on the third floor and we can look down on the trees. The branches are not swaying. Their leaves are not moving at all. The air outside is deathly still and the sky has gone an ominous green-grey colour. 'Warning or watch?' she asks. 'Which one makes that sound?'

'Whichever, we shouldn't stay here.'

We grab our purses and head down the hall to the elevator. I'm not sure if we're supposed to use it or not. As we walk we each remind the other that there was no warning on TV this morning, nothing. Nothing at all. She says that if it's a watch not a warning, then this is a pointless thing to do, to go down to the basement, that we should just try to get home. 'It'll pass,' Helen says. 'I'll call Tom. He'll know what to do.' Then we decide to go down the stairs.

The vast concrete stairwell echoes. The clatter of our feet sounds back and forth, like a monument to fear, and then we are joined by a few other people that we barely know: two from the ticket offices, the night-shift janitor and a woman from the kitchen. Jackson, the janitor, confirms that a warning has gone out on KATT-FM. He's got the radio with him, which is good thinking.

Helen can't get a signal for her cell and I realise that, though I hope Mikey is okay out in the suburbs, I don't want to talk to him. I guess I can't anyway. If Helen's phone doesn't work, mine won't either.

We get to the basement and proceed along the hallway in the bowels of the building. Bare walls, no carpet. Bare pipes above us.

I wonder if this evening we'll go the whole hog and sit with our backs to the wall and knees up and head down between them, like in elementary school: rows of kids lined up in the brace position. Looking around, it's clear that only Helen and I are remotely limber enough to do that now, so I guess probably not.

A large woman whose name badge says *Doreen* and that she works in the restaurant asks, 'Anyone got any food? I'm starving. We might be here a long time.'

'Nuh-uh,' Helen says. She gives me a look that tells me she's also thinking that if anyone should have thought about bringing some dinner to this party, it was Doreen.

When we sit down the concrete cold seeps up. It's as cold here inside as it has been warm outside the last few weeks.

Doreen produces a deck of cards from her apron pocket. The two women from the ticket office, Jean and Janet, scoot up close to join in, and Jackson turns up the radio. There's a lot of interference, but we can hear some music and everyone lightens up a bit. We might become friends even. Who knows how long we're going to be here? It'll be a story to tell.

Two hours later, the radio starts to report on the fallout of the numerous tornadoes that hit the city outside. People have been killed and a number of buildings flattened. I recognise the name of a neighbourhood near Mikey's.

I phone Mom when I finally get home and there is no answer. I phone Mikey and leave a message on his answerphone saying I hope he's all right, that I'm all right. I figure if his phone is still there, his house is still there. I fix some food and put on the TV to watch the news. I try to get hold of Mom repeatedly during the evening, and by ten-thirty her time I'm getting worried. She should be answering. It rings twenty, twenty-five, thirty times. I hang up and count out the rings again. Then I try her cell phone. No reply, either.

I phone Mikey again and this time he answers. He says he's been trying to call, but my line has been continually busy. He's breathless as he tells me about his tornado experience. He spent it in the basement of his house alone. A building not far away from him was completely demolished. 'It's a miracle I survived,' he says. 'A goddamn miracle. I'm alive. Amazing.'

I tell him that I'm worried about Mom.

'Hey, do you want me to come over? I can come over. Keep you company. I'm on my way.'

He's hung up before I can reply no.

By the time he arrives forty minutes later, Mom still hasn't answered the phone. I'm just about ready to book a flight but I can't remember which is cheaper, American or Delta. Mikey tells me not to worry about her. Maybe she can't hear the phone. He says that old people get deaf, that she's probably asleep. 'Deaf and asleep,' he says. 'Honey, there were no tornadoes near her.' He moves his head to stare hard into my eyes like he's a hypnotist. He can be such an idiot.

'My mom *never* sleeps,' I say. 'You're just not taking this seriously. Something is going on.' I burst into tears.

'Well, I gotta say, you are looking mighty sexy right now.' Mikey puts his arm around me and pulls me closer to him on the couch. 'Mighty sexy,' he says. I can feel his breath on my ear. He strokes my neck with a single finger. He slides his hand up my thigh.

Then the phone rings. Mom's voice. 'Where have you been?' I ask.

In front of me, Mikey starts to undress. He takes off his T-shirt and slips off his shoes. He unzips his jeans.

'Busy,' she says. 'But I heard about the tornadoes.' She tells me what I know already about the damage and that they expect more people will be found dead. 'Are you okay, honey? Is your building still standing? What about tomorrow?'

'Of course it is. You're talking to me now. Where were you?'

'I've got to go. Catch you tomorrow. Sleep tight.'

'Is Philip there?' I manage to say quickly but there's no answer. She's hung up on me.

Mikey is down to his now grey, once white, undershorts. His stomach has grown since the last time I saw it naked. He's got a hard-on.

It's been a long time.

I hardly ever talk to Helen in any detail about Mikey but the next morning I tell her, 'Mikey came over last night and we had sex. He stayed over. I left him lying in my bed this morning.'

'So, you think it's going to work out?'

I shake my head. 'No, but I'm stuck with him. The guy spent three hours in the basement of his building on his own last night thinking that he might die, and then found out afterwards that he nearly did. He said that his depression is finally over. Gotta tell you, it's been ages.'

'Ah... Oh.'

'That's the only reason why we had sex last night – because he nearly died – and honestly it wasn't that good.' I don't know what else to say. I *am* stuck. It's me as much as him. I wish that I were in *The Wizard of Oz* and whisked away by another tornado, but that's Kansas. 'The whole situation is crap,' I say. 'I don't know what I'm doing. I know, it's nuts and something is going on with my Mom. Hey, this is pathetic. God, Oklahoma really sucks. I'm pathetic.'

She nods.

'I've got to do something.'

Her head is still nodding.

And then I just make a decision.

I pick up the phone and ask Brad for urgent time off work to visit my mother who has just had surgery, and then I book the flight for the evening. Helen says she's pleased that I'm finally doing something definite. Apparently I've been dithering all over the place for months. 'Go, girl,' she says. 'Go!' She gets up from her seat and does a little dance and that Ricki Lake thing with her hands in the air. I suddenly feel sorry for Tom. If he doesn't get his act together soon, he may be stupid enough to lose the best person in the world.

Now I'm on a roll and am encouraged enough to phone Mikey and tell him the news. The new me. I refuse to use his babyfied name. 'Mike,' I say, 'It's over. I'm leaving. I'm going to see my mom. I've come to a crossroads and need a vacation.'

'Great! I'll come with you. I woke up happy and I knew it was going to be a fantastic day. Marry me, honey. I love you,' he says. 'We'll do Vegas.'

I don't reply. It's too late. That ship has sailed. I put the phone down, pick up my bag, give Helen a hug and get the hell out of there.

1995

On Becoming a Fish

This is how my mother arrives. She doesn't come the day before the surgery when I'd expected her, and when I wanted her. She arrives at Mercy Hospital while I am already under anaesthetic and this means that I return, horizontal, from the recovery room to find my mother sitting there alive and well, not killed in a plane crash as I had worried right up until they put me out at seven o'clock that morning.

'Oh, Mom,' I call out as she comes into view. 'You're here.'

Johnny is there in the room as well. He says, 'She got the date wrong.'

By way of apology, perhaps, Mom manages to shrug, wink, and grin at the same time. She puts down her magazine. She and Johnny stand up for my designated nurse, Sam, and the recovery nurse (whose name I don't know) who has escorted me back upstairs from the basement operating room. The two of them slide the bed into place and reposition all the wires and tubes that are attached to me.

I find that, now that I am living in the after, instead of being angry at all the anxiety she's put me through, I'm just very pleased to see Mom, to know that she's alive as well. She's far from a spring chicken but still looks pretty good in her red pant-suit, all dressed up and wearing heels. Despite her supporting role in this situation, she never fails to appear the important one in any gathering.

When they're finished moving stuff about, Sam starts talking to Mom like they're old friends. Someone has given her a cup of coffee but Johnny, in his T-shirt and jeans, doesn't have a drink and he looks restless and irritable. I expect he's very hungry, because he usually likes to start his lunch at eleven. We've been here since five a.m., which is when they told me to arrive. I reach out to grasp his hand. This movement is strangely awkward and uncomfortable. I am tightly bandaged, but now I realise that I still have my left breast. Why haven't I thought of this yet? Nothing exactly hurts, but I do feel the pressure of the bandage.

It turns out, if there is any concern about cancer, there is nothing as definitive as getting in there and rooting around and chopping bits of flesh out. When I had my pre-op assessment I consented to the removal of whatever was necessary once they had 'opened me up'. In addition to worrying that Mom was dead and that was why she hadn't turned up this morning, I had spent the time from then until now wondering what it would be like if 'necessary' turned out to be more than a small amount. At the same time as wanting them to get on with it in case it was malignant, I did not realise how attached I felt to my body, how distressed I could feel at the prospect of losing any part of me.

As I lie here in my hospital bed post-surgery I next find myself concerned about the fact that I have told the doctor who met me in recovery that he looks like a teddy bear. Now that it's over and I'm still alive and no longer so worried about losing half my breasts, I really wish I hadn't said that. He probably thinks I'm a moron. I remind myself that, when I told the nurse in recovery about it, she said not to worry, that he won't think I'm nuts, it was the anaesthetic, and he'll totally understand.

'But he does really look like one, doesn't he?' I asked, and I went on to tell her that Barbie's boyfriend Ken is the one who did my nose job, which is one of those true-false memories. It's all perception, after all. A person is vulnerable under the influence of drugs.

I know, really, that it wasn't Ken, but I can vouch for him being very gentle, even if a bit plasticky, when he spoke to me and told me I'd be fine. In return I'd told him at the time that Barbie was very lucky, and that I envied her. 'The thing is, I really love teddy bears, and the teddy bear look,' I said to the recovery nurse. 'In fact, I think I'm in love with Dr Frostrick,' I concluded.

She smirked a bit, but she was also nice and told me not to sweat it. I don't mind being one of those patients they can laugh about later. I'll never see her again.

Now I try to explain something to Johnny. 'It's not unusual for patients to fall in love with their doctors,' I say. He just looks puzzled. 'I'm not in love with anyone,' I add, which doesn't help anything because we've been going out for months and perhaps Johnny thought that I was in love with him. 'I guess I'm a bit shocked. It's the drugs,' I say next, and he seems to accept this explanation. 'I'm kind of stoned.'

'What'd she say?' Mom asks, looking up from the *Reader's Digest*.

'Nothing,' Johnny says. 'She's talking crap. She's fine.'

When I've been back in the room for a while, Dr Frostrick comes to talk to me again. I'm impressed when he asks my mother to wait outside. She always wants to butt in on these things and no one, including me, has ever had the resolve to ask her to leave. She doesn't put up resistance today, even when he suggests that Johnny stays with me. Perhaps he thinks we're married or something?

Frostrick *still* looks like a teddy bear. A very cuddly and attractive bear. He sits down on the bed, pats my hand, speaks for a few minutes, and smiles at me. I smile back. When he finishes speaking and waves goodbye as he leaves I turn to ask Johnny what he said, because I haven't understood it. It was all gobbledygook.

'You haven't got cancer. They're doing tests to be sure, but he thinks it's fine.'

'Tell Mom,' I say, 'she'll be worried.'

A minute later she rushes back in. 'See, I knew it would all be okay, honey. I knew you were worried about nothing.'

This is the first time she's said anything like this. Up until this very moment she's only offered gloom. Instead of reassurance she chose to tell me about her sister Sheila – one of my two aunts (both of whom I never knew) – and how she died of cancer. 'I'm pretty sure it was breast cancer too,' Mom said. 'When it runs in the family, the Big C is just a ticking time bomb waiting to go off. That's why a person needs good insurance.' And, with regard to my problem, she said it was just as well they caught it early for me, that treatment nowadays has improved. In fact, the most positive thing she said throughout all the build-up to this surgery was, 'If you're lucky, you might have a couple of years.'

Johnny goes off to get something to eat. He'll be back in an hour, he says, and Sam brings Mom a tray of food. It's something the two of them must have arranged before I got back to the room. People always like to take care of Mom. She's got some woman, a woman her own age (not a girl) from her Mah Jongg group, cleaning the house for nothing, and some guy from the church she belongs to shows up every week to mow her lawn and do odd jobs without pay, or even acknowledgement that this is a kindness. She says she gives him a coffee and a couple of cookies and that, as he's a Christian, she's helping him by giving him the opportunity to do good works. 'He's the one who should be grateful.'

I wonder, often, if I'm just jealous because she's the sun with a powerful gravitational pull that everyone recognises, and in contrast I'm just a very minor planet in her wide orbit. Even Dad always did exactly what she said.

Now that the crisis with my health is over, she decides to pull her chair close and reads aloud jokes from her magazine. I know they're jokes because she's reading from the *Reader's Digest* joke page, but, listening to one after the other, I am confused. Again and again, I don't get them. They're not funny. They make no sense. Not one of them makes any sense. She picks up another issue and we go through more jokes, but they're still not funny, still all complete nonsense.

I ask her to read the last few again slowly and I concentrate but still I can't understand what they mean, why they're supposed to be funny. I begin to panic. I feel on the outside of everything. I am again the person who doesn't speak the language, who doesn't know what's happening, and who can't keep a grip on reality. I am someone who, at some level, still thinks it's possible that a children's toy could be an accredited plastic surgeon.

'Stop now. Stop telling me these so-called jokes,' I say to Mom. I feel breathless. 'This is setting me back. It's not helping my recovery. Please don't read me any more.'

'Recovery? What's to recover from? You were always just fine.'

'Well, from how I feel right now. I'm still going to have a permanent scar. A scar, Mom. Just stop, please. I'm freaking out. I can't understand anything.'

A stabbing pain followed by a sharp ache suddenly comes up at me and I shut my eyes. Whatever chemical block they put in earlier is wearing off. 'I just hurt, bad. I'm sorry. I'm just hurt,' I say, and she tells me gently to lie quietly. She says that everything will be fine. Her voice is soothing. It's irrational; around her things are often not fine, but still this is the effect she has on me. I relax.

She tells me, 'I'm changing the subject now, to take your mind off yourself. You think about yourself too much.' She asks me, again, where I met Johnny. Of course, she doesn't say it like that, she asks where the hell I dug this one up.

I think I've told her before that he worked for the city, but maybe I managed to avoid telling her anything or maybe she's really forgotten. Keep it simple, I think. That's the trick to lying.

I say, 'You know, Mom. I told you. I don't know anything right now.'

'Well, you should put him back,' she says. 'And where'd they get this crappy pudding from?' It's the only thing she hasn't eaten and she pokes at the container with her forefinger. Then she sets it aside on the cabinet next to her chair, probably to save it for later. Finally, she puts her head back to get some shut-eye and tells me to do the same.

Infuriatingly, Mom is able to doze in waiting rooms, on trains and planes, even at a party if she gets bored, whereas for years I've struggled with bouts of insomnia. I try to sleep now. I really try.

Johnny returns after a while and I whisper to him so as not to wake my mom. I tell him about the pain and how I seem to have lost some of my brains. He goes to tell the nurse and, while we're waiting for Sam to come back to see me and fix things, Johnny decides that maybe he will be able to explain the jokes.

'Beans can't run,' I say, still whispering. 'They don't have legs. You need legs to run, and a reason.'

'It's a joke,' he says. 'Just a joke. Like, if beans had legs they could be "runner beans". It's not clever, just funny. Don't think so much. You're always thinking too much. You should cut that out.'

'But they don't have legs.'

Sam interrupts us to see what's up. As Mom is asleep, he whispers as well and asks about the pain which is getting much worse. 'I'll see what I can get you.' He takes my blood pressure, which is fine, and goes off again.

After twenty minutes or so, pills have helped the pain, but have made me feel a bit dizzy, like I am drunk. Maybe I sleep for a while but, later, I am looking right at my mother when she opens her eyes. I tell her hi.

Whenever Mom wakes up, she's like Woody Allen in *Sleeper*: it's as if she's been asleep for hundreds of years, not minutes or hours, and she doesn't know where she is, as if she's been pulled back from some other, more real place. She slept with her mouth open and now she licks her lips. Her voice is dry.

'How are you doing?'

'Less pain, bit dizzy.'

As if she has been called in for a second opinion, she wobbles to her feet and puts her cheek against my forehead. She has always taken my temperature this way. After a while, she says to me, 'You're looking a bit green about the gills,' then she repeats it to Johnny who also looks like he's been sleeping, but he often looks a bit dopey so he might not have been. 'She's a bit green about the gills.'

I am horrified as he nods agreement.

'Maybe,' he says.

I clasp my neck with both hands, and run them up to my face, to my eyebrows. 'Where are they? What are you looking at? I haven't got gills,' I say.

'They'd be right there.' She points to the area just below the left side of my jaw.

'What colour are they normally?'

'Pink maybe, beige – flesh, I guess,' she says.

Johnny says, 'It doesn't mean anything.'

'I can't see your gills. Do you have gills?'

He shakes his head. 'Don't be a dumbass.'

'Why is it just me with gills?'

'I don't know. Forget it,' he says.

I look from one to the other, searching for something that will explain my gills.

'What did they give her?' Mom asks.

'I don't know. Something. Some drug. She's just talking crap again.'

'Maybe it's a reaction,' she says. 'You'd better check. Get the name of it. I want to know.'

My chest really hurts again and the bandage feels even tighter and more confining. I feel increasing panic as I wave my hand in front of my face. If I were a fish it would explain a lot of things. Fish don't get jokes. Fish have gills. Do I have legs? Do I have breasts? I signal with my eyes to Mom that

I am thinking about something serious. I mustn't say these things aloud because then I'll look crazy and, even if I have gone crazy, I don't want anyone else to know.

As the panic increases, I send my thoughts to her. I don't think she understands at first, but, then suddenly she does understand. 'Go get that man, that nurse, now,' she shouts at Johnny, and I strongly nod my approval by whacking my head up and down against the pillow. I lift up my hands again to look at them and check that they're still there, that I am not losing all my limbs.

'Calm down,' Mom says. 'All that thrashing about won't help.'

And I transmit more thoughts to her, staring at her eyes, boring my concerns into her mind. She gets it. I know she gets it. 'Why have I got gills?' I whisper. 'Tell me the truth.'

'Honey, gills are no big deal,' she says then she sits back on the upright chair and puts her head back again and shuts her eyes.

If she's not worried, I don't need to be worried. My mother is like a talisman. I know that when she's with me nothing really bad can happen to me. I try not to think about it. I must not think about it. If I am a fish, then I'll have to get used to it. Life can be like this. Surprises happen. Fish get ill, I guess. She still loves me. She always tells me the truth. There is nothing to be worried about.

I don't want her to go off to sleep and leave me like this so, just to keep her talking, I ask her if she's tired.

'I am,' she says.

'Very tired?'

'Try to rest now.'

'How long have I been a fish?'

'Not long. It'll pass.'

Finally, I shut my eyes too. I float off. I dream about swimming in clear water and I am not a fish, I am a mermaid and I have a very strong tail which works just like flippers to send me this direction and that. I can swim the oceans and right around the world.

When I wake, Johnny is back and Mom is also awake. She's got another cup of coffee and he's got another magazine and is crunching through a bag of potato chips. He reaches over me to offer Mom one from the bag, and then she sees that I am awake.

'You're back with us,' Mom says.

'Sorry about that,' I say. 'The fish thing and everything.'

'It's no big deal,' she says. 'See, everything's all right.'

'I'm glad you're here, Mom. I just wish you had come when you were supposed to. I was worried.'

'I think I should go. I need to sleep,' she says. 'Do you get CNN here? I can't miss O.J. It's better than *As the World Turns.*'

'We get everything here, you know that.'

'Well, you need your rest too. Jimmy, can you give me a ride?' Neither of us corrects her about Johnny's name, and, though she kisses me on the forehead and tells me she loves me, he doesn't even say goodbye as they walk out.

A few minutes later, Sam comes to help me to the bathroom. I am very unsteady on my feet. When I return to the bed I am violently ill and vomit bile everywhere. Sam gently puts me in the chair vacated by my mother while he changes the sheets.

'It's probably a reaction. The anaesthetic, and the morphine. It happens.'

Now that my stomach is empty I feel a bit clearer. 'It's been a big day,' I tell Sam. 'I feel very relieved … Hey, you don't notice anything funny about the way I look, do you?'

'You mean the surgery, or are you a fish?' He laughs. 'I heard. Your boyfriend told me. He thought it was hilarious. Said he wondered if we needed to get a shrink in.'

'Did he? Well, I know I'm not a fish,' I say hoping that I sound convincing. 'I've never been a fish. Why would a fish be in here?'

Sam laughs again. 'You look fine. Don't sweat it. Let it go, Louie.'

The slogan is from an ad but at first I can't remember what it was for. I guess and ask if it's Budweiser.

'Budweiser,' he repeats. 'Budweiser, for sure.'

Now he gets another gown and loosens the ties on the one I'm wearing. He changes my nightwear discreetly and politely, without allowing me to feel cold or vulnerable. He holds the flapping back shut as he helps me to stand up again.

A psychiatrist? I can't share anything with Johnny. He doesn't know the first thing about me. He's so fucking grounded he can't come with me anywhere interesting. Instead of making me feel special, he makes me feel like I'm weird.

Sex is not enough to stick us together. But this is not a disaster. I know things are never actually static and that a person can be a variety of things in a lifetime. No one should be tied down to any one incarnation. I'm okay and life is fluid. It's keeping track and keeping up that's difficult.

'I guess I'll have to tell him we're finished. I can't be with someone who thinks I'm crazy,' I say to Sam.

'Unless you *are*, maybe?'

'I'm not. I'm sure I'm not.'

'Well, I'll tell you, your Mom is one special person,' Sam says as he delicately cleans my face with one of those wet wipes, before he helps me to sit back on the bed. 'She seems very sweet.' As he continues I think how much she'd hate to be described as sweet. Sweet is little and gentle and she's always been gigantic and fierce. Now he lifts my legs on to the sheets and puts on those special socks that will keep my circulation in action. He plugs these in one at a time as he tells me he's going to be going off duty soon, but that he'll see me tomorrow. 'Tomorrow you'll feel a whole lot better,' he says. 'The first day is the worst. You will be fine. Tomorrow we'll change this top dressing and you'll want to watch TV. But now you just need to rest. It's been a big day.' He gives me the thing to press to get a nurse if I need one.

I tell him thank you and settle back on the fresh linen. The entire floor has gone quiet now that all the visitors have left. The pillow is cool beneath my neck and it's a good feeling as I fall fast asleep.

1994

Butterflies

'I'm like a dog on heat,' I say to the nurse who has been taking my history before my GYN exam.

'Uh huh,' she says, like she hears this from every woman. Does she hear it from every woman?

'Do you hear that a lot?'

'Uh huh,' she says, 'Can you step on the scales there?'

She frowns as she brings the rod down on my head to measure my height, then she slides the weights across and taps them to get them to balance. 'Okay,' she says. 'Can you sit down again?'

Here she puts the blood pressure cuff on my left arm. She appears to be concentrating hard as she lines up the tube with the midline of the underside of my forearm. 'Please keep still and quiet,' she says.

Half an hour later, on my back, with legs in stirrups while Dr Gauntlet (as he has introduced himself) unpacks the swab for my pap smear, I try again. Better vocabulary. 'Doctor,' I say, 'I've noticed a surge in my libido.'

'Have you?' he says, sitting down on the stool between my legs and now becoming a disembodied voice. 'Horny, huh? Urge or orgasm? Multiple orgasms?'

I don't know how to answer and now I don't want to as I can feel him begin the examination. 'It's just that I want to do it a lot,' I say quickly.

'You're not married?' he says.

'No. I'm seeing someone. I have sex with him.' I sound like an idiot.

'We should do an STD screen, and I'll get Angela to give you some sample condoms,' he says. 'We've had some terrific choices come in.'

'STD?'

'VD.'

'I know what STD means.' I don't tell him that we haven't been bothering so much with condoms after the first couple of times. He is now beginning to wind up the speculum. Best to be silent. I wait until he's taken the sample – which feels like someone scraping at my innards – and has unclamped the instrument again.

'So it's not unusual, being horny like this? I wondered if it's my age, or my hormones aren't balanced or something.'

'Well...' He pauses. 'Libido is a very difficult thing to pin down. What might seem a lot for some, well, it might not be a lot for others,' he says. He stands up again and looks, between my bent knees, at my face at the top of his examination table. 'Once, twice a day?'

'Yes.'

'Well, is it a problem, then? Is he complaining? Is there a mismatch? That can be very tricky. Real tricky.' He looks genuinely concerned.

'No, it's not that,' I say. 'I just wanted to check if it's normal.'

'Well, I guess, life goes like this. Feast or famine, eh? I suggest you enjoy.' He bags the swab. 'We'll phone you with the results.'

My mother has a nose for evasion like a bomb disposal dog for explosives. She'll circle and bark when she finds it. 'So, what does he do?' she asks. I've just told her that I don't have time to talk, that all she needs to know is that I've been seeing someone and that it's working out so far. It is true I don't have time to talk, but I also don't want to.

'He's got a job. And I've got to get the kitchen clean. I'm cooking for him tonight.'

'Go out,' she says. 'Go anywhere, or get something catered. Ring the Piggly Wiggly. You've got one there, haven't you? Their gourmet section...' She keeps talking but I stop listening. I'm not worried about the food because I'll probably serve ready-made and pass it off as home-made, but I am worried about the layers of grime on the stove and everywhere here. It didn't look clean when I moved here from Tulsa but I didn't care at the time and, when I did discover that it was filthy, I did nothing to improve the situation until today when I started with the cabinets, then the countertops, and now I'm on to the back door.

Mom has drifted on from promoting the Piggly Wiggly and is now talking about the health benefits of blueberries and then she wants to know if I'll be there for Thanksgiving. 'It'll come soon enough,' she says. 'I need things to be firmed up.'

My neck is killing me. I can't clean with the phone propped like this on my shoulder. 'I don't know. Look, I'm gonna have to hang up,' I say, tilting my chin down to hold it but nearly dropping the phone.

'Wait,' I hear her yell. 'I haven't finished.'

I look, really for the first time, at the screen door and start to wipe it over with the ammonia-laden cloth that I've used everywhere. At least my kitchen will smell clean even if it isn't actually clean.

There are three holes in the screen. The one in the corner is big enough to let in butterflies, let alone bugs.

'Where did you meet him? Just tell me.'

'Mom, I'm trying to clean up.' My fingers explore the limits of the final hole and as I do this I manage to push the whole thing in. Half the screen is flapping out now. 'Shit, I've just bust the screen door.'

'Why did you do that?'

'I'm hanging up.'

'What's his name? At least you can tell me his name,' she shouts as I rest the phone back in the cradle and get back to work.

To the detriment of any food, and the rest of the apartment, including the bedroom, I have wasted a whole hour hacking away at the screen with a now blunt kitchen knife. The mesh is gone and there are jagged edges all around the inside of the frame. I should never have started. Why do I do these things?

The phone rings at the same time as the doorbell goes. 'It's me again,' Mom says. 'Don't hang up.'

'Mom, he's here. My date is here.'

'Ask him about Thanksgiving.'

'No.'

'What did you cook?'

'Nothing. We'll get takeout.'

I open the door. Johnny looks great. He's wearing a dress shirt over black jeans and holding a bouquet of flowers, and has a bottle of wine tucked under his arm. 'Come in,' I say.

'Let me talk to him,' the voice from the phone says.

'No,' I say. 'I'll speak to you later.' I press the button to end the call and I tell him, 'Sorry, it's my mom. She lives in Phoenix.'

'Mom, huh?' He nods. 'My dad calls me. Yeah.'

'Where does he live?'

'Who?' he says.

I take the flowers to the kitchen to find a vase to put them in and to get some glasses and the bottle opener for the wine. 'We'll have to get takeout,' I call back over my shoulder. 'Pizza?'

'No problem.' He appears intrigued by the bottle opener. He twists it in the air and presses the arms down to force the screw out. On the third time, I take it from him as I've spotted the bottle is a screw top. This is when he says that he thinks my place smells weird. I hope it's the ammonia.

The next day the doctor's office phones to say there's a problem with my pap test. I've got to have another one this week. It's annoying because we've got a big event on and his office is all the way across town and they can't offer me any convenient times, but she says Dr Gauntlet has instructed her to book it for this week, as soon as possible. I can't possibly do Monday because we've got all the set-up and preparation to make sure everything is ready. I'll just have to be away from work on Tuesday, just when the delegates will be arriving. It's some Spiritual Warfare thing, which sounds a hell of a lot more exciting than it is. The only bullets are verbal and, like where I worked in Tulsa, most of the rest of the admin team here are born again and hoping to get involved. Experience tells me that at this conference if anyone acts out of line there will be twenty or more people eager to lay hands on and cast the demons out of him or her. For Christians, perhaps the social embarrassment of being thought to be possessed is what keeps them in line, even those whose booking we've screwed up. So on the whole it's an easy gig.

'Okay. I'll take Tuesday morning, then,' I say. 'Ten o'clock.' My mammogram is due too. If I have to have the morning off, I can get that done then as well and check off all the well-woman boxes my primary care physician told me to complete. It's the same building, but Dr Gauntlet's office can't help me with this. I have to ring another number to get an appointment for the mammogram. I make that appointment for forty minutes after the GYN appointment. That should be enough time.

Johnny's dad lives on a farm out of town and on Saturday Johnny says that he thinks we need some fresh air. A walk and good blow through would do us some good. It's true, we've really only spent time in the bedroom and a couple of movie theatres. We even met in the evening. He was posing for an evening class in the Civic Center and I was there, working late after a conference I'd been in charge of had ended. It *has* been all very nocturnal. A day's outing will be a novelty.

We stop at his apartment on the way out of town. When he parks, I realise how much I was expecting something else. This building is square and squat, very plain. I know it's getting colder, but there's no foliage at all – no evergreens.

The three trees in the front lawn must be diseased or something because their leaves are already gone. There's nothing to give the place any character. 'Second floor,' he says. 'Hop out.'

And, inside it looks like he's never decorated it. Not one picture on the living room wall. All pale cream and beige. The kitchen is immaculate. 'I hardly use it,' he says after I comment on the pristine appearance of his place. He goes into the bedroom and I trail after him. He changes his clothes – he showered at mine – and puts the dirty ones in the wicker basket outside the bedroom. Other than these new arrivals, the basket is empty. The fresh pair of jeans and shirt appear exactly the same as the ones he just removed except now he's wearing a blue, rather than green, shirt, and these pants have a small tear above his right knee.

'Set?' he asks, like I've been holding us up.

Then the urge comes at me again. Lust is a kind of itch. An excitement of possibility, but I don't want to delay us and I don't really want to make love here. It's too un-lived-in, like a show house or something.

I resist the temptation. 'Yes, let's go.'

When we arrive, it's obvious 'the farm' really is not a farm at all. Johnny has told me, on the way, that there are no animals, or land, but that his dad's place *used* to be a farm. The veranda is wide and there's one of those old-fashioned swings with sun-faded cushions on it, which makes the place look like something out of *The Waltons*.

Johnny opens the door and he calls out for his dad as we walk right in. Dave is in the kitchen. It's an old-fashioned homey kitchen with higgledy-piggledy cabinets separated by irregular gaps. There is no countertop joining them and not all the units have doors. There's a patchwork curtain stretching across the space under the sink.

Dave doesn't look old enough to have a son Johnny's age. They could be brothers. His face has the same square features and heavy browline but the full head of brown hair on the father is a surprise, since Johnny's hairline is receding. I wonder if Dave's had a weave, or is wearing a wig. At the very least it's dyed. 'Great to see you,' he says as we shake hands.

'Got a beer?' Johnny asks his father. 'Want one?' he asks me.

I say I'd prefer a soda, so he passes me a Mountain Dew. We sit down at the kitchen table. The sweet fizz of my drink floats up as I sip from the glass, and it tickles my nose.

'Long drive?' Dave asks.

'So-so,' Johnny says. 'So-so.'

He has told me that Dave is a widower. Johnny's mother died of breast cancer when he was fifteen, and I know he was an only child and Dave never remarried, so I'm surprised when a woman bounces into the room. She appears very much at home. Despite the fact that it's October, she's wearing cut-offs, and I've got to say her legs are amazing – long and firm.

'Jo-Jo!' Johnny jumps up and kisses her on the cheek. 'Good to see you.'

'Hi,' I say and then he introduces me to Jo-Jo, but all he says is, 'This is Jo-Jo.' I am waiting for someone to explain exactly who she is in relation to them, but no one does. It takes me a good half-hour to figure out that she and Dave are a serious item.

I've already imagined Mom meeting Johnny and then meeting Dave. Now I try to imagine her meeting this Jo-Jo as well, Johnny's surrogate stepmother, but it is all unimaginable.

On the drive home Johnny asks me what I thought of the place.

'Your dad seems nice,' I say. 'He can really cook, and he has fabulous hair. It's phenomenal.'

'Jo-Jo made him get a transplant.'

'How long have they been together?'

'Since we split up.'

I ask him to repeat himself, and then to clarify further.

'She and me, we used to go out. It's not a problem. Don't turn it into one.'

'When did you break up?'

'A couple of years, maybe. I don't know. It was before her birthday. I remember that because I didn't have to get her a birthday present.'

'Glad to see you have your priorities right,' I say. 'The whole thing is weird. I don't get it. How did they get together?'

'Through a threesome.'

I gulp. 'Maybe I don't want to know.'

'No, not me with my dad. He was with another girl who introduced Jo-Jo to Dad. It was after we split up. *That* was the three-way.'

'So, she's bisexual?'

'Maybe. I don't know. The other girl was a hooker.'

That's the limit for me, I think. I don't want to be uncool, but I really don't want to know anything more. 'Oh, right,' I say. Then, when we get back to my place, I say that I'm really tired.

'No problem. It's been a real long day. I'll just catch you later.' He kisses me goodnight and I get out of the car. He waits until I've put my key in the front door to the building. I turn and we wave before he pulls away.

It's Tuesday and I've left Steve in charge at the centre and headed across town for the repeat pap smear. Turns out he just didn't get enough cells for them to work with. This time he does it in a perfunctory fashion, no need for conversation.

I guess he's as annoyed as I am that he has to repeat it because he didn't get it right the first time. 'Thanks, doctor,' I say when he leaves me to get dressed. I notice that he's still got gloves on when he does a finger wave as he leaves the room. I think about the fact that my germs are now on the door handle.

I hope they factor all that in.

After I dress, I open the door using a tissue stolen from the examination trolley.

The mammogram suite is downstairs and along a long corridor. There's a whole load of women waiting here and I'm half tempted to just walk out. It's not essential at my age. I had one two years ago and this is just another money-maker for HMO, but if I leave I'll have to go back to work and I don't want to do that. Steve can cope. I decide to stay. I sign my name in at the reception desk and settle down on a seat in the corner, next to the magazines. There's not much choice, but there is an ancient copy of *Cosmo*.

Ten minutes later I decide that 'Ways to Drive your Boyfriend Crazy,' is not that informative. Over the years, *Cosmopolitan* has become tame. The *Audubon* magazine probably offers as much instruction on sex. In another pile there's also a *Reader's Digest*. I am reading the article 'Ways to Protect Yourself from Crazy Boyfriends' in an old edition when my name is called and I'm taken through one set of doors to remove my upper clothing and put on a gown and then told to wait in another, smaller, waiting room.

This room has no windows. There is one other woman here. There are no magazines or any other diversion except for a clock on the wall. The other woman and I sit facing that wall. She looks nervous, and from what I can tell she appears to be very flat-chested. Women with small breasts have the hardest time with this procedure because there's less to grab hold of. A technician once told me this fact at the very same time that she grabbed hold of my right breast and shoved it into position on to a metal plate – as if serving me up for slicing in one of those delicatessen things.

Then a door opens and the other woman is called by a big black woman in a too-tight uniform into one of the rooms off this waiting room.

Only a minute later, I am called through, and I allow myself to be directed, pulled and pushed into position. I stand passively as my left breast is flattened like a pancake. I am squeezed, and squeezed breathless. We do it again with the plate at another angle, and then the whole process is repeated on the other breast. Finally, we're done.

'Can you just wait outside, honey?' the technician says. 'I just need to check we've got everything we need today.'

The waiting room is now empty. The clock tells me that the delegates at my event at work will be coming out for lunch in an hour. I hope Steve made sure that the girls who processed them when they arrived checked the dietary requirements. There's always one we haven't planned for. Kosher catering is a nightmare, but these spiritual warriors can also be very picky, with special diets devised to enhance their spirituality through deprivation or perhaps malnutrition.

I've been obedient and switched my cell phone off, so I can't call him to check that everything is going okay. It's very quiet here. I suddenly start to wonder what if there was a real emergency somewhere – would I ever know? What if this building were overrun by crackpot terrorists? What if a SWAT team were called? Should I hide under the bench if I hear gunfire, play dead on the floor, or just put my hands up and hope for the best?

Finally, a door behind me opens. A man comes out and calls me through into a new room. He indicates one of the two chairs in the room and asks me to take a seat. He does not sit down. He stands looking down at me while he explains that there's something, 'just a shadow,' he says. 'We want to take a look further.'

'Which one?'

He points to my right breast. 'Probably nothing, but we want to check further. Have you noticed anything when you self-examine?'

'No.' I don't say that I don't examine myself, because what would be the point in making myself look so careless when they'll be taking a look themselves soon? 'My breasts are lumpy,' I add. 'Generally, you know, just lumpy. Not like mashed potato lumpy, more like fibrous lumpy, cooked celery, or overcooked broccoli stems.' Even as I say all this I realise I sound like a fool.

'Uh huh,' he says. 'Well, we'll want to do a sonogram now. Can I just get you to sign here?' The paperwork is already done. There's my name and date of birth at the top of the form allowing them to bill HMO for more money. 'Won't take long.'

He leaves and a woman comes in. She looks Chinese, with a beautiful curtain of long black hair loose down her back. 'Hi,' I say.

'Hi.' She has a quiet voice. In this soft voice she tells me to lie down on the examination couch and then she starts. She lifts my right arm up and examines my breast with the flat of her hand, then she feels into the area under my arm, prodding deep. She is silent throughout. Then she pulls over a trolley with a big monitor on it, and starts the sonogram. This thing gets rolled over my flattened right breast while she watches the screen intently.

Her face is perfectly still. No frowns, no smiles. Then I spot the first guy by the door in the corner. Perhaps he came back in, or perhaps he never left, but he must be the person who switched out the lights just before she started. He appears to also be watching the screen, but I don't know what he could possibly see from so far away.

'Well,' she says, finally, 'I think we'll just want to do a tiny biopsy, while you're here.'

Above us, the light flickers on.

I am still lying in position with my arm over my head. I pull it down, try to cover myself. My arm across my chest can at least cover both nipples. I don't want to be in this horrible airless room with these strangers pawing over me any longer.

'I really need to get back to work.'

'It won't take long. There's a little bump, just here.' She lifts my arm away and prods into the breast. I can't feel anything but her fingers digging into me. The man in the corner jumps forward with another form for me to sign, for them to claim yet more money from HMO for the 'extended examination'. When I read this form, I learn that a needle is involved. It's a needle biopsy, and a five minutes later I discover that the needle is big, and it hurts.

'I have to wait for the results,' I tell Mom down the phone. 'It's nothing to worry about,' I say, even though I do not believe this and I am terrified.

Yesterday I was reassured about the pap test and was told that the STD screen was clear. I'm waiting for the results of the needle biopsy of the lump that they discovered. There was a message on my cell phone to say that they'd ring me to discuss the result this evening.

'Happens all the time,' Mom says. 'Mistakes like this.'

'It's not a mistake. The lump was a finding and they investigated. I'm waiting for the results of the test.'

123

'Well, it could be a mistake, still. But one of your aunts had cancer. I think it was her breasts. One or both of the breasts.'

'Who?'

'Not your dad's. One of *my* sisters. Sheila.'

'What? Did Dad have sisters?'

'No.'

'They asked me about family history. And I didn't know this. What else don't I know?'

'You don't want to worry people needlessly with stuff they can't do anything about,' she says, 'Don't worry about it *now*. Now that you're in this situation, when it's too late. So, it is cancer?'

'I don't know that yet.'

'But probably?' she says. 'That's terrible. It was Charleen's primary too. Oh, dear. The treatments are awful, honey. But finally maybe you'll lose some weight and that's a plus even though your hair will fall out. We can get you a wig. Oh, God ... Will they remove both breasts?' Then she says, 'Don't worry. You're not going to die right away.'

'I'm hanging up, Mom. I'm expecting Johnny any minute.'

'Aha! Is that his name?'

I end the call.

I'm about to fake an orgasm. I'm still waiting for the phone call. If I don't pretend to be joining in, we could be here forever and I won't hear the phone.

I don't want to tell Johnny that I've been thinking about cancer all day. He's not the most observant person. He doesn't even know that I've had the biopsy done. I've kept my bra on and he hasn't noticed the bandage.

Cancer. That's a conversation I'd rather we never have. It will change things. It would change everything.

He's picking up the pace, slightly.

When we finish, he's not going to want me to say, 'A for effort, but it's just not doing it for me today because I'm scared that I'm going to die.' But, if I don't come, what will he think? That I've suddenly become frigid? What can I do now? It's too late to tell him to get out of me and explain why while he wilts. It would put him off sex with me forever, and he is just so darn good at it.

I arch upwards and start moaning. I could be an actress.

There will be fallout, though – if my faking is too good. He might hurry things along every time, and often I want us to take things a bit slower.

I continue with the repetition. 'Ah! Oh! Ah.' (I don't know how to be more original, but it doesn't seem to matter). Let me be clear: I invariably have an orgasm when we make love. I am very attracted to him, and, though intellectually it might not be the most satisfying relationship, our sex life is extremely satisfying. It has been from the beginning. He knows how to excite me and I have never been bored or disgusted.

I should have told him I had my period.

Suddenly his pace leaps ahead. His eyes take on a particularly vacant expression. I try, 'Oh, baby,' for variation. Then, 'Yes! Yes! Yes!' I am a cheerleader.

It works.

Eventually there is the unravelling of our arms and legs and we are reinstated as individuals again. I roll on my side and out of the bed and into the bathroom. When I come back into the room he's looking very pleased with himself. I must have been convincing.

I tighten the bathrobe about me. He says he'll shower, do I want to join him?

'No, that's fine,' I say. 'Go ahead.'

He has left his wallet on my bedside table. It's an old brown leather wallet – rather old-fashioned and fat. The underside has a butt groove, where it's shaped to his body.

The shower starts up.

His billfold is thick, but not heavy. There's a whole lot of cash in there. Couple of hundred dollars in small bills. It doesn't look as if there's anything larger than a twenty. The card flap is full. There is also a passport-size picture taken in a photo booth somewhere. Guys crammed in and goofing off. I remove this to see if there's a date on the back, which there isn't but I discover, beneath it, a similar picture of a group of girls. College kids maybe. None of them is Jo-Jo but maybe one is the hooker.

Then, finally, the phone rings. I half expect it to be Mom wanting to continue our conversation, but it's not her.

1991

Fireworks

Pastor David always said that understanding and subscribing to a concept intellectually is totally different from translating an idea into action. 'Faith is where the rubber hits the road,' were his words. And now, though I still probably agree with Dad's view that ninety-nine per cent of the things the pastor said were total crap, in my present situation I have to agree with his insight.

After the break-up of a relationship, grown-ups are supposed to move on. I know that this is the truth, but I have not moved on, and seeing how much Chip has moved on is unbearable. He was actually moving at the time. I was two cars behind him and there were packing crates crowding his back seat and the trunk wasn't properly shut. It was held closed with rope.

'Was he in the driving seat?'

'In more ways than one,' I report to Mom on the phone that night. 'And she was there with him. They must be moving in together.'

'Oh,' Mom says. 'I guess you have to expect that. It shouldn't surprise you.'

'A person can hope.'

'A man like him would always run to another woman. Straight into another relationship. You knew this was going to happen. And you're over him. It's in the past. Water under the bridge. Spilt milk. His loss. You've got to make the best of this. Learn and progress.' Then, to add weight to her position as an expert, she slips into phrases I remember hearing her old hairdresser Maurice throwing around in his salon. 'C'*est la vie. Ne fatigue pas,*' she says, '*Je ne regrette rien.*'

'What do you mean, "a man like him"?'

'Well, just that: a man who can't do without a woman to take care of him. I read somewhere that eighty-four per cent of the time when men leave relationships it's because they've got another woman lined up to go to, whereas women frequently leave relationships just because they've had enough. For men, enough is just not enough.' She pauses for breath. 'So, was he leaving Tulsa?'

'So, that doesn't make Chip a *type*, does it? It makes him typical.'

'For example, your father, who was by no means your typical man—'

'Don't talk about Dad,' I interrupt. I hate it when she talks about Dad.

'Look, it was in the *Reader's Digest*. And I've just seen a book in the drugstore, *The Ugly Things Women Do to Make Men Leave*. You could really do with taking a look at that.'

'I don't know where he was going. I didn't follow him. I turned off, and parked, and cried my eyes out in some strange neighbourhood. I feel real bad, Mom, and I need a date. For Donna's party. I can't be date-less Saturday.'

'So, go and get yourself a date,' she says. 'And lock your doors when you're driving. You never know what's around the corner. You might see him again. If you do, you might want to follow him, find out exactly what's going on. Catch them in the act. Now that would be taking action. Try that.'

'What would be the point?' I say, for the millionth time wishing that Mom would be on my side. Not exactly that she isn't on my side, it's just that she never sees it the same way. She doesn't keep up with what I'm saying about my life. Now she's cheering from the sidelines without understanding how much this whole thing hurts. It's not a matter of just moving on. I'm lagging behind. I've fallen out of the race. I'm standing on the kerb. I'm in the gutter looking up at the world that I've lost. 'The divorce is over, and we split up not because of me, but because of him. That's what he said.'

'They all say that. It means nothing. *Nada.*'

We said so much stuff, all that bickering then shouting, that there's a mountain of words. I can't even remember now where exactly my marriage started to go from healthy to coming apart. 'Oh, hell,' I say, 'Did I tell you why we first began to argue? I can't remember.'

Mom says she doesn't know, that I never tell her anything, ever.

'I give up. What issue of *Reader's Digest*? And what was the name of that book?'

She says just read the article. It's in March's, last month's, edition of the magazine, then she asks again if I want to move back home to live with her, I say no and goodbye; we'll speak tomorrow.

Afterwards I go to bed considering my options and wake in the morning feeling strangely more optimistic, until I realise that it's not all that easy finding someone to date and I've got to get on with it – the party is Saturday.

Over my cereal, I decide to settle for Louis in Accounting. The guy's been pestering for months, if not years. Not that I've got a lot of choices lined up.

'You look adorable,' he says when we meet in the bar before Donna's party.

Adorable? Isn't 'adorable' the same as 'cute'? I was aiming for adult in this get-up. Why do men think describing a woman as a child would be flattering? However, it's clear Louis has also made an effort with his appearance. He looks clean and pressed and, even though there is a small dark inkstain on the shirt, for once he doesn't have six identical pens winking at me from his pocket.

'You look good too,' I say.

'So, how well do *you* know Donna?' he asks in that sleazy way which makes me wonder how well he knows Donna. Louis speaks like that when asking directions for using the copier, down the phone to clients, to his boss Lenny when asking if he wants a coffee. He can't say anything without it sounding smutty.

'I knew her from when she was in our department. She started there, taking bookings and working on the brochures. She's moved over to where you are now, but a couple of years ago she used to be at the next desk from me.'

'So, she's leaving?'

130

'You know she's leaving. I was there when you signed the card.'

'I'm just making conversation,' he says. 'Small talk. You know. Preliminaries.'

I just know he wanted to say foreplay and I want to be sick. 'Can you get me a drink?'

'Sure, let me fulfil your desires.'

'A Coke, please.'

'I don't know, he's sort of Italian,' I am talking to Mom on the phone the following morning.

'Oh. Nice-looking? They can be.'

'He's a creep.'

'So, how far did you go?' She asks as if she's been taking lessons from Louis.

'To the party and back.'

'Did he kiss you? Is he a good kisser? Dry or wet?'

I am not answering those questions.

'Well, it's a start,' she finally says. 'At least you went.'

'I had a life and it didn't work out. I can't believe Chip is with her.'

'He's the father of her child. Even if apart, a man and a woman will always have a special tie if they have a child.'

'Thanks, Mom.'

Then she tells me that the daughter of her old friend Charleen has got a new job. When Pan Am went bust last December she managed to get another job straight away with American Airlines – how lucky, but she deserves it – and then she says that Louelle's daughter has moved to Manhattan permanently, and in return I ask what do I care where Louelle's daughter is living?

'Just, *that's* a place to live. Who wants to live in a state known for its panhandle? You don't have to stay, you know?'

131

'I hope Susie knows she's joined a second-rate airline.' This is a very mean thing to say and I hate myself for saying it as soon as the words leave my mouth.

'I'm hanging up now,' Mom says. 'I've got plans.'

The party wasn't much of a party. Louis and I left at eleven and he drove us back to the bar, where I picked up my car. I'd told myself that if I was driving it would prevent me from drinking, which would prevent me getting into something I might regret with Louis, but not drinking just kept me from enjoying anything and I had a twenty-minute drive from the bar home feeling like a spoilsport and then feeling sorry for myself.

My pity party continued right up the stairs, through the door and into my empty apartment. I suddenly missed not only Chip, but Dad too, all over again. It's impossible to think of life going forward when all I can feel is that I've lost all my past and the future that I should have had.

At least I should replace all the artwork that Chip took. The walls are bare. The bookshelves are half-empty. It's been cold since Mrs Waterman downstairs went to live with her daughter midtown. Everything echoes. Every single thing is impossible.

The truth is, Louis didn't even try to kiss me. I didn't really want him to, but I thought he'd try. Am I so disgusting to men that I'm not worth trying to kiss?

On Monday morning I decide that I should do something – a diet and makeover would be a help, and might offset the bloating that accompanies the PMS now beginning to kick in. Lunchtime I call into Woodlands Hill drugstore to pick up some Slim-Fast as well as Kotex, and some new make-up.

When I get to the counter to pay, Nathan is standing behind the cashiers. 'Hey, clumsy!' he greets me.

Nathan is a sweet guy. I'm surprised to see him here at twelve-thirty because he's the night manager, but he tells me that he's been promoted to day manager now. He takes over from the woman at the till and packs my bag and then carries it to my car. He says that, now he's not working nights, he's in a position to ask me out on a proper date. 'What do you think? Maybe Friday?'

I first met Nathan when I'd stopped off at this mall late one night on my way home. We'd done a late function at the convention centre and, as I entered, this young guy, Nathan, warned me, 'Only weirdos come out to shop this time of night. Watch your stuff.' I didn't expect to buy much so I tucked my purse tight under my left armpit and put a hand basket over my other arm and proceeded around the nearly empty store.

I collected some mascara and eyeliner and a couple of lipsticks in the basket and balanced them on top of a *National Enquirer* magazine to prevent them from sliding out through the mesh. I'd put in shower cream and deodorant by the time I got to aisle eight, and just added some cleaning stuff when a glass quart jar of Gatorade crashed to the ground next to me. I must have brushed it with the wayward basket. The juice splashed everything and the glass was everywhere. Nathan came to the rescue.

He nicknamed me Clumsy that night and we've been friendly ever since. He's got puppy appeal but he's years younger than me – he's only maybe twenty-five – and I've never even remotely considered him as date material.

I'm thinking all these things as I realise that Nathan is still standing next to my car waiting for a reply. He's harmless and I like him. What's the problem? So, I say yes but I can't do the weekend at all as we've got an event on, what about Wednesday? We agree that he'll meet me at my apartment, and we'll go to a movie. He enters his number on my cell phone, and makes a note of mine on his.

As I drive back to my desk for the afternoon some of the thick gloom I've been feeling since I last saw Chip on Highway 64 starts to disperse. I might never fall in love again, or be loved again, but it doesn't mean that I can't have friends. Friends are the cornerstones of our lives, the family we create for ourselves, the people who we encounter who make our lives meaningful. Life is for the living. KBEZ on the car radio chimes in; 'A rut is a grave with the ends kicked out.'

Anyway, Nathan is cute. I can rely upon him to be presentable and even if someone thinks I'm his mom there are worse things that could happen. I wouldn't be embarrassed to be his mother. His mother should be proud of him. And, we can still have fun. I haven't been out to the movies for months.

The first thing he says when he arrives is, 'Gee, my mom would have loved to live in a place like this.'

And I say, 'Where *does* she live?'

'I don't know, now,' he says. 'I think she's still alive. I grew up in Osage County. Mom left my dad when I was thirteen. Hey, this is a great apartment.'

'Must be hard if you don't know where your mom is.'

'I still miss her, but not as much as I did when I was a kid. That was tough.'

By the time we reach the concession stand at the movie theatre I have abandoned any diet I might have started, but I don't want to be a complete pig. A medium popcorn will be fine for the two of us. Nathan hasn't eaten dinner so he buys some candy as well. When you're young you can eat whatever you want.

Nathan tells me that he's an only child and that his dad now lives over an hour away. I realise that over the months that we've been saying hi he's managed to learn a great deal about me but I know hardly anything about him. He was always making conversation and asking questions, and he was kind to me when Chip left and I turned up there three nights in a row at one o'clock in the morning unable to sleep and looking a total wreck. I'm embarrassed to acknowledge that I've never given any thought to him as a person, what his life might be like.

As we walk into the movie theatre, he takes my free hand and this is sweet. He asks me to choose where we should sit, then he steps back and follows me along the row of seats. He talks during the film only at just the right times and, even though I know he must be hungry, he doesn't hog the popcorn.

By the time it's over, *Life Stinks* has made me feel sad. Mel Brooks wasn't very funny. It wasn't what I'd expected and I'm glad I didn't watch it on my own. I'm relieved when Nathan says let's go get coffee at an IHOP for a bit of reality. 'It's like you can read my mind.'

To get there we have to get back onto the I44 and go past the Broken Arrow expressway. He's a steady driver and he concentrates, but he still has a gentle smile on his face. Memorial Drive is not the best place to stop at eleven o'clock at night but Nathan knows the place, and the head cook, and finally he has a proper meal. He says since he worked nights for such a long time his body clock hasn't properly adjusted. 'You know how you used to turn up all hours in the night when – ' he pauses delicately ' – you know, back when you split up … ? Well, it's like that. I can't sleep when I'm supposed to and I get real hungry at the stupidest times.'

He doesn't talk with his mouth full and doesn't eat with his mouth open. He's made an effort this evening, swapped his khaki-coloured shirt and slacks for some smart jeans and a clean, pressed button-down shirt. His hair curls slightly on his shirt collar. When we walk back to the car for him to drive me home under the moonlight I realise that it's the exact colour of caramel popcorn.

'You're really nice,' I tell him at the door to my apartment. I won't invite him in. It's late and it would ruin the evening. I just want it to finish now.

He bends down and kisses me on the cheek. 'I'll call you,' he says, then he grins and waves before he bounces down the hall to the stairs and back to his car.

His teeth are white and even and his breath smelt warm and clean against my face.

The next day I get a horrendous migraine. It begins at five o'clock in the morning. Mom phones me at seven, my time. She's going over to Vegas for a few days. I explain that I'm sick. I can't go to work and that I need some meds so I've got to see a doctor. She says that my migraine is probably caused by guilt. 'What did you do last night?'

'I had a date with a boy.'

'A boy?'

'He's twenty-five, maybe twenty-four. I didn't ask.'

'Did you make out?'

'Nobody "makes out", Mom.'

'You want to be careful not to get pregnant. Younger men have super-potent sperm.'

'Oh, yeah! I'm hanging up. So, have a good time. Be good.' Only when I get off the phone do I realise she's not said if she's going alone, or who she's going with. I realise I've no idea what she's up to lately.

My primary physician, Slovackney, doesn't insist that I schlep down to his office to let him have a look himself first.

He sets up for me to see a neurologist. It's now ten o'clock and, once the migraine is over, the flashing lights in my head and the pain like a drill boring its way into my skull have left nothing but a dull ache, and a peculiar feeling of vulnerability. I feel like crap. I take more aspirin and lie in the dark until the afternoon, when the neurologist's secretary phones and says they've got an opening at five, if I want to take it.

'I'll be there.'

The drive to this new guy's office isn't complicated but my head still feels blurry from the headache. I wonder if the analgesics are just masking a continuing migraine or something. There's no wait in the waiting room which is just as well because, though I can't consider reading as the glare from the pages would remind me of the visual aura and bother my head, it's easy to see that the magazines are boring. Why does nobody realise that *Good Housekeeping* is a terrible name for a magazine?

The nurse takes me through and weighs and measures me, takes my temperature and my blood pressure. She is silent, but smiles relentlessly without actually looking at me.

There are bits of my biography at doctors' offices all over. And none of them makes a whole. Just a catch-me-right-now, take-a-peek today, this hour, this second, this moment. Pieces of me. Parts.

I undress to my bra and panties and put on the open-backed gown she hands me, and then all there is to do is wait in the cold examining room to meet the doctor.

Dr Finegold has a firm handshake and the sort of fatherly manner that makes for a good doctor. He grasps my shoulder as he looks with a light into my eyes, waving it around, telling me to follow it. He asks me to track his finger as he moves it across my view.

Dad would have liked him, I think. Finegold looks like a golfer. If they lived in the same city they might play at the same club. Then I remember that Dad is dead, that they probably wouldn't be friends even if they had ever met, and that I am here because I've had a scary migraine. 'You know, I'm not sure it's over,' I say to him. 'It began twelve hours ago but I don't feel myself.'

He begins to ask me hundreds of questions. I explain that Dr Slovackney said that I had to see a neurologist before he would put through another prescription. I've had ones this bad before, I tell him, just not for a long time.

'And you say it began with fireworks in your head?'

'Not fireworks. Fire crackers. Nothing pretty like fireworks. Just crack crack.'

'There was a sound?'

'No, not sound, I don't think. Just flash flash flash. Maybe like gunfire? Silent gunfire?'

'Silent gunfire,' he says, as he writes something down. 'Do you get any other aura?'

'Sometimes, I get olfactory hallucinations – like bubblegum or Juicy Fruit gum, or maybe spearmint.'

'Always gum?'

'No, not always. Other things that aren't there I can smell sometimes. Strong, but they don't last long.'

'When was your last EEG?'

'I've never had one.'

He says I should have this done; he explains that he wants to rule out temporal lobe epilepsy, but he does not – he emphasises this – think that I have that. It's a precaution. He'll set it up.

We get to the medication questions. I tell him I'm on an antidepressant and a very low-dose pill. It helps to regulate my periods. I haven't had children and won't. I can't. But it seems to help a bit with PMS. He says he's not convinced that I should stay on it. I only get to leave after he's listened to my heart, palpated my abdomen and checked my reflexes with his miniature hammer and given me a prescription for a drug I've not had for years as well as a foolscap, single-spaced migraine prevention diet, which seems to have doubled in content since the last time I got one, and strict instructions to stop taking the pill immediately. Even though until now I haven't had a migraine for six months, I have to keep a diary of what I eat and drink, how tired and stressed I get, and I have to see him again in six weeks. 'Migraines can last days,' he says. 'Take it easy until you feel yourself.'

I wonder how safe I am on the drive home.

Nathan calls me later. I tell him that no, I'm not at work so I can talk but that I'm off work because I had a bad headache and had to see a neurologist. His concern is alarming. I end up trying to reassure him, and me at the same time. 'I get them infrequently, really. He said I've got to avoid some foods and come off the pill. He gave me some meds for if it happens again. I think I'm going to stay at home tomorrow too, just try to relax a bit, you know.'

'So you've got to come off the pill.'

'Yeah, it's no big deal.'

'Well, it's *something*,' he says and, although this is the chance to tell him that it is not ever going to happen between us and I am not going to get pregnant even if we did, I say exactly nothing. Then he says he'll phone tomorrow to check on me. He tells me to get some rest and he says goodnight. 'I'll be thinking of you,' he says quietly, right before he hangs up.

'Oh, shit,' I say aloud after putting down the phone.

Nathan and I should not get involved. It would be really dumb. However, despite the fact that I know this and I know I need to make things clear to this poor guy, every other part of me, without exception, is telling me something different. For a change, I feel excited and hopeful and good. Distraction might be a good thing; where's the harm in that?

The Lorelei Haddon Program is scheduled for an event in eight weeks and I ask for the week off. I don't want to be involved. The idea of being surrounded by hordes of pregnant teenagers is bad enough, but a number will be bringing along the products of earlier pregnancies. We are expected to provide a crèche while the mothers-to-be listen to advice on childbirth and attend a fashion show of modest born-again maternity wear.

Here in Tulsa my views are in the very small minority. I believe a woman should have the right to choose when she has a baby, and that teenage pregnancies should always be discouraged. This goo-goo event is ridiculous because it enables irresponsible behaviour.

But when I ask my supervisor, Eleanor, she says they need everyone here to help out. I leave work feeling frustrated as well as disappointed. And later, at home, when Nathan calls unexpectedly, I end up griping about it. 'Why is it that I can't take time off when I want? Every year they come and do this stupid thing. It's not even a convention, it's a free-for-all, the most stupid, chaotic and stressful event you can imagine. We always have to call an ambulance for something. One of the thirteen-year-olds will go into labour – because they always do; a fourteen-year-old will lose her baby at the last minute and end up bleeding all over the mezzanine floor and crying for her momma – because they always do. It should take place in a hospital.'

'I know about that programme.' Nathan sounds a bit sheepish. 'My church raises money for it.'

'Your church? You belong to a church?' But, of course, this makes sense. How could I have not realised that he was religious. Nathan has never been at work on a Sunday, he doesn't cuss like other people, he talks to everyone, he's nice, and despite four dates he has not tried to lay a hand on me. 'Oh, my God! When were you going to tell me?'

'Tell you what?'

'About your religion.'

'I told you I went to ORU.'

'You did?'

'I *did* go to Oral Roberts University, and I *did* tell you that I did.'

I have no recollection of this vital piece of information. For a couple of moments I try to review every conversation we've had, and I realise that I knew he went to college, but we talked about this when he'd been asking a lot of questions and I wasn't paying attention.

'I'm sorry, I just didn't take it in,' I say. 'I didn't realise.'

As he says it really doesn't change anything, his voice down the phone sounds sad.

'Well, yes, it kind of does, doesn't it? Because I'm not. I'm not going to ever be.'

'Give me a break.'

'Don't even think of trying to convert me.'

'I'll see you tomorrow at ten,' he says referring to our plans to go to the zoo.

As I'm falling asleep I think about this again. Sometimes when you have one small piece of information everything changes. Things shift. Nothing can be understood in isolation. Everything is interdependent. Nuances might well mean something else now. Nothing is certain. How often do I do this? How could I have missed this fact? I'm sure he did tell me. But I didn't listen. He hasn't pretended otherwise, hasn't disguised anything, or been deceitful. Anyone who goes to ORU has got to be born again. Those sixty-foot praying hands and that crazy prayer tower where the big man himself takes requests for his direct line to God are the architectural proof that they're all crackpots. And Nathan is one of them.

When he arrives in the morning I've thrown out six different outfits and I'm wearing a below-the-knee skirt with a high-necked blouse. When I stub my toe on the bookcase before we leave the apartment. I find myself saying, 'Gosh darn it.'

Once we're in the car and he's heading towards the highway, I remember that I've forgotten to switch the bedroom alarm off. It's still on snooze. At some point within the next hour it will begin an ever-increasing shriek-eek-eeek-eeeek, which will irritate the happy young couple upstairs – and mess up my chance to be a good neighbour.

Suddenly I am cussing aloud: 'Fuck it, fuck it, fuck it.'

And he starts laughing. 'What's up?'

When I tell him the problem he offers to turn the car around and go back. His response is irritating. I am trapped in this tidy, no doubt well-maintained car with Pollyanna. I'd bet money that if I popped the trunk there would be a first aid kit and a 'what to do if your vehicle breaks down on the highway' emergency box in the trunk. My life has never been like this. This is not who I am and, whatever this is, it's not what I need to be doing at this point in my life.

I tell him that the alarm will eventually wear itself out, so don't turn around – I don't want him doing me any favours – just get us there. 'Try and drive like you mean it, for a change,' I say, and he doesn't even take offence.

All through the drive I oscillate between self-loathing and him-loathing. As we arrive and I spot a sign advertising

Tulsa's amazing ape house, I say, 'I bet you don't even believe in evolution.'

'I don't know. I don't think about it too much.'

'You must have a view on it.'

He stops the car in the middle of the road and twists around to look at me. He's upset, and angry. 'I guess I don't, then. If I have to have a view on it, I don't. It might be a correct theory, but it also equally might not.' Then he falters. He says, 'If God created...' His face changes. He's cornered and nervous – as if he's just been asked to do a speech at a funeral or something because the guy that was supposed to do it has dropped dead himself. In fact, he looks ten years old and I'm bullying him and he's always been such a nice guy to me. I am a total bitch.

'Forget it. Sorry.' I take his hand. It must be really embarrassing. He can't help it. It's nearly impossible not to be a Christian here, maybe. He lost his mother, he grew up in this place. His father probably relied upon church to help out. I don't know. 'It's not important,' I say. 'Don't sweat it. I'm sorry. I'll stop it. I'm sorry.'

For the rest of the morning I try not to think about it and just enjoy his company. I'm being silly, I should just appreciate him for what he is: a friend. He's kind and considerate. Then when we stop for lunch and I'm waiting at the table for him to bring the meal over I watch an exchange between Nathan and the girl behind the till. Though I know it's part of his ready, friendly charm and that it means nothing when he starts talking to her, I feel irrationally jealous. I can't hear what he's saying but I can hear *her* voice when she replies, 'Yeah, but standing is better than sitting for this.' She turns slightly to invite him to admire the view of her very pert-looking ass.

Nathan averts his gaze, and decides to wave at me. He makes it clear he's not buying whatever she's selling.

It is at that moment that I experience a significant shift of something I thought impossible: this man's loyalty and decency is attractive. It's a mighty mess of attraction, flattery and admiration that produces a definite buzz. So, when he puts his hand over mine and says that he's really enjoyed the day but that he's got to take me home, from all the excitement I am feeling in my body you'd have thought he'd sworn his undying love, not that he's got to get back because he's got bible study that night.

Thursday the next week I prepare for the EEG that Dr Finegold set up. I've got the day off and my appointment is at ten. I re-read the instruction sheet in with the appointment letter. Seems the only thing I have to do is make sure my hair is clean; there must be no gel or hairspray residue. I decide that this means I should avoid conditioner on my hair because that can be pretty gloopy, and, even though I've finally found a product that prevents frizz in even the highest-humidity conditions, I mustn't use my new straightening gel.

I arrive five minutes early at the outpatient facility and report to reception. They are running an hour behind. The receptionist suggests I get a coffee or something and come back later. She does not mention my Ronald McDonald hair.

Fifty minutes later I return to the waiting room and the technician who will be doing my test is irritated. I start to explain that I was told to go away and come back in an hour and therefore I'm right on time now, but she's not listening. Her high heels clip clip clip away along the corridor in front of me and I follow.

Ms Technician's hair is short and spiky. She's wearing big bright red earrings. I wonder for a moment if she's a Christian. Do they allow hair and earrings like that?

'You can get yourself ready there. There's a locker for your purse.'

'Do I get undressed?'

'The electrodes go on your scalp.'

'So, I don't need to get undressed?'

'Keep your clothes on. Go ahead and put your purse in the locker, and come and take a seat. She indicates what looks like a dentist's or optician's chair – high and mechanical, a hospital throne. She begins to pick through my hair and then takes a tray with some wires and begins to apply them to my head. They're surface electrodes, she explains. This is a non-invasive procedure. All I need to do is let her do her job.

I am transfixed by her earrings and wonder where she got them and how much they weigh. Her earlobes are stretched, but perhaps it's not these cheap earrings that caused it. Maybe she's worn heavy earrings since she was a kid.

'I washed my hair like the sheet said. I'm glad to get this date so fast. I don't think I have epilepsy or anything. The doctor is investigating migraine, but I've had that for years. I think he's just, you know, being sensible.'

'Uh huh.' I feel her poky fingers separating out strands of my thick frizzy hair. The tray is emptying fast. 'I wonder what it looks like,' I say. 'It must be an interesting job you do, meeting people all day, helping people, you know. Nice, I guess.'

'It'll be over before you know it.'

Now she plugs the ends of the wires into a box thing and puts a strap across my middle. 'I'm adjusting this to a reclining position,' she says, and the chair buzzes into action and stretches out until my legs are raised and my head lowered to nearly horizontal. Once this is done, she retreats to the other end of the room. 'I need you to just relax and be quiet. You can shut your eyes for a while just while I get set up. I will ask you to open them in a bit, and then shut them again. Then you need to open them again and look directly ahead – you'll see some flashes of light from above you. This is nothing to worry about. It's all part of the test. It's very unlikely that you'll have a seizure of any kind, but, if you do, don't worry. Are you okay there?' She says all this in the same flat tone, without any breaks.

I note that this is the first time she's actually inviting a response. I say I guess so.

She dims the lights. I shut my eyes. I try to think happy thoughts, giving my brain the chance to demonstrate how relaxed it can be. I think about Nathan and what happened, and how sweet he was when Chip and I split. When things are happening it's too easy to get caught up in events. That thing about time healing things is true, but the other thing about time is that it's wholly dependent upon what's going on. It seems to slow down and speed up.

Then her voice interrupts my thoughts. I find myself back on this bed, in this room and an object again.

'Open your eyes, please. Keep still.'

The ceiling looks like it's false. Tiles inserted in some scaffold construction. The real ceiling is beyond that, and in between there will be the air-conditioning ducts, insulation, all the wiring this kind of building needs. I wonder how many sockets there are in this room alone. Without moving my head or eyes I do that thing where you try to remember what's around you even though you can't see it. There's the computer she's looking at; there was a sink, no electrics there. There's the machine that's measuring my brain waves, watching me watching nothing and thinking about everything.

'Okay,' she says, 'you can shut your eyes again now.' Then she asks me to breathe deeply for a couple of minutes, which makes me feel dizzy.

'Breathe normal now,' she says. After another few silent minutes, she says I should open my eyes again and look straight ahead. There are a series of fast flashing lights like strobe lights.

When she says, 'Good,' I wonder what she's seen: something or nothing. Then the lights finish and I'm allowed to shut my eyes again. For a while the pow pow pow of the lights remain in my eyes, the negative on my eyeballs, the phantom picture of the light – and finally the image fades and she tells me it's over and we're done.

I can go home. The doctor will get the results, she is not able to tell me anything, except that to the best of her knowledge the test was performed adequately.

She waits while I collect my bag and she strides in front of me down to the main doors. She dismisses me by telling me to have a nice day without even bothering to look at me. I go home and take a bath. I wash my hair properly and use a whole bottle of conditioner and handfuls of gloop to get it right again.

I must take some control in my life. I want to get myself back.

I phone Mom. There's no reply.

I have to be true to myself and so I must make things plain with Nathan. I feel that if I don't I'll disappear. I love spending time with Nathan because I like him. Nathan makes me feel hopeful, less serious, happier, but it's a ridiculous idea. We have no future. It's inevitable that we'll break up.

I tell myself that I'm worried he's become too attached. The longer we are together, the more heartbroken he will be in the end. But, truthfully, it's me who is too attached. I'm scared. If it's going to happen, I'd rather jettison the relationship now.

Fifteen minutes later I'm dressed and driving to see him at his workplace. We met there; we can finish there. I don't want any misunderstandings if I have to call into the drugstore for any reason in the future.

He's in his office and I shut the door behind me.

'We can't go on like this.'

He looks genuinely puzzled.

'It won't work.'

'What are you talking about. Are you okay? Have you got your period again?'

'Wrong question, buster. Are you monitoring my cycle?'

'No, come on, relax. Sit down.'

'I've been for the EEG.'

He tells me to wait for a minute. He goes out and comes back with two cans of 7 Up. 'Are you okay?'

The bubbles fizz in my mouth. He's got the drink straight from the fridge and it is delicious. He always knows what will feel good. He is waiting for me to collect my thoughts but my mind wanders further. He's so sensitive and considerate, I've never had a doubt that he'd be dynamite in bed if only he tried it out. 'So, do you want to sleep with me?' I say. 'Or not?'

He takes a large gulp from his can – too much. Some of it dribbles down out of his mouth.

'Well, do you?'

'Gee, you do like to pin things down, don't you? Did they say something was wrong with your brain?'

I go right over and kiss him. He tastes as delicious as I've suspected. Now his tongue is hot in my mouth and his hands are sure enough doing all the right things. He wriggles out from under me, locks the door and comes back. His desk chair has no arms and we do it right there in his office in the drugstore with the sound of 'Clean up aisle seven... Could Joe help out on checkout C...'All that beeping and bleeping and nothing stops us. Finally I hear nothing and I am exploding. My head is going blam blam blam and it's actual beautiful fireworks. 'This is great,' I whisper, opening my eyes to see that he's kind of not with me and looks like someone else. He's nearly there too.

Afterwards all that tension is gone and we clean up, dress, and try to finish our sodas as if nothing has happened.

He finally says with a sigh. 'I'm worried you're not on the pill.'

'I can't get pregnant.'

'Gee,' he says. 'Oh.'

'It's okay.'

'Was the test okay?'

'I don't know. Probably. It's just headaches.'

'I did kind of want it.'

'It was good. It was fine. I knew we'd be good together.'

We both smile at this, and clink our nearly empty cans.

He is a good guy, with way more principles than me. I can't tell him that he's at the age when things happen that really shouldn't have consequences. And that I am at the point when things must have consequences, which is exactly why this is where any idea of 'us' must end. My marriage failed and I've been feeling bad, lonely, desperate and unwanted. It's not a good time to make a choice involving someone else. 'I love being with you but we won't do that again. It's not right,' I say.

He nods slowly. 'We can be friends.'

When I finally get hold of Mom to catch up with her I ask her where the hell has she been. 'You've been gone two weeks. You are so inconsiderate.'

'I went with the flow and stayed. All those lights, all the colour. Vegas is great. So, did you worry?'

'No. And don't tell me about lights. I had a test. The doctor thought I might have epilepsy.'

'You went in with a migraine and got epilepsy?'

Then I tell her that it turned out Nathan was a Christian. 'We're just going to be friends.'

'How do you find them?'

'For God's sake, Mom, you belong to a church.'

'I'm a Presbyterian. There's no funny stuff going on. Nothing out of control. You can't be friends, you know. There's a natural law that says that men and women cannot be friends. In fact, some men can't even be friends with other men. Your father—'

I interrupt. 'Well, we did sleep together,' is what I say next, and then explain that Nathan and I agreed we won't ever have sex again. 'We both wanted to end on a high.'

'Maybe you're terrible in bed. I'm sure there's a book you can buy—'

'No, Mom, we can have sex with other people, just not with each other. Well, I can. I guess he can't.'

'You'll always have the memories, I suppose.' She sounds wistful as she says this, but not for long, because she goes on to tell me that I must watch out, that I'll be wearing a headscarf by next week. 'He'll buy you one for a gift. Then a bible. Evangelism by seduction. I'm sure I read about it somewhere. Anyhow, I've got to go, I can't sit around forever, I've got things to do.' And she hangs up straight away, before I can point out that I'm a grown woman capable of making my own decisions.

I've decided I'm going to apply for another job. If Chip is staying in this city, then I'm not. I'm going to move on.

1988

Fireflies

There's a pause in the conversation. Whenever this happens, that aching hole-in-my-middle feeling seeps back.

'I know exactly how you feel,' Mom says. 'When Dad left—'

'Dad didn't leave you,' I interrupt, the sad feeling replaced with frustration. 'He died. Because of what happened, he died. Died is not the same as left.'

'I don't think you can get more left than dead,' she says. 'He's not coming back. Whereas you might find—'

'This is not helping.'

'Do you want him to?' Before I can even consider my answer, she says, 'Let's have another glass.' Even though we are in Phoenix, and at her home, I am doing the pouring and this is the second bottle.

She met me at the bus station this afternoon. I got off the bus grungy and stiff-legged from the overnight confinement and swearing that I'd never travel by bus again. She gave a wave and a sturdy, brave smile, and at this I felt relieved to see her – perhaps she could be on my side without being against everyone else as well, as I'd hoped – but before we were even in the car she clutched my hand and said, 'I'm telling you, I never liked him. I don't know what you were doing with a guy like that in the first place,' and within ten minutes I was wondering if the idea of the visit was misguided.

Now she says, 'I know you think you won't ever be okay again, but you will.' She scoots her rear close to the edge of the sofa and swills the white wine around in the glass. 'It's just a matter of time. People get used to all kinds of things, if they have to. Life doesn't turn out as you expect it sometimes, but you're like me – someone who overcomes problems. It's not where you start, it's where you end up. This won't get you down. So, do you want to watch the telethon?'

'He didn't say it was definitely over. He just wants some space. He's got his new place.'

'Space! One word that means it's over,' Mom says. 'If you'd only admit it, you didn't even like him, honey.' She turns on the TV. Jerry Lewis is looking ropey and slightly confused. Dolly Parton is about to sing. Then she does. She sings a full-throttle depression-making song. I don't want to hear about any babies, or their baby sighs.

'Turn this off, Mom, please.'

She mutes the sound on the TV.

'Okay,' I say, 'perhaps that's true, but I didn't want him to leave. I wanted to be the one who left. I feel abandoned. I've been abandoned.'

'Don't be melodramatic. It doesn't suit anyone, least of all you.'

You can talk, I think.

When I tell her that I'm tired and want to sleep, she takes me down the hall, and we take our drinks along. I have never lived in this house, but she's made sure that I have a room here. Dad never lived here either, but I am pleased to discover as we pass her room that it is the same as I remembered from their earlier home. It's a mess but she's not gone all fluffy-pink-and-white furniture now that she's a woman alone, which is what I half expected.

'Do you still miss Dad?'

'Maybe,' she says.

'I miss him.'

'I expect you would. He always loved you. He really, really wanted you, you know.'

'And you.'

'Maybe,' she says again, which riles me. She never appreciated him and he put up with a lot. Even his death was a matter of her selfishness. She'd gone off for two days, no note, nothing. He'd been frantic and phoned me several times to ask if I'd heard from her. Did I know where she was, why she'd gone?

She said that when she came home and pulled up in the driveway he was on the roof; apparently he was fixing the aerial. She'd been complaining about the reception for months. She said that, when she got out of the car and called to him, he waved an excited greeting with his free arm. I think that in his glee at seeing her he lost his balance and couldn't hang on. 'He was so happy,' was what she said at the time, that and, 'I was so surprised to see him on the roof like a young man, like a red-blooded guy who could fix something. I never expected him to get up there himself.'

It was a long fall and he crashed and bounced on the roof a bit before he rolled off and finally hit the ground. He sustained a fractured pelvis, numerous broken bones and a bad head injury. He ended up in a coma and on a ventilator. After a week, we turned him off. Well, not exactly. Mom and I stood there while someone else removed the ventilator and the two of us watched him make small noises over the course of two hours until he finally went quiet and still and when we called the nurse she said he'd gone.

Mom will relate to anyone now that we agreed to what the doctors advised, and implies that she was reluctant, but it's not true. There was some concern over the insurance and she argued with Uncle Pete, Dad's brother, on the phone. Pete wanted us to pay whatever, or at least wait until he got to the hospital, but when she got off the phone Mom announced that she had decided. She said, 'We can't play God. Even with Blue Shield, medicine can't go on forever. We've got to turn him off and let him go.'

I know there wasn't really hope of reasonable recovery. If he'd have woken up he'd have been paralysed, and chances are very badly brain-damaged too. Yet the doctors were remarkably silent about what we should do. When Uncle Pete arrived – too late – he was beside himself upset, and kept clinging to Mom, and hugging me, even though we were virtual strangers.

Uncle Jack offered to do the eulogy. Unlike Pete, Uncle Jack isn't related to us at all. He popped up in our life periodically as he'd been Dad's best friend since they were at college together, and he was also his lawyer. He was okay. He was always nice to me, but there was always something missing with Jack – maybe because he never married. Mom says marriage knocks the edges off of a person and Jack was like a kid in lots of ways: selfish and self-centred. When he was around he always demanded Dad's complete attention. I think Mom was jealous of him, and Jack was jealous of her.

Anyway, at the end of the visit Mom got Uncle Pete to tell Jack that he wasn't to say anything. I overheard that conversation, but not the one Pete had with Jack. The fallout was loud and everyone who was still around heard it. Jack got angry and he shouted at Mom before he stormed out and back to Chicago. Pete stepped into the breach with the eulogy, which was brief and inadequate. Jack *would* have done a better job, because Dad and Pete never saw each other and Jack and Dad were close.

It's only a blurry memory now, but I remember feeling that it wasn't fair, it was a disappointment, and that what Pete said didn't seem to be about Dad.

We're at 'my' room now and Mom sits down on one of the twin beds. 'Do you want me to sleep in here with you, honey?'

This offer is startling, because it is out of character. But I tell her that there's no need, that I'm a big girl now.

This night there is a full moon and the room glistens. Except for the new bed, and the firm mattress, the furniture is from my childhood bedroom. I think about Jerry Lewis's past-it voice on the last song, and then, as I slip to sleep, I think about catching fireflies. They are best captured at dusk. When it's too dark it's impossible. They're only random sparks and never close enough to catch. One summer I spent every evening leaping about in our front yard, a big glass sauerkraut jar in one hand and the lid, with its nail-punched holes neatly spaced, in the other. I don't remember how successful I was or how long they lit up once I captured them, but even now I can remember the weight of the jar and the feel of the stretch in my arms.

Then for a few minutes more I think about Mom's life now without Dad. She seems to have made neighbourhood friends and she tells me about them on the phone. I fantasise about just upping sticks, quitting my job, and moving back here to be near her instead of a thousand miles away. It would be nice to be near her. I could get another job. The warm weather is appealing. I wouldn't be lonely. I only moved from Phoenix with Chip – for him and his job. Without Chip there's nothing to keep me in Tulsa any more.

In the morning, I risk a bath. Mom disapproves of baths. She says showers are much better because they don't take so long. She's not worried about the environment, it's just one of her obsessions, but water is healing and a good soak would do me good.

I've lost weight, and when I lie down my stomach seems even flatter than it did yesterday before I left home. I lather up the soap and then it falls, sliding between my fingers like something alive. I swish around but, every time I catch hold of it, it slithers from my hand, slipping away from me and hiding again. I realise I'm making a lot of noise, so instead of soaking as I'd intended to do I end up climbing out quickly and draining the water. I dry the bath and find myself pouring some water on the shower screen to mislead her but this doesn't work. When she comes downstairs she says, 'You should have cleaned the tub. I hate soap-scum tidelines.' But she doesn't give me the lecture I've heard a hundred times before so I think she's making an effort to be nice.

The news is on TV while we're eating our breakfast. 'When did the weather man get promoted?' I ask. 'That fat guy is now news anchor.'

Mom says that he's not Jim-Bob, he's gone over to KCRW Radio. Back east in Chicago or somewhere.

'Sure looks like him.' We both study the set. Maybe this guy isn't quite as fat as I remember, but he's got the same goofy grin. He's saying that there's a new clinic opening up offering IVF to women over fifty.

Mom says, 'Do you think in the end it was the kid thing?'

I suspect she's been holding on to this question for a week now, since I told her Chip had left. In fact, Chip had been gone nearly two months by the time I told Mom. I couldn't tell anyone what had happened, because I didn't want to acknowledge it myself. I couldn't sleep, I barely dragged myself into work. I'd never felt so bad, and the worst of it was that I felt ashamed. He said it was nothing to do with me in a way which made me sure it was only to do with me.

'No,' is what I answer. 'There's much more to it than that.' I don't say that it's clear now that we were too different. He doesn't have any imagination. I have too much.

'Is Chip gay?' She asks. This must be her theory B, but she explains that the weatherman gone to do radio was gay, that's why she thought, while we were talking, that she'd ask. 'Is he?'

'But KCRW is LA.'

'That explains it,' she says. 'A person can get away with more personality in California. California has a lot to answer for.'

'I *don't* think he's gay.'

'I read about it. He is.'

'Not him. Not Jim-Bob. Not the guy on TV. Him. Chip.'

'A lot of men pass. I'd say it was extremely common – gay men getting married to put people off the scent.'

This is not a comfortable conversation. 'Mom, I really, really, really don't think he's gay, but of course I can't be sure.' It's the truth because how much does anyone know about someone else in reality? That's the next thing I say: that a person can't ever be sure of anything, not one hundred per cent sure.

She grins. 'Well, honey, that's a change, for you.'

'What do you mean? How come you said that? I don't think it's a change for me.'

'Nothing,' she says, but I want to know. She squeezes her eyes shut. She decides to tell me that she means nothing, doesn't have any idea why she said it. 'Forget it,' she says with her eyes still screwed shut. Then she starts to tell me about one of her friends, who she plays Mah Jongg with. The connection is that it turns out this woman had a husband who turned out to be gay. She caught him in bed with another guy. It was a shock but the signs were there all the time. 'I'm telling you, it happens a hell of a lot of the time, and we should feel sorry for these men. Imagine the shame. And their poor wives who have to live with it. What a terrible thing to marry someone who doesn't want you, to live with that. It's a disappointment to be rejected by someone who is supposed to love you, who has promised to love you. Imagine the sorrow.'

'Huh, Mom?' I can't listen to all that she's saying. I am calculating what time it is at home now and what Chip is likely to be doing, when she suddenly says, 'Anyway, enough of gloomy talk. Mandy said to me the other day, "Cindy, you are consistently lucky." She thinks bridge is a matter of luck,' Mom says, 'which explains her half-wit playing. If you think it's luck it takes away any incentive to improve. She's useless.'

'Why'd she call you Cindy? Your name isn't Cindy.'

'She probably thinks it is.'

'Why would she think it? Have you given her a phoney name? A pseudo-name?'

'A name is not important. She probably thinks I'm some-one else. It's no big deal. Sometimes it's hard to remember things. We're getting on. All of us. None of us are kids.'

'You're not that old.'

'Some days I am. Some days I'm ten years older.'

I tell her that I think it's weird that she's spending time with a bunch of people who can't even remember each other's names.

'Mandy sounds a bit like Cindy. Maybe she's got me muddled with herself. Maybe she thinks we're sisters – twins, maybe.' Mom giggles. 'Twins ... It would be nice to be a twin.'

'I wanted to be a twin,' I say.

'I could never have had another child, honey. Because you were enough. You were perfect.'

My mother has never said anything like this before. I am touched, and softened by the fact that I was enough for Mom and Dad. At some point in my life I was adequate.

'And your shitty idiot husband. He is *such* a schmuck to let you go,' she says.

I don't point out that we didn't leave it long enough for him to let me go. He went.

Four hours later, over lunch and with another bottle of wine open between us, I ask, 'So, if I'm so perfect, what did you really mean about what you said, earlier?' I ask. 'About me.'

'Nothing.' Obviously we didn't have alcohol with breakfast, but we ploughed through a hell of a lot last night and here we are about to do it again. I wonder how regularly Mom drinks now as I watch her downing her first glass.

'Yes, you did mean something. Tell me.'

'It's nothing.'

Then I do it. I don't have to, I know I shouldn't, that there is nothing to be gained from pushing this point, but still I go and say, 'Just tell me, what you meant. I won't get mad. I just want to know. What did you mean?'

She places her glass down. 'The thing is, honey, you said it: nothing in this world is ever actually black and white. People are complicated. I just think that finally understanding that everything is more complicated than you might realise is a real change for you.'

'It's not that nothing is. I wasn't talking about everything. I know things are not *always* unambiguous. But sometimes they're clear-cut.'

'You've always wanted to straighten things up, straight lines – like how you lined up your dolls. Sometimes it can't be done, that's all. You don't need to pick at everything. Some things are best left. Let sleeping dogs lie. Live and let live. Don't sweat the small stuff. In fact, you're very controlling, honey.'

'You're calling me controlling? You with the no-soap and the bath thing.'

'You're upset,' she says. 'You said you wouldn't get upset.'

'Dad is dead,' I tell her. 'He didn't leave. He fell off the roof not because he lost his footing but because you weren't there. You could have saved him but you killed him.'

She doesn't look at me. She says quietly, 'It's too late.' But I'm going on, breathless. My heart is thumping. 'And now my husband has left. It's made me feel real bad, Mom. I didn't expect him to. I didn't think it would end like that. Why can't you understand? I feel terrible and you just want to tell me what's wrong with me.'

'No, honey. You can't know everything. That's my point,' she says. 'That Chip, he's one fucking idiot.'

We drink all day and then, in the evening, I phone Chip at his new apartment.

160

He answers on the second ring. He doesn't have the decency to sound different; his voice is exactly the same.

I don't say hi. In an even voice I say I'll be back by the end of the week. He'd better have hauled every bit of sorry-ass crap of his out of our place, or else it's to the Goodwill, and he should know I'm changing the locks as soon as I get home because I don't ever want to see him again.

Even though I tell myself it's probably better to be the person who tells the other to go, when I slam the phone down I discover my hands are shaking.

'Good for you,' Mom says. 'That's telling him.'

'But maybe I still love him.'

'I know, honey,' she says. 'That's because he was the love of your life. He'll always be the one. Especially now he's gone. But you can get on with things. You'll love again, I'm sure, but you should know he'll always be the one. That's the gospel truth.'

'What a shitty thing to say. How can you say that? How's that supposed to make me feel?'

'Well, think about it. What a waste it'd be. I mean all this feeling. What would it all mean, what would it be worth if you didn't love him a whole lot? Don't you get it? It's okay. It makes sense, you'll see.'

Finally, I cry, and cry, and cry.

When I'm in bed, she kisses me on my forehead, like I was a little kid, and she sits with me until I pretend I'm asleep. The sound of her tired sigh as she leaves the room is soft and warm. It's totally real, and totally sad.

1985

The Seahorse

Dad has opted to stay up at the lodge and Mom and I are on the grass resting in the shade of some big prickly tree. Chip referred to his guide book about Utah and when he set out the loungers for us he announced that above us was an Alligator juniper. He didn't notice the sarcasm when Mom said, 'Thanks for putting my mind at rest.'

Right now, he and Kimberly are at the lakeshore throwing rocks in. The faded guidebook bulges from his back pocket. It's the sort of hot and hazy and too-humid day that makes my mind as well as my hair go all frizzy.

Mom looks nearly asleep but I know she isn't. She's waiting for me to say something because, though she might not know exactly what I'm riled about, she knows I am fuming about something. I caught her watching me from the back seat of the car on the drive here and she can read my mind.

Every time I look at Kimberly I see Joanne, her mother, Chip's ex. He insists that Kimberly phone her mother every evening and before they talk he spends a couple of minutes telling Joanne the things that we've done each day, even though this is exactly what Kimberly will be repeating. Last night he called me Joanne in his sleep. We can't have a vacation without dragging Joanne along with us.

When Kimberly turns to wave up at us now, I grin and wave wildly back, rocking the lounger. She's not yet ten but this girl is not just cute, she's well on her way to beautiful. She's like a chestnut colt.

'Well, that's a nice picture.' Mom opens her eyes. 'The two of them.'

'Don't,' I tell her.

'Don't what?'

'You know. Leave it.'

She settles back down and waves her hand in the air, brushing me away.

'What time can we go back?'

'We're going back for lunch. We're here until it's time to eat.' We came out here because he and Kimberly could do a hike; and since the route, Chip explained, was circular, Mom and I wouldn't have to go along, but the idea was for us to be together, sort of.

'You're as bored as I am. Admit it.'

'We can't leave.'

'I want coffee.'

I leave Mom to walk down to Chip. He's holding his daughter's hand and I see how she really is growing like a weed, just as he teased her at breakfast. She'll soon be as tall as he is. This is the first of the two weeks she spends with us in the summer.

I feel like an intruder but, even so, I take his other hand to get his attention. 'I know it's early but Mom's had enough,' I say. 'It's real hot.'

'What about you, sweetie?' Chip turns to ask Kimberly, instead of me.

'I'm okay. I don't care. Whatever you want to do will be fine.' Kimberly says, directing her Miss America smile at me. I've been calculating the monthly alimony until Joanne remarries, and the child support Chip has to pay for the next eight years, but I now note that at least she won't entirely clean us out financially: she won't need thousands of bucks for braces. Her teeth are absolutely perfect.

'We wanted to do a hike,' he says. 'I thought you'd like that, Kimberly.'

'I don't care,' she says. 'It's just walking, anyway.'

'I guess this sun isn't good for your skin,' he says. 'You take after your mom.'

'It's okay. I've got stuff on,' she says, smiling at me. I let her use my skincare (one of our little bonding things, another attempt not to be the wicked stepmother) and then bought her an entire collection of unnecessary creams and make-up when we went shopping for some vacation outfits. I want her to like me better than she likes her mother, because I want Chip to love me more than he ever loved her mother. Being nice to Kimberly is all part of my project; I'm being Disney Mom so I can keep Disney Dad interested.

Chip thinks I like the idea of having a daughter to fuss and he encourages it. He doesn't know he's been paying for all of it. I use his credit card every time I spend money on his daughter.

The lodge coffee shop is part of the gift shop. There are the usual T-shirts and caps, pens, notebooks and garish clocks built into inappropriate items. Chip has gone in search of Dad, to tell him we're back. Kimberly is fondling a ceramic seahorse on a gilt chain. 'I've got a real one of those,' I tell her. 'At home.'

'A real seahorse? They're not make-believe? I thought they were mythical.'

'No, they're real creatures. It's the skeleton that I've got, of course. Not a live one.'

'Where did it come from?'

'I don't know. I've had it forever. Probably came from a place like this, somewhere.' I picture it now, in the tiny faded blue box, between two pieces of tissue wadding. A seahorse coffin. It's incredibly light. I remember now the weight of the tiny skeleton. It was brittle and prickly, but fragile like strands of spun sugar. It still had an eye, or maybe it was just something stuck in there, to look like an eye.

'Does it look like this?' She's holding the clumsy, ugly ceramic in the palm of her beautiful hand.

'No, it's much finer. Nature is immensely more delicate than anything man-made.'

'Will you let me see it?'

'Sure. Some time. In fact, I'll give it to you. You can have it,' I say impulsively. Then I choose a yellow apron to buy for Mom. She likes to take home mementos when we go places.

Mom is at the cash register paying for a book entitled *How to Change your Life in Five Minutes a Day*. She hands it back to me to look at before it goes in the bag. The book has a glossy cover and is the size of a man's wallet. There is one sentence on each page. The first page says: 'Wake up five minutes earlier and spend time thanking God you're alive.' A page in the middle says, 'Take your make-up off before going to bed.'

'What do you want to change?' Kimberly asks her.

'Lots of things,' Mom says, looking at me rather than Kimberly. Then she looks at Kimberly and opens her mouth. I quickly point in the direction of the ice-cream counter and ask Kimberly to go over and choose us the flavours, before Mom can say something poisonous and completely wreck everything.

Up in the room, Kimberly tosses her Minnie Mouse suitcase on to the rollaway bed. We've booked a super-king bedroom along with the rollaway, but I can see that her bed is really far too small for her to sleep in comfortably. If she stays in a room on her own, Chip will be awake all night worrying about her. I figure if I mention the problem of the size of her bed, he'll probably suggest that he sleep in a room on his own and I keep her company in here, or that he and she share a room and I sleep on my own. But, as neither Chip nor Kimberly has said anything about the miniature bed, I decide I won't point it out, though I will remember for next time. Then suddenly I realise I am wondering if there will be a next time because actually, lately, I think Chip also prefers to sleep alone – or at least not with me.

This evening we're going out to eat and I take a shower and get changed before we meet Mom and Dad, as arranged. The lodge steakhouse was only good for one meal, and that was last night. I'm hoping we might have something better tonight. We saw the restaurant when we drove through the town trying to find the motel. It's only a short walk away. There's country-and-western music playing and the five of us slide into a booth, Kimberly gets sandwiched between Chip and me. The room is square and the walls are wood-clad except for one, which is entirely taken up with a mural. Mom and Dad have their backs to the painting, and neither Chip nor Kimberly appears to notice it, but I am mesmerised. The picture depicts Joseph Smith, in bed in his nightshirt, in earnest discussion with the Angel Moroni, who is looming over him. Not only is the content disconcerting, so is the shocking lack of artistry; it's like a terrible cartoon. Angel Moroni resembles Superman.

For a moment I don't realise that Dad is trying to make conversation with Kimberly. Then I hear Chip say, 'Go on, tell Grampy what you like best about school.'

'I'm not a dwarf,' Dad says.

'There's nothing wrong with dwarves,' Chip says, picking up the menu to show it to Kimberly. He lifts it so that it's a big plastic wall between them and us.

'Don't take it personally,' Mom says from beyond the barrier.

'I don't like school,' Kimberly says.

Mom says, 'You can call me Grandma, Kimmy, I don't mind.'

'Don't call her Kimmy,' I say.

'Have you taken any steps with the adoption?' This is Dad.

Chip says, 'Kimberly has a mother already,'

'We're not adopting,' I say. Dad is not referring to Kimberly but to a conversation Mom and I had last week, one we had before Chip called me Joanne in his sleep. I had said to her that maybe we'd look into adoption or something, that I wanted Chip and I to bring up a child together, our child. Mom must have told Dad. I think what I wanted was something that would tie Chip to me more than marriage.

Something that he couldn't escape, even if he wanted to – that was the thing with having a child together.

'Oh, I see,' Dad says. 'But an adopted child would become just like your own in time.' He pushes his glasses up his nose. They're always sliding down, and I've noticed that he only pushes them up when he's about to make a point.

'She's happy being a stepmother,' Mom says. 'And that's fine. You're happy, aren't you?'

'Sure,' I say. 'Very happy. Ecstatic.'

I am really hoping that all this crap is going over Chip's head. This whole family vacation thing was a dumb idea. Why did I think we could pull it off? The more we pretend to be a family, the more we aren't.

Dad twists on the seat to get his wallet out and pulls out a business card. He slides it face down across the table to me. 'Hang on to this,' he says. The card feels slimy, which, when I turn it over, is apt. He's passed me Uncle Jack's business card. 'You might need it,' he says.

Finally, the food comes and we can eat and drink and forget this discussion. Chip doesn't ask anything of me on the way back along the road and up to our room. Kimberly is sleepy and he tucks her into the too-tight rollaway bed. They forgo the nightly phone call and I'm grateful. Now he looks at me with a disappointed expression, but still says nothing, and I feel like I'm lying, even though I've not said anything untrue to him.

1983

The Egg

'You know motherhood is not all it's cracked up to be.'

This is Mom trying to be helpful. We are in a bridal shop, sitting on red velvet upholstered chairs watching models demonstrate the dresses. It's much easier than trying them on. We've been doing this for years, in various shops across the city, because it's a good way to get a free glass of champagne and spend time away from real life, like going to a movie. This time, though, it's for real. The same week that I've been told I am unlikely ever to conceive a child, I am choosing my wedding outfit.

Mom has taken the news about my infertility well. However, Chip, the man I am to marry, has yet to be told.

'Maybe you don't have to tell him,' Mom says. 'What a person doesn't know can't hurt them. But I think you should. I'm going on record one hundred per cent to say that you should tell him... Being tall helps,' is the next thing she says, straight away, as if to erase her earlier statement.

'Chip isn't very tall.'

'Everything looks better on women who are tall.' She is looking doubtfully at a girl significantly younger than me, and who looks, up there on the little platform, more than a foot taller. 'Is the first wife going to be there?'

'No, but there's no ill feeling. Joanne's okay with it.'

'Um,' she says. 'The kid?'

'Maybe the kid. Not sure.'

'At least he's had one already.'

Can't she be sympathetic? Does she ever think about what the things she says might sound like to those of us who have to listen? 'I'd have liked a child,' I finally say. 'I really would.'

'Would you, honey? Of course.' She waves the model away and finally turns to look at me. 'Have they said definitely?'

She knows this but I tell her again anyway that yes, pretty much they have.

'What about freezing an egg or something?'

'It's not like going to the freezer and getting one out.'

'What is it, the kid? A girl?' she says.

She knows this too. I nod.

'She should be there. You can bond with her. Make her a bridesmaid. No, don't. Child bridesmaids always look so... I don't know – so desperate.' She turns to look at the new girl who has just come in, wearing some shapeless short shift-type dress. The only thing that makes it a wedding dress is that it's white. 'Now that would suit you.' She points.

'Thanks a lot.'

'Well, they could fix it up. At least we're not buying at the wrong time. The dress will fit. Actually, you might want to talk to Dr Dan. There's a gorgeous you in there wanting to come out. I just know it.' Mom has been on Dr Dan's diet plan that includes injections of some shit, and, ingestion, I'm sure, of ordinary street-quality speed. She's lost twenty pounds in a month and perhaps a bit of her memory. She pats her stomach to remind me that now she's the skinnier one of the two of us.

What I want to say is that I am this person, now, in front of her, not someone else waiting to come out and surprise us. God forbid I be a clone of her, or even an extension of her, but I don't say that. I say, 'I think Dr Dan is sleazy. He's scumbag-level sleazy,' and she just shrugs.

In bed that night I try to decide how Chip, lying beside me now, will feel about my news. Will he ask lots of questions? Will he believe me when I tell him, truthfully, that this is not a result of a past botched abortion?

He shuts himself down to go to sleep. He does this thing every night and he does it now. Right before he goes to sleep Chip punches the pillow lightly, and sighs and turns over to face the wall. He always sleeps soundly and wakes easily when the alarm goes off, whereas I always fight sleep and then, if I do sleep, I have to be dragged to wakefulness in the morning.

I make myself take deep, slow breaths. I count the flow in and the release out. Without obvious movement, I tense and relax my thighs, my stomach and my arms. I go over what the doctor said, again. It's not as if I wasn't some way prepared for the news. At some level, for a long time I'd known something was wrong.

I guess I'd found it difficult, but not impossible, to imagine our wedding that is shortly to take place. With courage, I've chosen a wedding dress, have committed a date to St Luke's Episcopalian church downtown, and have booked time off work for our honeymoon. I've sent out invitations and accepted presents at my bridal shower. The marriage is all done except for the transaction.

But my obsessive longing for a baby is like a physical ache that alcohol and analgesics cannot alleviate.

'*Absent* is a strong word,' the doctor had said to me more than two years ago, about my fallopian tubes. '*Demolished* describes our findings a bit better.'

'Demolished?' I'd asked, thinking in what world is that word milder than *absent*. 'Did any dye get through?'

He shook his head. 'You'll be aware of this new technique called *in vitro* fertilisation and I think it holds lots of possibilities. It's the treatment we should go for, when you're ready, of course.' He went on to explain that 'ready' meant a stable relationship and strong desire to undergo procedures designed to challenge it.

With Chip I had met the prerequisite requirement, and so I'd booked my appointment with confident optimism, but the most recent consult with my new OB-GYN man, to talk over all the tests they'd done, had informed me that over the last couple of years the unexplained depletion in my eggs, even with hormone treatment, meant harvesting sufficient numbers for IVF was a long shot. That was how he explained it, after questioning the veracity of the previous guy's investigations. 'Long shot. Was always going to be a *hell* of a long shot. You have to think whether or not it's worth trying at all. On balance, I'd advise against.'

Now, in bed, Chip asleep beside me, I am bereft, and feel as if what the doctor really meant was that my entire life has been a long shot. A risk. Enormous gaping gaps are everywhere ready for me to slip through. I see holes in everything now, waiting to swallow me, because, really, if I can't have a child, if my body has failed me like this, can I do anything right? I might as well admit it: my whole life has been a mistake.

I realise how easy it would be to turn into one of those women who tries to kidnap an infant. I confess I have thought about what kind of security they have in place in maternity wards and whether or not I could pretend to be an aunt and get hold of someone else's baby that way.

I want to be a parent. Shouldn't anyone who wants to be a parent and who is responsible and could give a child a good life be allowed the opportunity to do this? But I don't think I'll ever be allowed to adopt. It's sad, but I'm not even likely to be a proper step-parent either. I don't know his daughter Kimberly at all, because the truth is there *is* ill feeling. Joanne doesn't want her daughter to spend any time with him when I'm around.

A mother is never alone. Joanne will not be alone, even without Chip. He told me the reason they broke up was because he was 'moving on' and she didn't want to. Chip deals with things in a very straightforward way and this practical streak was the first thing in him that I admired. He likened his relationship to Joanne to a car that wouldn't start and had to be left behind. I remember a conversation I had with Mom, about him. 'You can just take what Chip says at face value,' I told her. 'No pussy-footing around. No guesswork. He's plain and straightforward.'

'So that's interesting, is it?' she said.

The truth is I know *he'll* understand about me not being able to have a child. He'll be okay. It's just me that's the problem. I can't deliver the news because I don't want it to be true. If I say it, it's real.

We have decided that we will leave it up to Kimberly whether or not she wants to be a bridesmaid, but here in the darkness I decide that I don't want one. Mom is right. It's a terrible idea.

Next morning, as I make strong coffee, I decide that I must tell him, now, before I've had the news such a long time that it's stale and he has reason to be annoyed that I didn't tell him earlier.

'We need to talk,' I say.

This doesn't get the response it gets in books and films. He doesn't even look up.

'I've been to the doctor.'

'Oh, yeah?' Now he looks at his watch.

I should just tell him. But, though I don't want him to be upset, I do want him to care, so I decide I won't tell him now. I'll wait for a more appropriate time when we can discuss it properly, rather than rush out the door for work. That would be better.

'Yes,' I say. 'Do you think I should go on a diet?'

Finally he looks at me. His gaze runs up and down my body. 'Maybe,' he says.

The low-cut princess line in ivory satin looked very elegant on the model. Heavy material, lots of drape. It is there on the hanger staring at me now, waiting. There is a three-way mirror in this room and I don't want my tentative illusion of beauty wiped out prematurely so I shut my eyes when I get down to my bra and panties.

The sales assistant doesn't say anything as she helps me hoist the dress over my head and down over my body. As she begins to fasten all the countless buttons at the back I take my first peek and it's not too bad. As instructed, I am wearing skyscraper heels, so that helps the overall effect. Unfortunately, Chip, at five foot seven, will now look like a midget next to me. I know I should say something today, while the hem can still be taken up to allow me to wear flatter heels, but I don't. With a wedding it's every man for himself. Chip can invest in a pair of lifts if he wants to.

The dress is to be boxed. Pale pink tissue paper crinkles luxuriously as the assistant places my wedding dress carefully inside. She smooths the tissue between folds of fabric, and lays it over the top before putting the lid on. 'It's going to be fabulous. You'll look great.'

I wish I had her optimism. 'Thanks – and for all your help.'

'A pleasure,' she says. It's true. It's easy to see that she enjoys working in this hopeful place. She's got a huge smile and very optimistic manner. Then I notice that she's not wearing a wedding band. She only ever sees the before.

The rehearsal is a simple walk-through, but daunting because of the echo in the otherwise empty building. Pastor David is charming; he is not being sarcastic when he says not to worry about the fact that Chip and I have never been there before. He's clearly proud of the building, which is impressive, and, presumably he's also pleased with the donation that Dad is making.

When he air-kisses me hello Chip's dad smells the tiniest bit of drink, or perhaps cheap aftershave, and his mother looks very anxious. She greets Mom by saying, 'So, here we are losing our babies.'

I'm waiting for Mom to remind her that her son has already been married and divorced, but she doesn't. I'm amazed, and relieved, when Mom says, perfectly, 'I know.'

In front of the others, Pastor David has a brief interview with Chip and me and I discover that Chip's first name is actually Joseph. Mom, behinds us, claps when Pastor David suggests that it would be appropriate to use Chip's proper name for the service, and now that he knows he has an alternative name I reckon Dad will always call him Joe.

I think the rehearsal meal goes just fine. Chip and his mom talk about Kimberly. Mom talks about Mah Jongg, which she's learning to play. Dad is quiet, as usual. I drink a lot and so does Chip's dad.

On the morning of the wedding I put on the dress and become the bride. Then Mom leaves me to go down to the church first, with the best man, Truck, who will walk her up the aisle and to her seat. Dad and I watch from the front door as she gamely climbs up into the pickup. The plan is that she'll check the flowers, fuss Pastor David and then hide out in the vestry until everyone arrives. We'll meet her there, near the side entrance, and she'll help me put on the veil.

Once she's gone with Truck, Dad pours us both a shot of bourbon in the den. He holds my hand and tells me that he's always tried to be a good father.

'And you are, Dad.'

'I hope so. I know it's not always been perfect. Your Mom can be a bit crazy, but I don't blame her. She had a tough time of it before we met and I blame me, really. We were young when we decided to get married. We weren't well suited. It was a long time ago—'

'Not now, Dad, please. Not today.'

'Okay.'

Then we both down our drinks before going out to the limousine, which stinks of cigarette smoke. As we settle back,

I wish I hadn't so rudely cut across whatever Dad wanted to say. He and I never really talk, and it would be good if we did, so when we are stopped at the first set of traffic lights I decide to confide in him. I blurt out, 'You know, Dad, what you said about being married ... well, I can't have kids and I think I haven't told Chip.'

There's a moment when he doesn't reply. I wonder if he hasn't heard me, so I'm just about to repeat it when he says, 'You *think* you haven't? Did you tell him or not? You can't go into this without full disclosure. It's not fair.'

'It's too late.'

'Call him. Call him now.'

'I haven't got my cell.'

'Jesus,' he swears. I see the driver's eyes check us out in the rear-view mirror. 'Did your mother think this kind of stunt was a good idea?' he says, rubbing his bony knuckles.

'Don't, Dad, please,' I say. 'Mom told me to tell him. Really, she did; it's my fault. And it's all too late. But he's got one kid already. He probably doesn't want another one, not really, so it doesn't matter if I can't have kids. I could always try to get an egg and freeze it. Maybe—'

'Maybe doesn't count,' he says. 'You should have told him.' He says something else about Chip, then neither of us says anything more on the ride to the church.

As planned, when we get there Mom is waiting in the vestry. I quickly tell her that Dad thinks I should have told Chip my news, but that I haven't, that I knew I should have but there hadn't been the right time.

'You should have told him,' she says.

Dad is shaking his head. 'What a mess. What a crock of shit.' Then we all at the same time notice that Truck is with us, and he's looking very worried.

Dad takes charge. 'You,' he says, 'take a hike.'

When he's gone, Dad tells us both to sit down. At this, Mom glares at him. I don't think she will obey, but she does. Then Pastor David appears at the door. I wonder if maybe Truck sent him. Dad tells him to come in, that we've got a moral dilemma brewing, maybe we are in need of some spiritual advice here, but what he actually says is, 'maybe we need a spiritual device here.'

Mom then tells Pastor David that it's nothing to be worried about, just a little hiccup, that she really doesn't want him to be troubled with it.

By now I am the only one sitting, so when I say, 'I'm useless,' I am shadowed by all of them and I don't think anyone hears.

'You know you can't base a marriage on deceit,' Dad says above me.

Mom comes back within a millisecond with, 'Oh, yeah? You think so?'

Pastor David says he thinks that perhaps I, the bride, could do with some calm, rather than stress, so maybe we should try having a little time of prayer. I shut my eyes because at least one of my parents is about to tell him to fuck off. But they don't. Neither of them says anything and Pastor David starts to pray.

I'm not listening to whatever Pastor David is saying, but his voice is soothing. The air stills and, when he winds up, it feels as though all the pressure has gone from the room. He leaves after patting me on my shoulder.

In silence, Mom fixes the veil: pulls the lace down, so that it falls in front of my eyes. My parents become blurry for just a moment before I find I can see through it okay. Dad and I watch as Mom uses the mirror on the wall to put her hat on and freshen up her lipstick again. She tells Dad to go and fetch Truck, and when it's just the two of us she tells me to put it all out of my mind. 'The doctors haven't said one hundred per cent, have they? We'll find you that egg.' Then she puts her face very close to mine, speaks at me through the veil and says, 'Trust me, it's no big deal. It'll be fine. Just put one foot in front of the other and keep going. That's the only way to handle life.'

Truck and Dad appear and Truck takes Mom's arm ceremoniously. They leave to go up the aisle before us.

Now it's just Dad and me alone again. Pastor David's secretary will tell us when we are supposed to come out.

Dad straightens his tie in the mirror. He won't look at me. When the secretary puts her head through the doorway to tell us everything is set, he finally speaks to me. He says, 'We can delay. Honey, you don't have to do this. Do you want to speak to him first?'

'It's okay, Dad. It's time. He'll be okay with it. Please?'

I take his arm and we walk up the aisle looking straight ahead.

Pastor David says the *who gives this woman* line and Dad takes my hand and puts it into Chip's. Chip is beaming at me.

Even as I smile back, an uneasy sense of loss runs through me. It sends out its tendrils and tangles its roots around my bones. I remember two things: how Dad, in the car, said Chip was 'a poor sucker', and how Mom has always told me, 'No one will ever love you as much as I do.'

Pastor David is addressing us while I am hoping my parents are both wrong.

1981

The Idea of Sushi

Mom parks the car at the strip mall near the doctor's office. It's nearly two o'clock, but the Japanese restaurant is still open. Inside, the entire wall which overlooks the parking lot is made of tinted glass, and through it the colour of the car outside changes from silver to brown. The tiny waitress shows us to a table covered by a stiff white linen cloth. Everything looks more manageable from here. The light was so white outside, it is a relief to be indoors. My head has been hurting for days.

I am depressed. Last month I decided that talking about being depressed was only making me feel more depressed so I quit my therapy altogether. I haven't told Chip yet about any of the stuff that was going on in my head, nor that I've quit therapy, but I did tell Mom. She said that before I gave it all up I had to see this psychologist she knew of. She made the appointment and I went along with it even though it was a waste of time.

Maybe the guy sensed I didn't want to talk about how I am feeling, because I don't, but he should have tried to get me to spill the beans. That's his job. Instead, I was doing all the running, and I don't think he was interested at all. Without emotion, to fill him in and save time, I outlined my situation.

'I'm told I'm bipolar and I can't stand my meds. I have issues with my parents, both of them. My mother is controlling and hypercritical. My dad is passive and distant. There's more but it's not relevant. I've been seeing someone seriously, but two months ago I found out that having a baby might be a problem. I want kids. I haven't told anyone about *that*. I've mainly been on lithium and tricyclics. I hate both of them; I hate the pills, not my parents, or maybe I do hate my parents too. I'm hoping to get into tourism. It's a growth industry.' I tried to end on another upbeat note. 'And I like sex, a lot,' I said, 'That's got to be a good thing, don't you think? In fact, I just love sex.'

All the doctors I've seen before are writing stuff down constantly, and they love to hear any mention of sex – it usually elicits copious amounts of scribbling. But he didn't take any notes.

When the waitress comes over now with the menus, Mom says, 'Don't know why this place is always empty. Everyone loves sushi.' She says she knows what we'll have, there's no need to look at the menu, and she orders for the two of us.

When the waitress has taken the order and left, I say, '*I* don't love sushi, Mom. I don't even like it. No one does, really. People like the *idea* of sushi.'

She looks disappointed. 'You were hungry. It was close.' She glances around. 'Wish this place were busier. Makes you wonder.' She chews her bottom lip, rubbing off her lipstick completely. 'Use the chopsticks. These people like people to try to use chopsticks.' Then she pauses and looks excited. 'So tell me, what do you think of the doctor?'

'I won't go back.'

'He was nice, though, wasn't he?'

'He wasn't a great shrink. He said to sit wherever. He made me choose a chair. There were five different chairs and a sofa. What kind of a guy makes you choose a chair like that? Who has a Goodwill warehouse for an office?'

We are interrupted as the food arrives quickly, but I guess if it's raw fish there's no cooking involved. I have to admit, it's very pretty, but there's not much of it. 'Is this it?' Six tidy pieces of sushi encircle a pair of minuscule shrimp sitting astride cucumber strips. The green of the cucumber matches the colour of the napkins exactly.

'It's sushi. It's healthy. No one pigs out on sushi.' Mom aligns her chopsticks by tapping them on the table. Then she rearranges her plate quickly, sliding the centrepiece to the edge.

'I guess that's why you don't see any fat Japanese people.' I wish I'd had a cigarette before we got here. I don't want to eat this cutesy fake food. What I'm craving is McDonald's and a hit of nicotine. I tap my fingers on the table.

She reads my mind. 'I wish you'd quit smoking. Did the doctor let you smoke in his office?'

I shake my head. 'Patty was chain-smoking yesterday. You don't tell her to stop.'

'It was a fashion show. They can't eat. What do you think people do at fashion shows?'

'There were *No Smoking* signs up everywhere.'

'Those aren't for the fashion shows, it's for the rest of the time.'

'I don't think so, Mom. Why did she say you were the same age? Patty has got to be over fifty.'

'She's entitled to an opinion, isn't she?'

'Age is not an opinion.' I'm always trying to force my mother to give me straight answers to questions and she won't. She says things like, 'Life isn't black and white, sometimes two and two make seven.' The latest nonsense slogan she's been throwing around is 're-framing the past is the path to the future'.

'Why do you always ask questions?' she says.

'I don't. You do.'

'Do I?'

I've never told her that what I really want is for us to be standing in the same place, to face things together. I want there to be starting and finishing points to things. I want things to be either this or that. But she can't understand. Sometimes I have the feeling that her past just floats away like a dream behind her, that there is nothing fixed anywhere. How Dad has put up with it for so long, I'll never know.

Then she says, 'What's the point of smoking?'

'You *used* to smoke. You did. I remember you smoking.'

She pours us each a glass of water from the jug on the table. 'Did I?'

'You know you did. Be honest, Mom. Stop denying everything. That's healthy.'

We have finished our food. She waves her hand at the waitress who brings the check and when she fishes out her credit card to get ready to pay she says, 'Not much.'

'Yep. I'm going to be hungry again soon.'

'I meant it was a bargain. Cheap,' she says. 'Sushi isn't like that. Did you think it was supposed to fill you up?'

We are out in the heat again, walking across to the car when she says, 'Do you think he'd make a nice dad?' She passes me a mint before I can dig out a cigarette to smoke.

'Who?'

'The doctor, who else?'

'Has he got kids?'

'Do you think I should marry him?'

I spit out the mint that I've just put in my mouth and it pings on the ground.

'Do you think it's a crazy idea?'

I feel I have to point out to her that she's already married, to Dad.

'Some people should never have got married in the first place. If a marriage is not meant to be, then once you find a way out, surely you should take it? How long do you think a divorce takes in this state?'

'I don't want to talk about divorce.'

This is not the first time my mother has told me that she married the wrong man. Only last year she tried to kick Dad out, and six years ago, when I was fifteen, she waved a book at me. It was called *How to Love*. 'Now this is the man I should have married,' she said. The picture on the back was of an overweight guy with long hair and a bushy moustache and beard, as different from my skinny, bald dad as white from black. 'He's understanding and understands the importance of everything, including a woman's perspective on intimacy.'

'You mean he's gay,' I said.

'He's not gay.'

Now I say, 'You don't even know this guy.'

'Don't you remember telling me I should see someone, professionally? Don't you remember me telling you that Patty recommended someone?'

'God, Mom. It's not real, those feelings that you get for someone taking care of you.' I know that this sort of thing happens. It's a stage to do with the treatment, this attraction between client and therapist. 'It's transference.'

She's annoyed. 'What would you say if I told you we've been physical?'

'I'd say he could go to prison.' I'm not sure if this is true, but it sounds like it should be. Stupid Patty has recommended a dipshit shrink who tried to get my mom into bed.

'He has feelings. He's a man with feelings. We kissed. We cuddled,' she says. 'Can you imagine feeling so loved? We—'

'Don't!' I interrupt. 'I don't want to hear.'

We are now at the car. She throws me the keys. 'Why don't you drive? Let's go to the drugstore for ice-cream on the way home. There are negative calories in frozen yoghurt. You use up calories warming it to body temperature. Did you know that, Miss Know-it-all?'

'I can't believe you'd do this to Dad. He loves you. Dad loves you.'

'Maybe,' she says. 'But is it enough?'

'You are not Ali McGraw.'

We fall silent as I drive over to the drugstore. I think over what the screwed-up shrink who wanted to screw my mom had said to me earlier. He said, don't let sex confuse things. That sometimes you might want to sleep with someone just because you want to be close; that a lot of people confuse sex with intimacy. That people even sleep around because they want to connect with someone and they don't know how else to do it.

Maybe he knows he's inadequate at his job. His compassion hit tilt or something. Maybe it was a hint. Maybe he wanted out of this business with Mom; maybe he could see he'd stepped over the line and was trying to excuse himself so that he could end it. I try to remember in what context he'd said this thing about sex. I think it was in relation to my describing a dream I said I had a couple of nights ago. It was a fabrication – I gave him the dream to start a conversation, to get some response. I have no desire to sleep with my dentist. I try to ignore his fingers when they're fiddling about in my mouth. Sex with my dentist is not something I fantasise about.

At Walgreens we go straight to the ice-cream counter. I order two scoops of pralines and cream ice-cream, not yoghurt, for each of us. Mom tells me the calorie count, then tells me we can ignore it because it's been a long day and we only had sushi earlier. We eat the ice-cream outside, spooning it with minuscule pink spoons from little cardboard tubs.

In the shade it's not so hot, and the ice-cream is smooth and delicious. The familiarity is soothing. We've been coming here for years, just for this.

I ask her if she's said anything to Dad and she says that it's possible he'd understand.

'You are off this planet if you think he will. Does Patty know?'

'No.' She shrugs. 'I don't think she knows.' Suddenly my mother looks very tired, and sad. 'Things don't turn out the way you want them to, sometimes. It's just incredibly sad. Can you believe that?'

'Of course,' I say. I see that her life has probably had lots of closed doors and I guess if one is open, or at least ajar, she might not want to walk right past it. Maybe she's just trying this on now, like the clothes yesterday. A person needs to peek inside, or to see if something might fit, so I say, 'Are you seriously considering leaving Dad for this jerk?'

'Yes. I don't know. Maybe I am.'

'Well, he did an unprofessional thing,' I say. 'It's really bad, Mom.'

'People do. Things get the better of them. It's life, and I've got to tell you, Mark's chairs never bothered me,' she says. 'It's not a test, choosing the chair. Things don't always mean something else. It's very limiting to be so restrictive. A person doesn't have to choose. Anything. The world is bigger if you don't try to box it in.'

I have no idea what she's talking about but I don't feel like either arguing or asking. Then, with a rush of excitement, I remember that the certificate on the wall said *Matthew*. A different disciple. 'Was his name Mark or Matthew?' I ask. 'Which one?'

'What does it matter?'

'How many times did you see him?'

'He's been married a few times before,' she says.

'How many times?'

'Three or four, maybe more.'

'Wives, or times you went?'

She shrugs again.

'So, are you going to leave Dad? Are you going to let him know? He deserves to know before you leave him.'

'Probably not. Maybe you could tell him?'

'Mom, this guy is a complete deadbeat. I don't think you even know his name.'

'You won't tell anyone, will you?' she says. The tired tone in her voice tells me she won't see Matthew or Mark or whoever he was again. I understand that she just wants me to know that she's not just my mom; she's always been a person with possibilities. I go over the whole rainbow from being angry about the set-up today to feeling sorry for her. Although it was selfish, it was a really pathetic move. But she's never had a career. She didn't have any more children. Her bipolar disorder is worse than mine and it's always just been her and me, and Dad. She hasn't got anyone else. This is it.

She doesn't entirely belong to me, but to all of her past as well as her present, even the parts and people that I don't know about. Because I am her daughter, we are forever part of each other. It's different for us because our lives overlap. We are in it together. We're in that Japanese restaurant and outside this drugstore together forever.

I don't hurry to speak. The ice-cream here in the shade is suddenly helping my depression. I tilt my head back to rest it against the brick wall of the store. She'll drive us back to her house and I'll have a cigarette in the car on the way home. I will offer her one and she'll laugh.

I'm scared of the responsibility of being the one person who knows this big sad thing about her. But I really don't want to feel sorry for her. I want to make this thing today small, as small as a joke. As we walk back to the car to go home. 'Hey, Mom,' I say, 'is he the one who turned you on to sushi? Did the two of you go to that place?'

'I think he likes it.'

'It? Or the idea of it? Or because it's close?'

'Why does it have to be one or the other? I really liked him,' she adds.

'They should yank his licence. Report him. You're way too good for someone like that.'

She's back in the driver's seat and now she starts the engine. I lower the window and blow smoke out into the heat where it disappears. For a moment I want to tell her that I think Chip and I are really serious; he wants us to move in together. But that news won't help. If I say anything there will be more to say and I sense that neither of us would benefit from a conversation that might potentially eclipse the present crisis.

She can be looking straight at me, and even through me, but I never know what she's thinking *about* me. She can read my mind sometimes. I've noticed that if I catch sight of her in profile my mother looks like a total stranger. Someone completely hidden from my understanding. I'm small in comparison. She's the sun and the entire universe combined.

'He's a total shit,' I say. 'To make a move on you. You deserve better. That's what I think.' And it's true.

1980

The Kokopelli

'So, here's the thing, Dad,' I say. 'I don't know what's up with you and Mom, but something's cracked.' I pause. 'Have you seen what she's done to her hair *this* week? You might want to take a look.'

He's watering the lawn, which doesn't need watering because the sprinkler system does this just fine. We're both trying to avoid being under the same roof as a crazy woman, but it's painful to watch his feeble attempt to look occupied with a dribble from the hosepipe just because he doesn't want to be in the house.

'And she's in there moving furniture again,' I say.

'Your mother needs some space. Everyone needs space.'

'Well, she's not making space. The space in the house is finite. In September I'm out of here, so the two of you can have all the space. But that's *if* you make it to September. If Mom doesn't go up in some kind of explosion from too much hair product.' He's not listening. 'Dad? Are you listening?'

'I think you're overestimating the problem.'

'Wake up and smell the coffee!'

'She's trying some new meds. Cut her some slack.'

'She's not taking any pills. She listens to her nut-job new friend Betty, and some book she gave her that says don't take pills.'

'Uncle Jack is coming over. We're having Italian out. Want to come?'

'Look, do the two of you hate each other?'

'Why would I hate Jack?'

'I'm talking about Mom.'

'Well, yes. Your mom hates Jack. You know that.' He bends down to turn off the tap and then he starts to slowly wind up the hose. Then he says, 'Honey, it's not easy to live with a person.'

I give up and offer to make him some lunch and tell him I'll bring it out.

Inside, everything in the den is shoved together in the centre of the room. She's piled an armchair on top of the sofa. At the other end of the room a lamp table has been upended and is lodged precariously. There's a half-full box of books that, earlier, were on the now-empty shelves next to the chimney breast. I can't see her, but I find her in the kitchen, sitting at the table. Her head is on her arms. I think she's crying, but there's no sound, or movement. 'Mom?'

'I can't believe it,' she says.

'It's okay. We can put it back. Don't worry.'

'The fucking Republicans are going to repeal the ERA. It's a crock of shit,' she says. 'And *he* can pack his bags.' Then she gets up suddenly and her chair topples backwards, a big clatter on the kitchen floor. 'If he doesn't, I'll do it for him. Nothing happens in this house unless I do it.'

This is mostly true, I guess. She stomps out of the room and I follow her heavy-footed march up the stairs. By the time I catch up with her she's yanking a large Samsonite case from the guest-room closet and dragging it into their room.

'Don't do this, Mom,' I say, trailing behind her. 'Please don't do this.'

She scoops armfuls of Dad's undershorts and dumps them into the case now on the bed. She pulls three suits from the closet and throws them haphazardly into the bag, squashing them down into the edges.

'He's got nowhere to go, Mom!'

'He can go to Jack and go to hell.'

'Isn't Uncle Jack staying here?'

'He's not staying here. Don't call him your uncle. You have an uncle. A decent, normal uncle. It's not my fault we don't see him.'

'They're having Italian, Mom. Why don't we all go? You like ravioli. We can go to that place that does vegetarian ravioli and non-meat antipasti. Come on, please.' I feel breathless, and trapped. I hate her. I hate this. I can't do anything. I'm stuck here. 'I'm going in September. I'm leaving,' I mumble.

She stops and looks at me. 'How did I raise a daughter who wants to eat ravioli?' Her eyes are black daggers.

'I'm getting a job.' I back out of the room. 'I'm going to get out of here.' And I leave her there and race down the stairs and out the front door, where the heat hits me like a slap in the face.

I tell Dad that lunch is not happening. That I'll come with him to the meal, and that he's going to have to prepare himself for a night in a hotel. He doesn't seem surprised. Neither of us goes back in the house. He puts away the hose and we get into his car.

We stop at the strip mall for him to buy some stuff he says he needs, then we drive down to where Uncle Jack is staying at the Ramada and, while we wait for Jack to come down to the lobby, Dad books himself a room ready for later. At the same time, I phone Chip from one of the phone booths. He's at work, and I ask if he can give me a ride home later. We fix a time. With any luck this'll be late enough and I won't have to speak to Mom tonight.

We don't have Italian because Jack is on a diet again and has to eat fruit instead, but his diet makes for interesting conversation. The trial of the woman who killed the inventor of the Scarsdale diet has just ended. Second-degree murder. She said Tarnower's death was an accident, even though she shot him four times and he was screwing around with someone else and now she's going to prison for at least fifteen years. 'Fucking crazy women,' Jack says. 'Happens all the time. Fifty per cent of the human race is subject to raging hormones one hundred per cent of the time.'

Dad nods. He orders another scotch.

I tell the two of them that it's not only women that kill; that actually men kill people more of the time. It's also all over the news that this is the two-year anniversary of the murder of *Hogan's Heroes'* Hogan. 'For example,' I say, 'no one has been put on trial for Bob Crane's murder yet. In the pictures, you couldn't even tell he was a person any more; his head was smashed to nothing. I'll bet anything it was a man who did it. And it happened right in our neighbourhood, Uncle Jack.'

'Not *our* neighbourhood,' Dad says.

'That Crane was a nice guy,' Jack says, and I look at Dad to see what he will say, because everyone knows now that Bob Crane was a pervert who had a library of videos of women filmed having sex with him and his bisexual friend.

Dad is looking at his plate. He's finished his steak. 'You shouldn't be looking at pictures like that.'

I don't know if he means the movies that Bob Crane made, or the ones of him dead which have been in the papers.

Jack is just picking at his food. He hasn't eaten anything and we've finished. 'Aren't you hungry, Jack?' Dad asks.

'Gives me the shits, all this fucking fruit,' Jack says. 'Atkins was simpler but then you get constipation.'

'You don't need to lose weight,' I say. 'You look just fine.'

'Well, you're a doll, honey. Larry should never have let you get away. I thought you two looked good together. We could be related by now. Wouldn't that be great? Making it a goddamn legal arrangement.'

'Well,' Dad says, and coughs. He doesn't want us to talk about Larry and I momentarily wonder if Mom ever said anything about what happened.

'I'll get the check,' Dad says.

When Chip is due to pick me up I leave the men in the bar and go to meet him outside, mostly so that Chip doesn't have to meet Uncle Jack. I don't ever want him to meet Jack.

Chip doesn't turn his head to look at me when I get into the car. He doesn't smile, or anything. 'Are you okay?' I ask, and he nods slowly, and starts up the engine.

'What's up?'

'Joanne. She's a real headache.'

'Oh,' I say. If he wants to talk about his ex then I'll have to leave it to him to tell me what he wants to. I'm not saying anything. 'A man with a past and a kid should be left alone,' Mom told me when I explained that Chip had been married and had a kid. 'Run a mile,' she said. So, if only to prove Mom wrong, I will make the relationship work. I won't be the one to trash the bitch. I'll be dignified and keep quiet.

He stops to get some gas and, unasked, buys me the Juicy Fruit gum that I like. He's very thoughtful. He tosses it into my lap and I say thanks.

'Want to stay at mine?' he asks. 'I could do with the company.'

'Sure,' I say, not sure at all. He should have got me a toothbrush instead of gum if he wanted me to stay over with him. I haven't got anything with me.

He guns the engine out of the gas station and, instead of taking a right and going up Sanders Avenue, we head up the highway to his apartment. I wonder if Mom will be worried, but she'll assume I've stayed over at the Ramada, and I wonder if Dad might be worried, but he'll assume I've gone home.

The first thing to say about Chip's apartment is the smell. In the hallway there is a strong fresh paint odour, but, as soon as he unlocks and pushes open the door, this other aroma hits you. It reminds me of kindergarten – a combination, perhaps, of Play-Doh and warm Crayola. The smell is distinctive but fleeting, and the three times I've been here before I've noticed it as well. As I follow him and walk down the hallway we pass his bedroom door, and the bathroom. I sniff the air like some kind of a dog, to see where the smell is coming from.

Chip shares with this guy, Benny, and Benny's bedroom door is open. I'm still sniffing when I look to the right and spot him sitting cross-legged on his bed in his undershorts, bent over a handheld mirror he has propped on his knees.

He waves as I pass. 'Hey, there.' He's holding small scissors in his other hand.

'Moustache day,' Chip explains as we get to the kitchen. He pulls open the icebox and passes over a very cold Bud. We pop the cans in unison and he takes a long swig and leans against the island between here and the den. I'm thinking so when do we go to Chip's bedroom and will Benny hear us and why does Benny have his bedroom door open and how much maintenance does a moustache take when I notice that Chip is preoccupied. There's this fixed vertical line between his golden eyebrows. He's not saying anything. He might be looking in my direction, but he's not seeing me and his frown line is new. I love his dusty blond hair and green eyes, but like this, he doesn't look so good. He's probably still annoyed by whatever Joanne said, or did, and I vow to say absolutely nothing until he invites me to do so.

I'm silent. I'm still. I'm calm. I'm peaceful. I'm patient. I'm inscrutable. Pretty soon I'm bored too.

I spot a pile of records in the corner of the den. This would be something we could talk about if we were talking. I already know his music preferences, and he's got better taste in music than me, but we can't have everything in common. Life would be tedious if we were all the same.

There's a picture of his daughter, Kimberly, on the bookshelf next to the TV. I've met her. It's a couple of years old; she can't be more than two or three in the photo, and she's dark and strikingly beautiful, like an angel, not just cute like every other kid. She probably looks like her mother, which means Joanne must look amazing, which is a real bummer.

Suddenly he says, 'Bitch,' so loudly that I jump. For a moment I think he's addressing me but, '*She* is *such* a bitch,' he adds, which is a relief. I look at the floor. He's very angry. 'She wants to restrict access.'

This whole relationship business is one hurdle after another. 'Oh,' I say, because this amount of interest must be permissible.

The next day Chip drops me off at the house and Dad meets me in the hall and announces, 'Let's go for a drive. Chapman's. We can talk. We can have lunch.'

There is nothing that I have to do and it is nearly midday and I'm starting to feel hungry. I think Chip and Benny live on Church's chicken and Hardee's burgers. The trash can was full but the icebox was empty this morning. Mom must still be upstairs in bed because there's no sign of her, or the disruption she causes down here, and her car is in the driveway, but he's all dressed and it seems like he's been waiting for me to come home, so I shrug okay.

In the few minutes I've been home, it's like the temperature has doubled. There's no shade over the driveway. The July sun has heated the metal of the car door to burning point. I gingerly open it, and climb inside Dad's Nova. The heat from the seat through my jeans into my thighs feels baking hot. I open my window. The idea is to let the warm air out before you fill it with new, cold air-conditioned air.

Chapman's is a big Chevy dealer. Dad wants to get a new car. I like the smell of the cars fresh off the assembly line, but although the salesmen, and Dad, talk as if the cars are astronomically different it's hard to tell the difference between the designs. I resign myself to another boring morning.

'I've ordered a Citation,' he says as we pull out on to the road. 'It's a new model. The colour you liked. Blue. We need a change.'

'Oh, yeah.' I can't remember expressing an opinion, but that's fine.

'Hey, let's go north,' he says, and something about the way he says this reminds me about a trip north of Chicago shortly before we came here. Suddenly I'm worried. Mom has been a shitload to handle recently. Perhaps Dad has killed her and she's lying in a pool of blood upstairs. There are no bloodstains on his clothes, but he could have showered and dressed while she lay there, unseeing – eyes on the ceiling, if she still had eyes by then.

I want to say, *Did you kill her, Dad?* But instead I ask, 'When are we coming back?'

'Later,' he says. 'No hurry.'

'Is Mom okay?'

'Sure. She just wants some space. I think maybe she's going through the menopause.'

She's too young for that and even if she were old enough I'm not so sure that the way Mom behaves has anything whatsoever to do with her age. She's been pulling this sort of shit forever. She's been headed into the stratosphere for many years. She needs to see a shrink.

'She should see someone.'

'I don't think it's *that* drastic.' Then he turns from the road to look at me, embarrassed.

Neither of us wants to discuss the past. There's no point. I shake my head and shrug.

We turn right out of the subdivision and along until the signs for the highway appear. We join Highway 17, heading toward Flagstaff. The air-conditioning is kicking in now and I shut my window and the car becomes instantly quieter. The road has disappeared and we're kind of floating along. 'Nothing wrong with this car,' I say. 'Perfectly fine, if you ask me.'

The landscape is passing by. I unfocus my eyes until it all looks completely blurry and think about what it would be like if we were going twice as fast as we are. Then I shut my eyes and I think about last night with Chip and how tightly he held me after we made love, which made me feel good, but also slightly suffocated. Then he rolled over and fell asleep while I lay awake listening to some music coming through from Benny's room. In the darkness I thought about how Joanne could still make him angry, even though they are divorced. She can phone him up any time and complain about things, and she gives him progress reports about Kimberly. Having a kid sticks people together forever.

I wondered if she knows he's dating me now, whether or not he'd told her. I don't know if I want her to know or not. Eventually I must have fallen asleep, because I woke up with Chip kissing me again.

Suddenly Dad says, 'There was a place near where I grew up called Road Kill, a truck stop kind of joint. What a name! Huh?'

'Have you ever hit an animal?'

He shrugs and blinks. 'What?'

'I mean, in the car. Would you eat road kill, Dad? If you had to? If you were starving and killed an animal. I don't know what kind. If you were starving, would you stop and pick it up and take it home to cook?'

'A person who is driving a car is not a starving person.'

'I'm pretty hungry right now.'

'So this guy doesn't fix breakfast?'

'His name is Chip.' I realise how stupid Chip's name is and change the subject. 'Do you think they'll catch the killer?'

'Who?'

'Hogan's killer. Bob Crane's killer.'

'Probably not. Too long ago.'

'Do you want me to move out? Does Mom?'

'Maybe,' he says. 'It might help. She's very uptight right now.'

There's a sign for Camp Verde and Dad says we can stop and have lunch when we get there. At the side of the road a sign announces the world's largest Kokopelli. I know this is a fertility deity. Ugly and red, and massive.

I think again about Chip and Kimberly and Kimberly's mom, and my mom, who had just the one child. I wonder if Joanne will meet someone else and stop bugging Chip, or if she just wants to get him back, in which case I might as well hand him over now.

If I had a child then Chip and I would be glued together. He'd be with me; we'd live together and we'd have a kid.

I don't know how to ask Dad to stop the car so that I can get out and touch the thing, or even if that's what you're supposed to do to make it work. I think about Larry and then Scott. I think about Jay, Carl, Rick. I imagine them standing in a line one behind the other, so that I can't see them individually, but just that there's a line of them and I feel disappointed, in myself, and in every one of them. Sex is cheap, and loving seems an easy thing to get into. Liking involves more of an investment.

'Did you and Mom want more kids?'

'Why would we? We got lucky. We had you,' he adds, as if I might not get what he meant.

'I think he's *the one*.'

'This Chip is *the one*, huh?' Dad says. He's not exactly making fun of me, but, for sure he's not going to agree.

'Yes.'

I'm sure there's not going to be any place to touch the Kokopelli anyway, so I don't say anything about maybe stopping to take a look at it. We go on to the camp and have a hamburger and walk around the scattered old buildings and I think why would anyone ever want to have to tame the land and hold back the Indians here instead of living back east in civilisation?

It's a dusty, empty moon here.

We're the aliens in Arizona.

On the drive back home, we pass the Kokopelli again. This time it is on the other side of the road. I fix my eyes on it in the wing mirror and see it small, and watch as it gets smaller and smaller until it's just a red outline moving away from me. When I shut my eyes the red shape is imprinted tiny on the back of my eyelids, but it's nothing. I don't think it's anything at all.

1979

The Cockerel

Outside it's humid and hot, but inside this too-small tent it's like a sauna. Scott is asleep next to me, and up close the paper-thin peeling skin on the top of his shoulders is irresistible. He shifts slightly, but there is no resistance when I begin to gently tug at the delicate white flakes, pulling inch-long then two-inch strips, producing a rosy pink and beige brown map on his back. At first the skin seems to melt on my tongue just like a snowflake, but then it wads up and is disgusting, like a newspaper spit-wad. I shoot it out of my mouth into the corner of the tent behind him and wipe away the taste with the back of my hand. My mouth is dusty dry but I can't drink. The nausea that hit right after the peyote hasn't completely stopped and I'm afraid of being sick.

We are in the Organ Pipe Cactus Park, and we've been here, near a place called Why, Arizona for days. Right now I can't think about exactly how long we've been here. That would take a mathematical genius, which I am not.

The tent is beneath some shade, but now that the sun is straight up – and I can see this through the canvas – we are being baked alive.

Then I remember that we're in here to avoid getting more sunburn and to rest a while. It seemed like a good idea at some point when Scott said this was what we must do, but he's asleep and doesn't know that he's being roasted. He has a higher boiling point maybe, because he's bigger than me. But on reflection I don't think that's logical. It must be to do with cold blood or something. Scott is a desert creature. He must have cold blood. That's why he's okay now.

We did the peyote together this morning standing at the side of the visitor centre. My first time. The plan was to do it at sunrise but we woke up too late. No one else was around anyway.

We sat, backs to the wall, in the shade, side by side. He said it was better not to try to walk, or talk – just allow it to wash over. I felt sick but he said not to throw up, whatever. Then I seemed to suddenly slip my mind – actually everything slipped: his face changed into a stranger's – first beautiful then old – and I felt my nose grow, my feet too stretched longer in front of me. I couldn't feel them. I tried to walk and fell over, I think. I was lying flat and I heard laughing. The sound throbbed and tinkled and shrieked and bounced all around inside my head and then bounced right out of it, right away.

I'd grazed my face, Scott said, and he helped me up. Then he licked the scratch and his tongue was like a lizard's and I saw how he belongs here and I felt sad and lonely because I don't. 'I'm not a lizard,' I said. 'I will never be a lizard.'

'Shut up,' he said.

'Okay.'

'Shut the fuck up. You're shouting.'

'I said okay.'

'Don't be a bummer, babe. People are looking. I can't fucking deal with that. I want to enjoy this.'

'Okay.'

'And stop saying okay. It's boring.'

I put my hand over my mouth but it bubbled out anyway, 'Uh huh,' I said. 'Uh huh. I'm not a snake either.'

And that's when he said we had to walk back to the campsite. Because I couldn't be cool about anything.

Now I check to see if there are any snakes in here. I can hear one hissing. The hiss worms its way into my ear, one at a time, right then left. 'Scott, Scott.' I shake him awake. 'There's a snake.'

'Shush, shush.' His voice is now the snake and I pull away and try to stand, but I can't stand – my head hits some soft resistance and I have to crouch. I push against the canvas ceiling with my head again, then my hands, my elbows.

'Let me out, let me out.' My voice sounds like a baby's cry. I am desperate to escape a womb. I am suffocating. I will die if I don't get out. 'I can't breathe. I can't breathe,' I shout.

Scott prods the tent flap open and I clamber over him out into the air. 'I want to go home,' I say to the sky, and then some woman in the distance speaks back.

'Are you okay, honey? Are you lost? You were crying.'

Out here in the middle of nowhere there's a fat woman dressed in shorts and a pink T-shirt that says *Florida* with an alligator wrapped around the lettering. And there's a little bald man behind her who is dressed identically, except that his T-shirt – same design – is blue. He is tugging at her hand, like Lassie trying to pull his master from danger, and I can hear him tell her, 'Don't get involved.'

'I just want to go home. I feel sick.'

She points to the tent. 'Is there anyone else in there? Where are your clothes?'

I start to cry. 'I am so uncool. That's my main problem.'

Scott throws my stuff out of the tent. My cut-offs and purple tank top and then my backpack erupt before him and then he comes out too. He's completely naked. When he stands up from crouching I see that his penis and scrotum are shrivelled up. Because of his tan everywhere else, he looks like he's wearing a stupid-looking swimsuit.

'She's got some problem. She's messed up. In the head,' he says making a crazy sign with his forefinger and his own head.

The woman picks up my top and shorts and hands them to me. 'Where are your parents?'

'I'm not a kid. I'm nineteen.'

'Where do you live?' Her voice is patient, like she's a guidance counsellor in real life or something. She's all round with no edges, even her face, even her glasses; everything about her is curved.

'I really do. I want to live.'

'Let's phone your mom,' she says. 'Have you got a mom?'

'Jesus H. Christ,' Scott suddenly shouts. We all step backwards with the force. 'You are so pathetic,' he says to all of us, but I know he really means me.

'I know.'

'You need to wash out your potty mouth, young man,' the woman says.

'You need to fuck yourself, lady, and this chick is nothing to do with me.'

'Loretta, honey,' the man behind her says, 'we're nearly in Mexico. It's obvious they've been doing drugs.'

'Nothing to do with me, man,' Scott says.

'No. No. I am not high,' I say. 'I am very, very low.'

It is Dad who collects me and Loretta sits with me in the visitor centre to wait for him. We've waited for hours. She lets me put my head on her shoulder. Her husband is annoyed because this is a major interruption to their vacation and also because he has to explain to Dad what happened. He glares at me. 'What am I supposed to say?' he asks Loretta.

'Oh, man up. Just tell him what happened,' she says.

Then when he's walked away because dad's car has pulled up, she tells me to not pay any attention. 'Hank might be height-challenged, but there's nothing my man cannot do.'

'He is very short,' I say.

Dad doesn't say much when I get in the car. Through the open window he thanks Loretta and Hank for taking care of me. A couple of hours later we stop off the highway at an Arby's and I eat a sandwich even though I still feel a bit nauseous. He tells me that he doesn't want to know exactly what happened, because people make mistakes. That making mistakes is not the problem as long as you don't go on making mistakes. 'Are you going to go on making mistakes?' he asks. Cheese sauce is dribbling down the side of his mouth.

'I really hope not.'

'This boy,' he says. 'You've got to find yourself someone decent.'

'Where's Mom? Is Mom at home?'

'I have no idea where your mother is this week. She's on some woman's thing, I think. Some event. Some thing...

I don't know.'

'How's work going, Dad?'

'Oh, you know,' he says, which is ironic because I really don't know and he knows I don't know, but this is what he always says whenever anyone asks him about his job.

'I love you, Dad. It's all okay,' I say next, because this is the truth. We have no conversation. It's the only thing left that I can say.

'I know, honey.' He looks very sad, like he might cry. 'You were the best thing that ever happened to me, and to your mom.'

'And I love Arby's.' Then I have to run to the restroom because I'm about to chuck up.

Mom turns up on Saturday. She's got a haircut, colour and perm and looks completely different and completely ridiculous.

Dad doesn't seem surprised. He goes to hug her and she wriggles out of his arms.

'Mom, your new hair makes you look like Daisy.' This is the Pomeranian dog that lives next door.

She ignores me.

'Is it what they call strawberry blonde?' he asks.

'I guess so,' she says. 'I'm still missing Maurice. God, I'd give anything for another Maurice.'

'Have you ever wondered if they know what they're doing?' I say.

'That's enough,' Dad says.

'We need to talk about arrangements this summer,' Mom says.

'I don't think we need any more instability,' Dad says.

'I'm not suggesting that. I just think we need to make some arrangements.'

'Not a family vacation,' I say. 'Please not a family vacation.' They both turn and look at me like I've just suggested a trip to Mars. 'I mean, I'm going to get a job. I want to get a job. I'm going to get a job. I can't do any vacation over the summer. I'll be working.'

She says, 'We're not talking about *you*.'

'We need to talk about her,' Dad says.

I get up and leave the room.

Upstairs the air-conditioning has been left on very low and it's cool. I change the sheets on my bed for fresh pink ones from the linen closet and strip off my clothes and climb underneath and sleep.

In the morning they're both gone and I watch TV and eat a couple of hotdogs and a bag of chips and then sleep again.

Mom is away until Tuesday evening and when she returns she slams the front door shut behind her and goes straight upstairs with her bag. The door to the hall is open and so I can see this from where I'm sitting on the sofa in the den. Dad has heard it too. He and I look at each other. A door slams upstairs and he shifts in his seat. I think he's going to go after her, but instead he shrugs and goes over to the TV and turns up the sound. *Happy Days* is on. He doesn't even like the show.

An hour later, she joins us in the den. Her hair today is like an Afro. 'Your hair is different again,' Dad says.

'It looks terrible, Mom.'

'It's a hairdo.'

'Say it loud!' I make a fist in the air.

'Stop that, young lady,' they both say at the same time.

'We need to talk,' Dad says.

I leave the room.

In the morning it looks like she's gone again and Dad's gone to work as well. The house feels cool and calm. I roll a joint, put a record on the stereo in the sitting room and lie down on the sofa. I feel every inch of my lungs fill as I inhale the smoke and I hold it until I'm bursting. I crank up the sound. I let the music into my body, into my veins, right up into my heart, which begins to beat in time to 'Sway'.

The clock in the kitchen tells me it's nearly two hours later than I thought. I am discovering how Captain Crunch is the most delicious food and I think it should be a food group on its own. It must not, it cannot, be compared to cornflakes, or Frosties, or even muesli. There's a bag of the stuff in the cabinet. I check it out. Muesli has regenerative qualities. In the bowl when you add milk it seems to grow and swell invitingly. It is a pulsing, nutritious, fibre-filled grain that wants to be eaten. A co-operative food. This sincere heart of muesli is something important and I think I'm getting to the bottom of what exactly this is, beyond the fact that it's just there for me – and I'm also getting to the bottom of the bowl – when the phone rings.

It's Mom.

'Are you up?'

I have to think for a moment. I say, 'Do you mean am I awake, or am I standing or maybe am I high?'

'Doesn't matter. Is your father there?'

'No. He's at work. He's at work, Mom. He goes to work.'

'Meet me at the Mall. Tommy's.'

My beat-up old Pontiac has just got back from the shop because I forgot to put oil in, and I think they must have sprayed it with something because it smells different, like what leather should smell like, or a terrible aftershave, and then I see that they've hung a complimentary scented thing from the rear-view mirror. It's got a picture of Superman on it. I unhook it and pitch it on to the driveway, but the smell doesn't go away. It's so fake and I am trapped in this smell. I wind down all the windows and head off to the highway.

Tommy's is a dingy fake Irish pub stuck on the second floor of the mall, next to the Kinney shoe store. The hostess who leads us to the table is dressed in a stupid French maid outfit – overflowing tits and short black frilly skirt – and the waiter is a leprechaun wearing *lederhosen* and I think he's got stick-on Spock ears. 'However much they're paying, you'd never, ever get me doing a job here,' I say when he hops away having brought us some water.

Mom lights a cigarette. I open up the menu. There's a whole load of food here. So much choice, it's amazing. Mom inhales and blows the smoke out through her nose, like a dragon. Then she takes the menu from me and looks at me. Thunder mode. 'Wise up,' she says, and I don't know what she means, but I'm guessing she's noticed I'm eating too much or maybe Dad has told her about the trip south.

She will erupt if I say the wrong thing. I must not ask her where she's been lately, or what she does, or what's up with her and Dad.

'Why'd you want me here,' I say.

She just looks at me.

'Where have you been?'

'What the hell are you doing with your life?' she says. And then she bursts into tears, the back of her hand on her forehead, just as the leprechaun is back with our coffee on a tray. She waves him away.

I take charge. 'We're talking. Could you give us some space?'

His expression says it all. He's already disappointed because we only wanted coffee and now I see what we must look like to him: one high chubby-ugly chick with one hysterical black-hair white woman.

Her hair really is awful. It's the sort of thing someone should be able to sue over.

'What am *I* doing with *my* life?' she asks next. She seems to be asking both of us, because the leprechaun hasn't moved away fast enough and she's looking at him as well. He kind of nods, then shakes his head and leaves the tray on the table in the empty booth next to us.

'What's the hourly rate, do you think?' I ask. Then, 'Can a person sue a hairdresser? Do they have lawyers? Is there any mileage in it? My car had a really bad smell, Mom. It was so fake.'

She uses a handful of napkins to dab at her eyes and then another lot to blow her nose. Her mascara has run. She looks even more crap. I've got to pay attention. I try to concentrate. I have to concentrate, but her hair is taunting me. 'Hey,' I say, 'Mom, is something wrong?' I try to say this as casually as possible. Do you want to talk to Louelle or Patty or Freda, or someone?'

'Everything,' she says then she gets angry again. 'They won't understand. I'm talking to you. Can't my kid ever listen?'

It's suddenly all too much to handle: this place like a cave, my mother like a clown. I don't know what she wants from any of us. 'I'm moving out,' I say.

She straightens up. 'Well, that's probably best. Good luck to you.'

Next day, Jay picks me up in his Corvette. He used to work at the McDonald's by the crossroads and that's where I first met him. He works in some warehouse now, but evenings he hangs about at the ice-cream parlour in the strip mall near the house and I asked if he could give me a place to stay. I have a garbage bag full of clothes and a red plastic vanity case that Mom gave to me when I was twelve. I've stuck my toothbrush and paste, hairbrush and shampoo inside and I can't think of what else I might need, but there's always a supermarket. Jay said his apartment is near a Target. Target sells everything. Mom has given me a hundred bucks and I make the mistake of telling Jay about it, when I say that we might need to stop at Target but it's okay because I've got some cash.

'Let's go score,' he says, and I don't contradict him.

Later, as he opens the door to his apartment, Jay tells me that he is a cat person. 'I hope you're cool with cats,' he says as a mangy, mottled grey thing begins to wind itself around my legs.

'Sure. How many have you got?'

'I don't know. I always leave that window open.' He points into the room beyond and I try to see what he's showing me, but my eyes haven't adjusted to the darkness in here. 'So, they bring in their friends, I guess. I feed a heap of felines. They come and go as they want. I like a free spirit.'

This is a bad neighbourhood and I must look alarmed because next he says, 'Don't worry, baby. There's a gun under the bed. You're safe. I'm here.'

The first night we make love on the floor next to the bed because there's a moving pile of cats sleeping on the bed and he doesn't want to disturb them. When he finishes, I feel the way the carpet beneath me looks: stained and used. And, after he pushes the animals off to allow us to get under the blankets, his sheets are grubby and worn. I want to retch at the smell. I try not to think about my clean sheets at home. If only I'd been nicer to Mom. I try not to think about Mom, who must be going through some sort of major mental breakdown the way she's behaving.

We smoke another joint and that helps reduce the nausea and also slides me into sleep.

In two days it's the fourth of July weekend and Jay is going to visit his family. I'd like to tell him that I want to see mine, too, but no one is answering the phone at home and I've no idea what's happening with either of my parents. I offer to stay behind in his apartment even though the prospect of spending a whole day alone in his stinky apartment with his flea-ridden cats is unpleasant, but he is insistent and, when we get going along the highway in his beat-up car, he says he's real pleased to have me along with him. He comes from a big family, he says and they have a party in the park every year. He didn't go last year, but wishes he had. It's a blast, he says: barbecue, hog roast, the whole nine yards.

Turns out he's not seen his mother for about eighteen months. He has five brothers and two sisters. He rattles off their names, and when we get there and walk along to the gathering he points out his siblings. His mother is sitting on a straining folding garden chair. She is massive, and her wobbly, fat arms flap wildly as she spots Jay arriving. When we get closer I can smell sweat coming off her, but he doesn't seem to notice. He has to bend right down to kiss her cheek. I guess she can't get up unaided, or else she's wedged in too tight.

'Finally, son,' she says. 'Finally you decide to come along. And you've brought a girl! Howdy.' She grins at me.

'Hi there.' I do a little wave with my fingers.

She looks me up and down. I wish I were wearing a tube top and cut-offs instead of this dress, which is too dressy for the occasion. 'So, where'd you two meet?' she asks.

'You know, around,' he says.

'He's a shy one, my baby Jay. Bet you had to ask him out, huh?'

'Oh, Mom,' he says. 'Don't. Leave it be now.' He points out his dad and we take our leave to go and say hi to him as well. His dad is standing around the barbecue with a couple of his uncles and cousins. Again Jay rattles off a shedload of hillbilly names. We pass a picnic table loaded with bowls of potato salad and coleslaw, marshmallow salad and one solitary bowl of green salad. None of the food is covered and it's over a hundred degrees in the sun. I'm already worrying about food poisoning before we get close enough to see that the cooked meat is on the same plate as the raw hamburgers and chicken legs.

I decide to be a vegetarian. I decide to be on a diet. I decide to somehow avoid eating altogether, forever.

We drink warm beer under the shade of an ugly acacia tree and stretch back to watch the littlest kids playing with water pistols, screaming as they chase each other around and around. If there's any family resemblance it is their universal pale colouring: stringy blond hair with sunburn. I wonder how long the family has lived in the area, but I don't want to ask Jay; it will only irritate him. He's already said, 'I expect you think my family is white trash, but we're not that, really.' He said this sadly and it reminded me of how he lets all the cats in the neighbourhood in. 'Oh, no,' I said. 'I don't think that. Not at all,' which is a complete lie.

One of his cousins, Truck, comes over to rustle up enough people to play softball. I haven't played since school, but Jay volunteers us and I don't object. I slip off my platform sandals and drop inches on to the hard scrubby grass. I'm not the only girl playing, but it's mostly guys, and the first time we field I'm directed to cover first base rather than outfield because there's less running involved. Truck pitches the ball and he's good, but then some of the other team are fourteen and fifteen years old, so it seems a bit unfair.

When we bat, Jay hits a great home run and our team high-fives him and he looks really, really happy.

Afterwards, Truck, Jay and I sneak back to Truck's pickup to smoke a joint. One of his friends joins us and the four of us sit with our backs to the hot metal sides of the flatbed. Our legs and feet stretch haphazardly into the middle. I observe how cute Truck's friend Chip is. He is fair and stocky, quite handsome. The first thing I noticed about him when he arrived was his confident walk – a chest-out strut, like a cockerel, older than the rest of us. Now he's says he's training to be an accountant and it's easy to see there's something solid about him that would immediately make any person feel safe and trust him. He's got a little girl, he says, but she's with her mom. They're getting a divorce; things haven't worked out. Truck tells him not to beat himself up. Chip shrugs and still looks a bit regretful. Jay tells the two of them to shut up and stop hogging the joint.

It's a gentle, dreamy high – the best kind.

I look at my feet back in my shoes. My toes look abnormally long today for some reason, but then I don't pay them any attention normally. I compare the guys' footwear next. Jay's right sneaker has a hole in the sole. Truck's look new; the white edging is still white. I think Chip is wearing more expensive shoes. I notice how short his legs are compared to the other guys. We share a packet of chips and smoke another joint. It begins to cool down and Jay goes alone to say goodbye to his mom before we leave. After a couple of minutes Chip says he's got to head off too. He asks Truck to get his backpack, which he left in the cab of the pickup, and, once we're alone, he reaches over and squeezes my knee. He looks me straight in the eye when he says he hopes he will get to see me again some time. 'You're real cute.' Then he clambers down and waves goodbye.

'So, what are you doing with Jay?' Truck asks when the other two have gone. 'Don't seem the type.'

'What type?'

'You don't work at McDonald's or anywhere like that.'

'No. I don't have a job. I'm going to get one,' I say, and this makes him laugh and the laughter is infectious. We're still sort of giggling about nothing when Jay comes back. He asks what's so funny and Truck says, 'I told her, I don't get what she's doing with you. What does she see in you?'

'She's a stray,' he says flatly. 'You know I attract them.'

On the drive back to Phoenix Jay and I talk happily all the way, about his idea of going back to school one day, about how his mom always thinks of him as a little kid, even though he's grown-up, and how, because of all her kids, he never had any space to himself, so he feels crowded whenever he's with them. 'I can't be around people all the time,' he says. He likes Truck well enough, but no one in his family really gets him.

'I know what you mean,' I say, even though I'm not sure that I do.

'So, are you ready to go back home?' he asks next, and I say I guess so. He must know how I'm longing for clean sheets and air-conditioning that works, and he must want more room in his bed than the two of us allows. He drives me to my house. He doesn't want to come in. He says he just wants to crash, will call me tomorrow and we'll hook up some time in the week. Then he kisses me goodbye and I climb out and wave as he drives off down the street.

Mom isn't home, but Dad is, and it's good to be back. He's real pleased to see me, I can tell, and the house smells familiar; the sheets are fresh and clean. He phones for pizza and orders enough for Mom, too, in case she comes home tonight.

1977

Big Bird

Everything now feels like it's in motion. People coming and going. Schools starting and stopping. The dreadful run-up to Christmas. Mom is preparing to stuff the Thanksgiving turkey, which is four times the size of our next-door neighbours' small dog Daisy who is yapping incessantly. Joe and Mary Wilkins, the dog's owners, are two of the guests with us for the day and they're now in the den with Dad watching the parade on TV. The dog seems real loud today as the back door has to be open to let out some of the frenzied heat of our kitchen in full use. It's not cold out, it's about seventy degrees. It's not at all like where we used to live; Hallowe'en marked the start of winter there, and by Thanksgiving it was cold, but here the seasons slip from spring to summer to fall to winter with only the slightest temperature shift. With all my meds I feel pretty well the same as the climate – no ups, no downs, numb. Nothing. *Stable* – they call this, but I do have a constant dull headache which I've been told is insignificant, a *long-term temporary effect*, whatever that means.

Mom is at that stage with the cooking that means that she cannot speak. I can see that her entire brain-processing capability is taken up with making sure we have too much food on the table at twelve o'clock. Year-round she doesn't care much about food, except making sure neither of us eats too much of it, but come the holidays it's this sea change and she wants to be Betty Crocker and feed everyone.

For a moment I consider asking her if I can help, but instead I ask where she's storing the Tylenol now and she tilts her head in the direction of the cabinet above the dishwasher. She speaks without turning, two hands in use – one steadying the golden bird and the other basting it with what looks like a giant eyedropper. 'Over there. And get something decent on.'

She hasn't noticed that I am already showered and dressed. She doesn't like me in jeans when we're entertaining and we could have a fight about this, but we don't need to, it'll only turn her into more of a basket case, so I ignore her comment, and fetch the pills and down them with a glass of water.

The front door chimes and she tells me to go and answer it. I get there right before Dad. He does this kind of fake salute to me before he opens the door.

Uncle Jack leads this new lot of visitors in. He lives in Chicago now and it's not very often that Dad sees him, so recently Mom and Dad have had fewer arguments about him. Mom still didn't want him to come today, but they've agreed an equal trade. Mom's friend Louelle is invited, and Dad has invited Jack. Jack introduces Larry who, we learn, is his half-brother. I can't figure this because he looks at least twenty-five years younger than Jack. Larry is a college senior. I'm only a high school senior.

Louelle is behind Larry, but I hardly see her. All I can think when Larry crosses our threshold is that someone should have shown me a picture to warn me, and I wish I'd done something with my hair, because lately it's looking like a massive furball rather than the luxurious locks that my bottle of shampoo promises. Larry is very, very cute. He smiles politely when I get introduced and this only improves his gorgeous face. I hope no one asks what I've been doing with myself this year. I hope Dad didn't tell Jack. At my neck, I feel an embarrassing blush beginning.

In the den I can see that the parade on TV is in full flow now and there's a new balloon this year. Kermit the frog has an endearing and hopeful face. Wearing a reporter's trench coat, Kermit the puppet stands in front of his own naked giant Kermit balloon to conduct an interview and then directs the camera to return to Ed McMahon in the studio just as Mom comes in and announces lunch is ready. When she looks at the TV she says, 'Who is this guy? Why do they have to change everything?'

Dad tops up everyone's glass, emptying a full bottle of Ripple before getting to Jack, who complains and asks him to get some real wine out. 'Gee, Richard, he says, what the hell has living in this godforsaken state done to you?'

'Young people like Ripple,' Mom says.

'Well, I'm not young,' Jack replies. 'And that means neither are you.'

Dad goes to fetch some other drink and meantime we begin to load the table with the food. The first thing is a cranberry Jell-O mould set with grated carrots and walnuts. I get to carry this into the room and Louelle gasps theatrically. 'Hey, baby!' she says. 'Get a load of that concoction.'

Louelle has wild blonded hair and in her high heels is even taller than Dad. She always wears vibrant colours. Today she is in a bright yellow pantsuit and the outfit makes her look like Big Bird. She and Mom met years ago, I don't really know where, and they seem to only meet up infrequently – years go by and then Louelle turns up again with a phone call: 'Hello, honey, what's cooking?' She says that sort of stupid thing all the time. I also hope Mom hasn't told Louelle about me. She's the most indiscreet person in the world. I'll avoid eye contact.

Mom's Jell-O creation has taken a lot of effort to make, and it's shaped exactly like an elaborate Christmas wreath. It is interesting and decorative but there is always something about this that doesn't work. Maybe the lime. It will taste disgusting and no one will ever have more than a small spoonful and I will loyally dump the unappreciated remains down the disposal later. I go back to fetch the candied yams and the other vegetables follow on to the table quickly, so that things don't get cold.

Mom likes to serve the turkey to the table herself. She carries it through on the big orange and white Thanksgiving platter at a height that obliterates her face. From where I am, it's as if the turkey is walking into the room itself, on Mom's legs. I don't know how she can see where she's going, but she has never once tripped up. She plonks it on to the table right in front of Dad. He's at one end of the table and she goes to sit down at her end and, from there, she volunteers Uncle Jack to say grace. Everyone who knows Jack knows he's a militant atheist so she's just doing this to piss him off, but he seems in good spirits when he says he will, because it is Thanksgiving.

While everyone else has their eyes closed, I take a look around the table. Louelle is probably going to drink too much. Jack will make some crass jokes. Mom will be tense until the meal is over. We're new to the neighbourhood so Dad will want to impress our neighbours and will not want anything to go wrong.

Larry is sitting next to me. He has a strong physical presence and the table is crowded; my right elbow connects with Larry's left. He smells of Herbal Essence shampoo and I notice that his pony-tailed hair is as shiny as mine is dull.

Jack finally finishes speaking and, at exactly the same time, Larry drops his hand to my right knee. I wonder if I should notice this or not. I decide to ignore it, that it's probably unintentional and that he's just forgotten what he is doing with his limbs. A moment later when he squeezes my leg I think that perhaps I should remove his hand, but I don't. It feels more warming than the drink or the food that everyone has begun to pass around.

Larry manages to fill his plate without removing his hand. Now he slides his hand up the inside of my leg, headed for the crotch of my jeans. I am terrified. I don't know what to do so I freeze and he still doesn't remove his hand even as Dad speaks to him from the head of the table. 'Larry,' he says, 'Tell us what it's like at Irvine now. Things improving?'

'You know,' Larry says, 'it's school. It's okay.' He is very cool, and I have the thought that just being next to him, like this, is liberating for me; he is above and beyond this parochial suburban cul-de-sac and has singled me out to be so too. His hand remains on my body even as we all eat our meal and, instead of jumping up to help Mom clear the table when it's time, I stay seated.

Louelle takes out the empty plates instead and Mom fusses in with the pumpkin pie, then a pecan pie, and finally an apple pie. These are all store-bought and they look perfect and will taste delicious but when Larry says he's replete I discover that I, too, have completely lost my appetite for more food. Instead I pour a glass of water, squishing the liquid discreetly through my teeth in case there are bits of turkey stuck between them. I begin to calculate when I might slip away from the table to brush properly in case he wants to kiss me.

I feel anxious about not being sure what time they will be leaving. If we are going to kiss, we'll need a bit of time for this. Surely they'll stay to watch the end of the football game? Then Mom decides to embarrass me by asking why I'm not having any dessert. 'Why does my pumpkin not want any pumpkin pie? My pumpkin loves pie. Are you alright?'

'Maybe she doesn't want pie 'cos she doesn't want to look any more like a pumpkin than she does now,' Louelle says. She throws back her head to laugh at her own stupid joke.

I am thinking that she can talk when Joe replies, 'I thought you Women's Lib types didn't worry about looks. Gloria Steinem might be a looker, but she's the remarkable exception that makes the rule. For ugly you can't beat that Betty Friedan. Pig-ugly, that woman.'

'Joe!' Mary says.

Louelle says, 'I'm not a Women's Lib *type*. I am no *type*.'

'Pig-ugly?' Mom says. 'Really? You want to use the words "pig-ugly" about feminists?'

'I don't think we men *can* judge this women's rights situation without understanding our naïve bias.' This is Larry.

Louelle looks at him suspiciously and Mom with surprise. Jack slowly nods his head, and Dad's eyes narrow at the other end of the table. Me, I freeze.

Then Louelle says, with her mouth full, 'Well, I'll tell you what, Joe, if you want to talk feminists, that Betty Dodson should be a saint. Have you read her? *Liberating Mastur-bation* is a masterpiece. Changed my life, but you're probably already an expert at jerking off.'

Dad looks appalled, but Jack laughs loudly as Joe begins to grin. Mary starts coughing and Mom rushes out to fetch her a glass of water. Larry says, '*Touché*,' under his breath.

I could possibly be falling in love. I put my hand on Larry's leg and squeeze his thigh. It's a bit ungainly, this intimate holding of each other's body parts, but a woman shouldn't leave this sort of thing to happen without a show of willing participation.

After the meal we watch the game. The Dolphins are playing the Cardinals at St Louis. Larry and I sit cross-legged on the floor next to each other. Joe keeps muttering that he can't believe the Cowboys aren't playing, that it's not Thanksgiving without the Cowboys. Then Mom tearfully says that the loss of Lorne Greene as presenter, who has today been replaced by Ed McMahon, is also tragic. 'He's a real man. He was the best. He made Thanksgiving for me,' she says. 'I always look forward to Lorne.' I didn't realise she was so drunk.

'Let's get out of here,' Larry leans over to whisper in my ear, and I offer to the Wilkinses that we could go next door and check on Daisy, who seems to have finally stopped yapping.

'I'll come too,' he says.

It's dark outside. Mary Wilkins' keys are heavy in my hand. They've got an alarm system installed, but she said it's very complicated and they never actually use it.

Larry is silent beside me as we walk up the path to the front door. It's all dark in the house except for the glow coming from the kitchen. The porch is crowded with rows of potted geraniums and the sweet stink is earthy. There is no light here, just shadows. His body is close behind me as I turn the key. I've only been in here in the daytime until now and am surprised how different the house appears at night. When the door opens, the dog starts up her noise again and Larry shouts through for her to shut up. As we enter the kitchen – me first – Daisy bounces up and begins throwing herself at my legs. Larry steps between us and kicks the dog away, which shocks Daisy, and me as well.

'You've always got to let an animal know who is in charge,' he says, and I bend down to pet the dog, who didn't deserve to be kicked. She's whimpering and cowering. I pick her up and stroke her as I carry her back into the hall and through into the dining room.

Without words it seems we have decided that we will not turn on any lights except for the one that was on when we came in. Light from the back yard is coming through the open venetian blinds and gleaming off the huge glass table. Larry puts his arm around my back and whispers right into my ear that we should put the dog back in the kitchen and get down to business. Then he leans over the lumpy squirming dog that I am clutching and kisses me. Whereas I expected and hoped for cool and romantic, the whole thing, particularly his mouth and tongue, is clumsy. And when he says, 'Come on, baby. Give me some,' he sounds like an idiot.

Daisy starts yapping again. I wonder if we can find something to give her that will keep her quiet. Do dogs like pumpkin pie? I am chattering fast when I tell Larry that we can't be unkind and that I'm not sure about this, but that we could explore the house, while we're here. That would be something to do. I untangle myself and begin opening doors. When we discover the guest bathroom I check out the medicine cabinet. It's virtually empty. Upstairs, Mary Wilkins' bathroom cabinet is a bit more interesting. I'm reading out the prescription labels and estimating how many Valium are left in one container and would she miss one or two when Daisy squirms right out of my arms. She drops to the ground and dashes into the bedroom next door, running off with one of Mary's scarves; she must have left it lying around.

'Damn it,' Larry says and we both chase her. He's in the lead. He manages to grab one end before the dog reaches the stairs. Daisy starts to growl and tugs it back. It's a game to her but not to Larry. The result is a loud tearing sound and Daisy tumbles down the stairs with bits of blue chiffon in her mouth. 'Shit,' Larry says. 'Stupid dog.' Daisy wobbles to her feet but looks okay.

I gather up the remains of the material and stuff it into my back pocket for disposal later. Larry is now just annoyed and I feel I have to do something so I kiss *him* this time. As we begin to make out at the top of the stairs I can see Daisy watching us from the bottom. Finally, as Larry tugs my jeans down and off and begins to undress himself too, I shut my eyes and hope that Daisy does the same.

When it's just us in the evening, Mom, Dad and I watch *Welcome Back, Kotter*. Gabe has a dream about life in 2050. It's creepy to think that by then no one here in this room is probably going to be alive, including me.

The phone rings and Mom goes out to answer it. She's a little while before she comes back and tells Dad that he's wanted on the phone. 'It's Pete,' she says. 'You should talk to him. He's family. Your brother, for God's sake!' But Dad tells her to say he's gone out, he won't speak to him, and she goes back to the kitchen and it's another ten minutes or so before she comes through again. Mom sighs loudly and drops back into her chair. She crosses her legs and her right leg moves up and down, like she's kicking an invisible and persistent balloon in front of her. Though it's irritating the way she says it, when she asks me about Larry it's a welcome interruption because I thought she was brewing for an argument with Dad again. 'You going to see Larry again?' she says. 'Are you?'

Dad says. 'Don't sell yourself short, sweetie.'

'I didn't know I was selling myself at all,' I say.

Then Mom just stares at me. She stops moving and squints at me. She looks at my face, my chest, my legs, my shoes and back to my eyes. I tell them I'm tired and want to go to bed. Dad says goodnight but Mom doesn't say anything. She knows everything.

It's two months later and we've only been back at school for three weeks when I say to Mom that I think I need to see a doctor. She phones for an appointment and then drives me straight to her gynaecologist.

I pass over the still-warm urine sample and Mom helps me to fill in the forms. When the nurse calls me through and takes me briskly along the corridor, Mom waits for me in the tidy green waiting room, flicking through *Redbook* magazine. Then, after the doctor has finished his examination, she comes into the room. We're left alone. I don't have to explain anything. I ask if she wants to tell Dad.

'We can get another opinion,' she says. 'Before anything is definite.'

'He's recommended a D and C. It's not exactly an abortion.'

'Did he say that?'

'No – not the abortion bit, of course. He said it wouldn't take long. It's a simple procedure.'

She says, 'Let's get out of here.'

We eat ice-cream sitting on stools at Walgreens and then she goes to the gas station and phones Louelle, who knows a female doctor who can see me the same day, that afternoon, downtown. We don't need an appointment.

This waiting room has posters plastered all over the walls, advertising concerts, yoga classes, all sorts and every kind of hippy shit. It is also full of women and there are six or seven little kids sitting on the floor playing with toys. The receptionist says there aren't any forms to fill in. We can tell the doctor everything ourselves.

Because there are no magazines, we play snap while we wait, with a well-worn deck of cards I spotted under the table in the corner.

When she comes out it takes a moment to realise that this must be the doctor and not another patient who is just calling someone's name. She's wearing a maxi skirt and white T-shirt, with no bra underneath. Her breasts are large and droopy and mesmerising.

When it's finally our turn, this time Mom comes in with me. The doctor introduces herself as Rosanna and she asks me the three questions: Could I be pregnant? Where does it hurt? And when was my last period? Even though the questions are short, she has a gentle, patient voice. I try to avoid looking at her unfettered breasts.

I answer and Mom explains that I've already done a urine test but it didn't tell us anything.

'You don't get false positives,' Rosanna says, 'but you can get false negatives.'

'It was negative,' I say.

'It's early. Tests aren't accurate so soon,' she says and proceeds to tell us that she needs to do an examination, is that okay? She suggests Mom waits outside.

When we're alone, I start to wonder if two OB-GYN exams in one day is a kind of torture, and then whether or not this torture is deserved punishment. When she's finished, Dr Rosanna says there's nothing that I have to do now. There will be no problem in waiting. She thinks that the pain is nothing to do with anything, that I don't need to worry: my period will probably come soon. I should go on the pill. She'll do a prescription. She pats my hand and I feel like crying.

While she was busy poking inside me and I was trying to pretend I wasn't in this room, I was thinking about Larry. I haven't heard from him. He didn't phone me, and when I phoned him at Jack's at Christmas to talk to him, and Jack said he wasn't available, I was sure Larry just wanted to duck the call. Jack passed on Larry's message that said he was too busy right now to meet up. Not ever speaking to Larry again for the rest of my life was my New Year's resolution.

'I wish I hadn't had sex with him,' I say.

'Ah.' Rosanna gets up from her stool and washes and dries her hands.

Even if I wanted to tell her that I think I'm all messed up, and that I'm a recently released mental patient, and that everything I can see and hear tells me that the world is crazier than I am, I wouldn't know how to start. She hasn't asked anything about any drugs that I'm taking – prescription or otherwise. I didn't speak for months, but now I just want to keep talking. I want this Rosanna to step in and save me. I want her to tell me how I should live, now. I want more from this stranger-woman than anyone should be responsible for.

'I thought I wanted to, or maybe I thought I should, I guess,' I say. 'It was supposed to be fun. All of that. He's got smarts; he's very together. He wasn't my first, but sort of.'

I can't really explain myself. I can never explain myself. I'm useless at expressing myself.

'You're fine,' she says when I've finished. 'You're young, that's all.' She squeezes my shoulder and tells me I can get dressed, there is nothing to be worried about.

On the drive home from the women's clinic I ask Mom, 'Are you going to tell Dad?'

'He doesn't need to know. Women have accidents. These things happen. The important thing is to keep your options open. We're not living in the fifties.'

I want to tell her that I don't want to go back to classes, ever. I want to be in my own bed, at least for the weekend. Maybe forever. 'Can I stay at home again for a while?'

'Of course.'

'I didn't really like Larry.'

'He's a lowlife. Like his brother.'

'The doctor was nice.'

'Louelle knows a lot of people.'

Another way she's like Big Bird, I think.

We go silent for a moment and then I ask Mom what she thinks happens to the balloons after Thanksgiving, between one year and the next. She says maybe they go on vacation, but I'm not joking. They must deflate them.

'Of course they do. They can't be big balloons all the time, honey. It would be a hell of a storage problem.'

'It's sad, really. Don't you think?'

'No,' Mom says. 'It's a day. Thanksgiving comes and goes and comes right back again, just as good as before.' Then she says, 'You'll be okay. I promise.'

1976

Silk Worms

Carl says to me, 'Wilbur's not all that bad. For a faggot.' He takes his pack of cigarettes from his pocket and shakes it until one drops out. 'Changed your mind? Want one?' I shake my head. He gets up and goes over to wave it at Dolly, who is on duty this afternoon. She is also just sitting and watching. He has to ask for permission to light up. There's a thing like a car cigarette lighter on the wall, but it has to be turned on from inside the nurses' room. He bends over to get his mouth to it. Carl is tall and lean with broad shoulders. He winks at me as he walks back.

That night he and I sit up watching TV. This is because Henry has pulled a double shift and wants to watch a film. He's got the okay to do this as long as at least two of us watch it too. No one else was interested.

I think the film is stupid and scary. I've never got the point of science-fiction. Carl keeps laughing, pretends to be eating popcorn and feeding it to me. Asks me how old I am. He keeps guessing, and when he gets it right I finally nod and he grins, shouts, 'Should have known. I'll bet you're a virgin.'

Even though it's only Carl making any sound, Henry turns to hiss at both of us, 'Shut the fuck up, you fucking mentals, I want to watch this.'

Carl started guessing with 'twenty-five'. I wonder if this is because he is twenty-five. When he puts his arm around the back of my chair, Henry can't see the move because Henry has his mind on entertainment and is leaning forward to watch the screen. And then he can't see when Carl leans over to me and lifts my hair gently. His mouth brushes my cheek. I turn and he kisses my lips. His thin, pointy tongue presses against my mouth and worms its way inside. Carl tastes of Camels and salt, even though the popcorn was only pretend. It's a delicious combination.

'Thank God it's a private hospital,' Mom says when she first sits down on the chair next to Wilbur. We are over by the window and she's just arrived. The moment before she saw me it felt like I was invisible, or maybe actually not here, or anywhere, at all.

It's hot all the time in here. It's never really cold enough in Arizona for a fur coat, but Mom loves her mink. Today it makes her look like a big brown bear. The coat comes out of storage in September and is returned at the beginning of every March.

She's bought more things for me, in a large white Neiman Marcus bag, but she just drops this down on the floor and goes to look out the window. I don't know why she wants to look outside. There's a park not too far away, but the windows here all have wire grills like chicken wire, and you have to see past those, and then the road and past the houses until finally you can you spot the park. I don't know if she has the patience to look that far.

Wilbur is interested in what she's brought in for me. He leans over and tries to peek inside the bag. I wonder if he'll start taking things out, but he doesn't.

She comes back. 'God knows what a state hospital would be like,' she says.

'Your luscious little girl wouldn't make it out of a state unit,' Wilbur says in his snakiest voice. Then he gets up and walks off, which he should have done earlier. It's an unspoken rule that other patients should respect. They are supposed to leave the visitors alone with the visitee.

'Did that boy have *varnish* on his nails?' Mom says. She takes a deep breath. 'Dad can't make it again this week, sweetie. But I said I'd give you his love. You're all right, aren't you, baby?' She reaches over to put her arm around me. I move a bit so that we fit together like a puzzle and snuggle into the warm smell of her perfume. I like the feel of the soft fur of her coat as it tickles my cheek but I try not to think about the hundred and fifty dead minks. Minks make a high-pitched squealing noise. People grow them on farms and there's a lot of noise on a mink farm because they must stir each other up.

Mom says, 'I've booked a conference with Dr Wilson and we'll see what he's got to say for himself. You are looking A-okay, young lady. We'll have a fresh start soon. It's always warm in Phoenix. Even in January.' She smooths my hair away from my face and kisses my forehead. 'I think you're looking darn good, honey. I think you've dropped a couple of pounds. What's the food like? It damn well better be great, for what we're paying. But don't worry. This is what insurance is for. That's what your dad's job is for: to take care of us. We'll get you over this thing. Do they have bathroom scales here? Maybe not. You know, don't worry about it. I know it's not a health farm. When you come home we could go together.'

I pull away. I want to tell her that this is like no other place and that this ward, as terrible as it is, is an improvement on where I landed on admission.

Only male nurses are allowed to work on the top floor. There was just a six-foot-square, carefully guarded communal area. People were restrained in straitjackets, or secured on beds with wrist ties. They said I could have no visitors until they were sure that I would behave myself.

I graduated down to this ward after a week and was granted visitor rights. Here there are women nurses and nursing assistants. I didn't realise how reassuring it could be to have women around instead of just men in charge. I felt I could breathe again.

I can't tell my mother that there are no baths here and we are watched when we take showers in a row, in grubby mouldy stalls that have no curtains. Yesterday, a nurse shaved my legs and under my arms for me. Afterwards she stuck a Band-Aid on the razor, and then wrote my name on that with a magic marker and dropped it, unwashed, into a shoebox with more than twenty other razors. Mom wouldn't understand that there are no weighing scales anywhere, and the only mirror is in the toilet block. I've never seen it myself. Why would I want to look?

Anyone refusing to eat for longer than a couple of days may be force-fed. If you refuse to swallow your meds, they put you in restraints, inject them and then leave you in one of the padded rooms at the far end of the corridor. You might even get moved back upstairs if you fail to comply with whatever you are told to do.

Just being here means I am beyond the pale. I will never, ever be able to tell anyone what this place is like. No one who hasn't been here could ever understand.

When Dr Wilson comes on to the ward today, Mom and I go with him into the conference room to talk. Wilson is the sort of man I think would be at home in the army instead of in a hospital. Wilson has a trim moustache. Upstairs he barked out orders at the staff like a sergeant. He's only on staff here, but Wilbur said that ninety-five per cent of inmates are Wilson's. He acts charming around the nurses when he comes to this floor and does lots of shoulder-squeezing, winking, and encouraging talk about the next thing 'we' need to do as he parades through, but everything he 'suggests' is an order.

Mom told me that she chose this hospital specifically because of Dr Wilson. He was a recommendation from her friend Judy, who is a walking user's guide to psychiatric services nationwide. She's had everything and he once treated her bipolar on a sun retreat. I know that Mom hadn't talked to her for years, but she phoned Judy from the emergency room when I was admitted.

Dr Wilson holds Mom's hand a bit too long after shaking it. He pulls out the chair for her to sit down and she slips off her coat and drapes it over the back. I deal with my own seating while he sits down on the other side of the table from us. He starts speaking. 'Well, how're we all doing?' He smiles at her.

I can see that he's doing just fine. Mom's not looking good. And I am totally shit.

Mom says, 'Let's be clear. I want my daughter to come home and for things to be back to normal.'

When the light from the table lamp catches the yellow lining of Mom's coat, the material glints like gold. I consider how many silk worms were sacrificed in its production. Manufacture of a blouse requires over six hundred cocoons and this must have taken two thousand. Only some of the moths are allowed to emerge from their cocoons in order to produce worms for the next cycle. The vast majority are never allowed to hatch. Silk worms eat constantly until they begin to make their cocoons. I wonder what noise they make. Quiet humming, crunching, or steady grinding?

They are both looking at me. He says, quietly, 'A suicide attempt is a very frightening thing in a family.'

'You said it was a gesture,' she says.

'A failed attempt could be classified as a gesture. It's hard to determine actual intent. However, we cannot ignore an overdose.'

'I think I'd like it to be a gesture.'

'We can refer to it as a gesture.' He smiles meaningfully at me. I give him another sort of gesture, under the table.

'These things rarely happen suddenly. Was there a precipitating incident?'

Mom appears to consider this for a minute. He will be imagining her reflecting about hints she ignored over the course of my childhood, feeling remorseful about her own failings, or my dad's failings as a parent, or neglect, or a sudden trauma. Perhaps he thinks she is climbing back up the family tree to re-examine her ancestors for familial mental illness. But she's not. This is the pause and this is the facial expression she uses when she's about to say, *No, I will not accept an exchange. I want a refund,* or, *No, I cannot help you at the PTA.*

After a while she says, 'She's my daughter. I know how she is. She's always been thoughtful and quiet. This is a blip.'

'She's acutely depressed and needs treatment.'

'She needs to be free and living her life, doing things, not stuck in here with a bunch of fruitcakes. That's what's depressing her. Being where she does not belong.'

'The drugs we have tried have not shifted her mood.'

'Find another pill. One that works. And let her come home.'

'I think that we should talk about another option.'

She suddenly rises and goes to behind my chair. Hands on my shoulders, she growls at him, 'What are you thinking of doing to my daughter?'

'A tried and tested treatment that we should consider.'

'I will fight you tooth and nail if you're thinking what I think you are. Not shock treatment. She is a minor. I do not give permission. It is an assault.' She is screaming now. 'I don't know what Judy Glutzman saw in you, but Judy Glutzman is an idiot. I am not. I will sue you and I will sue this crappy joint right into the gutter if you go anywhere near her precious brain. Don't think I don't know. I know about these things.' She is panting when she finishes. She clutches me to her tightly and I can feel the heat from her body.

He shakes his head. 'I can see that this is getting us nowhere,' he says, and slowly backs out the door, shutting it behind him, leaving us alone.

I shut my eyes. All I can hear is noises. Everywhere.

1975

Whispering Pines

There is a six-foot rat snake baking in the sun on the middle of the service road that runs beside the pool house in this subdivision. The development is new, like they all are out here. In our case, moving here was nothing to do with urban spread, or (as my friends' parents complained about) increase in crime and property devaluation as a result of the number of black families moving into the suburbs; our move to Whispering Pines was because Mom just up and listed our house and then sold it. There were vacant units here and we have to live somewhere.

The townhouse has lots of space inside. My room is on the top floor and big, and a block away there's a clubhouse for residents of the subdivision with two swimming pools in the pool house, one indoor, one outdoor. But I miss the house I grew up in and I miss the old neighbourhood and my friends, and almost every house in this place, like ours, is rental. Everyone here will be moving on sometime. Us included. Dad still doesn't want to move to another state, and he hasn't got another job yet, but we will go. Mom won't talk about it; they're not arguing any more, but she won't take no for an answer. It'll happen. 'Getting rid of the house is step one,' she said. 'He can get with the programme.' Once Mom is set on forward motion, nothing can stop her.

'How do you know it's a rat snake?' I ask Kelly, who seems to know everything.

'The colour, dummy. Go ahead and stroke it. It's cool.' She bends down and pats the snake's midsection like a person petting a dog.

'Well, sure. That's because it's cold-blooded.'

Just then Rick, the lifeguard, and Darryl, the creepy maintenance guy, come out from the side of the clubhouse. Darryl is the last person I ever want to see.

'She's scared to touch the snake. It's non-venomous.' Kelly says.

Darryl sniggers when Rick says, 'I dare you.' Even though Darryl is there, I'm excited that Rick has noticed me. He's never spoken to me before today. I decide to do it.

The snake is not really cold but it feels like solid muscle, strong and thick beneath my hand. The shiny black skin is rough, even though I can't really see any proper scales. I fix my attention on the small section under my hand. I hear some kids squealing in the pool behind the fence. I stretch my fingers and fix my palm on it. I'll count ten Mississippis, which I think will be fine for a first effort. Maybe the snake finally feels the pressure because, at seven, it twists suddenly and I jump back.

They all laugh then Rick goes to fetch a broom. Darryl winks at me like we're friends or something, which makes me feel sick, and then Kelly and I watch as Rick gently prods and encourages it off the road on to the scrubby grass. We don't wait around to see it disappear into the woods. Later, after we get out of the pool and Kelly goes home, I go to look where the snake headed for, but it's so gone, it's like it was never there.

The day before yesterday I walked into Dad's study and thought someone had broken into the house because Dad was supposed to be at work. Then I saw what I thought was a girl with long hair kneeling in front of this man in my dad's chair. The man turned out to be Dad. I didn't recognise him at first and I didn't realise it was even a guy with him there until Darryl looked up when I knocked the trash can over. I stumbled over it as I backed out. Dad grabbed a magazine and tried to cover himself.

Darryl was there, in our house, with my father, on the floor in front of him.

'You know Darryl,' Dad said. 'He's been doing the grass. It's perfectly innocent...' he called after me.

I ran down to the clubhouse, and Kelly was there. We got wasted on Quaaludes. She wanted to know what was wrong, and why I'd been running, but there wasn't anything I could tell her. Before we left, Darryl slunk in to put something away and he sidled over to where we were lying, fully clothed, on the sunbeds by the pool. Everything was happening in slow motion. 'Hey, sorry,' he whispered, 'Forget it, huh?'

I didn't answer him, and I wouldn't look at Dad when I came home. I still can't speak to him. Later that evening

I asked Mom if she knew Darryl was hanging around the house lately. Darryl, the faggy guy with the long blond hair who did the lawns and worked out of the clubhouse. Did she know he was here? Did she know him as well? Or was he just Dad's friend?

'I don't know him,' she said. She slowly shut her eyes and eventually I left the room.

Rick's friend Fernando arrives in his pickup. He wants some help. Rick does this when he can. Today he says he's noticed I never have anything else to do but hang around here, so do I want to come with the two of them? It's business.

Fernando waves at Rick from the driver's seat. I climb up the other side of the pickup then slide over to the middle to make room for Rick.

'Hi,' I say, but Fernando says, over me, to Rick, 'Hey, she's a kid.'

Rick says to Fernando to shut up. It's not like that. I'll be cool.

Squeezed between the two of them I speak. 'I'm nearly sixteen. I have a name.'

'Yeah, it's Jailbait.' Fernando revs the engine and accelerates up the hill to the highway to take us into the city. Forty minutes later we're downtown.

As far as I can tell it's Rick who is doing all the work. Rick makes the deliveries and collections while Fernando waits in his truck with his arm stretched behind my shoulders on the back of the seat. He taps the fingers of his left hand on the dashboard. 'Hate this place,' Fernando says out the window more than once. I figure it's best to keep quiet. Even though he's slight and energetic, from the side view of him I see that his neck has wrinkles. He might be nearer my dad's age than mine.

Finally, after the last stop, Fernando relaxes. He puts a tape in the player. He whacks up the sound and sings 'Takin' Care of Business' as we head back. *The scenic route,* he calls it. We drive through the first of the suburbs on the outskirts of the city, and spread out sound as we wind through roads beside larger houses with wider and wider lawns, then out beyond the empty afternoon roads back towards my subdivision, but before we reach my suburb Fernando takes a sharp left right where St Mark's Hospital is set back from the road and we head west. I guess this is where he lives.

Apart from the massive glass coffee table with thick chrome legs there is hardly any furniture in Fernando's apartment, so Rick and I sit cross-legged on spotless white carpeting and he sits on his black leather chair. Fernando gets Rick to roll a couple of joints while he takes a shower. Rick explains that this is the build-up to him getting paid and we have to be patient. Hardly anyone comes to this place. 'He trusts me,' he says. 'He'll take us back when all this is done. Won't take long.'

When we finally leave, Rick asks if I'm okay and he squeezes my hand.

His red Mustang is still parked outside the clubhouse. We go to get something to eat. He tells me he loves this car. And, when we get there, that he loves Arby's. The smell inside is amazing. We sit side by side in a booth. Everything is red.

'My mother is crazy and my father is a big fat liar,' I say. 'I can't tell you about him.' Rick pats the top of my hand, says he understands, says he knows that parents are always a disappointment. I don't have to tell him the details. I'm too ashamed to, anyway. Darryl is just a nobody and, even if Rick has to work around him, it's not like they're friends. It's obvious Darryl is a creep. I feel like crying, then Rick says that he believes in me, he knows I will be okay, this is just how it feels to be my age. It'll all change. I don't need to be scared.

Later we find that while we've been talking it's got dark. When he drops me up at our townhouse, he tells me to relax and then he kisses me. It's like I'm falling in a spiral and it makes me dizzy and breathless. Like I haven't got any edges. When we stop he says he knows nothing can happen; I'm only a kid. I might be precocious but he's not going to be stupid.

Doc, Kèlly's stepfather, runs a diet clinic in a strip mall near the subdivision.

Doc is not a real doctor, he's some sort of chiropractor who decided to help fat people. Kelly says his clientele adore him and he can write prescriptions. He's also always good for money. When we go in, the receptionist knocks on the door to his office and he doesn't make us wait.

'Hi there, doll,' he says. Kelly's long blonde hair falls in front of her left eye. She's always sweeping it away and she does this now. Then she cups her hand around her mouth and whispers into his ear like she was seven instead of seventeen and then Doc peels off bills in exchange for her kiss on his cheek in his waiting room.

We've been gone minutes but the car is baking when we get back. She turns the engine on with the doors open to get the AC going. 'Great,' she says. 'Funds. Let's go get some candy and play.' She laughs.

Back at Kelly's house the furniture is big and dark. The TV is always on, which makes you feel like there are people around downstairs, even though it's only her and me up in her room. She rolls a joint. Her folks don't mind, she tells me, whatever she does. 'They're really cool.'

Her pointy tongue licks the paper shut; she twists the

end delicately. When she smokes she holds it lightly between her thumb and forefinger, like it's a cigarette holder or something.

We sit on her bed, backs to the wall, and listen to music. We both think school is pointless. She wants to be a vet. She'll graduate high school next year. We both don't want the summer to end even though it will soon be over. I start to notice how much her laugh is like a waterfall so I ask her to laugh again and again.

When Doc comes home he comes upstairs and right into her room and sits on the floor. He asks for a toke, asks about friends, about boyfriends. He says he can put me on the pill, if I want, that Kelly is already taking it. 'Oh, Doc,' she says. 'Don't bug her. She's a kid.'

'No, I'm interested,' I say.

There are cat hairs everywhere here. It's like her whole bedroom is furry. I ask Kelly if she remembers *The Cat in the Hat*. She laughs again. 'Because I think I am the fish,' I say. 'That's my problem. I'm the fish. I see everything and no one believes me.'

Doc gets up off the floor. He leaves the door open, but she bounces off the bed to slam it shut behind him.

This morning I face six empty boxes stacked in my bedroom. Mom says that they've agreed on a house in Phoenix. Dad's got a job that starts in six weeks and we'll be moving to Arizona within the month.

Last night when I put on the halterneck dress to go out with Rick again it made me feel grown-up. I haven't told my parents about him. Neither one will ask what I'm doing. And, if they ever do ask, I'm learning how to lie.

Though my dress has been washed a hundred times, a perfume lingers: the smell of the dyes and the patchouli-filled head shop where I'd bought it. Now there are bright purple stains around my neck and shoulders; bruises splodge my arm, one on my breast.

My outside matches my insides.

A T-shirt just about covers all the worst love bites. But in the kitchen Mom looks at me sidelong and then decides not to say anything. I think up until the other day we'd hardly spoken for weeks and now we won't.

Today Mom is busy stuffing ketchup, mustard, salt, pepper, cinnamon and allspice into an already full container. All the cabinet doors are open and some of the shelves are already empty. I grab a bowl, some Cap'n Crunch and a carton of milk from the refrigerator and go to watch TV while I have my breakfast.

The phone rings before I'm finished eating. It's Rick and I tell him I've got to pack, there's stuff I've got to do, and he says, lightly, 'Too bad. Catch you later.'

Upstairs the cream walls are pristine. My closet doors glide smoothly open and shut. The green carpet still smells of plastic. This room looks exactly the same as when we arrived.

I stand still and think about Rick's red Mustang and how far it could take us. I think about my dad and his pitiful red face. My mom and all that anger. I think about what's happened here, and what it might be like in the new place. I have no choice about anything and I can't escape. It's like being on a high sided travelator and unable to turn around or get off.

Even though the AC is on and I'm not supposed to, I edge along the glass of the window to let some real air in to my room just so I can breathe. Ours is the very end townhouse at the top of the hill, the end of the subdivision. I am very high up here on the top floor. To my right, through the fine mesh of the screen, I see the hodgepodge buildings in timber and stone with matching wrought-iron balcony rails and, below, the green between them. The flat mown lawn runs right to the border of the darkened, uneven wooded area to the left. Suddenly only the white wood windowsill seems solid and I want to rest my head here before I fall.

The restless tops of the pine trees are murmuring. They tell me that they whisper all night and that I've not been listening. I should listen while I have the chance. I think about how we, too, will soon be only ghosts here.

Nothing is important. Nothing lasts. Nothing is real.

1974

Magnetism

We've been driving through the Midwest from south to north for hours and I'm starving. This is not a bad sensation. I've learned to love feeling hungry. My stomach is concave and shrinking and every time I stroke my middle this fact pleases me.

Mom and I had an argument earlier. She wanted me to eat breakfast.

'You're always forcing food down my throat. I'm not a baby. I'm going to be fifteen in a matter of weeks,' I said.

'Everyone's supposed to eat breakfast. It's good for you.'

'Who says that? And what do they know? I'm just fine. I have the right to make choices for myself.' This is the sort of thing she says herself, so she could hardly complain.

Mom has become very big on equality lately. She asks people in stores how they feel about their work, she yells at the TV when the oppressor persecutes the underdog, cheers at it as if she can be heard when some bad guy in a movie gets his come-uppance. She's taken to clipping odd articles from the newspaper and putting them on the dinner table for us to read and discuss. Yesterday it was about Nixon's impeachment. Most of the time I don't know what to say so I just ask her what she thinks and then don't listen to her 'blah, blah, blah' reply. Dad says that we need to be patient, that she'll settle down again. I'm not so sure. Not now that she's decided to leave him.

She told me that I was going with her on this adventure yesterday and swore me to secrecy. Mom says Dad has some thinking to do and this will help him. He was at work when we left the house. She said we were going to see her oldest friend Charleen, that the trip would do us both good too and Charleen and her haven't seen each other for years.

I put on the radio and tune in a local station. She reaches over and clicks it off, then she seems to remember that she's not like that any more, that we're equal, and she switches it on again. I tell her thanks because she's also always saying about how a person needs encouragement, that without encouragement people wither. This makes me think of the wicked witch in *The Wizard of Oz* suddenly shrivelling up in hissing smoke, which seems to be what's happened to Mom's brains lately, but I think she means what happens when you don't water plants, which, in fact, she doesn't. In our house the plants gradually wilt and then turn brown and have to be thrown away.

I am the navigator. The map pages are slick. The smell coming up off the book is a mix of newspapers and gas stations. She ordered it in the mail using Dad's Triple A membership and this will be a clue to him when he tries to find us. There are only thirty miles to a page and then you flip it over and start a whole other page. I wonder when he will know where we've gone. Who will he ask about us? Who will he tell?

As I settle down to navigate the traffic gets thicker. It's a Friday night and rush hour is starting early. People are zigzagging around us. She is clutching the steering wheel. She refuses to change lanes and sticks to forty miles an hour. I have no idea where we are and tell her so.

'That's what the map is for,' she says. 'To tell us exactly where we are and where we are going, and how to get there.'

'I know that, Mom. But I need to know what page to start on. I don't recognise anything.'

'Look at the road signs, then. Figure it out. I'm just trying not to get us killed here by all these fucking idiots.'

I think about asking her to rephrase this in an encouraging way, but that could make things worse.

I finally work out that we are on page twelve, which means we have another fourteen pages to go. 'I need the bathroom,' I tell her. 'We should stop. It's getting late. I'm tired.'

'We're not even in Chicago.'

'We've made it nearly to Joliet and I need the bathroom. I'm a person too.'

I'm quoting her again. She said that last bit when she was yelling at Dad about the letter from one of his students. I heard the argument through the wall. He pleaded ignorance and accused Mom of false allegations, then there was no sound at all for a while. When he spoke again, his voice had shrunk and hers had grown, filling the room and bursting through the walls. She shrieked commandments at him: 'You will not do this to me. You will never do this to our family. You will not humiliate me. You will not shame us. You will not do this after everything. Everything! You hear me. You hear me. I'm a person too.'

She showed the letter to me yesterday, before we put our suitcase into the car. 'Read between the lines.' She thrust the paper at me. I couldn't see what she was so upset about. The guy wasn't complaining about Dad, it sounded like he liked him a lot, but I didn't say that. It wouldn't have helped.

We were going to do the trip in one day, but we set off later than she originally planned because she couldn't decide what to bring. It's getting darker and darker. Eventually she agrees that we should stop for the night.

As we undress to climb into the king-size bed that we will share, I begin to dread having to listen to her tell me how awful Dad is again. I wonder if Dad knows that she does this. I want him to know I'm not on anyone's side. 'I'm real tired,' I say.

She doesn't reply. She points the remote and the TV blasts into life.

With my eyes shut there is still a steady flickering flow of colours because she is constantly changing the channel, click, click, click, click. I lie stock still, pretending to be asleep, but I wonder how still a sleeping person really is. I suspect that someone who doesn't move at all looks more fake so I shuffle my feet and mutter, 'It's cold,' like I might be sleep-talking. She turns the TV off and rolls over. The bed shifts beneath us as she moves away from me to face the wall and I'm left to wonder alone whether Dad is missing us and if he's okay.

I wake some time in the night. The room is lit by strong moonlight coming from a slit where the drapes haven't quite come together. Mom has thrown the blankets from her and she is on her side, curled up. Her mouth has fallen open and her long hair is spilled on the pillow, on her shoulders, all over the place.

When I turn on the bathroom light, it is amazingly bright. In the huge mirror I see my reflection. My pale skin and white PJs appear yellow. The sound of me peeing echoes and, at the same time as I am sure that the sound will wake the whole motel, I also feel sealed in and sure that no one would ever hear, even if I screamed at the top of my lungs. Hundreds of people have sat here, also on their way somewhere else. I wonder how many of them didn't know exactly where they were going, and why.

On my way back to bed, I smooth Mom's hair and tug the covers over her. She rolls on to her back and makes tiny, reassuring snoring sounds that punctuate the deep humming sound of the air-conditioner.

In the coffee shop in the morning, I order French toast, just to cheer her up. Mom says she didn't sleep well and only wants coffee. This is not a good sign.

We get lost in the Chicago Loop. This is even though I have the map on my lap and am referring to it regularly, and have also been watching the street signs. I thought I could find a quick way through, but it hasn't worked. Three times we passed the Cadillac Palace Theatre. There have been signs directing us towards the Lake Michigan beach and this has been hopeful, but, every time we get close to turning off, the signs disappear and we're back driving around in circles again. When I explain to Mom that we are totally lost she's annoyed but doesn't seem to understand that we really are totally lost. The Chicago Loop is a loop we'll never get out of and we have no hope of ever escaping this trap. She says she'll stop at the next gas station and ask.

I stay in the car when she goes in. It's a small place and there's a big black guy behind the till and Mom makes little gestures explaining things to begin with, then she waves her hands about her head. I see him shrug. She hands over her credit card to pay for the gas. I think that this will be another clue for Dad.

When she comes out she's carrying a new map. 'This is just a blip. It's a detour,' she says to me. 'Don't feel bad. Anyone could have made the mistake. You're doing a great job.'

There is nothing that might remotely support that summary. We've wasted more than two hours. Together we stare at the folded-out map on my lap and she says she needs glasses, that today she can't read the road names clearly. We decide that my plan to follow the shoreline is a good one. We can go this way right to Milwaukee. Then, against my protests, she grabs the Triple A guide and dumps it out the window. I open the door to go and collect it but she starts up the engine, so we leave it behind on the gas station forecourt.

Much later we both cheer when we finally clear the Illinois state line and enter Wisconsin. For just a moment I forget that Dad is left behind and feel really happy that we're just not lost any more.

We get a new map and it's useful when we begin the hunt to find Charleen's street. Her house is set back from the road and we park in the driveway behind a beat-up Pontiac. 'Don't be surprised at what she looks like, honey,' Mom says. 'She's pretty sick. I should have told you. She's practically dead, really.'

This is news to me and, if Mom is warning me, this is going to be bad. She's right. She should have told me sooner.

I recognise Charleen's daughter, Susie, from the photo Mom showed me before we left. When she opens the door Mom steps forward with a happy yell and gives her a hug.

They walk through the wood-panelled hallway into the kitchen hand in hand. I am left watching their backs until I follow them, shutting the door behind me.

A black Labrador comes out of a room on the right and sniffs at my legs. She's old; the whiskers and hair around her mouth are white. When I stroke her smooth coat she leans in to me, getting closer. We're together at the doorway to the kitchen and she is a comfort because she seems to understand I don't belong here and that I don't know what to do or say.

Charleen is sitting on a chair by the stove and, even though Susie was clearly expecting us, Charleen's face looks overwhelmed, a bit surprised. She's very thin. Her head is covered by a scarf. Mom bends down to kiss her while Susie stands back and watches the two of them with a grin on her face. It's like Susie is Charleen's mom, not the other way round. It makes me feel sad and no one but the dog is noticing me, so I step back to stand in the hall and sit down on the floor to make a fuss of the dog.

Charleen's husband Bob died in a car crash a long time ago. I know from what Mom has said that his insurance paid for this house, and that Susie's brother Todd has left home for New York, where he's a wannabe stockbroker. It's now just those two women in this big house with an old dog.

Charleen shows us the downstairs of the house. The dining room, which turns out to be where the dog was before she came out to greet us, has been made into Charleen's bedroom, and the downstairs guest bathroom is full of her personal things. Medical things, too. When I have to use the bathroom I try not to look at the objects next to the sink.

While the dinner is cooking, we sit at the kitchen table. I am on one side, and Mom and Charleen are opposite. Susie's place is next to me, but she's busy doing the cooking so there is no one on my side. The dog is lying down underneath the table. They're laughing and joking but the whole house smells funny. It's full of this sickness, like a real hospital or an old people's rest home. I don't know how we're going to be able to sleep here.

Susie opens a bottle of red wine. Mom and Susie drink it, and Susie smokes a lot. Charleen sips at her glass and holds a cigarette but doesn't light it. The three of them sing 'Born to be Wild' together, badly. I can't hear Charleen's voice, but she's saying the words and enjoying it. I have a glass of wine too; Susie pours it out as though I've been awarded something wonderful. When I gulp it down and return my glass to the table empty, she applauds and Mom tells me not to be so greedy.

When it's finally dished up, the pulpy texture of the pasta makes me gag. No one notices as I spit some of it into my hand and offer it to the dog under the table. First I feel the breath from her nose then a nudging as she nibbles at the food. Her tongue is rough and thick and warm on my skin, and it slides the length of my hand. I try not to stare at Charleen's scrawny fist clutching her knife and fork opposite and look at the cheerful curtains instead. A yellow background with cartoon fruit: enormously fat cherries and giant strawberries. The designer should have painted faces on to them, I think.

Then I realise that Charleen is looking at me; she's evaluating me. I force myself to smile back and say, 'My Dad says hi.' From the corner of my eye I see that Mom is surprised. I am lying and of course she knows this.

'Haven't seen him in years. Or your mom,' she says. 'What a treat this is.' Then they talk about old friends. She says Louelle and Patty phone sometimes but no one else has come to visit.

By the time Susie starts to clear the table my plate is empty; most of the food is in the dog. But Charleen has eaten even less than me. She's pushed the food into a pile in the middle. Susie doesn't say anything when she scrapes it into the waste disposal.

It's ice-cream for dessert. Mom says how she loves this but Charleen waves her hand 'no' when Susie slides a glass bowl of chocolate chip in front of her. 'Go on, Mom,' she says. 'You have to keep up your strength.' Then Charleen shakes her head and the head scarf slips backward. She has only clumps of hair, like the mangy fur on the cat Dad rescued from a storm drain last summer. Susie delicately moves the scarf into place again. 'I've had enough,' Charleen says. Her voice is the most real thing I've ever heard when she pleads, 'Let me be.'

Even though I don't want to, I eat all the ice-cream in the dish just to cheer Susie up and then it's time for bed. We're going to sleep in the master bedroom. This is Susie's plan. Mom tells her that she and I can share the bed. I don't know how to feel because there will be Bob's ghost and Charleen's nearly ghost in there with us, but at least I won't be on my own.

There is thick dust on the banister going up the stairs and in the bedroom when we get there. Susie kisses Mom goodnight and waves at me when she shuts the door. The dust is also on the bedside lampshades; the pink colour brightens where I use my finger to make a large cross. We whisper in bed, in the dark, our heads on cold, hard pillows.

'When are we going home?' I ask.

'Why?'

'I miss everything. Please can we go?'

'I've come for Charleen and Susie.'

'I don't know why *I* had to come.'

'For me. You're here for me.'

She puts her arm up. I rest my head on her upper arm. Her smell is layered: there is the smell of the wine and the garlic bread, the perfume she squirts all over herself, her special soap, and finally the smell of her skin itself. I whisper into her armpit, 'Whatever he's done, he loves you a lot, Mom. He might not say it, but love means never having to say you're sorry.'

'That's crap movie talk,' she whispers back. 'It's not about being sorry, saying sorry, or not. None of that. Love is easy; it's living that isn't sometimes, and I'm tired.'

In the morning light Charleen looks even more shrivelled up. We say good morning while she is still in bed. Susie is preparing some medications in the kitchen. The dog is very pleased to see me, and while Mom sits with Charleen I go into the back yard with her to play fetch. She is slow and not very enthusiastic, but it's good to be outside. It's not quite summer, but it will be soon. I wish we could get our own dog, or even rescue this one and take her home with us.

Mom and I go out so that Charleen and Susie can get on with what they need to do. On the way to the neighbourhood mall we get lost again. I can't read Susie's scribbled diagram, and Mom can't either. When we stop Mom says she's sure we're near the stadium, but there are no signs. She says it's just a feeling, that sometimes even if you can't see signs you can sense where you are. It's a kind of magnetism, she explains.

'You know you're nuts,' I tell her and we both laugh.

We go into a Walgreens and there are no other customers in it. We go to look at the cards. There is a whole aisle of greetings cards here and I find three funny ones that I collect. When I turn to show her, Mom isn't there.

I scoot along where all the aisles intersect with the main space, looking down each one to find her. Finally, I spot her sitting at the ice-cream counter at the back of the store. 'You disappeared,' I call over. 'I didn't know where you were.'

Back in the car she says she's decided that we will drive home later. 'Then I want to move,' she says. 'A fresh start. He can get a job anywhere, even here.'

'Not here, Mom, please.'

'Or Arizona. I like Phoenix. That has possibilities.'

'Have you even been there?'

'I've seen pictures. The roads are laid out in a grid, like Chicago, but there's no Great Lakes to disrupt things. There's space and warmth there, room for the roads to grow and breathe. I think it would be great.'

'Roads don't breathe, Mom. We can make it okay at home.'

'I know that,' she says.

The drive back is quick and we miss all the tangle of Chicago. We are home before eleven o'clock. Dad is pleased to see us. She beeps the horn and he comes outside and rushes up to the car. 'Don't tell him anything,' she says. 'He doesn't need to know where we've been.'

'What am I supposed to say if he asks?'

She says he won't. He doesn't want to know. That she will tell him if he does. She makes me promise not to say anything.

That night, under my own blankets, I think about what Dad does know and what he might think. When we were alone, all he said to me was, 'Your mother is lucky to have you with her.'

In a few days Dad has some news. He tells us that he's going to start applying for jobs in Arizona. Mom's face doesn't move but I am shaking with anger. This is my life too, I want to scream, but instead I run upstairs and when Dad calls after me I don't reply. I slam the door to the bedroom behind me.

An hour later I come downstairs and find Mom. She's outside the back door holding a steaming mug between her hands, staring up into the dark sky. I plead with her to reconsider. She doesn't look at me. All she says is, 'Blame your father if you have to blame anyone. I don't want to talk about it.'

He finds us there too late to hear that, but not too late to hear me crying.

'What's up, honey?' He draws me away from the door, to him in the light. 'What's the matter?'

I shake my head because I don't know what to say except, 'I'll miss my friends.'

'It'll be okay,' he says. 'You'll see. We'll be together.'

I sit down at the table and she steps in through the door, stands behind him. She is watching the two of us. Dad can't see her expression, but I can.

It's not that she is happy, but her face tells me that she knows she has won something and he and I have lost. Not everyone can win, I know that. Some people are stronger than others. The effect of them is greater. That's how it works.

She stares at me. My mother waits for me to turn away.

1973

The Armadillo

Dr Turner's white coat across the desk is whiter than white, like the after part of a washing powder ad, and it matches his gleaming teeth.

'It's a very early birthday present. She'll be fourteen before long.' Mom explains to him. 'But I want her to have something that will last forever. No one should be disadvantaged in high school.'

Dr Turner flashes his smile again. I recognise that his are an example of 'positive teeth' that Mom has been going on about. I see now that, as she has complained, Mom's teeth are too small and hesitant for her face. She's deciding whether or not to do anything about it.

'What a lucky young lady you are, honey. Your folks sure do love you, don't they?' When he turns all that glow on to me, the attention hits me physically. I am beginning to blush as I nod. I mumble, 'I know,' looking down and trying not to open my mouth much.

Mom explains my unintelligible speech. 'She's a bit shy.' Then she turns and says to me, like she's talking to a three-year old, 'Dr Turner is going to have to study your face. Go ahead and let him.'

My blush deepens. I feel the heat at my neck and I remember how Dad always says I should demonstrate curiosity, that people like answering questions about themselves and this is a good way of getting over my personality. My heart pounds as I thrust my hand and point to the top of his bookcase and blurt out, quite clearly. 'What's that, I wonder?'

He gets up and comes around the desk and takes my glasses off. Everything blurs and his face suddenly swarms in front of me. He holds my head firmly in his hands, tilting it upwards and smoothing both of my cheekbones simultaneously with his thumbs. 'It's an armadillo,' he says, breathing the words on me. 'It's dead.'

His nose is not so elegant this close. There's a stray black hair drooping from his right nostril. Though it's coming straight at me, I try not to inhale his warm exhalation. If I have to be careful with the cat sleeping in my bed because her breath is dangerous, presumably I should demonstrate caution in this kind of situation too. 'Well,' he says, now sliding one forefinger down the length of my nose. 'Um. Uh huh,' he says to himself. Then he pulls his hands away and tips my head again, straight this time. I don't know what he's looking at now, but my view is his crotch, where his white coat has flapped open. I shut my eyes. There's a clock ticking and Mom is doing her deep yoga breathing beside me. I can smell her new perfume from here.

Then he releases me and returns to behind his desk. 'I'll do it,' he says to Mom. 'But you have to understand some facts. A good nose can be made beautiful, but a bad nose will never be perfect. You can't create a really great nose from something that's not at least good.'

Mom asks eagerly, 'It'll be better?'

'She'll have a real cute nose.'

I put my glasses back on and look at the two of them. Mom is bewitched by all that hope. There can be no other reason for her vacant expression as he dismisses us to make the arrangements with his secretary outside. 'Been a pleasure,' he says, winking at me and offering her his handshake.

'Why do you think he's got that dead armadillo?' I ask when we are getting into the elevator. I picture it. It wasn't posed; it was just standing there, in a glass case, like an aquarium.

'People like critters,' she says pressing B for the basement car park. 'What did you think?'

'I think an armadillo is a strange thing to stuff and keep on display like that.'

'No, about fixing your nose, honey?'

'I don't care what happens to my ugly nose.'

'He said it was a bad nose, not that it was ugly.'

At home later I get the *Encyclopaedia Britannica* volume 'A' from the *Encyclopaedia Britannica* bookcase in Dad's study and take it up to my room.

When I open the door my new bright furniture is still a surprise. Mom said that my old desk needed to be replaced and she ordered the huge vanity unit opposite. 'It's better for a girl's room,' she said. 'When you're a little older you'll want to do your make-up and make sure you look nice.' But all it means to me now is that I can view my ugly nose in the triple-aspect mirror instead of scoring ink daydream squiggles into dark wood. My sturdy old bed has been replaced with French Provincial style – white and spindly. There are two delicate chests of drawers to match and I've got a new white rug over the rose-coloured carpet.

Miss Tibbs has followed me up. I sit on the bed with her on my lap purring softly. 'He had a stuffed armadillo,' I whisper to the cat. 'What kind of a person keeps something like that?'

Miss Tibbs is very sympathetic and doesn't know either.

In the encyclopaedia I learn that armadillos are native to this landscape, that they are poor-sighted and use their strong forearms and claws to burrow. Despite their hard exterior armour, they have soft, vulnerable underbellies. I like the word 'underbelly' and have just flipped the accommodating Miss Tibbs over to expose hers when Mom shouts from downstairs that dinner is served.

I didn't hear Dad come home but he's there at the dining room table, pouring himself a glass of red wine. He downs his drink in two deep gulps as Mom plonks the casserole on the table and announces that tonight it is broccoli chicken.

Though it's highly unappetising to look at, I remind myself that, if you ignore the gloppy white sauce, it's probably nutritious. Chicken is good protein, after all. The broccoli is because Mom has been in love with broccoli since Mrs Glodsky's Welcome Wagon Fourth of July picnic. It's very healthy for us. We've had it in salads and hot pots, disguised and plain, steamed and boiled and even raw. I think the A&P has an ongoing special. Dad thinks Mom just has an obsession; he says that she gets like this now and then and not to be worried about it. She works it out of her system.

The one-dish meals are another of her recent crazes. Mom says they're efficient. I know Dad hates them. You can't separate and prioritise your food for eating; it's just all there in one mass. She's got a whole fat cookbook of one-dish meals. She's wading her way through the pages, dragging us along.

Today Dad doesn't even seem to notice that he's eating, let alone what he's eating. He rhythmically puts forkfuls of the stuff into his mouth, chews and swallows while he hoists up another lot. 'Have a good day?' he asks with his mouth full.

Mom recounts how we've been to see about my nose while I push my food around, wondering if I could slide some back off my plate without either of them noticing. One of the benefits of one-dish meals.: it's impossible to see what you're leaving behind. Mom says the nose operation is all fixed up for the first week in August.

'He's cutting off my ugly nose and sticking a fake one on.'

Mom glares at me.

Dad says, 'Does she really need a nose job? How much is it going to cost?'

Mom puts down her fork loudly and picks up the serving spoon. 'We've talked about this.' She jabs the spoon in Dad's direction. 'Her nose comes from your side of the family. Your mother had a nose like that.'

'I know, but an operation? She's only twelve.'

'I'm thirteen,' I say.

'She'll be fourteen and in junior high soon,' Mom says.

He pours another glass of wine and looks at my nose appraisingly. I remove my glasses so that he can see it better and so that I can't see anything.

'She didn't need braces. We don't want her disadvantaged,' Mom says.

'So how much?'

'You can't put a price on everything.'

'A plastic surgeon can. I'm not made of money.'

'I read that it's a growth industry,' I offer, but neither of them is pleased at this contribution. They both scowl at me. 'If you two are going to argue about my nose, go right ahead, but I've got better things to do,' I say, not that this is true.

As I leave the room Mom tells Dad that we should all be pleased Dr Turner was even willing to take on the job.

She stops by my room later on, when I'm in bed. She sits down on the covers and fusses my hair. 'What do you want?' she asks.

'A pretty nose,' I say.

'Your father doesn't understand that being a woman takes effort.'

'He works hard.'

'With women, a lot of it is presentation.'

'Like advertising?'

'Sort of. Maybe. Not really,' she says in quick succession. 'It's a very quick operation.'

'I don't like my ugly nose.'

'You are not ugly.'

'My nose is ugly,' I say quietly. 'Why do you think he had that armadillo?'

'Maybe it's a college mascot or something. Or belonged to his family. Who knows?'

'Do you think it died a long time ago? Maybe it was road kill?'

'Road kill isn't something you ever need to think about. I promise.'

'He had very positive teeth.'

She nods thoughtfully.

'You don't have to have the operation,' she says.

'I really want to,' I decide.

My bedroom is above the garage and at some point in the night I think that the big door whirrs open and shut but I can't be sure because I don't know all the noises here. Miss Tibbs wakes too. She stretches and kneads the blanket then rolls on to her back.

My furniture glows in the moonlight. Once school starts I'll see Kirsty and Misty and I will make new friends too. I will study and work hard, get straight A's and also be beautiful and popular. This is what I think about as I fall back to sleep.

This hospital is designed for little kids. Everywhere there are posters and Disney pictures. Dad points out as a joke that, given his main facial feature, Woody Woodpecker's portrait on the mural which takes up an entire wall in my hospital room is very appropriate.

After a while Mom tells Dad he can leave because it doesn't take both of them to do this, and she settles down with an old copy of *Reader's Digest* while I take a shower with this stinky pink stuff the nurse gives me. Then we just wait.

Eventually Dr Turner comes in, wearing green scrubs. Grey hairs from his chest are fluffing over the V neckline.

I'm very conscious that I have no underwear on. Mom couldn't tell me why I had to take off my underwear when it's an operation for my head. 'But I promise no one will notice,' she said.

'I still feel naked.'

'Ready, honey?' Dr Turner asks me now.

'I guess so.'

'Great. It's a date, then. See you down there.' He winks at me and squeezes Mom's shoulder.

The nurse arrives then and she tapes up my hair and tells me to leave my glasses with my mom, that I won't need them now. I ask her, please, can I take them? I can't see anything at all without them. Suddenly this is the scariest thing about the whole operation: that I'll lose all my bearings and won't even know where I am when they put me to sleep.

Mom tells the nurse that she needs to speak with her outside. She returns alone. Mom says that she will come with me right to the operating theatre and take the glasses at the last moment and that she'll wait right there for me until I come out. They'll make an exception. She's cleared this with everyone who needs to know.

I wave goodbye to Woody Woodpecker and say, 'See you later,' to the picture. Mom holds my hand as the orderly pushes the bed out of the room and down the corridor. She never moves from my side. Even though it's a very tight squeeze, she holds on when we are in the staff only elevator. Finally she kisses my hand, then my cheek and lastly my ugly nose, right before she takes the glasses from my face. 'You'll see. It'll be perfect,' she whispers. 'I love you.'

When it is unwrapped eventually, my new nose looks pretty darn good, but once the swelling settles it turns out the new delicate bridge is quite narrow and this is a problem. My glasses sit on my face and slide down continually. I hate this, and Mom sets about persuading Dad that I should get contact lenses. He doesn't think it's necessary.

She is undeterred and tackles it methodically: she mentions that my glasses are causing acne irritation one day, then tells him a couple of days later that the Clearasil isn't working. The next week she says that the problem is increasing, I might need to see a dermatologist, and then that she's anxious that my recurrent zits are going to scar me for life, and finally, a week before school starts, she tells him that if he loved us he'd understand the problem and fork out the two hundred bucks and be done with it. She thinks I'm out of earshot but I happen to be at the door when she says, 'We can't neglect her. My daughter's future depends on simple decisions like this.'

Dad can see me, but he's looking at Mom when he answers. 'Get the goddamn contacts. I don't give a good goddamn about any of this cosmetic crap. I've been taking care of the two of you since before the day she was born. Don't accuse me now of neglecting her future. You should know that, however things began, she means everything to me and I will always want the best for her.'

Before Mom can reply, I quickly step back and creep a retreat to my room.

Miss Tibbs is waiting upstairs. In this room there's another something new: there's a lock on the door, and a key. I turn it for the first time ever before I climb into bed. I don't want Mom to come up and boast that because of her efforts I'm getting the contact lenses that I want, because she'll present it as if she's won the battle on my behalf. I will have to be grateful.

The sheets are fresh and cold. I like my nose and I know that I do want the contacts and am pleased that now I will have them, but right now I just want to be on my own without interruption, or interference.

Miss Tibbs curls up beside me and her fur is silky soft.

Maybe Mom does come and try the door, but I don't wake. I don't hear a thing at all.

1971

The Foetal Pig

Mom is out somewhere and Carmela and I are in the back yard under the shade of the trees. This corner is dark, and the grass doesn't grow here. There are pine needles and long-dead, last-year-dead leaves stuck together in clumpy piles. She is talking about her brothers and how much they stink.

I sense the beginning of a headache like a watermark inside my head and I half wish my friend would go home so that I can lie down in the dark. I don't want to have to listen to her any more and imagine the stench of her smelly brothers, but she is my best friend so I can't tell her to shut up. Instead I say I'm thirsty.

While she waits outside I get two cans of soda from the kitchen. The screen door is light and flaps back too quickly. It ricochets and surprises me with a light tap on my back. It's cool and quiet inside and the soda is ice-cold. I hold a can to my forehead before I walk back outside into the sun. My eyes have to adjust – everything is whited out, except for the violet blotch, a paisley shape, that is growing in my right eye.

Carmela has moved to sitting in the sun and she's found a broken knife. 'Look at this,' she shouts, waving it about. Part of the blade, she says, snapped off when she pulled it up out of the ground. 'It could be a murder weapon.'

This knife does not look familiar. It must have come from next door.

'It's a dinner knife,' I say. 'That'll be Greg.'

Greg is always throwing things into our yard. Boys like to project themselves, Mom says. They walk around poking at things, the ground, whacking the leaves. It's part of being a male animal. Greg's back yard has trees scraped and stabbed to bits.

'Who's Greg?' she says. Even with her four stinky brothers Carmela is boy-crazy. I don't know if boys will ever like her, or me, but she stares at them in the schoolyard, nudges me on the school bus, and practically pants if any of the boys behind the counter at McDonald's even looks at her.

I don't want to be like Carmela. When I told Mom that this obsession of Carmela's was getting on my nerves – that they don't notice us, so why should we notice them? – she said it was just a phase. 'She'll learn they're nothing to run after. Some things are best not watered,' she said and that boys really hate the girls that chase them. 'They only want one thing and it's not getting married.' I didn't ask her anything else. I didn't want another talk about S-E-X. But I can see that boys have their uses. How else would a person get married and have children, without boys?

'Nobody,' I say now. 'Greg is nobody to worry about. I think he's a girl.'

We both roll over on the grass. The sprigs are springy underneath my hand. It was only cut last week. I imagine the worms resting underneath in the soil. It's too hot for them to come out and wriggle their raw pink segments around. We'll dissect an earthworm again this year in Science. It gets all pinned open so we can see all of the alimentary canal. Then we'll do a foetal pig. They abort the pigs for science classes just so we can look inside and see how things work. I don't know how big it will be, but you can't pin a pig open, surely? We'll have to take it apart. The pig's inside will be the colour of the blossom inside my eye. Fresh blood, pink in places.

'Tomorrow they're launching Apollo 15,' Carmela says. 'Imagine that. All that way away. Living for three days on the moon out there in space.'

'They've been up there loads of times already.'

Half of Carmela's face is fading in and out as I look at her. I try to figure out which half stays, but it's too difficult. I take off my glasses and shut my eyes. The colours behind my eyelids now are a beautiful kaleidoscope.

She takes a swig from her can. A dribble of foam slides down her chin and she wipes it away with her forearm.

We're silent for a while. It's a good time to get her to go home. She always wants to be here at my house because she says that it's too crowded at hers and that there's more to do here because I am an only child, but I don't see that that's true. Anyway, it's too hot to lie around outside any more and I don't want to do anything inside. If we went indoors all we would do is watch TV and that would hurt my head even more. Quietly I say, 'Hey, do you want to go home? My mom will be home soon. She'll want me to help out with doing *something* and my eyes are all funny.'

'Your mother's a cranky old bitch,' she says. 'It's summer vacation.'

I open my eyes to a squint. The half of her mouth that I can see grins at me and she says, 'Just joking.'

Now Carmela says to put the sprinklers on. I don't want the trouble of it, but I still can't figure out a polite way of saying that I really want her to go home and leave me alone – so I get up to do it. I have to put my glasses on. Things are still swimming around and disappearing in front of my eyes.

The hose is coiled tightly. Only the gardener uses it. It takes the two of us to un-stretch it to the middle of the yard, and then, from the garage, I get the thing with all the holes that makes the water swish in an arc over back and forth like a jumping rope, and we connect it. But when I turn the tap the water doesn't come out at all because there's a twist in the hose. Carmela flips this to straighten it and the water suddenly bursts out of the end. She's drenched and her sneakers are soaked, and then she's mad. She shrieks at me to stop it. 'Fuck it! Turn it off.'

I turn it off as quick as I can, but the sound of dripping water continues as the arc dies down and fizzles out. Her long black hair is now stuck to her face and chest like a piece of wet cloth. She stamps her foot, like a two-year-old. 'Look at me. Jesus.' She steps backwards and stumbles. She ends up on her butt sitting at the edge of the flower bed. She's squashed a whole bunch of flowers. 'You did it on purpose.'

'It was an accident.'

'Get me a towel or something.'

'No.' I just want her to go more than anything, ever. 'I can't. I don't want to. You'd better just go home.' I can feel the headache growing like the start of the drop on the big rollercoaster at Six Flags. I push my hand against my forehead trying to stop it coming. I feel nauseous.

She stands up and brushes off her legs with her hands.

What will it take to get her to go? I imagine using the hose to hose her right out of my life. Down the drain. I swap hands on my head and point at the smashed-up flowers. The pink and red colours are garish and grotesque as they appear and disappear. 'You'd better just go home,' I repeat. 'Go home. I'm going to be sick,' I say. I go over to the flower bed and try to throw up.

'You are so gross. You're so, so weird,' she repeats. 'I'm outta here.'

When Carmela has gone, I head straight back into the cool of the house. The air-conditioning is soothing. I lie down on my back in the den. I lie perfectly still and feel the ache behind my right eye slide out and fill my vision like *Fantasia*. In the dark, lying down, my head doesn't hurt so much. The jagged colours swarm, collide, dance and stab at me behind my right eye; I have never imagined such beautifully clear colours. They are now vibrant pink and yellow and blue, all of them in triangles and tiny squares. They mix and spread in my head like melting Crayola between pieces of tracing paper when you've applied an iron.

I don't know how much time passes before Mom comes home. I hear the shopping bags come into the room. I cannot open my eyes. 'What are you doing in here?' she asks.

'Headache and colours. The colours hurt.'

She gets me some aspirin and sits down next to me and strokes my feet until I go to sleep.

The next day, Mom arranges a physical with Dr Freddy. Dr Freddy is a children's doctor and at his office there is a whole wall full of pictures of sick kids that he has helped. There are so many that they overlap now and I feel sorry for the kids underneath that are buried under other, newer kids. Even some of the pictures that are on top – in the corners especially – look old and faded. Those kids might be all grown-up now, maybe with kids of their own who they take to another doctor, or they've moved out of state. And some of them, the Polaroids, aren't old, but are fading anyway. The kids are disappearing. Mom said that she would give Dr Freddy's office a picture of me to go up, but she never got round to it – so *I* am not sitting there with big bug eyes and gangly arms looking down on the other kids in the waiting room.

Some of the kids on the wall, though, are not alive any more. The receptionist puts a tiny yellow halo on the picture if any of the kids die. I watched her do it once when we were here. I guess their moms and dads aren't going to call in here again to complain and ask for the picture of the sick kid back, are they? You can see a few yellow halos sticking out from the deepest pictures.

It's busy today. When we finally get called through, I have to take off my clothes down to my underpants to wait. The nurse puts a thermometer in my mouth and then she weighs and measures me. She pokes me in the stomach with her cold finger. 'My, my,' she says as she pulls out the thermometer with her other hand and looks at it. 'You *are* growing up.' She says this like she knows me, but I'm sure she wasn't here last time we came.

Dr Freddy is bald with thick glasses. His white coat has his name in cursive embroidery over his top pocket. Red letters. It's not his real name, which is long and unfriendly. It says his kiddy doctor name: Dr Freddy. Since last time we were here, last year, someone has embroidered a yellow happy face after his name. Dr Freddy himself does smile a lot.

'So, you just graduated sixth grade, huh?' he says to me.

'Yes, sir,'

'My little baby all grown up,' Mom says. 'Seventh grade in September.'

'So, any problems?' he asks. His eyes are big through his glasses and sort of watery, like a creature who spends a lot of time in water, but not underwater particularly, maybe a hippopotamus.

'Headaches. I get migraine. I think she's getting migraine.'

'And stomach aches,' I add.

'Periods?'

I'm not sure who he's asking so I wait for Mom to answer.

'Not yet.'

'Not yet,' I repeat because I guess I could have spoken up. Maybe I should have answered. I don't want him to think I don't know what a period is. I try to sound both disappointed and hopeful but, instead, my voice sounds stupid and squeaky.

'Well, I'd guess they're right around the corner. But there's time … for these things,' he says. 'Have you got any friends?'

'I guess,' I say. I think of Carmela who is my best friend. I think I am her best friend too.

'She's got a couple of friends,' Mom says.

'Okay, then.' He takes the stethoscope that's over his shoulders and puts the ends in his ears and the other bit on to my chest. 'Breathe in … Breathe out … Again …' Then he feels my neck and under my jaw with his fingers. His hands feel warm and soothing. He pats me on the top of the head and tells me to stand up. I have to stand on my tiptoes, then on one leg, then the other. Then he suddenly pulls my underpants away from my stomach and peers down them. Just as quickly, he snaps them back.

Back on the examination couch again, I lie down and he prods my stomach and asks if it hurts. It doesn't. He asks Mom if I go to the bathroom regularly, and me if I have any problems when I urinate. She says yes, I say no.

Now I sit up and he tells me to pass my glasses to Mom. 'Watch my finger,' he says. He leans in close and moves his forefinger from side to side, then to his nose and over to mine. It makes me cross-eyed and he grins.

'Okay,' he says. 'Your periods will start pretty soon. Migraine onset now is typical.' He points. 'Your chest is sprouting. You'll need a bra very soon; maybe get one before you start back to school ... There are other signs. He points now to my underpants, to my new pubic hair. 'Aspirin for the headaches, and rest. Dark rooms. Do well in school. Plenty of time to make lots of friends,' he says to me. 'Take her shopping,' he says to Mom. 'Get things ready.'

It's the end of the summer now and we are at Carmela's house for a meal. The house is big, and dark. Lots of dark wood panelling. Rugs, not carpets. You can hear footsteps but don't know where they're coming from. Mrs Marino seems okay. She yells a lot, everywhere, but not at me, and she also smiles a lot. Today she said she likes my hair. It's taken ages to grow out, but I'm pleased with how it is now. It's nearly to my shoulders and I got bangs cut in yesterday, all ready for school, which begins next week.

I've also got new shoes, two new skirts, four new turtlenecks and two bras. I think about the first day, Monday, almost every morning: if this was day one, what would I wear? What if I get my period at school?

The school board is set to discuss whether or not girls can wear pants. Maybe even jeans. In the winter, last year, some of the girls wore them under their dresses and skirts and left them on when they got to school and no one said anything. Mom says that's because the stupid rule is that girls must wear skirts or dresses, not that they can't wear anything else as well. The jeans under the dresses looked dumb, but I bet the girls wearing them were warmer when it got real cold outside. Mom told Dad she wants to get involved and make a stand. She's going along to the PTA to say something. I'm not sure how I feel about that. She probably won't remember anyway.

It's nearly seven o'clock. The table is not set, but Carmela tells me to sit down. She says dinner will be coming out soon. Her mom is in the kitchen clanking around cooking. But when I go to sit on the first chair, she says, 'No, not there. That's Tony's seat.' The next one along is Joey's, and Frank's and Marco's. Her seat is around the other side. In the end Carmela pulls up another chair for me and squeezes it between where Tony and Joey will be sitting.

I realise I want to use the bathroom but, now that I'm sitting down, I'm too embarrassed to ask where that is.

When Mrs Marino comes in, her face is wet – either with perspiration or steam. Through the open door it looks like the whole kitchen is full of fog. She's carrying a large bowl full of plain noodles, some of them are dribbling over the edges. 'Sauce, Carmela,' she says, and Carmela jumps up and goes to get it. She brings another big bowl and a ladle to the table.

Using some special utensil I've never seen before, Carmela's mother puts scoops of spaghetti on to plates as the family arrive. Then on to each plate she ladles the meat sauce. She hands out the plates like the cafeteria ladies at school. No one except me says thank you. 'I love spaghetti,' I say.

'It's vermicelli,' Carmela says.

Carmela's brothers are all older than her. They appear big and nearly men – with lots of black hair and tanned faces. I think they all look like Joe Namath, another one of Carmela's crushes. I wonder if Carmela has thought about that, but that would be gross. I won't mention it.

Neither Tony nor Joey acknowledges me even though my chair is between them. They have to put a leg over their respective seats and wedge themselves in. Either side of me male elbows encroach on my space. No one eats despite the steaming full plates.

Then Carmela's father strides in. I've never seen him before. Mr Marino sits at the head of the table and everyone copies as he puts his hands together to pray. Except me, of course. I've never done that.

Unfortunately he notices. 'What are you?' he says to me, then to Carmela. 'Some fucking atheist you've brought home?'

I freeze. I think we are Episcopalian.

'Leave the girl alone! Can't you see your sons are hungry,' Mrs Marino shouts at him.

'Don't you tell me what to do.' He stands up to yell back at her with his knuckles on the table like the gorilla at the zoo.

Carmela's mother says, 'Sit down; you're frightening her. She comes from a civilised family.'

I don't know what to do. To be polite, I shake my head to deny that my family is any more civilised than this one, but what I am thinking is exactly the opposite.

Now Mr Marino speaks directly to me. 'For your information, my wife,' he says, 'is a very religious woman and she successfully imposes it upon all of us.' He clasps his hands again and everyone falls silent. Tony nudges me and I copy the others.

'Heavenly father, Lord Jesus, Blessed mother of God and all the angels in Heaven, and all the saints in heaven...' he starts. I imagine a crowd of winged creatures looking down on us around the table, as if we were specimens under a glass dome. But just as soon as he's begun he's finishing. He says, 'Anyway, bless us as we eat this food today,' and everyone picks up forks and spoons.

There is the sound of slurping all around the table. I try to catch a piece of the stringy pasta using my fork, but it keeps sliding off. I watch Carmela, opposite me, suck up the strips dangling from her closed mouth. A trail of sauce is on her chin. Her brother next to me twirls his fork against his spoon until it makes a manageable glob and then he sticks it in his mouth.

I'm not hungry. I really wish I were at home.

'So, tell us about yourself, mysterious atheist.' Carmela's dad pours himself a huge glass of red wine from the bottle on the table.

'I said leave the girl alone,' Mrs Marino says.

'Have you got something to hide? Crackpot politics perhaps? Women's Lib? Where did your parents stand on Amendment 26? Important decision. Will you be ready to vote in seven years?' He rattles out the questions at me without break. I have no idea how to answer but I reckon I should be able to learn how to use a voting machine when my time comes to vote so I tilt my head slightly and thoughtfully and then I nod, just a bit.

'This kind of stuff will ruin America. Watch my words.' He taps his forehead with the back of his fork, leaving bits of spaghetti sauce scattered around his face which he wipes off with the table napkin.

When she clears the plates Mrs Marino is kind enough not to point out that I've hardly eaten any of the pasta. It's all rubbery and stuck together in one glutinous mass, with the greasy sauce glistening away on top. Everyone else's plate is empty. 'Thank you,' I say. 'It was a very nice meal. Delicious.'

School starts and, not only does Mom want to get involved in the pants versus skirts debate, she wants to run for the PTA. I don't want my mom within a million miles of my school but she says she needs to do this. She doesn't care if she's the president or the treasurer, she wants to get right in there and be involved because we can't always sit on the sidelines with everything. Dad said he'd rather she be involved with getting the house straight and making a decent meal, but she told him that if he acted more like a man, maybe she'd act more like a woman. We are both going to the Start of School Year meeting. She will put her hand up and find out if anyone seconds her and then there will be a vote.

When she comes downstairs, at first I am relieved. At least she's not wearing that red pantsuit. She thinks she should dress like Mary Tyler Moore, but Mom is short and a size 12. But then I realise that things are not good. She's not wearing a bra. Her breasts are too big and are just hanging there, obviously braless. I can't exactly see her nipples through the material, but I don't want to look too hard because then I probably will and, if I can, other people will be able to as well. I notice that the plaid skirt she's wearing is way too short for anyone over thirty. Her legs are like carrots. She has thin ankles and broad round thighs, which are dimply at the back, and when we get in the car I notice that she's forgotten to do her make-up. Her face without make-up looks so ordinary and – I don't know – poor, I guess.

She drives too slowly, in silence, which means she's mad.

If we're late, everyone will see us come in, but I can't say anything because when she's in this kind of mood it's best to just sit quietly and wait until it goes away. Sometimes, though, she can be jollied out of it if I show some interest in *her*. So I ask, in a normal voice, 'How was your women's group?'

'Interesting,' she replies, sounding suspicious. 'Very interesting.' And then she goes quiet again. We're now going slower – we're doing twenty miles an hour. There's a line of cars forming behind us.

'What did you talk about?'

'Consciousness-raising.'

'Is it all Women's Lib or do you do any beauty stuff, or Tupperware? Avon?'

'Avon?' It's as if I've asked if they crap on the floor. 'No, we don't do Avon.'

'Paint Me Wonderful? Carmela's mom was telling me about that. She says she thinks my best colours would be indigo and moss.'

'Moss, huh?' Mom says. 'Green looks shit on everyone.' Only two months ago, she wouldn't have said anything like that.

'Is there a lot of cussing in the group?'

'No.'

'So, do you talk about your husbands? Or books?'

'Sometimes books.'

'Can I come?'

The traffic light ahead is green and we could get through, but we're going so slow, by the time we approach it it's turned orange and then red. She stops. 'No.'

For a moment I think she's going to just come out and say it: that her life with this group, the stuff she does now, is more important than us. She spends more time with other women raising themselves than being at home changing the sheets every third day (which she used to do, and which was my best smell and sensation in the world – clean fresh starched sheets – and which we have no more). Now our home is dusty and the bedclothes all warm and crinkled and Dad is right, we never get a decent meal any more. It's all TV dinners since she decided to liberate herself – from what, I'd like to know? She hasn't exactly been in prison.

I think she might as well just come out and own up to the fact that she doesn't want to be my mom any more, or Dad's wife, but she doesn't say this. She says, in a very calm voice, 'Today I looked at my own cervix. We all did. It's in the vagina. At the top.'

She is still not looking at me and I don't look at her, either. We're both looking at the red light.

'Oh,' I say, because what can you say to that? That this sounds like a good thing, for a bunch of moms to sit around looking at their own private parts? I think about how they would do that, but don't say anything.

'We used doctors' instruments and mirrors. Our bodies are nothing to be ashamed of.'

I don't want to think 'why' in case she tells me that she's turned into a lesbian. All her friends that I've met, looking up their insides, together. Mrs Brown, Diane's mother, goes to that group. Why can't Mom stick to the yoga? I try to think about yoga. Yoga. Yoga. I turn to look out the window. Yoga.

The fact is that my crazy mom wants to march into my school and ruin my life. I've got to do something. I grab my head, then clasp my stomach. 'My stomach hurts, Mom. I'm going to chuck.' And it works. Because I'm feeling sick, she lets me wait in the car when we get to school. This means I don't have to watch what happens with the election.

They don't appoint her. When she gets back in the car her mouth is fixed in a straight line, but I can tell she wants to cry. 'It's a humiliation. I should have known they'd never elect me,' she says. 'People like me don't win elections.'

Feeling sorry for your mom is not a good feeling.

On the second week of school, I have to go to the dentist. Not a kiddy dentist, but the one that Mom goes to. There are no *Highlights* magazines to read in the waiting room. It's all boring stuff. Mom thinks I might need braces. She talks about this in the car. She says that Dad will have to understand, that it's not the end of the world if I do. 'There's a lot of crowding in there, and we don't want crooked to set in, do we?'

'Why doesn't Dad like braces?'

'It's not that he doesn't like braces. Everyone likes braces. There's no reason to not like braces. That's not it,' she says.

'I don't want braces,' I say. 'I want to be cute.'

'Cute? Cute? Who wants to be cute? Women today have all sorts of choices. Cute is for babies and little kids, not for young women.'

'When do you think I'll get my period?'

'We'll have a women's party to celebrate when it arrives, like they do in other cultures. What do you think? Lots of my friends are doing that for their daughters.'

None of my classmates have mentioned anything like this. But then, my friends' mothers are not friends with my mine.

'I think that's a parking spot.' I add, 'Please, Mom, please don't tell the dentist about me and periods. Please don't tell Dad. Please let this one thing be private. Please.'

On the drive back, Mom is quiet. I've learned that I don't have to wear braces during the day; he says I'll get away with just a retainer at night to nudge my teeth into where they should be all the time. Actually it was kind of bad news, but it's better news than having to have a lot of wire in my mouth all the time. Dr Tromane explained there'll be something to wear over my head that I have to sleep in and elastic bands to tighten as we go along.

'Are you sure she doesn't need real braces?' Mom asked him, more than once, and he said that he thought not, that things were basically sound, just needing a bit of tweaking. Then he looked at her and, just as plain as that, asked had she thought about doing something about her receding teeth? He could give her a price. She said she'd have to think about it.

Come to think of it, though I don't *think* she's thinking about her teeth now, she might be worried about her teeth. Just in case, I need to take her mind off of it. I see a sign for a carpet store, 'Have you ever thought about our carpeting, Mom?'

'Carpeting?'

'We could put down rugs instead of the carpets. Maybe rugs. They provide a lot of colour.'

She laughs, and it's the kind of fake laugh that tells me that things are not going to go well, now. There is nothing I can say but I think hard for something positive to say when she suddenly says to the windshield, 'For the record, I love rugs. In my childhood a rug would have been wonderful, and carpets like we've got, well, they were just a pipe dream.'

She turns into the parking lot, which is empty. She parks the car over the line between two places and opens the door. I get out, but she doesn't. Instead of getting out, she is sitting with her legs out of the car. I come around the front of the car to her side. It's hot now without the air-conditioning of the car and the shade of the shop fronts is inviting. The sun is beating down on my back. 'Mom, are you thinking about your teeth? About what the dentist said. Don't worry about that. Your teeth are fine.'

'No, not really.' Her face, now that she doesn't wear make-up, looks like it's caving in. She does look very sad.

'Well, I'm really happy that I only need a night retainer. I won't complain. It'll be fine. Come on,' I say. 'Let's get us a praline and nuts, please. Double scoop? Pistachio? Fudge brownies? Rocky road? You love rocky road, Mom. Please.'

I feel desperate and helpless. I hate this. Finally, she gets up and takes my hand. I have to shut the door because she seems to have forgotten she's responsible for the car. We go inside, into the cool air and the wonderful smell. Rexall's drugstore is a mixture of perfumes and paper: books, notebooks, greeting cards, and ink.

We sit and order the ice-creams at the counter at the side of the shop. On hers the top scoop is rocky road – our very favourite – and she has pistachio on the bottom. I have rocky road and fudge brownie; fudge brownie is the top scoop on mine. Then she starts to talk, slowly. 'You see, honey – ' she licks the pistachio ice-cream as it begins to dribble down the cone ' – the thing is you have to decide what kind of a person you're going to be. We all do, and it's important not to get it wrong, even if sometimes you do at first. It sets a trajectory and it can take you in the wrong direction. I've wanted your dad to be someone he can't be and I've tried to give you a good life – better than the one I had. But I'm not the right sort of person either.' She pauses for a deep sigh. 'I've been lonely, I guess. That's all.'

'No, you're not. Come on, Mom,' I say. 'You've got me. It's okay.'

On the way out, we stop at the school supplies section. She doesn't hurry me. I choose four notebooks and a compass and a new pen set. 'I'm going to work hard,' I say. 'I'm going to get straight A's. You'll be real proud of me. Just you see.'

She smiles limply at me, like now she feels sorry for me; like I don't, or like I can't, understand anything.

1970

Baby Bird

Mom and I are working in the kitchen, making an angel food cake, and Dad is about to come home from work. I crack the eggs and roll the gloppy white from one half of the shell to the other before dropping the bright yellow yolk into the small bowl, for another time. The egg whites go into the mixing bowl. I whisk them by hand for a minute and she sets up the mixer and it whirrs into action. It vibrates and rocks on the table top and makes a mighty racket.

She shows me how to fold the flour and sugar into the whites by turning with the spatula gently over and over, then I take charge. She sits down at the table and lights a cigarette. I hear her inhale again, and on the next exhale she says it's ready: the batter can go into the cake pan.

Then I put it into the oven, and begin to wash up the utensils. A good cook cooks in a clean kitchen. I tell Mom about how by next week I'll have earned my cooking badge. We just need to do a one-pot meal and a snack, maybe Friday? I'm doing sour cream mixed with powdered onion soup for my snack, with chips. We could have that as an appetiser. She'd better include some cream of mushroom soup too when she gets the groceries; I'll need it for the base for my casserole. I explain that, as it happens, I am also working on my sewing badge. I'm already a competent swimmer so the swimming badge won't be too hard and I want to get that too by the summer.

'Well, chatterbox,' she says, 'can't you earn your sewing badge by sewing on your cooking badge yourself?'

'No way. It's way more than that. I have to make a whole item of clothing, like a half-slip – that's pretty easy – or maybe a skirt. You have to use the zipper foot for putting in a zip.'

'You'll zip through the zip,' she says and we both laugh.

Just as I finish putting the mixer away, Dad comes in. He asks what his two girls are doing and I say that we're making something de-e-e-licious for his dessert.

'Did you wash your hands?' he asks.

I ignore the question. This is the first thing you have to do when you're cooking. Then he tries to kiss Mom but she leans away. She walks past me to stub out her cigarette in the sink. I won't tell her that Mrs Palmer, our troop leader, says that smoking is a dirty habit.

Dad says he's sure I'm right, that it'll be very tasty, before he leaves us to watch the news. Mom finds the news too sad to watch and doesn't understand why he has to have it on while we have dinner. He said last week that he doesn't know why she's changed. 'Pot and kettle. Leopards and spots,' she said, and I don't know what either of them was trying to say.

In bed that night, before I turn my light off, I recite the oath: I will do my best to be honest and fair, friendly and helpful, considerate and caring, courageous and strong, and responsible for what I say and do, and to respect myself and others, respect authority, use resources wisely, make the world a better place, and be a sister to every Girl Scout.

I don't bother with making the salute, because I am holding the card, and also no one is watching. I have to check the words twice the first time, and only once the second. Unless I get the whole promise right all the way through I don't think the badges really count for much. A person is her values. If I don't even know what they are by heart – and Mrs Palmer says it's not 'by heart' by accident – what kind of junior Girl Scout will I be? I could be a troop leader one day if I work hard at it. I fall asleep wondering what it would be like to be in charge of people. I reckon I could do it.

In Home Economics on Tuesday afternoon. Miss Manning says a half-slip is the ideal project for those who are inexperienced dressmakers (which of course we all are; we're only kids). This is because it involves only seams, darts and hems. And, if you want to make it easier, then doing an elastic casing can substitute for darts. It will get me my badge and no one but Miss Manning would ever be interested in what it looks like at the end, unless I have to take it in for Mrs Palmer to examine. I hope not, because sloppy hemming could be my downfall. For some reason I find it difficult to make my stitches even in size; they always look uneven. Miss Manning said that my running stitch gallops at times. I'll have to watch that.

Miss Manning calls us to the front one at a time while everyone else looks on. For a full slip you measure waist, hips, nape to waist and bust. Our measurements are written down in four columns on the blackboard against our names. I have exactly no bust. That's what Miss Manning says, and she also says, 'You have a very mature face with that extraordinary nose, but a remarkably immature and short-waisted body.'

Then we spend an hour comparing our actual measurements with the pattern so that we can calculate adjustments. In order to get the sewing badge you are required to demonstrate an ability to adjust a pattern to personalise it, even if you don't actually have to make it. Miss Manning agrees a half-slip would be a good project for me. It might last me longer if I ever develop a figure.

'Only Dorothy Ellis in our class had a perfect body,' I tell Mom when I get home.

'What do you mean, "perfect body"?'

I explain how Dorothy Ellis's measurements matched the Butterick pattern exactly. That mine will always need a lot of adjustments because of my short-waistedness, and maybe another thing I'll have to think about is the type of hats I can wear, because of my nose.

Mom says that I am perfect, that I mustn't take any of it seriously, but I reply that I'm not worried. This is not a problem to me. Miss Manning was pleased with my ability to adjust the pattern. I've always been good at math. What I look like will not hold me back.

'Seems unfair that this Dorothy Ellis with her "perfect" body can get a badge for doing nothing.'

'It's just the luck of the genetic draw,' I say, which is what Miss Manning said when she reviewed our figures. 'She lucked out. Not her fault. You can't disqualify her. *That* would be unfair.'

But when Dad comes home Mom tells him that she's going to complain to the school board. 'Do you want your daughter to get a complex from her Home Economics class?'

'Things aren't perfect. She may well be short but she's fine.'

'It's not that I'm short,' I say. 'I just have a large nose and a short waist. It's how I'm made.' I point to the back of my neck and start to describe how the short waist refers to the measurement from the nape to my natural waistline, but he's not listening.

'The news is on,' he says.

'We are your family,' she says, 'She needs your support. You're supposed to be her father.'

But Dad has already left the room, heading to the TV.

After school Thursday Vanessa comes over to the house and we walk over to the swimming pool. Today I'm the one who's got gum. Sometimes it's her. Sometimes it's me. One of us always has gum. I pass her a piece, and lick the powdery surface before I pop the other stick into my mouth. It gives way and quickly becomes as soft as a melted marshmallow and sweet as sugar.

Vanessa is very good at blowing bubbles. One emerges now from her mouth like a pink balloon, eclipsing her face, covering her nose as well as all of her mouth until it pops with a sharp smacking sound. She sucks it back in fast and nothing is left on her face. I can't blow bubbles like that yet. I make tiny tentative bubbles with my tongue and pop them with a snap. Vanessa says I just need to practise a bit more.

It's May, but the weather is already hot. Even with my shoes on, I can feel the heat of the tarmac beneath us, and it makes me think about barefoot walking. Barefoot is for when school is out, when the rules vanish and every day is empty and hot and lazy. Cookouts and cold soda in the back yard.

I love swimming and this is the pool where I learned how. Dad showed me the jellyfish float first. I had to get used to having my face in the water and holding my breath. Then I learned back-float. Dad held me with one hand underneath my back until I stretched out and relaxed enough to let the water support me and then one day I floated right out of his hands. I couldn't change position to see his face, but I knew he was happy because he's a really good swimmer and wanted me to learn how to do it too. That was a long time ago now, but the back-float is a very useful thing to know. It's something you can do whenever you get tired of actually swimming. It's good for thinking.

Inside the swimming pool part of the Athletics Center the air is thick with humidity and even the high-ceilinged entrance has that stingy chlorine smell. We are members and I show my pass. I sign the book, putting a check mark in the box to say that Vanessa is my guest. As we go through to the changing room, I feel the moisture in the air worm its way into the ends of my long curly hair.

'Look at it.' I clutch a handful and wave it in Vanessa's direction.

Her mother is half Japanese and her hair does not frizz. Now, as she looks at mine, she blows a thoughtful bubble. 'It's very thick.'

'I'm thinking of cutting it. All off.'

She allows the bubble to expand to bursting. 'What if you look like a boy?'

'I don't care.'

We change into our swimsuits. I have to leave my glasses in the locker with our clothes. When we walk down the passage to the pool I'm blind as a bat. I'm used to it, but don't like it. I can't make out that Vanessa actually is Vanessa and I have to feel along the side of the wall. Once there, I can make out some moving fuzzy blobs, splashes of colour in the water. These are the other swimmers.

I get in fast and swim right to the deep end. The water is cool but not cold. Vanessa follows me. We mustn't get in the way of people doing laps, but we play Marco Polo. Some other kids join in. I don't even have to shut my eyes but I do, because otherwise someone might think I'm cheating.

Afterwards we go to her house and have peaches to eat. My legs and arms ache and I have that bleached-clean feeling from the pool. The fruit is fresh from the icebox and dense with cold and the fuzzy skin sets my teeth on edge. We talk about my hair again which hangs in heavy clumps onto my shoulders and back. 'When are you going to do it?' Vanessa asks.

'I don't know. Just some time soon.'

She puts down her half-eaten peach. 'How about now?' She gets up and begins to look closely at my hair, picking up strands, softly sweeping the dangling bits that lie on my cheeks and tucking them behind my ears.

'I think I don't want to do it today,' I say, feebly.

But Vanessa is already running to fetch the scissors, calling back, 'You said you wanted to do it. Lock the door. I forgot to lock the door when we came in. And take off those glasses.'

Friday morning, I wonder if Mom or Dad will notice I'm wearing one of Vanessa's mom's scarves at breakfast.

Mrs Stroming, our neighbour, was babysitting when I got home because Mom was sick. She said my mom had a bad head and she should be making an appointment to see the doctor soon, she should get someone to take a look at it as they're terrible, and that my dad had to go out, which is why he called her to come over, and did I want to eat something or watch TV with her or could she go along home now? I said she should go and I had two bowls of Cap'n Crunch and went up to my room to go to bed.

Mrs Stroming might be so old that she doesn't pay much attention to anything, but today Mom and Dad will find out what's happened to my hair. What Vanessa did to it is terrible, maybe worse since I slept on it. I look so ugly I don't ever want to go out of the house again.

I go as far as the kitchen door, just poking my face in. I listen to Mom telling Dad neighbourhood news, how there are plans for a big Fourth of July picnic in the park in a couple of months and that she's going to be responsible for organising games and put his name down now to do some of the cookout. She gets like this – all talky – after she's had one of her headaches. It's like she's got a new battery in her or something, but it doesn't last. Later she'll be crying and then tomorrow, maybe, she'll be normal. She's speaking while setting the percolator on the stove and he's concentrating on putting his tie on. I notice this because Dad hasn't worn a tie since we went to church at Christmas.

'I don't feel well,' I say. 'I can't go to school.'

Neither of them bothers to look in my direction, but Mom says, 'What's wrong?'

He says, 'I don't know how you can think about the Fourth of July. You want to play Leave it to Beaver when, in real life, the world is in revolution. Things are changing.' And then he's gone. He slams the door to the garage behind him and I can hear the car engine start up. He didn't even say goodbye.

I back out the door, saying, 'Stomach ache. I've got to stay in bed,' and go back up to my room, aware that I have broken the first promise and also promises seven, eight and nine, and even the last one, because I definitely hate Vanessa now.

I climb into my bed considering how my scouting career is over, and my school life is also over. I won't get my cooking badge because I can't even think about cooking now. I can't make the one-pot meal, or even the dip. And Mom will come up soon and take my temperature. I should pull the blankets up and get myself as hot as possible or else I'll have to go to school with this hair and everyone will laugh at me. The scarf idea is stupid. Who wears a scarf except someone wearing curlers? Maybe if I can just wait until Monday it won't be so bad. Hair grows fast. Maybe I could get a wig, or something.

I try to think about my problem and then think about how, when I was disappointed that we had to cancel Easter vacation because Mom can't stand Kenny and Jennifer, Dad said a broader perspective helps a person cope with personal setbacks. I think about the riots and the marches against the war. All the soldiers getting killed and the draft. Dad thinks about this stuff all the time and it's always on TV. I know that civilians are killed over there too, and that it's all wrong and that the President is an idiot.

I shouldn't be worrying about my hair. It'll grow back. There are more important things going on in the world. However, I'm still not feeling brave enough to go to school, so I get out of bed and put the scarf on then get back into bed, even more disappointed in myself. All I keep coming back to is my stupid hair, which is my own fault. My looks. I let this happen to me. I am so stupid.

I bury my head beneath the blankets when I hear Mom's footfall on the stairs. The door opens and she sits down on the bed. I mutter from beneath the blankets that Vanessa and I ate a punnet of peaches at her house yesterday, which is nearly true. 'I feel real sick,' I say. 'I might chuck up.'

'Sit up instead.'

I obey, and she yanks the scarf right off my head.

'Vanessa did it.'

'Why?'

'I let her. I didn't want that hair any more. It was frizzy and ugly.'

'It was a feature. You've always had that hair.' I didn't know that she thought anything about my hair. Mom is not angry, she just looks sad. 'Are you sick as well?'

I shake my head. 'No, it's just the hair thing.'

'I guess nothing lasts forever.' Her voice is wobbling.

I don't want her to cry. 'I didn't want to be features. I want to be normal. It'll grow back, Mom.'

'Well, we can't leave it like this. Come downstairs,' she says. She phones Maurice, her hairdresser, and makes an appointment for eleven o'clock. He has just *got* to repair my haircut. I hear her tell him on the phone what's happened. 'A game gone wrong,' she says. 'These kids do such stupid things. They don't understand consequence. She was so beautiful and now she looks like some bald baby bird or something.'

I stare at my face in the mirror after she says this. I never saw the beautiful and I don't see the bald bird. It's not *that* short. I'm not *bald*.

Maurice does frosting and sets. I don't think I've ever seen a kid in there actually in one of the seats to get her hair done, though there are usually three or four of us waiting on our moms. It'll be a bus ride up town.

Mom is quiet for all of the journey. She has let me wear a baseball cap and now she holds my hand tight even though

I'm way too old for that. She just holds my hand and looks out the window. She sighs a whole lot.

Maurice is excited about some riot that happened last night. For a grown man, he does look silly waving his hands around so much. He falls upon Mom when we arrive, with his phony accent, and goes on about what might happen next. Dad always says about Maurice that he is probably Canadian and a crackpot, even though I don't think he even knows him.

Anyway, when we get inside, Maurice completely ignores me and my dreadful hair, which is still hidden under the cap. If Dad wants to worry about something, it's Maurice and how he kisses Mom and touches her back all the time and how they laugh together. She goes all giggly and he is all over her. Her mood is all gone in minutes. Then, finally, Maurice turns to me and demands that I remove the hat.

'Ça alors!' He pretends to faint. 'How could such a catastrophe happen?' One of the girls behind the till sniggers loudly. Maybe it's about the state of my hair, or maybe she, like me, just thinks the fake-Frenchy speech and behaviour is big-time dumb.

Mom, holding my glasses, settles down with a magazine and he ushers me to the basin. A girl washes my hair twice and I'm led back to the big chair in front of all the mirrors and Maurice, behind me, sets about his work. When he's finished drying it and Mom comes over to hand me back my glasses I see that I have the kind of haircut that I have always wanted if only I knew it existed. My hair looks now like it belongs in a magazine. I look like I belong in a magazine. In the mirror I watch my hand touch it, just checking that it's real, that this is not a wig.

'It's terrific. Don't you look fabulous?' Mom says. 'You are a saviour, Maurice.'

Maurice has an expression on his face that tells me that he knows lots of people think he's wonderful. 'It's a simple cut, feathered. *Très chic*,' he says, to the hair in the mirror, then smiling at Mom.

It's short but it doesn't look like any kind of bird.

When we finally get on the bus for the trip home I feel very happy. When Mom asks for one adult and one kid's ticket, the bus driver asks me how old I am. I explain that I might look like I have to pay for an adult ticket, but that is because of my new haircut. While a line forms behind us, he admires my hair and says, 'Well, it sure is pretty, missy.'

We stop at the market and pick up the ingredients for a casserole and the dip. At home I start work on the meal. It's been a very productive day.

When Dad gets home the first thing he notices is my hair. 'How about that! What happened?'

'That was Maurice,' Mom says. 'This morning.'

'On a school day?'

'On a school day,' she replies.

Before dinner I serve the appetiser and practise reciting the pledge, with Mom and Dad as the audience. I throw in the Pledge of Allegiance, which I've got down pat, like a warm-up into the Girl Scout promise.

Dad seems to be listening, they both do, but then he suddenly asks Mom, 'Should we encourage this? What is it with militaristic organisations and young people?'

'I might ask what is it with *you* and young people right now? You think growing your hair, wearing blue jeans and spending time with twenty-year-olds makes you twenty again?'

We eat at the kitchen table in silence. No one says it's good, but the meal *is* pretty good for a change, and then Dad

goes to watch TV. After a while he comes back and orders
Mom through from the kitchen to watch the news with him.
He tells her she can't avoid it forever. Even though I am too
big, she pulls me on to her lap when she sits down. The news
is all about the riot last night. Not far away from our home.
'Surely you – ' he is talking to Mom though he's looking at
the two of us on the chair together ' – want to be informed.
Or do you really not care about what happens anywhere but
inside this house?'

'I care plenty. I'm not as ignorant as you seem to think.
I know plenty about what's going on. I know what I care
about and where my responsibilities are.'

He doesn't reply, but we stay there in the same room
until my bedtime. I'm tired. I'm excited about taking my hair
to school on Monday, and that's what I am thinking about
when I fall asleep.

One month later Mrs Palmer issues the troop the earned
badges. I collect three: for cooking, sewing and swimming.
Mom helps pin them on to my green sash. Then I quickly
tack each of them down with a basting stitch and use a
careful overcast stitch to secure them properly.

I model the uniform and completed sash together and
Dad agrees with Mom that it looks like professional work.
'You could be a seamstress,' he says.

'Or a troop leader.' I make the salute.

Dad says, 'Or even President?'

'Maybe.' I laugh and feel very happy about Dad saying
that. 'But no one likes him.' I'm also thinking that I'm a
girl. There's never been a Mrs President. Who would do the
cooking and who would take care of the kids?

Mom says to Dad, 'You think we'd ever have a woman
president?'

Her new pills are working; she's not so angry and sad all the time and the long, hot summer has already begun. It stretches out before us now in a sigh. I will wear just cut-offs and T-shirts over my swimsuit and dry in the sun after running through the hosepipe to cool off. I can see the yard sales, hear the lawnmowers of the morning, the cicadas of the afternoon, the sound of ice cubes in glasses, taste the fizz of soda-pop in my mouth. I will peel the satisfying papery layers of sunburnt skin from my shoulders in the evening. I'll always be friends with Vanessa, forever and ever.

Summer makes the grass grow fast. It is stubble, then prickles up against the soles of my bare feet.

This is how I feel time passing. My own hair relentlessly wilts longer and longer until I have to brush it away from my eyes again and it begins to tickle against my neck. We go on vacation out west. Dad's brother, my Uncle Pete, lives there and he's really nice when we visit. I can see he and Dad don't get on well, but Mom makes everyone laugh and we're only there for a day.

The Grand Canyon is amazing and too big to understand – impossible to look at all at once. You have to choose chunks of it and focus on that and then refocus somewhere else. It's so bright it hurts my eyes to pay attention. I look without my glasses and for some reason this feels safer, like I won't fall into this massive hole and be lost forever.

When we get home Mom makes an appointment for me to see Maurice again. He decides to cut bangs into my hair and I look different again for a while, and suddenly I'm getting a new lock for my locker, choosing fresh school supplies at the drugstore and going with Mom to buy all new clothes from J.C. Penneys. There is the excitement of trying them on and then hanging them up carefully in my closet when we get home, imagining all the combinations I can wear.

The leaves turn red and brown and the morning air is cool when I'm standing alone waiting for the bus the first day, nervous and eager at the same time to see my friends again. I hope that the bus is not already so full that I will have to walk all the way to the back to sit next to someone I don't know. I hope too that my new schedule and home-room means I can easily get to classes on time.

The bus finally arrives and there is the swish of the doors as they open. I climb up the steps. The new driver nods as I tell him my name. A few kids say hi as I begin to walk down the aisle. It's really noisy and then I spot Vanessa halfway along and see that she's saved a seat for me with her books. She lifts them up so that I can sit down next to her. It's good having a friend.

The bus starts up.

1969

The Wattle

The pumpkin outfit has been transformed by brown dye applied in speckles. My leotard and tights as well. A few feathers are stuck on to the body of the costume, to suggest lots of feathers. I have a pink swimming cap on and Mom is now attaching a semi-inflated plastic pink glove, with a hairband, under my chin – which is to be the wattle.

This wattle is my idea. Although it is ugly, it is a realistic feature of turkeys. I've got a thin beak to put on as well, but will save this for when we get to the Thanksgiving party, as when I wear it I feel that I can't really breathe.

Dad comes down the stairs and looks through the door. 'What do you reckon?' Mom says. She jumps up from kneeling. She grabs the beak and puts it over my face to complete the look.

'You are absolutely the cutest turkey I have ever seen,' he says, 'And you have the most determined mother in the world,' he adds. 'Nothing has ever stopped your mother once she wants to do something.'

I pull aside the beak. 'It's not about being a cartoon turkey,' I say. 'Does it look *real*? I want to look like a real one.'

Mom says, 'I bet you'll win.'

'If I've done my best, I don't care about winning. That's what Mrs Skinner says is the right attitude.'

'How're you planning to get this amazing bird to the party?'

'Same as Hallowe'en. She'll lie down on the back seat. It's fine. No sweat.'

It is the fifteenth of December when I am sent home from school because I fail the eye test. The nurse phones home and tells Mom she has to pick me up. Then she gives me a sealed note to pass to the doctor when we see him. She says they are expecting me at the Children's Hospital.

On the way back from the doctor's office, we stop at the mall. From the last week until Christmas Eve, Santa is scheduled to sit smack in the centre of the four concourses and we're going to see him while I'm not at school and all the other kids are. Information-gathering, Mom calls it, this talking to all the children. 'He's making sure he's got his lists right.'

Mom reckons I could do with something to perk me up now that I am going to have to wear glasses. I'm still thinking about the consequences of the visit. Following the technician's advice, I've chosen sparkly frames. 'If you have to wear them, make them a feature,' the woman said.

I have accepted that this means I am going to be ugly forever. This is who I am going to be.

The snow is deep and most of the parking lot hasn't yet been ploughed. We find a space that used to be a handicapped space, near the entrance. You can't read the sign any more. Mom says that makes it exempt, that today anyone can park anywhere.

'Where does he get all the stuff from?' When I speak, my breath puffs into a little cloud in front of my face, and when I draw in air it feels like a shock to my insides.

'That's why they give him the prime location, so he shops here,' Mom says.

Santa's sleigh is empty when we get to it. It is huge. Mom says that maybe there's a problem with Rudolph; she thinks she heard something on the news in the morning while I was at school. 'He's probably taken him to the vet for an overhaul before the big day.'

'So, who pays for the presents?' I ask.

'The government. Taxes. Which is why, if you earn a lot, Santa has got more money and your kids get better presents. There's a whole heap of book-keeping involved.'

'I'd like to be a reindeer,' I say. 'Instead of a candy cane.' This is for the Christmas party.

'A candy cane is more cheerful. A reindeer is huge. A lot of work involved.'

'I don't want it to be like the turkey. I want to be like the other kids. I guess I could be an elf?'

'The wattle was a great idea.'

'It was dumb,' I say. 'No one got it. I looked stupid. I felt stupid, Mom. People laughed at me. I've got to be inedible for the Christmas party. Something not so original, I think.'

She laughs and hugs me. 'You've always been good enough to eat; you can never be inedible.'

'When I have my glasses, if I get eaten by a lion, I will crunch.'

Santa phones the house that evening, before I go to bed. I answer the phone and am very surprised when he knows my name. He says he hasn't yet had my requests for presents, and he needs them to complete his list.

'You weren't at the mall this afternoon,' I say.

'So, what do you want?'

I'm trying to listen to him and think but Mom is trying to get my attention. 'Shush,' I hiss, finger over my mouth, just like she would if she were talking to someone very important. I tell Santa I want a Schwinn bike, in yellow or pink, and a stamping set with rubber stamps and ink. He can find the set in the big Walgreens store, behind the puzzles and games. He'll have to go to the bike store for the bicycle.

'Have you been good?'

'Pretty much. Not too bad.'

'Be sure and go to bed on time on Christmas Eve. I can't drop by unless you're asleep.'

I tell him that I know this and that I will, and thank him for phoning, he must be very busy, but he says he wants to do the job right.

Mom asks me to repeat word for word what he said when I hang up and says she never, ever had a phone call from Santa herself. 'Your friends at school will be impressed.'

I'm not going to tell anyone at school about the conversation. I'm too old for Santa. A lot of the class don't even believe in him, but I can't tell Mom about that. 'I know it's not the real Santa,' I tell Mom, 'that sits in the mall.'

'No, of course not. It can't be him. It's his representative, like a babysitter when we go out.'

'So, is there a real Santa?' I ask.

'Who was on the phone?'

'Santa.'

'Well, then,' she says.

There are pink hearts, yellow moons, orange stars and green clovers in my bowl of Lucky Charms. It's the sort of food Christmas elves might eat. I save the crunchy pink hearts for last but the milk fades the colour. Mommy is having coffee and fidgeting with her cigarette. Daddy is having a bagel.

It's the day of the Christmas party at school and I will be the best ever elf, with stick-on ears and a green leotard, with a red skirt that Mom made for me, over it. Karen Zuckerman is an elf too, so when we get to school we get to sit together. No one laughs at us. No one points.

After the success of the party, Mom takes me after school to get my new glasses. I take off the fake pointy ears but I'm still wearing the elf outfit. No one seems to notice. Mom doesn't say anything about it either. If I'd been a candy cane, she'd have to explain to the receptionist, and I wouldn't have my hands. An elf isn't *very* unusual but I don't think they really exist.

I'm in the middle of telling Mom what I've been thinking about this when the nurse calls us through into the dark room.

I have to sit in the chair that's like a throne, again. This time to let him measure how much I can see with them on. He comes up close with his light, shines it in my eyes, then adjusts the arms and the nosepiece to fit my face better. 'There now,' he says. Then he fetches a hand mirror. He switches on the lights and hands me the mirror to look at myself wearing glasses. I don't know what to decide about how I look because, even though I know it's me behind the glasses, I look different. I'm not the same me as before.

'What do you think?' he asks.

'It's okay.'

Mom is sitting in the corner of the room. She calls over that I look like the brain of my class. She doesn't seem to see that I'm someone entirely different from when we walked in.

When we get outside I look up at the trees and buildings around and see things I have never seen before. There are thousands of leaves in the trees and hundreds of windows in the buildings. It's very cold and I want to get across the road into the car, but everything looks so new and complicated, I can't stop looking.

I like this feeling, but there is so much to see, it's a bit scary. When we get in the car I tell Mom that I can't wear glasses all the time because I am seeing too much. She says she understands, that I can get used to them over the holidays.

When Christmas Eve arrives I know that I have to go to bed on time, but it's very hard to do because I feel bubbly inside. There's an announcement at six o'clock on the news, that an unidentified flying object has been spotted heading south from the Canadian border. Then some new man comes on and says they've identified the UFO – it's Santa's sleigh.

At this the bubbliness gets bigger inside me. He's on his way.

'Do you have to be asleep before Santa gets to us too?' I ask Dad.

He's not sure, tells me to go in the kitchen and ask Mom. She's not sure either, but she says to be on the safe side, they'll go to bed early too. I relay this news to Dad.

I am awake when Santa arrives in the night. I hear the bells of the reindeer harness right outside the window, and, even though I am not asleep, I pretend to be and keep my eyes tightly shut. I hear footsteps downstairs and then a door shutting. Finally, the bells start up again with the movement of the reindeers lifting off. I get up out of bed and go to the window. I poke my head out between the drapes.

The moon is bright and reflecting off the thick layer of snow. The sleigh is already in the sky. It's still climbing higher, just clearing the trees at the edge of the Jacksons' back yard. Then it turns right and I can see the reindeer, stretched out in a line, with Rudolph in front, his red nose flashing and Santa in the back with his bags of presents.

I want to open the window and shout, 'Hey!' but this would let him know I am awake which is not allowed, so I go back to bed and try to sleep.

In the morning I am awake before Mom and Dad. Downstairs there are sparkly footprints from the fireplace to the tree and my new bike is underneath with a ribbon on it. I fetch my glasses from where I put them next to my bed. Once I've got them on, I look at the bike again, carefully. Wearing the glasses makes the pink brighter and the chrome shinier. It has a bell and a basket and it is just exactly what I wanted.

Because of all the snow, I can only ride it in the kitchen, and not properly because there is not enough room.

'It's the kind of thing Santa doesn't think about,' Dad says. 'The practicalities of particular presents. And this mess. The floor ...'

'There's always the mall,' Mom says. 'She can ride there. And meantime,' she says to me, 'you can play with the stamping set. Did he leave that?'

'Probably,' Dad says. 'I bet he did.' And it is there; I find it at the back of the tree.

That night, Dad carries the bike upstairs to stand in the corner of my bedroom. If I wake up in the night, I will see it there, and it will be there in the morning, waiting for me, whenever I open my eyes.

Perfect.

1968

Wonder Woman

The bed is shaking. I push the button for the nurse to come,
like my mommy said I should if I need anything.

'The bed is shaking,' I tell the nurse when she finally
turns up. 'I don't like it.'

'It's not shaking.'

'My stomach hurts.'

'See this here clock?' She turns to point; it's above her
head on the wall. In fact, everyone who comes in here stands
right under the clock to look at me. I can't read the time. It's
too far away. 'When it's ten o'clock you can have another

shot. Now you have to wait.' Then she takes the button from my hand and slings it over the rails at the back of my head, where I can't reach it, even if I have a problem. 'Try to sleep,' she says.

'What about the bed shaking?'

'There's nothing wrong. It's your condition. Your mom will be back in a minute; she's just gone to fetch a coffee. Be a big girl, now.'

'I'll tell her about the bed when she gets back.'

'You just do that, honey.'

It is eight o'clock. It's dark. The lights in the hall outside the room are bright, but there's no light on in here.

When my daddy left he said, 'Honey, it's tough but you're going to need to man up to this.' And Mommy said, 'Shall I remind you that your daughter is an eight-year-old girl?' That was right after the operation and she was still angry with him because in the morning when Dr Leonard said I needed the operation she tried to phone him but no one could tell her where he was. She told me she knew exactly where he was and who he was with, but couldn't prove it.

The bed is shaking in judders. The water in the jug on the cabinet beside me sloshes back and forth.

Mommy doesn't come back until nine o'clock. She gets them to give me a shot straight away, even though I'm supposed to wait.

This is the shot: it stings for two seconds then it's feels like a long, slow sigh or uncurling fists. My fingers grow longer and my legs grow lighter. I feel I am growing my own wings and can fly. After ten minutes, I shut my eyes and float high above me on the bed, out of the room, beyond what I can see now. Then I zoom down on to parks, and up from swings back into the sky. Then I am not zooming but sort of zinging in the clouds for a while. After a while I come back to this bed and feel that cool, smooth, melting-ice-cream-on-my-tongue feeling from the sheets, followed by the slippery before-you-fall-asleep feeling.

And then I get the feeling that I am just a little kid again, tiny as anything and happy just to sit on my mommy's lap. Still and sleepy and nothing else.

The night nurse is a short fat black lady with a shape like the Pillsbury Doughboy. I like her because she's smiley. She's so fat I wake to hear the sound of her stockings rubbing together as she crosses the room. She tells me it's three-thirty. I can see the water in my glass shimmering with movement, and the bed is definitely shaking. I tell her this.

There are bars up on both sides of the bed to stop me from falling or getting out. She puts her hand on the metal. 'No, it's not. I can't feel any shaking, honey.'

'But I know it is.' I feel like flour being sieved: up and down, side to side. 'Where's my mommy?' I give the nurse a big smile and hold it on my face even though I am suddenly feeling really scared.

'She can't be here all the time, baby.' She checks the tubes and bags, picks up the chart from the bottom of my bed. 'Are you hurting? Maybe that's the problem?'

'A bit,' I say, still smiling. 'I'm thirsty too.'

'I can just give you a little something to help the pain, but this drip,' she points to the stuff hanging above me, 'means you can't be needing a drink. I'll get hold of some ice chips, you can suck on some of those.'

Mommy is back very soon, before the nurse returns with the shot. I tell her about how the bed has been shaking. Not all the time, but just now and then. She says that maybe it's just being in this place. It could drive a person crazy and we're way up high. It's pretty unnatural. I say, 'Well, one of the nurses is getting me a shot.'

'That sounds like it'd be a good idea. Might help you sleep.'

'Yes. The shots help a lot. I really like the shots. The needle doesn't even hurt.'

Then she tells me that Daddy is going to come in the morning before he goes to work, and that she's going to sleep right here with me, on a rollaway bed that they are fetching for her. She says, 'I can't leave you here alone. Someone's got to keep an eye on you.' This gets me back to worrying again about what she said in the emergency room before they took me for the operation. I asked Mommy what was going to happen next and she said, 'I've told them we'll sue if anything goes wrong. These people are less likely to kill a patient if they know there will be repercussions if they do.'

'Am I going to die?'

'No. That's what I'm telling you. It's not going to happen. No one is going to die, I promise you. Not on my watch.'

Then she went to get a coffee and to try to phone Daddy again and while she was out they sneaked me out to have the whole thing done before she could come back. I don't know what she thought about what they did, but it happened. They just put me to sleep and then I woke up in this room with Mommy next to the bed and the operation had been done and I was still alive even though she wasn't watching.

Daddy did finally turn up about an hour after I woke up from the operation. He was all wrapped up with a hat, scarf and gloves, which surprised me because it's so warm in here – more like summer – that I'd forgotten that it was November outside when we came in. He said the view from the window was amazing. We are real high up and everyone says this the first time they come in, that the people and cars down below look like ants and toys. Aren't you lucky to have such a great view of the city? Daddy asked.

I nodded. I don't say to anyone that the view is for people who aren't stuck in this bed and I haven't been out of it. If I turn my head, all I can see is the sky. It's like the rest of the world doesn't exist any more, but none of them can understand that because they can look down and enjoy seeing things.

Mommy wouldn't look at him then because it had taken an age to find him. Then he had said the 'man up' thing and that he had to get back to work. He'd see me later. He bent down to whisper to me. 'Don't let your mom rattle you. She's mad at me, that's all, but be a big girl now.'

'Sure, Daddy,' I said, 'I'll try.'

Then he tried to kiss Mom but she pulled away, so he was left puckered up and no place to put it. 'Jesus,' he said to no one as he walked out the door. 'Jesus H. Christ.'

Now, after a bit, the Pillsbury Doughboy nurse returns and gives me a shot. I'm asleep even before the rollaway that my mommy will sleep on arrives.

In the morning, Daddy is there when I wake up. He tells me that Mommy has gone home to take a shower and change her clothes. The bed is not shaking. Everything is too bright and too still. The sky is still very blue through the window. The doctor comes. He's the one with the beard. Yesterday he looked to me like a goat for a while, but he looks normal today.

Daddy asks him lots of questions. They talk about my temperature, which is raised, and that the night nurse made a note of the bed shaking.

'Hallucinations,' the doctor says, and they both stare at me.

I stretch my smile as big as I can until my mouth hurts. 'I think I need a shot.'

Daddy looks at me with a funny expression and then he turns to the doctor. 'Have you turned my daughter into an addict?'

'We don't want her in pain,' the doctor says.

I try to join in the conversation by shaking my head while still grinning. 'I really need the shots. They're great,' I say, but this doesn't help, I guess.

The doctor just says to Daddy, 'We can't do cold turkey. We'll wean her off.'

They are now looking at my stomach. The doctor lifts up the hospital gown. There's lots of bandaging which he starts to peel off slowly. It hurts. 'Maybe just rip it off quick, one pull,' Daddy says, and the doctor does this.

My belly is red and swollen. It all hurts. Using tweezers, the doctor pulls out gauze from a hole right to the inside of me and it unravels as he tugs it upwards. It's yellowy as it hangs over me. It stinks. Daddy backs away.

'It's infected. Antibiotics. IV,' the doctor says. 'I'll write it up.'

Then he goes and fetches another shot to give me before he begins to pack new stuff inside me. The pretty day nurse is with him. She has long blonde hair and when she gets close I see she's got thick freckles all over her face. I turn my smile on her as she pats my hand. I think that the doctor doesn't need to be so careful now, because the drugs are beginning to work and I am completely still. I feel how all the gauze goes back into me like a backwards worm. Then he wipes over the surface of my skin with some yellow stain and puts the top bandage back on. Finally, he steps back and he and Dad watch while the nurse rolls up the top of my underpants.

Mommy says it's ten-thirty when she comes back. Daddy is gone. She feels my head with her cheek to check my temperature. With her I don't have to try to smile. She smells clean and she's wearing her red and blue striped dress that I like a lot. I tell her that the bed has stopped shaking.

She sighs and settles back in the chair. I ask if she wants to put the TV on. She says no and we are quiet together.

After a while I remind Mom that I should have another shot and she goes to get the nurse. They've changed over and the new nurse looks grumpy. She takes my temperature and feels my wrist. When she asks how I feel I tell her the truth, that I don't feel good. I smile and ask if maybe I'll feel better when I've had the shot. She shakes her head and then tells Mom she's going to page the doctor because she's not authorised to give me another shot. He's not written me up for one. They want me off the shots, so I'll have to wait. Mom follows her out of the room.

When they leave I feel like I did when Dr Leonard told her that I had to have an operation. They'd left me alone in the examination room and went across to his office. He'd made me take off my clothes except my underpants in order to take a look at my stomach, and he hadn't said I could get dressed so I was cold lying there on the examination table. The door was open and I heard Mom ask to use his phone. Then she started crying and he got his secretary to fix them coffee and to get a Danish. He said that Mom had had a shock and I could hear them talking about what was going to happen next.

The doctor eventually arrives and Mommy is behind him, followed by the nurse. He checks the drip, gets the nurse to take my temperature again and finally he asks how I'm feeling. 'Not good,' I say. 'I'm sure I need a shot.' I tilt my head to the nurse to alert him to the fact that she, and only she, can account for the hold-up in this regular delivery. He will understand and fix the situation.

'You're being very brave, aren't you?' he says.

'I guess so.'

'I need you to go on being brave.'

Mommy starts crying. She sniffs as she tells me that they've got to do something else to try to fix me. The infection has got worse.

Ten minutes later I am watching a tube disappear up my nose. While he feeds it in, the doctor explains they are emptying my stomach before they do another operation. I want to tell him I haven't eaten anything for three days now, but he must know this. He says I don't have to keep grinning. I can relax; it'll be over in a minute. Maybe he's realised that I'm not happy, that I am not brave, that I don't really like any of them and I'm just doing what they say so they don't kill me while I'm here.

Mommy holds my hand, but she turns her head away so she can't see what's happening. He tells me to swallow and I want to, but it hurts. I wish they'd given me the shot.

After the second operation, I don't feel any better, but Mommy says it was a success. She tells me that at the first operation there was a mistake; that's why I got infected. She says that the doctors won't admit anything but I'm not to worry. She was here the whole time. She's got her eye on the situation.

They add another drip.

When I wake up the shaking starts again. Mommy is with me. It's the middle of the afternoon.

'It's shaking. The bed is shaking.'

'Try to relax, honey.' She stands up and puts her hands firm on the mattress on the left side of me. Then suddenly the whole room, not just my bed, is shaking and I see that she can feel it too because Mom's face changes and then the clock falls off the wall.

There are screams from the hallway. Mommy shouts, 'It's an earthquake.' She begins to unhook the bags above me and lays them down beside me on the bed. The room is going from side to side and she's struggling to keep her balance. People are rushing around outside the room but no one comes in to help us. I hear Mommy grunting with effort as she goes around to behind the head of the bed and begins to push it. She is making it move. As the room continues to shake from side to side we're picking up speed, rolling right through the door and out to the nurses' station, where we take a right turn and head straight on. And then, as suddenly as it started – though people are still screaming and shouting – the terrible shaking stops.

Mommy, though, keeps going and doesn't stop until we get to the elevator and we have to. She presses the button. There is an old lady with a stick who is sitting on the floor. I wonder if she fell or if she sat down.

The elevator doesn't come. One of the nurses comes to round people up and get them back to their rooms. She says it's all okay and that it's over but her face doesn't look very convincing. 'There will be aftershocks,' Mommy says.

'I don't know about that.'

'Don't any of you here know anything?'

'I know you can't leave this girl here.'

'Aren't you evacuating?'

'We're not evacuating, ma'am.'

Mommy doesn't want to give in even when the grumpy nurse comes and joins in the argument. She says that the elevators can't work in this kind of situation, that this is the fifteenth floor and that if she's that worried she should leave me there and go down by the stairs. Mommy says, 'What kind of a mother do you think I am, that I would abandon my child?'

'You tell her,' the old lady says, still on the ground. I lean over to look at her and wonder why no one is helping her back to her room, or at least on to a chair where she'd be more comfortable.

Finally, Mommy sits down on the bed by my feet. She is beautiful in her bright brave dress and I love her more than anything. She's like Wonder Woman but I think all her energy is gone. After a long while two nurses wheel the bed back to the room and Mommy walks beside me.

There are no aftershocks that we can feel. On the television they say it's the New Madrid Fault and there are reports of people all over the city hurt by falling bricks and stuff. When he comes at six o'clock, Daddy tells us that in the place where he works there's lots of broken glass to clear up.

Mommy is very pleased to see him and they stand together side by side and look down at me. He knows what happened to us. He says to me, 'You could feel the pre-quake tremors. That's what it was.'

Mommy says, 'She's a very sensitive girl.' I see her reach to hold his hand and he doesn't let go.

The nice night nurse walks in. She's just come on duty and listens when I tell her all about what happened. She suggests my folks leave so I can sleep properly tonight. Mommy says she'll come back, but will get something to eat with Daddy downstairs. When they've gone, the nurse comes back to gives me my shot.

'I told you the bed was shaking last night,' I say.

'Just because you're right once, don't go thinking you know everything.'

I have the feeling that she's the kind of person who doesn't need me to pretend. 'I was frightened,' I say. 'You should have seen my mommy, though. Nothing would stop her.'

'I heard. It's good to have a mom like that.'

I can feel the drug in my body, slipping into my brain and now I shut my eyes and I am flying outside the building and seeing all the people all over the city fixing to go to bed to rest through the night, and I am just one of them. There is nothing to be scared of.

1964

The Stone

'Big day for you,' Daddy says, grinning at me. 'How are you feeling?'

Mommy says, 'Don't make a big deal of it, Richard.'

But I say that I feel good and I do. I want to meet my new friends. Daddy says that I'm ahead of the game with my reading and there is no reason to be worried about the first day in kindergarten. He pours himself a bowl of cornflakes and a bowl of Sugar Frosted Flakes for me. 'These are g-great,' I say.

'How are you doing?' he asks Mommy, who is smoking, but not eating.

'Don't want to be late, that's all. I need the car,' she adds, like he might have forgotten this, even though she's already said it a couple of times this morning, and at dinner last night she told him too.

'No problem. I told you it was okay. What are you doing later?'

'Shopping. I'm meeting Charleen downtown. Susie is starting high school today and we're going to a lecture about the Peace Corps this afternoon.'

'TV dinners are getting tedious.'

She gives him a look. 'I can't cook all day.'

'It'd be nice if you cooked sometime,' he says. 'Maybe you want to take a class?'

'I can cook fine, but I don't want to cook and I don't want to take a class.'

Instead of in the back, I sit next to Mommy on the drive to school. The seat is slick and I slide across it when she pulls out of the driveway. She turns the radio on. They're talking about an interview with some woman in the *St Louis Review* and that makes her angry. She's looking at the radio and talking to it. 'If she believes all the other stuff she says about keeping women tied to the home, why is she getting involved in politics? Talk about a hypocrite.'

Down the road we get stuck at traffic lights and a bus pulls up next to the car. A fat old negro man wearing a blue baseball cap stares down at me from one of the windows. Then he waves at me. It makes me feel funny as I wonder if he can tell that my mother is still yelling at the radio. I wonder if any negro kids will be at my school this year. Daddy told me that negro people can, for sure, go to white schools now everywhere which is a good thing, but Mommy said there are no negro families that live in our neighbourhood.

Then the bus turns and it, and he, is gone forever. The main thing is you have to practise what you preach, Mommy tells me next as she clicks the radio dial off.

When we get there it's not noisy, like Daddy told me it would be. We're way too early, but Mommy decides we might as well go in and get the jump on everyone else.

The hallway is wide and the walls bare. There's a smell of Elmer's Glue and that doughy-paint smell that I recognise. Mommy takes me to my new classroom and this is different; it's bright and there are lots of pictures everywhere. There are three easels in the corner with big blocks of paper ready for painting. Alphabet posters march round the top of the walls. There are two-people desks for the children. I am to share with a boy named Jimmy, Mrs Daniels says.

In the summer I came to meet my new kindergarten teacher, when there were other children here – the children she took care of last year. They've graduated to first grade now. Mrs Daniels' hair has been cut since then and it makes her look even more grown-up and grumpy. Maybe she's missing the kids from last year. She doesn't know what's going to happen with us. Mrs Daniels is not as pretty as Mommy but Mommy is not a teacher even though she said she could have been if she wanted to.

My own hair cannot be cut. I will grow it forever. Today it's in a thick braid down my back with a ribbon at the bottom and bobby pins in to keep it all in place. 'Don't you look cute as a button,' Mrs Daniels says. She has noticed that the ribbon matches my blue dress.

In reply I tell Mrs Daniels that she might want to know that I can write my name in cursive already. My mommy has taught me at home.

Then Mommy kisses me goodbye on the top of my head, and tugs the braid. This morning Daddy said not to let anyone do that but here is Mommy just doing it. She says, 'Good luck,' to Mrs Daniels before she leaves and I sit down at my desk and watch her go out of the doorway. Mrs Daniels starts to straighten out the books on her desk.

After a few minutes, other children come in and the desks start to fill up, and it gets noisier. There is still no Jimmy for a long time. The other half of my desk is empty for ages and everyone but me has someone sitting with them when, finally, Jimmy arrives. He has a small face, with freckles. He fidgets in his seat all the time. He says hi to me and I say hi back. He says he lives in the next block. His mom lets him walk to school. 'I came in the car,' is all I can think to say, and then we sit in silence while Mrs Daniels takes roll call.

'Me,' Jimmy says, instead of 'here', when his name is called. Mrs Daniels looks up at him like he's someone she'll have to watch.

At the end of the day Mrs Daniels lets us choose our own books to take home. She puts two books on the desk that Jimmy and I share. I can't decide between them. The first has lots of photographs in it. It's called *Nature in all its Glory* and I like it because of the pictures of interesting animals. Jimmy also likes this book, he says, because he's counted five pictures of tornados. The other one is a small book and there are only drawn pictures inside it. I can read most of the words. I decide to take this one home because that means that Jimmy can take home the one he really wants.

My book is called *The Stone*.

The pages are yellowing and the print is a bit fuzzy. Daddy reads it to me by the light of my bedside lamp – the one with Snow White and the dwarfs at its base. He slides his finger under each word in the book as he says the words aloud. It's a story about a prince who doesn't know he is a prince because he is stolen from his family and brought up by someone else.

I let my eyes close. I hear Daddy shut the book quietly after he's finished the story. He leans over and kisses me on my forehead. 'Good choice,' he says, then he tells me that he loves me. He is going downstairs to check on Mommy, he says. 'What a big girl you are, going to school now. You have a wonderful future ahead of you. I'm going to turn the light out now. Sleep well, sweet dreams, honey.'

I don't need to answer. I like school and I like this feeling of excitement about tomorrow coming in the morning and I feel happy. I snuggle down and turn over and curl into sleep.

1961

In and Out

Mommy lifts me on to her lap. We slide together; I squirm until the fit is just right. My head rests against her shoulder, and the soft thump of her is as close as can be.

Her breath is on my face for a whisper and her perfume pricks at my nose. Her long yellow hair brushes mine. We're tight like this. I feel like I am good enough to eat – melted butter on toast, with cinnamon and sugar, cut into squares. Sweet. Delicious.

Daddy is watching us and smiling. She says I am just so the apple of his eye and then she fixes to start our spider story. She puts her lips right up against my ear.

I feel the fizz in my middle as she begins. '*Incy Wincy spider*,' she says, and I feel the tiniest trail that the story spider threads on my arm, as he inches his legs this way and curls back that way. Her breath warms my skin as she whispers, '*Climbed up the spout.*'

Her pink nails continue their curly climb right up to my shoulder. I have to be still and quiet now until, finally, she says in a louder voice, '*Down came the rain, and washed the spider out*,' and her fingers whoosh down, right down to my own hand, where she rests hers – palm on palm.

Her big hand is on top, hiding my hand. It is warm. This is our story and we tell it together. 'Now what happens? Is it a happy ending?' she asks.

I turn and take in her smile. It lights my face and swallows me up. 'Yes.'

She says, '*Out came the sun, and dried up all the rain, and Incy Wincy spider climbed the spout again.* Isn't that great, honey?' she asks, even though she knows. 'Don't we do it great together?'

'Again,' I say, all ready for more.

I know I'm greedy because she tells me that this is how I am, and she doesn't mind because we are the same. There is nothing between us. We belong together.

1959

The Lamb

In her mind she thinks of herself as just lightly pregnant and today she is wearing a watermelon-blush dress that suits this contention. It falls below her knees and the small bulge in her waistline is completely concealed. She is twenty-seven – older than she ever thought she would be on her wedding day – but it doesn't matter. She can feel the gentle chiffon against her legs. Life, she thinks, is often like this – just brushing her softly; she doesn't have to pay too much attention if she doesn't want to.

'Watermelon-blush', of course, is not from her vocabulary but a gift from the enthusiastic saleswoman in the department store who, without knowing her or her circumstances, said she knew just the right thing for a 'special occasion'. It was the first dress she tried on. Thus, she allowed her dress to be chosen for her, but bought the veil she's wearing from a proper bridal shop.

She'd expected trouble, but when she warned him that she wouldn't be wearing white Father Thomas said nothing. He seemed to understand how life might get complicated. But a wedding needs something so, after speaking to him, on impulse she went and got the veil that now softens her view. It adds to her sense of separateness today, but when it's done the veil will come off and she'll have to live with all this.

From the back of the church she looks for, and then spots, her older half-sisters in the second pew on the left: one with bobbed light brown hair, Sheila, and the other with dark brown hair, Hannah. There aren't many people here other than the die-hard regulars that attend this church in a town containing only a handful of Catholics. Those that have come have turned out for a show, and all of them present, except for Sheila and Hannah, turn to watch her arrival. The two women she is related to refuse her important day. Their heads are directed stubbornly forward to the altar. Close in age and in disapproving temperament, the two of them can stay here forever. She wants something different for her life. She treasures the fact that she has a different father and is getting married to a man with education and a future ahead, as a promise towards this possibility.

Today both her sisters are wearing colours that clash with her dress: Sheila is in mauve and Hannah in lilac. Even this morning they still thought she'd change her mind and wear their mother's white-white wedding dress that they hauled down from the attic and hung like a ghost in her bedroom. No amount of pleading will work, though. She's been told since she was three that she has her father's irreligious temperament and now this has come home to roost. Serves them right.

As she comes down the aisle on her own – she has no uncle or brother to give her away and both her parents are gone – she sees Father Thomas's kind face guiding her to the front and the two men standing there. One will soon be her husband. Richard is a good companion and a loyal friend who doesn't care about her family, and won't hold it against her. He won't remind her of her origins in their life together. She wants to live somewhere clean and fresh. She wants rid of the poverty that clings to her – to her family name, to her home, to this derelict town.

There are ten more steps. As she walks she reminds herself that Richard can't help the type of man he is and she understands the limitations. She will give him a wife and child and he will give her his name. She might not be, but *he* is the sort of person who wants to do the right thing. He will take care of her.

She has now arrived at the front and the music stops. Father Thomas steps forward and momentarily she turns and smiles to Richard. He is nervous, but eager. She pats his hand and thinks how peculiar that she, the bride, needs to reassure the groom.

He has chosen Pete, his little brother by five years, to be the best man. Pete stands on the other side of Richard and looks scared. She wants to reassure him, too, because she knows he doesn't like anything serious and has made her promise that she won't tell Richard about how the two of them were briefly involved. He doesn't know she's pregnant, nor, of course, that it's his child. Richard does know about the baby but he has asked that she not tell the father of the child – 'whomever he might be', he said rather pompously.

He doesn't want another man potentially 'staking a claim' later.

The brothers both have new haircuts. Richard's looks smart and grown-up. Pete looks like a shorn lamb.

She wants to tell both of them that it'll be okay. She smiles again at them, and at Father Thomas and then, unbidden and against protocol, she turns to face the congregation and grins through her veil because she's got all the gumption she might need to pull this thing off and show them. They'll need luck, but she's always been lucky, and the child will look like Richard.

Father Thomas begins and I give her a sharp, hard kick. For the first time, I'm sure she feels it. We're in this together. Forever.

2013

An Angel

When I turn the lights on in the kitchen the dark outside is even darker, as if this is a stage set. This has been the first night I've spent in my mother's house for years and I haven't really slept. 'My mother has died,' I say aloud, to remind myself that this is how it's going to be from now on.

Outside, a coyote howls woefully in reply. The sound makes me jump first, and then it makes me cry and I can't come up for air. I get into the shower with tears still pouring down my face. And then I go out for a walk around the neighbourhood before the sun comes up. All the while I walk

I hold her keys in my hand and, with my thumb, I stroke the fragile bones beneath the fur on the rabbit's foot.

When I get back, I set to. I collect the dishes scattered throughout the house, and get the dishwasher going. I pull out the vacuum cleaner and begin to get the living room straight. At eight-thirty I call and arrange to see the funeral director at ten o'clock, which is the earliest he can see me.

I take a cab there, because I've not yet rented a car, and when I walk up from the sidewalk into the funeral home I suddenly panic. I must be in the wrong place, because this is not my life. None of it seems real, at all. I'm still waiting for my mother to arrive and tell me what to do next, and to berate me for being so worried.

The mortuary is a big old house set within pristine lawns. Except for the fact that the sprinklers are going, I'd have thought the grass was great quality Astroturf. The office is immediately on the right inside the double doors. I ask the sombre girl if I will be able to see my mother this morning, but she says it might not be possible, and I'll have to discuss that with 'Andy' when he comes through. 'There's stuff to prepare, before she'll be up for visiting,' she says. I register that this is just another of the absurd things people say and that if I had the energy and inclination I could tell her that this wasn't the best way to discuss viewing a dead relation. But I am no longer the kind of person who rises to an opportunity to correct. Instead, I nod and keep my mouth shut.

'Coffee?' she suggests, and then the funeral director appears and says that we might have this together; he's ready for a cup as well.

This stranger in his dull black suit tells me his name is Andy. We shake hands and he says it will be more comfortable to sit side by side on the couch than opposite at his desk. We are to begin the conversation about what needs to be done and I hope that this is the best possible funeral home. My mother deserves the best. Gus's recommendation doesn't mean I have to keep Mom here. I remind myself that I can still take my business elsewhere because nothing to do with this is yet final. If Andy is not up to this – if this place is no good, if his ugly couch is uncomfortable, or if that girl says something stupid again – I will go elsewhere. I'm not worried about the cost. Although I want an efficient service, I want one that she would be pleased with.

'My mother's friend Gus recommended you,' I say. 'So, I thought I should see what we need to do.'

Andy again beckons me to sit down and plonks himself beside me. Then he pats my hand. The contact stings for some reason and I pull back from him, but he's just trying to be nice and I'm afraid I might have offended him. I presume the bereaved are supposed to be grateful for all attempts at comfort, so I try to explain. 'I know you're being kind.' The sound of my voice surprises me. 'I'm not myself,' I say. 'My brain isn't working right.'

'That's okay,' he says. 'These are unusual circumstances.'

For me, not him, I think. We get back to the task at hand and there is sincere sympathy behind his blank patience as he waits for me to make a decision, any decision. I look at pictures from his brochure and laptop, and examples of the printed information they provide, and then in the display room I touch the various woods he has on show. The problem is that I can't decide on anything. He is infinitely patient and I sense no irritation and this, finally, makes my choice clear. This is the place that she'll stay, and he will do this. 'Andy, why don't you choose for me?' I say. 'You know what you're doing. You must do this all the time and I don't.'

He said he understands and suggests moderate pricing for everything. Not too much. Not too little. Not too dark, not too light. But nothing will be just right, ever again.

There are notices to compose for the papers and then forms to sign and, every time he passes me a pen and points to where, I obey, writing my name more illegibly each time. I disappear in my signature. I discover that death is a whole load of business and with every dotted line money is leaking. I calculate the additions to my credit card balance. Then he begins to explain the marathon of hoops to jump through. He hands me the death certificate to check, after suggesting that I should order more as I will need a number of copies at twenty dollars each – 'the bank will want one, the insurance, the house'. I glance at it. They've marked 'natural causes', no further details.

'Gus said she had a stroke,' I say. 'They've left that out, and the age recorded is wrong,' I say. 'This section. Here.' I point. 'She was seventy-four, not eighty-two.'

'Well, that's the hospital. I didn't realise she was seventy-four.' He's genuinely puzzled. 'We can get this changed. It needs to be accurate. I'll give them a call.' He pauses. 'In fact, I'll get Jeannie to do this while we finalise things. 'I don't think it will hold things up.'

He leaves me a moment to ask this Jeannie to do this while we talk, and I look around at the furnishings in the room. It is all very tasteful: beige wall-to-wall carpeting, deep maroon chairs, and three oversized Davenports. Heavy drapes. He's told me that sixty people can attend a visitation here comfortably. They don't allow food or drink, but they can provide coffee and water near the entrance. We've decided on a closed casket. The funeral can take place here too, but I'll leave this until I meet Gus's pastor. She wasn't religious – even when she attended church she went with barrels of cynicism – but I mustn't hurry. I'd like everything done; I'd like it all over and in the past; but that's impossible. This is something to get through, and right now I have to accept that lots of things will remain on hold for a while.

When he comes back he tells me that the hospital admissions records indicate that the age on the death certificate is correct and that the cause of death being noted as natural is standard.

'But she wasn't that age.'

He says that numerous hospital records confirm that this is actually my mother's age. 'Some funny mix-up.' Andy sounds embarrassed as he tells me this. 'I guess it happens.'

'But my mother wouldn't lie to me.'

He doesn't reply. He turns his sympathetic look towards the floor.

Eventually I say, 'Well, I guess it doesn't change anything.' But in the cab on the way back to her house, I begin to consider how much it does change. Why would she lie to me?

By the time the pastor arrives at the house in the afternoon, I've gone past feeling confused. I am angry because her lying about her age – even though I was bound to find out eventually – shouldn't be a surprise. It's typical of our relationship. I'm the one who doesn't understand, who can't keep up with what she's got going on. And the one who has to deal with the fallout. Like today. Like now. I'm made to feel an idiot, and someone not even worth the truth.

When the doorbell goes, I'm in her bedroom. I've considered her unmade bed and the piles of Target trash and cheap keepsakes on the cabinet against the wall. In her bathroom there are piles of half-used and discarded tubes of cosmetics and a dental floss container that didn't make it as far as the empty trash can. The sink is filthy with make-up and toothpaste spills. The toilet, too, is stained and will need a proper clean. I shut the door carefully and take my time walking along the hallway to the door.

Gus's pastor has long grey hair tied in a ponytail but otherwise he's wearing the costume of the office: a shiny black suit with a white priest's collar at this neck. He tells me his name is Brandon and that he's sorry for my loss.

'Come in,' I say. 'The family room is through here.'

He follows me. While I show him through the house, I think about what my mother might make of this man. Maybe she wouldn't like him. He looks like an old hippy.

'Gus was concerned that you need some support.' He tells me this as he sits down, then he says, 'So, why don't you tell me about yourself.'

'Let me get you a coffee or something.'

'I'll take a soda if you've got one.'

She's got two cans of Fresca in the icebox and I find two matching glasses.

'Always liked Fresca,' he says. 'So, when did you leave Phoenix?'

'Oh, long time ago now. I got married and my then husband and I left together.'

'You're not married now.'

'No. No. Divorced.'

'Children?'

'I never had children.'

'Ah.' The silence sits between us like a huge wall.

'Do you have family?' I ask.

He nods and tells me that he has three children. The middle one has got problems, but she's doing okay right now, he says. His wife works for the city.

'Oh, I work for the city in Oklahoma, too.'

'She likes it.'

'So do I. I used to do events management for a commercial business in Tulsa – big auditorium events, you know? And then when I moved to Oklahoma City I saw a job advertised with the city that was pretty similar, organising tourism, shows and conventions in the Civic Center. It was more money, regular job, benefits, and I got promoted.'

'You never thought about moving back here?'

'No. Not seriously. Not really. No. My mom would have liked that, but I had my own life. She did too.'

'So, this is really sad news for you, isn't it?'

It occurs to me that this is a really stupid thing to say; we are sitting here discussing my mother's death. Of course. But, instead of telling him that or agreeing, I find myself telling him that I found out today that my mother was years older than I thought she was.

'Do you think your dad knew? Gus said you lost your dad a while back.'

'He had an accident.'

'Here? At his work?'

'No, not here. Not at work. It was at home, before she moved here. They had a big old house, but Mom wanted a single-storey house afterwards.'

'How old was he when he had the accident?'

'Well, I thought he was much older than her ... but he wasn't, I guess. Not very old, I guess. Too young to die, anyway.'

'He was disabled?'

'No, no. He died. He survived what happened but he couldn't live and then he ... he died ... She just didn't want anyone else to have an accident like he had so she wanted a ranch-style place.'

'Ah, I see,' he says. 'Gus said he didn't know of any close friends. Do you know who will want to come to pay their respects?'

'She had a few friends locally. I found her address book this morning and I'm going to phone around this evening, let people know, but none of her good friends live around here now.'

'Well, making contact is good. It'll help to bring your mother more present for you.'

I think that this is an odd thing to say. My mother is so present now, she could walk into the room. In fact, it's odd that she hasn't walked in here and asked the two of us what the hell is going on. Suddenly I just blurt out, 'Hey, listen. Can you do the funeral? Can you just do it? It would help. A lot.'

He appears to be surprised. This is not what he's expecting and right before I said it I didn't know I was going to ask him, but it feels good to have done something. He tells me that he's just come for me, not to talk about the funeral. Gus asked him to call in to meet with me, because I've not got any other family here in Phoenix. He asks if she had her own pastor, or if there's some other church she might want to use for the funeral. 'What's her affiliation?'

'She was originally a Catholic, but she wasn't religious. We don't have to go with that, do we?'

'Ah, I see. No.' And then he says he'll be happy to do the funeral. I don't care that I think he feels sorry for me.

When he's gone I abandon cleaning up Mom's room and make a start at letting people know. I begin with the As in the address book and work my way through. It's hard because I have to keep it together when I tell all these people what has happened, and I don't really know what most of them were to Mom. Patty is listed by her previous married name, so that means I get to her when I reach the Ds.

'Oh, honey,' she says. 'I haven't seen your mother since the wedding and she was so sick then. Still came, though.'

'Well, she wasn't really ill. She was just…'

'And now she's died. Lived on borrowed time, I guess. When is the funeral?'

'We've not yet finalised it. I can let you know.'

'Oh, yes, please do. Gary and I will be there for you.'

Louelle's surname is listed as Edwards. This, too, is her previous married name. I'm glad, though, because otherwise she'd be at the end of the book and I might not have the stamina to make it all the way to the Ys. She answers my call on the first ring. 'Hey, honey,' she says. 'How are you doing?'

'It's me, Louelle, not my mom. I'm phoning because I've got some bad news.'

Immediately after I explain that Mom has died, she says, 'I'm there for you.' Minutes after I get off the phone, she phones me back to say she's got a flight and will be here in two days' time, at ten o'clock, and I say that I'll pick her up at the airport.

There's a Frank listed under the Fs, but when I phone him he doesn't seem to recollect my mom and is not interested when I tell him that she died. It makes me want to cry that he doesn't remember her. My mother had two sisters but they both died a long time ago. I never knew them, and their names, addresses and numbers have been crossed through in the book. There is no reply to my call to Dad's brother, Pete who is now my only blood relation. I leave a message on his voicemail. Then I put aside the address book and return to Mom's room. I clean it to within an inch of bare and I move my stuff into there. Then I give the guest bedroom the same treatment in order to make it habitable for Mom's best friend and, finally, I scrub the kitchen. By the time I'm done the house is gleaming and I'm exhausted but I still make my way all through the rest of the address book because if I don't do it now, then I won't ever do it.

After this I take a look through my Mom's supply of drugs. I choose one of her sleeping tablets and climb into her bed. Though I've washed all the clothes she'd dropped on the floor instead of in the laundry basket, I didn't change the sheets.

The adrenaline has vanished all together by the next morning. I can't get up. Instead, I take another one of Mom's sleeping pills as the sun comes up and when I eventually wake I just turn on the shopping channel and watch in bed until sufficient time passes to allow myself another pill. Instead of cooking, I phone take out and they deliver pizza. I finish off four bottles of wine in two days.

On the morning that Louelle is due to arrive, I get up and shower and get out to the airport. She comes down the escalator wearing a cream kaftan, arms outstretched, like Jesus himself, ready to save me. She puts her arms around me and hugs me forever. In the car she tells me that she'll field all the telephone calls and will arrange all the outstanding details of the funeral.

Andy and Louelle talk. Gus's pastor and Louelle talk. Gus finds someone from Mom's Mah Jongg group who will say something at the funeral. This woman talks to Louelle and Louelle tells me that she will do a eulogy as well. Louelle phones Patty who will come, but says she can't possibly say anything at the funeral. She is beside herself, Louelle says, and then laughs. 'As if she could actually be beside herself,' she says. 'Last time I saw her she was the size of a small room.'

Louelle takes the returned phone call from my uncle Pete and says that he can't come – his wife is ill and he can't leave her – but that he wants me to call him when I can. 'He sounded concerned,' she said. 'He really wanted to talk to you. He'll be a help.'

'We haven't seen him since Dad's funeral. He did the eulogy because Mom wouldn't let Jack do it. I don't think she's spoken to him since then.'

'Well, maybe talk to him about what happened. You owe it to the future to try to make things in the past right, if you can.'

'Mom was older than she told everyone. That was really shit.'

'Uh huh.' She looks sheepish. 'Listen, your mother was embarrassed,' she said. 'She never got a high-school diploma, did you know that?'

I shake my head.

'Well, I guess that made her feel defensive for a start. And, despite those two proud sisters – who did nothing to help except complain about their stepfather and younger sister – the family were really piss-poor. Your grandmother, her mother, died when your mom was not even twelve, and soon after that your grandfather ran off. As soon as she could your poor momma dropped out of school to work. She was way clever enough to stay on, but she couldn't. It wasn't that long after the Depression. She had to lie. I know she added years to her age so she could get a job and later on she subtracted them back, and in the process decided to drop a few extra. She was a bit vain, you know.'

'She could have told me. She didn't have to pretend with me.'

'Maybe, but habits die hard, don't they?'

Louelle doesn't stop me taking the pills. I see that she understands me and for the first time in my life I can sleep at will. Wonderfully, I sleep dreamlessly and wake in the same position as I settled down.

On the morning of her cremation I kiss her waxy, meat-cold cheek knowing that it is the last time I will touch my mother. Louelle holds my hand and I say that Andy can now close the casket. It is okay, I say. It's time. But, as I hear the sound of the heavy wood moving, I shut my eyes and long to be in there with her, curled up beside her forever instead of with Andy and Louelle, watching this dreadful thing happen.

Then I allow the two of them to walk me through what has to be done; they guide me away from the casket and to my seat.

Half an hour later people begin to arrive for the visitation. I speak only when spoken to but Louelle sits next to me and chatters up a storm to everyone who comes to pay their respects so that I don't have to. Andy circulates and makes sure that everyone signs the condolence book.

I realise he was right when he said that I'd find it hard to remember today. I'm forgetting it even as it happens.

Louelle stays on with me for a week after the funeral. Though she is not motherly at all – in the past I wondered if she even likes her own daughter – she does mother me. She sits with me in silence, holding my hand, hugging me when I cry. She reminds me to brush my teeth and tells me to wash my hair. At one point I say, 'I am motherless. I am an orphan.'

'Now no need to go crazy,' she says. 'You're a grown woman. You'll be okay,' which is the best thing to say, of course.

'I just didn't get enough of her.'

We drink a lot and after a couple of days she insists that I get dressed in the mornings even though we don't go out anywhere. She makes us both fat BLTs and serves up whole tubs of Häagen-Dazs for dessert. I want her to tell me what it was like when she and Mom were young and she replies, 'We met when we were both struggling with life, I guess.

She'd got herself into some trouble. People from where she lived as a child, with those kinds of circumstances, hardly ever get away, but she did.'

'What would I do without you?' This is true. 'Nothing. I couldn't have done anything this week without you.'

She smiles. 'Oh, anyone would have been the same... Your mom was something else.'

'Dad was crazy about Mom.'

'Crazy doesn't make for a good marriage. There's more choice for people now. She was pregnant with you, you know.'

This news should surprise me, but for some reason it doesn't. Louelle gets up and starts to pull the drapes across the window. We are in the den and it's that time of the evening when anyone outside can look right into the house. Her hair is no longer full and blonde, it is thinning and white at the roots, and I don't know when she stopped wearing heels, but she seems to have shrunk. She's smaller than she was.

'Are you saying she wanted to get rid of me but couldn't?'

'No, honey. She didn't want to do that. She got pregnant and needed some help. She wanted the best for her baby, and your dad... he stepped in and helped her out and it suited him, too. It was those times. It was Pete who fathered you but Richard brought you up. Your dad made a good home for you both. Your parents really did love you. You need to speak to your uncle. Phone him.'

It's late when we decide finally to go to bed. The news about Dad not being my dad should surprise me, but I feel numb. I take a pill and go into Mom's bedroom. I still haven't changed the sheets. I put my head down on her flattened pillow and imagine that I can still smell her there. I want to still smell her. I want to be with her, her arms around me, her hands on mine. I don't care that we might argue. I don't care about any of it, good or bad. I just can't bear that I can't talk to her about this – about her crappy childhood, her age; about my beginnings; about her and Dad.

Louelle wakes me in the morning. I know she only meant well, so over breakfast I thank her for telling me what she did. We don't talk about it again and I don't ask questions because I don't need to. I understand because everything suddenly fits. Out there somewhere there is still someone I'm related to by blood, but I don't know him.

The following afternoon, when I get back to the house after dropping her at the airport to fly back to Minnesota, I start trembling and my legs stop working right. I thought I knew who my mother was, who my parents were, but none of it was the truth.

I go to get a cup of coffee and I drop on to my mother's kitchen floor hard and fast – straight down. I finally crawl to Mom's armchair in the den, where I sit for an hour and watch how the blood from my grazed knee soaks into the Kleenex and try to recall how tall Mom was when she sat here, compared to me now. Am I closer to her when I sit here now than I was when I sat over there, during the time Louelle was here? I spoke to Mom only the day before Gus phoned, so she hadn't been dead for long, but still I can't get over feeling that I'd abandoned her. I didn't care for her enough. I wonder whether, if I'd paid more attention, I could have known her better, and then she might have trusted me. But it's all too late.

2014

Prince Poopy

I still have a leave of absence from my work. Jerry said he understood and I know Cotton has recorded it as ill health because we discussed it. I said there was no other way of describing the effect of everything that happened since I had the phone call from Gus to say my mother was dead.

After the funeral and after Louelle went home, I finally put everything into boxes, closed up her house, left it to the realtor and came back to Oklahoma, ostensibly to figure out what to do next, but in fact, to do nothing at all for a while.

Today the dog is delivered from the kennels Gus put him in on the day he found Mom. There are people who do such things – people who lifted my mother's precious body and put her into a box, and people more than happy to collect animals from the homes of the newly deceased and to house them indefinitely, for a price. Then there are young men like this one who transport pets hundreds of miles and convincingly behave as if they care for them.

The boy, whose badge reads *Jordan*, ruffles the fur of this nasty little dog and allows it to lick his ear before he passes it over to me and stands waiting for a tip. It's already cost me a fortune, but that's not Jordan's fault. He says that my dog will be pleased to be back home with his mommy. I don't explain that this is not my animal, and that we have never lived together before, and that he won't be here for long.

It squirms in my arms. I drop it on to the floor in the kitchen and command, 'Wait.' When it whimpers I tell it to shut up and it lies down contritely, head between its paws. I shut it in there and take the note I want from my pocketbook for the tip. As Jordan takes the offered money our fingers lightly meet and it feels electric. It's as if I have been alone for a hundred years.

This, the dog, is the final unwanted thing I will have from my mother. I drove back from Phoenix in a hired U-Haul, which was loaded up with boxes full of papers and her personal items – shoes, jewellery, frail wispy scarves which gave off puffs of Shalimar, some trinkets and memorabilia, handwritten letters mostly from people I've never heard of, her collection of perfume bottles, and also the boxes of things she'd kept of mine from childhood and then Dad's stuff, from when he died and we packed it all up together. All of that is stuffed into my portion of the basement store room, for whenever I have the courage to deal with it.

After two months away from work, I am no longer being paid, but I am still on the payroll. They can't replace me and maybe things are mounting up. Jerry's referred the issue to someone in HR who phones just after Jordan leaves. She asks when I might be back; I have to decide today when I am going to come back. 'You do know no one can remain on the books indefinitely. We need a date. I'm asking you for a date for the paperwork. The thing is, we're wondering if you really intend to return at all?' she says tentatively and too faintly, courtesy of the phone company who never fixed the line properly.

I tell her to write, that I'm not sure. 'I can't hear you properly and my return all depends on variables. Hey, maybe don't write. I'll write to you. Soon. I promise. Say hi to everyone.' I hang up.

It is an entirely unsatisfactory conversation, from her end. My side of it feels complete and full, a statement of how I am – I don't know anything. I make promises I won't keep. I'm out of touch.

The dog sniffs at my feet. Poopy is spoilt rotten, and I hate him and his moronic name. It might have seemed a cute name for a puppy but 'Poopy' is now just a reminder to me that I have to clean up his crap. I can't see that loving him would ever be possible but I'm not yet ready to put him down. I should find out how long these animals live.

It's not disliking dogs which prevents me loving him, I often wanted a dog when I was a kid, but Poopy was *her* dog and the truth is for a long time I've been jealous of him. When I'd visit her, she'd wave goodnight to me, and bend down to scoop him up to go upstairs to her bed, whispering into his tiny, but cavernous, ear. I know dogs don't actually have expressions, but whenever they left the room together to go off to her bedroom he sure looked smug. Poopy knew where his bread was buttered. She recklessly treated him to handfuls of bacon bits and gourmet food from the delicatessen. He had his own miniature electric blanket and claimed half of her double bed for his own.

Poopy's unconditional love was a wonderful thing, she said, and even that made me feel like I'd let her down. I had, I reminded her, tried to be the perfect daughter for years. 'Well, missed that by a mile. Maybe you should have tried harder,' she said.

The dog also happens to be neurotic, and his new, proper poodle cut done courtesy of the kennels can't be helping. I expect he's embarrassed because he looks ridiculous and frivolous. The only good thing about him is that he doesn't shed. He's lost a little weight since I saw him last, but he was way too fat and he's still overweight. Now when I stroke the tight brown curls of his coat I waver between a strong desire to push him away from me and another to pick him up and bury my face in his podgy little side.

Nathan phones to find out how I'm doing but I don't really want to tell him. He's a good friend and I like him but he can't help with this. I ask questions about his family instead and end up listening to what's happening with Cassie and their eleven-year-old twins.

When I hang up, I am again forced to face the fact that I am the last of a very thin, short and crooked family line and all I have to show for it is this pathetic dog now sidling up to my ankle.

I still haven't spoken to my uncle. I know I promised Louelle but I think a relationship with anyone else now that Mom has passed is impossible. I'm too old to get to know anyone new. There's too much to tell, and too much I wouldn't want to tell, I suppose. She was the one person who always knew me. How can I hope that anyone else might really know me without knowing everything? A lifetime. My lifetime. It's all too complicated.

And, of course, the truth is that Pete was *not* my father. My dad brought me up. He was my real father. Uncle Pete was just a sperm donor.

I really wish that Dad might have known that it makes no difference to me. I loved Dad, and he loved me.

In the evening I phone Louelle and we talk for an hour. She says that she'll come and visit me here sometime and meantime I should try not to worry, or beat myself up about Mom. 'Have you phoned your uncle?' she asks.

'No.'

'Are you scared?'

'Maybe,' I say.

'Do it anyway. How's the dog doing?'

'It's a lot to get used to, that's all. I guess he's okay.'

She says again that she's going to visit, or I could visit her, and we end up both promising to keep in touch.

After I hang up the phone, the animal starts to snuffle and whimper and I realise that he must be missing Mom too. His devoted transfer of attention to me should be endearing but it's not; he ignored me when she was alive so why should I respond to his obvious cupboard love? But, perhaps, the dog is afraid of losing me as well now. He'd have nothing then. I'm all he has, I guess.

I have allowed him on my bed – down by my feet, where he curls into a warm clump when we go to bed at night. He cries in his sleep and I comfort him and sometimes he wriggles his way up into my arms. But when the sun comes through the drapes and he rushes up and tries to lick my face as soon as I stir, I push him off me, then off the bed on to the floor. I don't want him to expect me to spoil him as Mom did.

'You're a legacy and a punishment,' I say to him now, and he looks up in surprise. He even wags his tail. It says something nice about the dog that he's grateful for any conversation, however insulting. He just wants to be acknowledged and, unlike every human I've ever known, he's easily satisfied.

I hear on the phone in the late afternoon the next day that Mom's house has now been sold. The agent cleared out the furnishings, crockery, knick-knacks that I left, and the appliances. He tells me now that he managed to completely dispose of all that stuff – some the buyers wanted; the rest went to the Goodwill. 'Made a lot of people happy,' he says. 'Your mother would have liked that.'

I don't correct him; I agree, because I think that's the sort of thing I should say.

Down in the basement I open the first container of my childhood stuff from their house. I find the small blue box that I am looking for. Even though it's been sealed it appears dusty on the outside, but the seahorse skeleton inside is just the same as I remember. I wrap the whole thing in bubble wrap and label the envelope to Kimberly. I've got her new address. It was on the invitation that I didn't even RSVP. I put a note inside, and a belated proper wedding present – a cheque for two hundred bucks. I try to keep the wording light and breezy: *Hope all went well. Thinking of you. Let me know how you are.* And I sign it with love and two kisses.

In the morning I take Poopy with me to the post office and I leave him in the car. There's a long line to be served. This I can endure, and I can endure the bored false politeness from the girl behind the glass screen as I explain I want it sent special delivery. 'Uh huh,' she says without looking up and so quietly that I have to strain to hear her. 'Anything valuable in it?'

I suddenly want to tell her that I'm mailing anthrax but, of course I don't. 'No,' I say. She's just doing her job, and why should she pay attention to every customer? I shouldn't mind being invisible. When I was a kid, invisibility was my most coveted superhero power, but, now that I seem to have disappeared, I want to be noticed.

When we get home I boil an egg for me and make scrambled egg for Poopy, which he loves. I plop the food down on his dish – one of my mother's gold-rimmed saucers. It is intricately decorated with a floral design. I wonder if he's noticed this loose continuity – that, despite my misgivings, I have honoured the fact that she wouldn't allow him a doggy bowl – and then I consider whether he knows what a privileged animal he is and suddenly envy grasps me again, like a lump in my throat, because he has someone to do this gentle thing for him to ease his grief, but there is no one and nothing to ease mine. I decide that tomorrow I will have scrambled eggs too and maybe on one of Mom's plates and maybe I'll get him a bowl that says 'Dog' when I go to the market. It's not too late to put some things right.

'You're a lucky little shit,' I tell him, and he licks my ankle with his tiny tongue until I shove him away with my foot.

Later I take Poopy with me to the hairdresser's. When I get out of the car he sidles into the driving seat to wait for me. He's assuming proprietorial privileges already. This is to be expected and it's okay. I tell him I won't be very long and that he should watch the car. He curls up on the seat and settles down when I blow him a kiss through the closed window.

Dreadful mirrors the length of the shop wall mean there is no escaping the row of women looking their vulnerable worst. For me, the fact that I resemble my mother is underscored. With my wet grey hair scraped back and face lipstickless, I look like her more and more every year. She used to say I looked more like Dad than her. It was an unnecessary lie. My mother was a liar. The fact that I ever believed her about anything angers me.

When my looks and hers intersected at a good juncture, perhaps at what would have been her pre-menopausal peak in her mid-forties – in her actual mid-forties, I remind myself, when I was around twenty – I didn't notice our similarities. She had all those crazy hairstyles and I was too busy getting on with discovering life and too preoccupied with myself to consider why she was trying to make all those changes to her appearance. But now before me in the mirror an old woman is creeping up on me or, rather, emerging from within. Dryness, wrinkles, a dullness. A *before* ad for face creams. A witch.

I decide I will not return to this place ever again when the girl says that colour and a perm won't suit the tone of my skin, now.

The next time they call, it is not Jerry, or his supervisor, making the call, but another administrator I've not heard of before now. He explains how short-staffed they are at present, and how I've been away three months, as if I couldn't have figured this out. He says that there is some concern that I do not seem to be 'proactive' about resolving this situation. I ask if he is human-resources-trained and he says a clumsy 'no', but that he's taken advice.

'Then, as I've told you before, write to me,' I say. 'I am not well. These calls distress me. I want you to know that I cannot think like this. Now listen...' I pause and he doesn't speak. He seems stunned into silence – which is very satisfying. It feels as if I've spent most of my life hoping that someone might listen to what I have to say. I stand legs apart with my one free hand on my hip and chin in the air. 'I'm gonna sue you,' I say finally, and then hang up. I continue to stand with two hands on my hips for a few minutes more and feel calm confidence surge through me. No wonder

Superman, Wonder Woman, Batman – even Robin and Commissioner Gordon – took this stance to contemplate things. It's a powerful stance.

In the afternoon, I have an appointment to see my primary physician. He says he also wants to discuss how things are going. He expresses some surprise that I still have little appetite and that I still cannot sleep at all. 'I take the pills you prescribed for my mood, and also make sure I get up in the morning,' I tell him. 'I don't lie around in bed all day. I *am* trying. The death of a parent is a shock. I want something to help me sleep.'

'What are you doing with your days?'

'I've done what you said. I go to the gym and walk the dog – my mother's dog; I have him now. I keep house. I've been doing an art class. I read,' I lie.

'Friends?'

'Oh, yes,' I lie some more. 'I meet up with friends when I can. They're mostly working so I can't do it all the time but I have around ten friends I see regularly.'

'So, what about you? Are you back at your job now?'

'Are you kidding? I can't work when I can't sleep. I'm exhausted all the time. It's an effort to get here to see you.'

He says I might benefit from some talking therapy, have I thought about that? Ever tried it? I could tell him that I've had more than my fair share of time with shrinks over the years, but instead I just say that I have and that it's a good idea. I thank him. Maybe he could set it up if my insurance will cover it? He writes me up for some more blood work just to see if there's any reason for me to be so tired all the time. He writes out a prescription for more antidepressants and, finally, some decent sleeping pills, then he shakes my hand. Before I've left the room he begins dictating a letter to one of his psychiatrist colleagues.

I fill the prescription for Lunesta but don't fill the others. I go home and stuff them away in the kitchen cabinet with my old birthday cards and recipes for stuff I will never try to make, but would like to. If I need them I can find them.

We go to bed at two a.m. and I lie there with Poopy, who is fast asleep curled up against me. Once again I listen intently to the silence around me, but no one is speaking. Is the fact that Mom has no opinion on my present situation a reward because there is nothing to say, or is she trying to punish me by not sending me a message from beyond the grave? Then, finally, in that shimmering state between wakefulness and sleep, I experience a loosening of reality, a little shake-up that releases the magic into my snow-globe, and I recall the smell of my mother; I remember her firm hand, the look of her smile. I feel sorry for her, as well as for me.

I drift somewhere further and feel the scrubby texture of summer grass underfoot. I remember the taste of bubble gum in my mouth and the sense of my own fluid limbs running, and dancing. I once thought I was a fish and I have been able to fly. I have had a bird's eye view of the world and saw Santa in his golden sleigh against a midnight blue-black sky. I can see him, and me and her, and even Dad again now, and it's all there whenever I want. I only have to shut my eyes.

The next day Poopy and I stop in at a Petco store. I am planning on buying the dog bowl for him, but instead find a bright blue leather collar, with fake stones set in and 'Prince' written in white.

He doesn't like the new collar when I strap it on in place of the thin plain black one he's used to, but he has no choice because I'm the one in charge. I think it suits him, this blue against the dark brown. The woman in the store admires him, bending down to stroke him under his chin and tickle him behind his ears. Then she asks me how long I've had him and I say, 'Since he was just a tiny puppy,' and then I tell her that he means the world to me. This is not entirely true but it sounds like the right thing to say.

'Well, he's a very lucky boy, then, isn't he?' she says to Poopy, who is sulking about the collar and looking very dejected down by our feet. He's a sensitive creature. The littlest things please this animal, which is rather a sweet quality, and it's a relief to both of us when I scoop him up and tuck him under my arm.

I can feel the faint thump, thump of his now happy tail against my side.

I can tell that since I've had him he's lost even more weight with all this pining.

I ask if she can recommend any nutritious doggy treats. While I'm waiting at the till for her return with the goods, I feel the dog warm against me and imagine his nut-sized heart beating away. I suddenly want him to live a very long time. When she returns I find I am asking her to also recommend a good vet and maybe a grooming salon. 'He needs a change,' I say, 'He does need someone kind. It makes all the difference, that attention. Things change; we have to move on.'

'Harvey Marsh is a wonderful vet,' she says. 'He'll take good care of your lovely little boy.'

This is what I tell them in the resignation letter that I write. I tell them that things have changed; that I want to stay at home and spend time with my dog. He can't be left alone because he needs me and I've got plans to travel.

I correct the pronoun before I mail the letter: *we've got plans to travel*, I write.

2015

The Bear

Prince is fast asleep in the basket on the window seat and, although I am able to suck one of the hard candies they just handed out to help our ears equalise the change in pressure, Prince can't do anything, poor thing. It's been a four-hour flight and there are still two hours before the sedation is due to wear off.

I'm sure Marsh wouldn't deliberately put Prince's ears in danger, but mine are popping and painful. Swallowing might help him. If he wakes I could slip him something to eat, so I lift open the basket lid and slip my hand inside to stroke him. I think about how many days and nights there were in the last nine months when I'd have done anything to get hold of whatever he's had that's made him sleep like this. My tolerance for sleeping tablets has increased lately.

The plane tilts and twists as we begin to make our final descent and the land below is coming closer now. It looks startlingly green and fresh. Fresh and empty.

I feel very nervous because it's been a long time coming. No number of phone calls and tentative, awkward getting-to-know-you-type conversations can lessen the importance of actually meeting him. We've exchanged recent pictures by email and I've checked him out on the university website. He still teaches Climate Science. Though Pete has a bigger frame than Dad, they share a resemblance, so I can't say that I think I look more like him than I do Dad, because I don't look like Dad at all, really, but I'm interested to see what we share and, of course, I want the full story. I'll soak up anything he wants to tell me, just because I want to try to make sense of it.

Pete told me that he held me on the day I was born, not knowing I was his kid, but when I was two months old Mom thought she should tell him the truth. He doesn't know what prompted her change of heart, but she'd told Dad as well and Dad felt doubly betrayed. He took the disclosure very badly. Neither Pete nor Mom could understand how a stranger would be preferable, but apparently that was the case. By that time, Dad had managed to imagine a future life with this, his family, and now, he said, she was determined out of sheer cussedness to spoil things.

The three of them argued. In the end she promised she'd never tell anyone that Dad wasn't really my dad. Pete promised he wouldn't interfere. Dad promised he would always take care of her and me, and that, whatever happened, he'd never leave her. And then Pete split. Dad was very happy about this. Pete was frank enough to tell me that, as a young man with his own future to think about, he didn't mind putting the Midwest, my mother and me – all of it – behind him. He also said that for a long while my mother sent him photos tucked into Christmas cards and how when we visited that once (when I was around twelve) it was civil, but the photos stopped after that.

'Did you ever love my mother?' I asked him.

'We had feelings, but not really. I think your Dad really loved your mom.'

'Everyone says that. Did you know about Uncle Jack?'

'Jack and Richard ... well, they were friends. Not lovers, I don't think, whatever your mom might have thought. Maybe, but I don't think so.'

'I think I caught him with a man once. It freaked me out, but Mom and I couldn't talk about it and he denied everything. I got sick after that. Maybe it didn't happen. It doesn't matter anyway.'

Pete and I haven't talked more about any of that yet. I don't know if we need to. I'll have to play that by ear.

He will be waiting at baggage collection, and we'll have some time alone on the drive to his home, where he'll introduce me to his wife, Roseanne, and I'll get to meet their sons. I'm glad they didn't have any girls. I've always thought of myself as an only child; at least in one way I won't have to compete.

Pete hasn't told Roseanne, nor has he told their boys. I'm just going to be their niece, their cousin, for now. Roseanne isn't well and the prognosis, he said, is poor. No problem, I'm used to keeping secrets, I said; it's a family tradition. Pete said he was grateful about our plan to finally meet in person. 'Life comes full circle,' he said. 'Closure.'

Everyone wants closure, I think, but for me it's impossible. Even meeting Pete doesn't change anything. Over the last nine months I've glided between being very sorry for my father, then for my mother, and then angry with her and then with both of them, and then I've cycled round to feeling sorry for him again. Mainly, I'm disappointed. Dad could have told me, and she had years after Dad died to tell me, and I might have asked questions but I would have understood. Promises don't stand once someone is dead, surely.

She either ran out of time or deliberately chose not to say anything. I prefer to think that she ran out of time. I know she loved me and I know she did her best, but is it unreasonable to want to know the truth about your parents? How much does a big secret take away from the rest of stuff you think you know? I can't answer that one yet.

The wheels touch down with a bump and I do that thing I always do when the plane lands: I imagine Fred Flintstone dropping his legs to the ground from a hole in the cockpit, and digging his heels in so hard that sparks fly. It takes my mind off the fact that I'm actually here. Then I panic for a moment. I haven't told him about Prince yet, but I'm banking on the fact that out here in the Wild West no one would be so precious as to really object.

I recognise Pete immediately I see him waiting at the baggage collect. He is solid and huge. He gives me a proper bear hug and tells me that he thinks I look like my mom. It's an eerie feeling to have this man's strong arms around me. He doesn't let go of me for a long time and, in an odd way, it makes me feel that Mom is with me, again. I wasn't expecting that. He reminds me more of Mom than Dad, which is weird.

With tears in his eyes he says that he's looking forward to catching up. 'A lifetime. God, there's a load to talk about. Lots of questions, still.'

Then there's a scuffle in the basket. Prince is waking up and he'll start barking soon. He's a powerhouse once he gets going. It's hard to hold the thing still. I should let him out. Pete spots Prince's nose peeking through the gap in the lid.

'Is that a dog? What the hell? You've brought a goddamn dog?' He looks alarmed. 'Are you crazy?'

I anticipated this and I know how it might seem, but it is minor. 'Don't sweat it. He grows on a person. You'll see and it'll be fine. I promise,' I say. I take a big breath of the clean air. I'm excited. Anything can happen and it might be good. It will be good. 'It's fine,' I repeat. 'We're glad to be here.'

Acknowledgements

I would like to thank Candida Lacey and the team at Myriad who have made this book possible, and I am particularly grateful to my very talented editor, Linda McQueen, who asked the right questions and helped enormously to get this story into shape.

A book takes a long time to write. I am fortunate to enjoy the regular company of other writers who read drafts and provided helpful criticism; I am indebted to them. These friends include Claudia Gould, Umi Sinha, Harry Barnett, Karen Bateman, Annie Callaghan, Rebecca Duffy, Judy Edwards, Michael Gould, Mary Green, Ruby Grimshaw, Peter Flaxman, Louise Flind, Sophie Kay, Chandra Masoliver, Clive Newnham, Duncan Richards, Sue Sharp, Paul Sharpless, Martin Spinelli, Stewart Ullyott, Russ Watling, Bob Whiting, Liz Wright and Helen Yau. I would also like to say thank you to Adrian Colwell, who provided a great venue for the creation of *Magnetism*.

My parents have always encouraged my writing. My mother, Margaret, has been extremely supportive, as has my brother David, and my sons Stephen and David. I have some wonderful friends and come from a large extended family – cousins, nieces, nephews, aunts and uncles, and sisters- and brothers-in-law. This love and support has been invaluable.

Finally, the biggest thank you is to my husband Robert. I'd like to acknowledge his sacrifice, wisdom and faithful encouragement, which has given me the confidence to write this book and to trust that one day it would be read.

Sign up to our mailing list at
www.myriadeditions.com
Follow us on Facebook and Twitter

About the author

Ruth Figgest was born in Oxford and grew up in the USA. She has an MA in Creative Writing from the University of Sussex. Her stories have been shortlisted and commended for the Bridport Prize several times, and 'The Coffin Gate' was commissioned for broadcast on BBC Radio 4. *Magnetism* is her first novel.